DETERMINED TO CONQUER

Kathryn had declared war, now Donovan intended to draw the lines of battle. His arms were around her, and she was caught against him, her body molded so intimately to his that she could not move.

His mouth lowered to hers and she uttered a muffled sound of protest. Then suddenly she was aflame, and the fire was consuming every ounce of resistance she was struggling to retain.

"Let me go," she whispered.

"No."

"You don't love me."

"But I want you."

"I will never love you."

"I have not asked for your love. That is too dangerous a thing to ask any woman for. But in a few days you will belong to me."

"You are making a grave mistake."

"Then I shall just have to pay the price for it. But what I pay for . . . I get."

SUMMER LOVE WITH SYLVIE SOMMERFIELD

FIRES OF SURRENDER (3034, $4.95)

Kathryn Mcleod's beloved Scotland had just succumbed to the despised James IV. The auburn-haired beauty braced herself for the worst as the conquering forces rode in her town, but *nothing* could have prepared her for Donovan McAdam. The handsome knight triumphed over her city and her heart as well! She vowed to resist him forever, but her traitorous heart and flesh had other ideas.

AUTUMN DOVE (2547, $3.95)

Tara Montgomery had no choice but to reunite with her soldier brother after their parents died. The independent beauty never dreamed of the journey's perils, or the handsome halfbreed wagonmaster Zach Windwalker. He despised women who traveled alone; she found him rude and arrogant. They should have hated each other forever, yet their hunger was too strong to deny. With only the hills and vast plains as witnesses, Zach and Tara discover a love hotter than the summer sun.

PASSION'S RAGING STORM (2754, $4.50)

Flame-haired Gillian Kendricks was known to the Underground Railroad only as "the Guardian Angel." In reality she was a young Philadelphia beauty with useful connections which she doesn't hesitate to use to further her secret cause. But when she tries to take advantage of her acquaintance with the very handsome Lt. Shane Greyson who carries vital papers to Washington, her plan backfires. For the dark-haired lieutenant doesn't miss much. And the price of deceit is passion!

SYLVIE F. SOMMERFIELD

FIRES OF SURRENDER

ZEBRA BOOKS
KENSINGTON PUBLISHING CORP.

ZEBRA BOOKS

are published by

Kensington Publishing Corp.
475 Park Avenue South
New York, NY 10016

First printing: June, 1990

Printed in the United States of America

To Lenny and Rose . . . two very special people.

Chapter 1

Sir William Frances Andrew Craighton, known better to his close friends as Andrew, waited impatiently in the anteroom. He didn't like to wait for anything and he was already suspicious of a middle-of-the-night summons by Lord Jeffrey Sparrow. It usually meant some kind of news or action he would most likely not enjoy.

Sir Andrew was a man of wealth and position in the English court. He was also one of the few men Jeffrey Sparrow trusted, and behind Jeffrey stood the trust of the king.

There were few who didn't feel the political earthquake that was now shaking Scotland. A father and son dueled for a throne. The outcome of the struggle was of the utmost importance to England. These thoughts made Andrew very uncomfortable. He was certain that Jeffrey's summons had something to do with the conflict.

Andrew paced nervously. He was a tall, strongly built man and his boots made a sharp sound he didn't try to muffle. He was a man used to riding and to wielding a sword.

Most of his friends were surprised that, at thirty-three, he showed no inclination to marry. He was a

7

well-educated, handsome man but did not share the refined handsomeness of the court dandies. His face was ruggedly cut, his jaw square and firm. Eyes of blue steel shone piercingly below ebony brows. Two scars enhanced his visage more than damaged it. One was high on his left cheek, from his hairline to the curve of bone below his eye. The other ran along his right jawline. Both were the results of courage. Other scars marred his powerful body, scars that seemed to intrigue women. All women—even those encumbered by the vows of marriage—cast their eyes longingly in his direction.

He stood now looking out the window into blackness, his mind wrestling with the late-night summons and its prospects.

A door opened behind him and he was annoyed enough not to turn around even when he heard it click shut. Then a mellow chuckle broke the stubborn silence.

"Ah, Andrew, Andrew, I see I've annoyed you. Surely a late hour is not so upsetting to a man like you. I've heard rumors otherwise."

Andrew turned around. He could not remain angry at a man he respected as deeply as he did Jeffrey Sparrow.

Jeffrey Sparrow's name was a more than appropriate description of his countenance. He was slender to the point of emaciation. A beaklike nose reigned over a thin, pursed mouth. His movements were birdlike, almost delicate. But one glance from his dark amber eyes told of the active and brilliant mind that lingered behind them.

"Scoundrel," Andrew smiled. "What skulduggery are you about now, and why did you not reserve an explanation until a more reasonable hour?"

"I would have liked to do that, but since your idea of a reasonable hour is near noon, I couldn't. I expect you to be well on your way by then."

8

"On my way? Where am I about to be going?"

"Scotland," came the quiet reply. For a long minute the two looked at each other. Then it was Andrew who spoke again.

"Suppose you offer me some wine. I have a feeling this is going to be even more than I bargained on."

Jeffrey smiled again and walked to a table where wine and goblets had been set out for them. He poured two, handed Andrew one, and raised his own in a toast: "To peace between England and Scotland."

"An optimistic toast," Andrew said, but he drank. "But that does not tell me what it is you want of me."

"I have a man . . . a spy if you will, at work in Scotland, but I have my doubts both of his loyalty and his motives."

"You want me to spy on your spy?" Now Andrew laughed aloud and drained the balance of his glass. "Spare me, Jeffrey, I've no time for your games."

" 'Tis not a game, Andrew, and that is not what I want you to do."

"Then for God's sake, man, tell me what all the mystery is about."

"You know of the situation between James and his son?"

"Of course I do."

"Whichever man wins we have to find out what we can do to ensure a peace between our nations."

"Neither man will accept it."

"Don't be so hasty in that judgment."

"You know so much more than you ever say. What is brewing for me in that mind of yours?"

Again Jeffrey granted him a smile that was much too benevolent to suit Andrew. "How are you at portraying a little deference in place of that arrogant attitude of yours, Sir Andrew?"

"To whom should I show deference outside of my king and those I respect?"

"How about a Scottish lord?"

9

"Ha! 'Tis unlikely."

"It had best be practiced, Andrew, because that is just what your king needs you to do for him. It is most urgent."

"Out with it, Jeffrey. Who is this lord?"

"Lord Eric McLeod."

"Why?"

"Because he can pave your way to the king."

"Just which king?"

"Whichever wins. Look you, Lord McLeod fights for James III, but Lord McLeod lives near the castle in Edinburgh, which will be the obvious place for James the Fourth to hold should he win. Either way you will be able to reach one of them."

"How am I supposed to accomplish this?"

"You will go at once, dressed in clothes somewhat below your station. There is to be a battle soon. There is little doubt of that. Join Lord Eric's forces and fight with them. From there I trust your ingenuity. I want you to get as close to him as you can. Close enough to be at Edinburgh at the right time. We must secure a peace, Andrew. Much depends on you."

"I would rather fight a man with a sword than work like a . . . a Judas."

"No, not a Judas. You seek no man's life. Lord McLeod can bring you close to the king . . . whoever it might be. There we expect you to speak up and try to negotiate a resolution."

"And if I fail?"

Jeffrey looked solemnly at Andrew. "It would be a very expensive failure. It might even cost your life. But what a bargain should you succeed."

"I shall have to become valuable to them in some way."

"There again I trust your . . . ah . . . creative imagination."

"Thank you," Andrew said dryly, "your compliments are beginning to make me nervous."

"You needn't worry; as a servant of sorts to Lord McLeod you most likely won't receive too many."

"That does not ease my nerves at all. How am I to be a servant?"

"Try to taste a bit of humility, Andrew," Jeffrey laughed. "It might even be good for your soul."

"Don't worry about my soul," Andrew muttered.

"I have more faith in you, Andrew, than in any other knight at this court." Jeffrey's voice had become deadly serious now, and he held Andrew's eyes with his. "We want to avoid a confrontation . . . with either king. We need a man on whom we can depend. The king has questioned me about the identity of this man and I have stated my complete trust in you. He has given you his as well."

For a moment Andrew was silenced. Then he smiled. "Scoundrel," he repeated softly. "You know your way to me well. No wonder you are the king's right arm."

"Then you will do what we request?"

"I will do my best. If I fail . . . ?"

"You shall not fail. You are much too clever to be outwitted by any Scot." Jeffrey's lips twitched in another smile.

"Stop please, one more compliment and I will be completely overwhelmed." Andrew laughed.

"The king and your countrymen will be in your debt if you can maneuver this situation. Lives will be saved, Andrew. The king will not hesitate to show his gratitude in a more substantial way."

Andrew's face flushed. "B'God, do you think I ask for pay?"

"No, Andrew, I harbored no such thought. I know you too well. I only repeat what the king has said, and," he walked to another long table that sat against the wall, "to offer you this." He removed a cloth that covered a sword—a magnificent sword. Its blade gleamed in the pale light. The scabbard that lay beside it was unadorned with the usual jewels. The hilt of the sword was of the same plain style. Yet the sword could take the breath from a man used to weapons.

"The king regrets that he could not give you a sword as magnificent as he feels you deserve. The jewels and adornments will be added on your return. He sends you this because it is the very best of its kind. He sends it with his respect, his admiration, and his wishes for your success."

Andrew was struck wordless. He could see that the sword was as nearly perfect as one could be. He walked to Jeffrey's side; then, almost reverently, he lifted the huge, double-bladed sword from the table. It seemed to fit his hand like an extension of his arm.

"It's magnificent," Andrew breathed.

"I thought you would appreciate it."

"When must I leave?"

"As soon as possible. Things are coming to a head there and every minute is precious." Again Jeffrey chuckled softly. "If there are many inconsolable ladies that you do not have the time to . . . console . . . I shall be happy to tender your regrets."

Andrew responded with a broad smile that immediately changed his features, adding a warmth that made him more handsome than ever.

"Don't worry yourself, my friend, any ladies of my acquaintance who need to be consoled, will be."

"Don't spend too much time doing it."

"I shall leave by dawn. Is that satisfactory, my dear inquisitive friend?"

"Excellent."

"Now, suppose you call for some more wine and we can sit down to discuss all the details."

"There is nothing to discuss." Jeffrey reached inside his doublet and removed a small packet of papers. "Everything is here. I suggest that you read it carefully, commit everything to memory, and destroy this as soon as you can."

"I take it there are some who . . . disagree with this."

"There are . . . on both sides. . . ."

"Some strong opposition?"

"Strong enough that it could be very dangerous for you. I will admit the truth. Some of our couriers have met with . . . ah . . . accidents. There will be eyes, and I would not like them to be on you. Ride very carefully, my friend, very carefully. Watch the shadows and your back at all times."

"I will be very careful." Andrew placed the packet in his shirt, next to his skin. Then he reached for the scabbard and sword. He held the sword for a minute, then slid it into the scabbard.

Jeffrey held out his hand and Andrew took it. The two men shared a respect and affection for each other and a love for country and king that had tested their mettle more than once before.

"God speed, Andrew."

"Thank you."

"Andrew?"

"Yes?"

"Next year my daughter, Elizabeth, will be married. I expect you here healthy and safe, to dance at the wedding."

"I wouldn't miss it for anything in the world," Andrew replied.

Their eyes held for a moment and more words were unnecessary.

Andrew rode thoughtfully through the dark city streets. He didn't feel fear, only the weight of the responsibility that had been thrust upon him.

Once at home he tied his horse outside, loosening the girth for the time the horse would have to wait for him while he packed what few things he would take.

He wakened none of the servants except his most

13

trusted friend, Charles, who had been with him since he was a lad.

"But sir, this hasty packing, what shall I bring?"

"Nothing, Charles. You're not going. This is one trip I must take alone. Just get me some food. I intend to stop as seldom as possible. The fewer people who see me the better."

"You go alone?" Charles's face wore a mixture of surprise and an almost amusing anguish. He had served Sir Andrew for so long he could not fathom Andrew being able to move without him.

"I'm afraid so," Andrew hid his smile, not wanting to offend a man who cared so deeply for his welfare.

"When will you return?"

"That I have no answer to either. It depends on . . . on so many things. Take care of everything for me, Charles. I entrust everything to your capable hands." He bent close to Charles so no whispered word could be overheard. "I go on the king's business."

Charles nodded and smiled proudly. He was worried, but he would abide by Andrew's wishes. Andrew could be assured of one thing. Nothing in his private life would be made known through Charles. The loyal servant would die first. Yet even he wasn't privy to the destination and purpose that took Sir Andrew from England.

Charles watched as Andrew dressed in his drabbest clothes, nondescript clothing he wore when the mood struck him to do some physical labor or practice with the sword. It was quite obvious Andrew did not want anyone to realize his station in life by the clothes he wore.

As he buckled on the scabbard and sword Andrew could have laughed at Charles's effort not to ask the questions that danced in his eyes. He clapped Charles on the shoulder, then turned to pick up his dark cloak.

"Charles, trust me that I shall tell you all on my return."

Charles nodded and listened to the jingle of Andrew's spurs as he left the hall and walked down the long corridors to the door. Then Charles went to the window and watched Andrew tighten the cinch of the saddle, and mount.

He traveled with only the bare necessities and none of these would be able to identify him in any way.

If anything went wrong it would be likely that no one would ever know what had become of him.

He thundered down the road and into the night. Charles watched until the darkness swallowed him up.

Five Weeks Later

When the two armies had clashed earlier in the day the sun had been a brilliant orange glow in the bluest of skies. Now it was late afternoon and the hills cut off the sun and laid shadows over the plain and valley of Sauchieburn.

The valley was bordered by tree-lined banks whose brilliant green leaves heralded the beauty of a Scottish spring. But there was no joy in the depths of the valley, for the exhausting battle was almost over.

Some distance away, north of the field of battle, a lone rider watched with the look of a dying man in his eyes.

James III of Scotland watched as an army of rebels, led by his own son, drank deeply of the victory. The clear water of the stream ran red with the blood of knights who had stood loyal to him. Knights and burghers had stood side by side and given their lives to retain his hold on the throne. But through bitter eyes he saw the defeat.

James III might have lived in peace had he been adroit or able to restrain his avarice; but greed had brought him into conflict with the powerful border family of Home and allied with the border family of Home were the Hepburns and the McAdams. The rebels had at first captured Dunbar and Stirling.

He had sent his closest friends into battle, friends who would have stood at his side until death. But over an hour ago he had known, and the failure tasted like ashes in his mouth. He sent them away, and watched the horror of final defeat alone.

The horse on which he was mounted was a sturdy steed, quite able to take him to safety, but the man who rode him was the most inadequate of riders and even the armor he wore was old fashioned and dulled.

He knew the battle was over and that his life would be forfeit should he be found. He knew he could find sanctuary in England. If he could escape he could gather his forces again. He would gather his forces again, he thought grimly, and when he did he would meet the enemy again. . . . Yes, he would meet the enemy again . . . his son. His son who had betrayed him and sought the crown that was slowly toppling from his head to the mud beneath his horse's feet.

Tears stung his eyes and he muttered a curse on his son through gritted teeth. This was the bitterest defeat of all, that his army of strong loyal men fell to his son, the royal betrayer.

After a moment he straightened his shoulders and turned his horse about. He urged it into a gallop. The great hooves dug into the earth. The horse had the power to take him to freedom. . . . He would escape to renew his army and strike his son a blow he would never forget.

The road was narrow and muddy, its course carrying horse and rider along the river. It would only be a short time until he could find a familiar shallow place to cross.

He found the place and splashed across the stream, weaving clumsily in his saddle. His hold on the reins was insecure and the horse sensed it and was alarmed and skittish.

A small group of houses lay before him and his intent was not to rein in his horse but to ride straight through.

But he didn't count on the two women who had been bringing water from a nearby well. Neither of them was prepared when the horse thundered about the curve in the road. Both women screamed and the already nervous horse shied and rose on his hind legs, his hooves pawing the air. The two women saw the rider dislodge and fall heavily to the ground. The frightened horse continued on while the two women slowly approached the fallen man.

"Mother?" The younger woman questioned her instantly.

"Hush," the older woman cautioned. She knelt down beside the fallen man.

Slowly James opened his eyes, seeing the faces wavering above him. But he could not seem to speak.

"Run for your father," the older woman commanded.

In a few minutes the girl returned with her father, who also knelt by the stunned man. The three laboriously dragged the man to a place where he could be cared for.

When his helmet was removed the man was stunned. " 'Tis him," he breathed. "We need some help."

At that moment the sound of approaching horses could be heard. The women ran out on the road to stop them. Had she known the three riders sought the fleeing man with murderous intent she would have silenced her call for help.

Her relief was obvious when she saw that one man was dressed in the flowing garments and cassock of a man of the church.

"Father," she cried. "Father!"

He bent down in the saddle. "What say you dame?"

" 'Tis a blessing you are here, Father. A man has fallen from his horse and is seriously injured. My husband feels he might be mortally so. We need a priest."

The three men exchanged silent but satisfied looks. The end of their quest lay close. Murder lay deep in their black hearts. The deceiver strode beside the woman to the side of the fallen king.

"Leave us. If he wants to confess and receive absolution we need to be alone."

The man stood from his kneeling position by the semiconscious king. He looked through narrowed eyes at the man who had given the order. Then with an intaken breath and perspiration on his brow, he motioned to his wife and daughter. Before they could question him he grasped their arms and began to drag them away.

"Come," he rasped. "This is no place for us."

The priest smiled as he knelt by the fallen rider. Was this the man he sought?

The king's helmet had been removed. His thick hair was rumpled and his forehead was beaded with sweat. His eyes were only partially opened. But his pursuers recognized him without doubt even in the light of the dying sun.

The priest bent his head and from beneath his cassock he drew a long, slender knife. The king's armor was old and fastened loosely across his chest. The chink in it could be seen plainly. The point of the blade was driven with a strong and merciless hand.

The king's eyes flew open and a gasp of recognition bubbled from his lips. A name was whispered as he died.

The priest wrapped the king's cloak about him and left his side. He walked to the small family who remained speechless.

"He has died with his soul cleansed by his confession. My men will see to his care."

They nodded and watched the body borne away by the heavily cloaked men.

The young girl's eyes raised to her father's but he

18

could only breathe one sentence.

"That was no priest . . . and someone must carry the word of what has happened here to Donovan McAdam."

Chapter 2

The dead were being buried all around Sauchie field. The man who had done murder without compunction rode away. His equally guilty companions rode under cover of darkness and returned to the campfires of the new reigning King James IV. None of the three would tell of the treacherous act. As far as the son knew, his father was going to be brought to him soon and that was what they wanted him to continue to believe for as long as possible.

Within the tent that flew the royal banner, James was asleep. He slept clothed and from total exhaustion. Yet even so he slept lightly.

Nearby a young lad lay coiled in a fetal position and deep in sleep. James stirred and wakened. He had slept less than twenty minutes and his mind and body both groaned as he moved to sit up. He was puzzled, wondering just what it was that had wakened him.

He looked about, his eyes skimming over the page who lay asleep. He smiled. Let him sleep a few minutes longer. For this few minutes he was blessedly alone with only his own thoughts.

He stood, and any observer would have named him king, for he looked, moved, and carried himself like a man born to reign over other men. James IV's energy, strength, and ability would soon become apparent. He had the inestimable gift of winning popular favor. To him the monarchy was all-important. It was the linch-pin that held society in place.

James had a sturdy body and a lively, inquiring mind, and dominating all was his determination to rule and govern, to make law effective and his kingship real.

What preyed on his mind now and kept him from sleep was the whereabouts of his father. He was more afraid than he would ever be able to admit that his father would die before he could be found and brought to him. He did not want patricide on his soul and he had sent men in all directions with explicit orders to find him and return him alive and safe.

Again he searched the inside of the tent, sure that something unusual had disturbed him.

He sensed rather than knew that the papers on a nearby table had been disturbed. Someone had actually had the nerve to come into his tent while he slept. He had to chuckle. This took either a great deal of courage, or a great deal of foolhardiness. He wasn't sure which.

Nothing in the papers would tell his intruders anything that they would not have gotten from him should they have asked. He made it a point to reward loyalty. It was a fact well known. The weakest of his men clung to it and the strongest dedicated their love and pride to it.

It had to be someone he trusted well, no one else would dare enter the royal tent. The thought made him inhale and straighten his shoulders. He had used men who were betrayers, and their code of honor did not preclude them from betraying him as well.

He walked to the table, gathered up the sheaf of papers, and returned to his bed. There he propped several pillows behind him and began to scan the papers randomly. He was satisfied with what he planned to do and the rewards he had given.

He thought of his most loyal and maybe the strongest of all his devoted men, Donovan McAdam. To him he gave the most because in him he had the most faith . . . and trust, trust that had been proven time and time again.

He could easily picture the lowlands and the border. He thought of Dunbar, and Hailes. Dunbar, the fortified harbor, was the key to Scotland. His utter faith told him that Patrick Hepburn had taken these cities by now and that he need only go to Edinburgh. His acquisitions through the bloody war would extend his power to Glasgow. He also knew that Donovan McAdam would be assessing the damage to the rebellion, and gathering what was needed to repair it and to make it a sound platform on which his king would stand.

The last thing he wanted was to give power in any way to any traitorous baron. He would be standing much too near his old formidable enemy . . . England.

It would be men such as Donovan who would protect these borders. There was no doubt that riders were already bringing word to England that the Scottish rebels under the young prince had won today. Now the English would face a man who would sit on the throne with strong authority. Instead of a frightened ally, Henry Tudor had a man who could not be bribed or threatened, a man with whom Henry would have to deal with respect.

James stood. He was a well-built man, handsome although he was badly in need of a shave. His hair was a deep, rich brown, and strength gleamed in his eyes. He walked to the sleeping boy and nudged him, laughing as the boy jumped to his feet, alarmed that his king was awake and might have been in need of something while he slept.

"Fetch me some water for shaving," he commanded, then smiled to ease the harshness of his voice so the boy's alarm would not grow.

"Aye, Your Grace." The boy was gone quickly.

James waited, expecting the boy's rapid return. But another arrived before him.

He was a tall, brawny man with a thick beard. Lord Douglas. Behind him was another man, John Fleming, a man whose eyes silently shifted about the room, moving to the bed where James had left the papers . . . and finally to James.

James was annoyed at their silence. He had sent them on a quest immediately after their triumphant battle and he was impatient for news.

"Well, gentlemen," his voice was deceptively soft. "You have been gone for hours. What news have you for me?"

Lord Douglas shook his head, and spoke in a voice that matched the brawn of his large chest. "There is no news, Sire."

Fleming smiled and this drew the king's eyes; then he spoke softly. "Your father has fled, Your Grace. He has run to cover, most likely toward the English border. A cowardly . . ." His voice froze and the smile faded when James's face grew cold and silently violent. He would not tolerate another to speak of his father this way. The elder James had been a man of merciful nature; this James was not so forgiving.

Fleming took a step back and grew silent in the face of a pure, cold rage. Lord Douglas felt he should say or do something before the king's wrath was felt a little more strongly.

"You gave me orders to find your father, Sire, and we have tried. We shall find him. Your orders were also that he was not to be harmed, on pain of death. No man will defy you and raise his hand against him. We will find him."

"Aye," James said quietly. "You have blocked all ways of escape?"

"Aye, Your Grace."

James remained quiet. He was filled with conflict-

23

ing and fiery emotions. He was angry at these men for their slur on his father's courage, yet he was filled with a sense of victory. True, he had wrenched his father's throne from him in a violent war, but he felt it had to be. Now he meant to hold it at all costs.

He knew the men who had betrayed his father and he wondered if they might one day consider betraying him. Well he would teach them a very different tune and they would dance to it. He would teach final and very hard lessons and he would teach them well. He meant to be a king who knew how to rule.

"Patrick and Donovan are in Edinburgh to secure the castle for me. It is time we take possession, gentlemen."

"We leave now, Sire?"

"Aye."

"We do not wait here for word of your father?"

"It will find me. I am assured, am I not, that you will find him?"

"Aye, Sire," Lord Douglas replied.

"Then you must prepare to ride, for we leave for Edinburgh within the hour."

This was the order of a king, and neither man gave one thought to adding a word of hesitation. They exchanged a quick glance, then turned and left.

James stood alone again. He wanted news of his father, news that he was alive. He meant to take the throne, not to commit a crime that would haunt him for a lifetime. For a minute the weight of the invisible crown seemed to be heavier than he had imagined it would be. Then he straightened his shoulders again and walked to the tent door to stand and look at the preparations being made.

Less than an hour later his horse was brought to him and he mounted. He had led these men in battle, now he would lead them in triumph.

He thought again of Patrick, and of Donovan Mc-Adam who held the city of Edinburgh for him and awaited his arrival. Why did he get the sudden feeling that these might be the only two men he could trust.

He rode toward Edinburgh, unaware of the events that had transpired elsewhere and that would have a powerful effect on his reign.

The city of Edinburgh seemed to be devoid of all life. Shops were barricaded, and the men who had run them had picked up their swords to do battle for their king, James III. Houses were securely closed, with the dim light from within unseen from outside. But the silence was a strange one, as if a darkness hovered over the city.

The men who had garrisoned the castle were gone, many dead. Ghosts walked the city.

In the finer sections of the city the residences of the great nobles were bolted well. Within, silent women waited for word of their lords, and of the battle that raged. None knew that the battle was already lost.

In one house, two women were alone in an oak-paneled room. They had not spoken to each other for some time. Their minds were caught with visions of their brother struggling in this mighty battle.

One woman was like a delicate flower, her skin creamy and pale and her black hair coiled about her head in a heavy rope. Everything about her seemed fragile. Her eyes were wide, violet blue, and innocent as they followed the movements of the second woman, who was pacing the floor in intense aggravation.

"Pacing like a caged tigress will not make the news come with more speed," the dark-haired woman said.

Kathryn McLeod stopped pacing the floor and turned to look at her sister. Where the first girl was fine boned and delicate, Kathryn seemed all flame and color. Her hair, a deep auburn, caught the reflection of the low burning fire and glowed with warmth. Brilliant green eyes dominated a face that was strong and rose tinted.

"Oh I wish I were a man. I would have ridden with them."

"But you are not a man."

"Damn! Cannot someone bring word! He could be lying dead out there."

"Kathryn, there is little we can do but wait."

"It has been so many hours, Anne. Surely it must be finished now."

"Oh, God, Kathryn, I am so frightened."

Kathryn looked at her younger sister, her face softening into extreme beauty with the affection she felt for her. "You are not well, Anne. The fever has not really left you yet. Why don't you lie down and rest."

"It is so hard to believe, Kathryn. Knowing our family and our love for each other. How is it that a son can turn against his own father . . . against his king."

"It is beyond my understanding. He wanted to be king so desperately. But he will never be king, and we will never submit."

"Kathryn, what if . . ."

"Don't say that!"

"But what if it's true and the king is defeated. What . . . what will happen?"

"Don't be alarmed, Anne. It will only make you ill again. Surely the son will not make war on women."

"But he will come here."

"Of course he must. Edinburgh is too important, too valuable to do anything less. But he will not be met as he hopes to be."

"If Eric is . . . what will the new king do with us?"

"We will be booty, I imagine," Kathryn said scathingly. "Most likely he will try to marry us off to one of his loyal generals. Well, it might come as a surprise that women will resist as strongly as men."

She saw her sister's face grow pale and her hands tremble, and was immediately sorry. "Anne, don't be frightened. Lie down and rest. Eric will be upset to come home and find you like this."

"Maybe I will," Anne said, and rose unsteadily to her feet. Kathryn would have gone with her, but at this time she had other plans. She had to find out for herself how the battle was progressing, how her brother fared. She had to know.

As soon as the door closed behind her sister, Kathryn ran to the window, pulled back the shutters, and looked down into the cobbled street. It was empty. Then she whirled from the window and left the room, leaving the door open in her haste.

On the ground floor all was silent. Leaving open doors in her wake, she moved quickly to the kitchen, where she knew she would find some of the men left behind to guard them. All of them looked up when she entered so abruptly.

"Have a horse saddled for me. We ride out now. It is time we found news for ourselves."

One man struggled to his feet, the shock making him frown. The group were all that could be spared to protect the house. A strange army of protectors: stable hands, house servants, cooks, a barber, a tailor, and only four men-at-arms.

"Mistress, it is too dangerous to ride out today, especially for a woman. There will be all kinds of brigands on the road. It's too soon and too unsettled."

"I didn't ask your opinion, Angus. Saddle my horse! If you want to follow my brother's orders and protect me, then you had best come along." She snapped at the stable hand, who rose quickly to his feet.

The man who had protested followed Kathryn. "Mistress Kathryn, Mistress Kathryn!"

"My brother may be wounded. He may even be dead. Would you have us just sit here and do nothing?"

"Aye. You have your brother's orders to do just that. And we have his orders to protect you and your sister," he said pointedly.

"Then don't leave my sister unprotected, I need only two to ride with me. The rest can stay. If you refuse to come, I'll go alone." Her eyes glinted with determination.

Angus knew this was dangerous. But as far as he knew no man or woman, including her family, had ever won an argument with Mistress Kathryn. She was worse than ten headstrong men. He smiled at her and she returned it. He tightened the buckle of his sword and followed her.

The stables were deep and dark. But they found their horses already saddled. Angus helped Kathryn mount, then mounted himself.

"Hurry!" Kathryn urged.

"I can't see a good reason to hurry into danger."

"Hold your tongue. If Anne hears you, your careless words will frighten her."

Angus wore the livery of the McLeods and was not sure that that was wise. Too many envied the wealth and power of the McLeods and their vast estates. He prayed that her brother had been among the victors today. Yet Angus was sure Lord Eric would make him pay for this bit of recklessness. He was damned if he did and damned if he didn't. He hoped Lord McLeod would be a bit understanding.

They raced through the city and Kathryn was filled with the satisfaction of action.

Kathryn held her head straight and rode easily in the saddle. Behind closed shutters, the people watched. She would show them the courage and honor of the McLeods. She would show them that she was unafraid.

They pounded toward the city gates, which stood open and unattended. Those open gates made Kathryn realize she was going where few others dared.

Kathryn, who used only one hand on the reins, lifted a hand to push back a long tendril of her sunlit hair that had come loose. The road lay free before her and the way to the south was straight ahead.

They rode three miles farther and topped a long, steady rise when she saw something that gave her pause. She reined in so hastily that her horse fretted. She sat very still and watched. In the distance a large body of riders approached with banners flying and sunlight glinting off the armor they wore.

"About two thousand horses," Angus said grimly, "and since there are two of us and you are leading, maybe they are outnumbered."

"Be quiet, Angus!" Kathryn snapped. "Whose banners are they?"

"Mistress, this is a very dangerous place for you. We should have awaited news of the battle before we rode."

Kathryn could plainly see that the horsemen were riding hard. The sounds of their approach could be heard in the clear air. But she felt they had plenty of time before the horsemen could reach them. They could ride to safety before anyone could get close enough.

"They are not his majesty's forces," Angus concluded finally.

"How do you know?"

"Because he had no large cavalry. These are borderers. I've heard of their power and the men who lead them. They are not men to be trifled with."

She had never seen Angus frightened, but she knew he was frightened now. But she refused to show any fear. She worried only about her brother's life and she was sure that a woman of her position would be safe even among the victors.

"There are too many trees about us," Angus continued nervously. He did not share her confidence.

"Trees," Kathryn said. It was the first time she realized there was a deep grove of trees to her left.

Not more than a mile away a troop of horses had just appeared over the brow of the nearest hill. Now she too became alarmed. She jerked on the reins and turned her horse, just as from the trees to their left came the unexpected attack Angus had feared. Men on foot, driven ahead of the victorious army, were moving in desperate flight.

Sure that these men were no more than common thieves, taking advantage of a lesser force, she gave battle to the limit of her ability, swinging her whip and effortlessly controlling her horse. But she soon found herself unseated. Still, she meant to fight until she recognized those in the group as friends. These men had fought today and, with a heart that felt like lead, she knew they had lost. Fear for her brother tore at her and she had to bite her lip to keep from crying out.

The small group that had attacked her and Angus was now surrounded by another.

"How could you set upon us like knaves?" she whispered to a man close by whom she recognized.

She could see the flush of shame on his face.

"You must know by now that we lost today, Lady Kathryn," he said quietly. "We needed horses to get to freedom." He could see the pain in her eyes. Then the two looked toward the man who seemed the obvious leader of the force that surrounded them.

The man next to Kathryn spoke. "This is the lady, Kathryn McLeod, and I am Sir Robert Campbell." With this he drew his sword and extended it to the victors, hilt first.

The horseman leaned down to take the sword. For a while he was silent. Kathryn could feel his eyes move from her to Robert and back. Then he said in a steely voice, "You are under arrest for insurrection against the crown of Scotland."

"I was fighting for my king as you were for yours. One can hardly call that insurrection," Robert replied. But he did not resist the two men who led him away.

Kathryn watched him go, then she turned her eyes to the other man. She could not really see him. He was wearing light steel armor. Under the helmet she could see that his eyes were silver gray and what she saw of his lower face was tanned. She had not heard him called by name. Kathryn was not used to pleading for anything, but now she was prepared.

"I have a brother, Lord Eric McLeod. Could you tell me if he is safe, sir?"

His gray eyes rested on her. She felt a kind of current flow through her and the shock startled her. She was unafraid . . . but strangely excited.

"He has escaped . . . so far." Slowly he dismounted and walked to stand beside her. As he reached up to remove the helmet, she was aware of his aura of strength and power. He exuded it like a fire gave warmth. Again his gray eyes rested on her.

He stood tall, nearly a foot taller than she. His hair was tawny gold and streaked by the sun. His eyes were wide set and his mouth was wide and finely curved.

Her first impression was that he was extremely large. The breadth of his shoulders was breathtaking. Her second impression was that he was ruggedly handsome . . . and very tired. She could see the beginnings of stubble on his clean-shaven face and there were deep lines etched around his mouth. Kathryn looked up at him in the darkening light and knew this was not a man with whom a woman could toy.

"You are a traitor!" Her voice was a sneering whisper.

"Why, because I choose to serve a different king than you?"

"Jamie may have seized the throne but he will never hold it."

"We shall see," he said. "What's your name?"

"Lady Kathryn McLeod," she tilted her chin proudly.

" 'Tis a strange place to find you, Lady Kathryn," his mouth twitched in an aborted smile. "Were you planning on wielding a sword alongside your men this day?" His attitude made her furious.

"Who are you?" she demanded.

"Donovan McAdam," he replied; then he turned to give a brisk order. "Bring Lady Kathryn's mount."

"I will not ride with you! I will not lead your bandits into our city."

" 'Tis no longer your city. 'Tis the king's and I have not asked you what you will do or not do. You will obey."

Kathryn was actually trembling with her anger. It was imperative that she show him just how strong her own resistance could be. She lifted her whip. Before he realized she would dare, or could raise an arm to stop her, the lash crossed his face sideways, catching the edge of his lip and surely leaving a scar he would wear always. Two of his men immediately grabbed her arms.

She glared up at him, caught in a magnificent, defiant anger. He watched her with a kind of admiring fury. She was more than beautiful, she was breathtaking in her emotion. It was then that a spark of an idea was struck in his mind. There were ways, and ways to repay such a blow.

He felt the warmth of blood on his cheek and lip, but did not raise a hand to touch it. Instead his eyes held hers, filled with a promise that jolted through her like lightning. For one second she almost backed away. But the immense pride that always filled her held her in place.

"Will you call your traitorous dogs to protect you from me!" she said scathingly.

The two men who had grasped her at her sudden attack chuckled softly. Donovan's eyes gleamed dangerously and he finally raised a hand slowly to tenderly feel his cheek.

"No," he said in a voice that seemed like steel encased in velvet. "It takes two of them to protect you from me. Now, mount your horse. We ride to Edinburgh."

She pushed aside the hand he had instinctively extended to help and seized the pommel of her saddle and swung gracefully into it. He gripped the bridle of her horse in a strong hand. She kept her eyes stubbornly away from Donovan as he mounted and rode to her side.

"Even if we lost today," her voice was thick with grief and tears she refused to shed, "don't dream that we will ever stop fighting."

"I'm not a fool to dream so," he chuckled softly. "Dreams are a fool's quagmire."

"You will not retain your hold. Too many people hate you."

"Maybe fewer than you think," he replied casually.

"You may have conquered today but there are those who will never surrender."

"You speak of yourself, mistress?" His face gave no hint of his thoughts, yet his lips quirked in the same restrained smile.

"You will never master me."

"Umm, I warrant it would be an enjoyable contest," he laughed.

She turned to look again at the man who sat his horse so regally and so close beside her. It was then that his eyes turned to her and she could see a look she could not understand. "But in time there will be changes. Whether you understand that or not, you will find out. And whether you choose to accept what is to come or not, it will be."

"What?" she breathed softly. "What must I accept? That my brother is dead? Do you think the murder you do this day will subdue me?"

"You will see."

"Am I under arrest?"

"I have not decided yet what I will do with you. I will of course make certain you do not have a weapon at your next meeting."

33

She laughed. But at his cool, calm silence the laughter died. "I do not choose to ever meet you again."

"But you will, Kathryn McLeod, you will." His voice was filled with a deadly finality. Then he began to move, and she was forced to ride beside him, an undefeated spirit facing a defeated city, and with their conqueror beside her.

Chapter 3

Andrew was beyond any recognizable state of exhaustion. Yet despite that, he was more than pleased at the way his plans had begun to work.

He had found Eric McLeod and, as a soldier of fortune, had fought beside him in two battles. It had more than surprised him that he had learned to respect Eric McLeod both for his ability to fight and for his tenacity. He had done battle like the warrior he was and his loss was with honor and not because of fear. Then he had ridden with Eric to the field where the final battle was held.

He had been separated from Eric in the heat of battle and a short time later a broadsword, swung by an ox of a highlander, had almost beheaded him.

He had managed to ride for nearly five miles before he found a dense thicket to crawl into. Then he could do little more than collapse. Now he lay face down on the damp earth. Slowly he opened his eyes, but still it took several minutes before he could even begin orienting himself. He couldn't remember where he was. In fact, he could not gather any idea of how long he had been lying here. He reckoned it must be a full day, and that made it the seventeenth of June. It was the day after the battle of Sauchieburn and — miraculously — he was alive. No thanks to Jeffrey Sparrow, whom he intended to chastise very firmly when . . . or if . . . he ever got home.

He could feel a thick matting on his head and reached a hand to touch it, only to have his hand come away bloodied. He didn't sit up, for the world was spinning, and he was sure if he did, he'd be sick. Tentatively his hand continued to explore the ragged edge of a still-open wound. But finally he assured himself it wasn't going to be fatal. He had had many wounds, some more grievous than this, and he had survived. He experimented with moving his head. He wet his lips and continued to move little by little until the world righted itself.

His horse had most likely been stolen so he gave up any idea of looking for it.

He could hear the birds sing and felt the breeze against his skin. He was relieved to hear the sound of running water and he struggled to his hands and knees and began to crawl to the edge of a small, clear brook. He cupped his dirty hands and drank; the water was deliciously cool. He put his hands in to gather more water to splash over his face and head; then he gingerly tried to wash the wound a bit. He was concentrating on not groaning aloud as the cold water sent a shock through his body, and he heard nothing until a voice came from behind him.

"Lie very still if you don't want to die where you are."

Andrew didn't move. He knew the voice and turned his head to look at the man who stood above him. It was only then that he was recognized.

"Andrew! God, man, I thought you must have died today."

Andrew remained silent, but Eric McLeod was more than delighted to find a man he felt he could trust. "Listen to me, Andrew. It's important that we get to my home before I am discovered and forced to surrender my sword."

"Why is that, sir?"

"My sisters. I'll be taken, but you, as a servant, will be free to stay and protect them. They will need a strong loyal arm to wield a sword. Two women alone, man. I need your help."

Andrew nodded while his wits spun. What better place for an English noble to be than in the midst of the action. He smiled. "I imagine it is necessary that I have some form of employment, just as it is also necessary that we find food and drink before we perish. Where do we go first, m'lord?" God, he hated to sound so . . . incompetent.

"We go straight home. My sisters could be at their mercy right now, and I shudder to think what that means."

"You will definitely be arrested," Andrew stated.

"Yes, I know."

Andrew could not help but admire the courage of a boy who was still less than twenty. He shrugged his shoulders, the motion making his head throb. "This way then." He motioned in the direction he knew the road to be. In twenty minutes they emerged onto the road he had left a full twenty-four hours before. Eric came to stand beside him. He stood for several minutes and looked around, a puzzled expression on his face.

"We are not exactly lost, sir," Andrew said with an effort to hide his amusement. "The city is there." He didn't want to answer questions, so he started to walk, and Eric followed.

The road was dusty and stony and walking was an annoyance to men more used to riding.

Andrew was annoyed about several things. One was that he had to remember to use a crude English border accent and the other was the knowledge that he was looked upon with disdain as a servant. He, a wealthy, educated noble. It had seemed a different story when he had conversed with Jeffrey. Andrew was not used to being subservient.

"M'lord?" Andrew questioned.

"Yes?"

"You would be less likely identified if you would discard your helmet and other signs of your rank."

Eric's pride almost rebelled at this, but he considered his new position and did as Andrew had advised. He removed the necessary equipment and tossed it into a ditch at the side of the road. Andrew knew this would be of little help. Eric McLeod walked, talked, and acted almost like royalty. And the winking jewels on his sword proclaimed his status. He would not fool too many too long. But Andrew hoped this would at least get them to his home and some medical care before they were caught. Without complaint he continued his long-legged stride.

Andrew had to fight the weariness and the pain that had begun to beat through his whole head.

"Where do you come from?" Eric questioned.

"Dorsetshire," Andrew lied automatically, while he drew on visions of the gentle hills of home.

"I suppose you regret your choice of sides," Eric tried to laugh.

"At times," Andrew chuckled.

"Right now I would give a fortune to see my home and . . . my family," Eric said.

In the distance they could see Edinburgh. It was this that made Eric speak again, as close to pleading as he would ever come. Andrew had not committed himself in any way and Eric knew he could simply leave him. Eric was afraid for his sisters and he needed protection for them.

"Andrew," Eric said as he stopped.

Andrew waited patiently. Eric hesitated because he had to battle his pride to ask a servant for help. Eric's eyes were on the city as he spoke. "Look, Andrew, you and I know it is only a matter of time before I will be arrested. You have a strong arm and a sharp wit. I need your help."

Andrew still said nothing. He knew Eric thought that, as a hired mercenary, he could be bought, and to Andrew's annoyance Eric's next words confirmed this.

"I will pay you ten gold pieces a month."

"To do what?" Andrew asked, although the answer was as clear to him as to Eric.

Eric was struggling with the knowledge that his life was in danger, and through him both of his sisters'. Maybe more than their lives were at stake. He was trying to shoulder the responsibility of their care and to do what he could for them against the time he had to face his future . . . bleak as it was.

"If I am arrested I want to place Lady Anne and Lady Kathryn in your care. You could be a secretary. I saw you fight, Andrew, and I know you can be trusted."

Andrew smiled at his naïveté, but he answered solemnly, "I thank you m'lord. I'll do my best."

Eric sighed in relief.

"I shall keep the welfare of your sisters first in my mind," Andrew lied gracefully.

They reached the city gates, where two guards were posted on watch for those returning from the battle. When they passed through the gates they were followed, as Andrew had known they would be. It would not be long until Eric was captured and Andrew would be safely established in the McLeod home to continue with his plan to bring James to recognize the possibilities of the alliance his king offered.

Andrew knew that fatigue and the pain in his head had certainly had their effect. His thinking was sluggish and he was just plodding on, following Eric through the unfamiliar city. Jamie or one of his followers would soon be here, and here was where he needed to be.

The pain in his head was now so bad that he began to think he was drifting around in some kind of nightmare.

Eric had stopped talking long ago, mostly because Andrew had stopped answering. He'd done that because Eric's voice was only a droning in his ear. Andrew stopped walking when Eric abruptly stopped.

"Damn," he whispered.

"What?" Andrew mumbled.

"I think soldiers are already at my house. I have to get in and see to my sisters before the soldiers find out I'm home."

Andrew had to blink his eyes several times to bring everything back into focus. "You are right m'lord. Is there a window somewhere that might be left unguarded?"

"Aye, around back. Follow me." They made their way silently over the slippery grass.

There was a small window in a shadowed corner where two walls met. It was dark within.

Andrew took his sword and broke out the lower panes. He cautioned Eric to watch for the broken glass, then let him precede him into the dark room . . . as a good, obedient servant would do. But Andrew had to grit his teeth to follow. He felt as if his head were about to explode.

Eric took several steps into the dark room, but Andrew's exhaustion seemed to have caught up to him and he remained where he stood, swaying unsteadily and trying to reach out a hand to find something solid to hold on to. He finally found the wide window-ledge and rested against it to wait. All sound seemed to be just distant echoes.

When Eric opened the door a beam of light crossed the floor and Andrew caught sight of a high-backed chair. He went to it and sat down. It could have been of rock and it would have felt comfortable. He allowed the momentary exhaustion to take over. For a short while he slipped into semiunconsciousness. While he was resting others entered the room. A fire was built in the fireplace and wine was brought.

He could not have been in that condition too long, for natural and protective instincts were too well ingrained. But when he did open his eyes Eric and two women were in the room and Eric was holding a goblet of wine toward him. The cup itself seemed to waver and fade in and out. He took it and held it between both his hands. Then he drained it in one breath. Eric poured another for him and one for himself.

Then he was drawn to the warmth of the fire by both exhaustion and the chill caused by his wound. He turned to face it and when he looked toward the hearth he saw a woman bending close to it. It was then that she turned from the fire and looked directly at him. For a minute Andrew, who had tasted all of feminine beauty he thought there was, felt as if his heart had paused, then had picked up a deep throbbing. She was the loveliest creature he had ever seen.

To him she looked like a fragile white rose. He could have spanned her willow-slim waist with his two hands. Her skin was cream and her great eyes seemed to melt something within him. He tried to catch his breath so he could ease the fear their arrival must have brought.

"Mistress, there is nothing to fear," he said softly, hoping to see color return to her pale cheeks.

"Anne is not afraid," the other woman said haughtily. "None of us are afraid. Anne has not been feeling well."

"Oh," Andrew replied, his eyes quickly leaving her and returning to drink in more of Anne's rare beauty. "I'm sorry to hear that." "Anne," he thought. Her name was as delicate and beautiful as she. In his mind he repeated it over and over like a piece of gentle music. She sensed his attention.

"Who are you?" Anne said softly. Her eyes held his and Andrew felt as if he were drowning.

"Eric," Kathryn said to her brother. "What in God's name does he do here? Are you mad to have brought him?"

"Be quiet, Kathryn. Andrew has saved my life more than once this day," Eric said; his eyes were also on his younger sister. "You should be in bed, Anne. You do look terrible. I leave you for two days and—"

"Two rather eventful days," Kathryn said fiercely.

"Eric, please, I don't need to go to bed. I'm fine and I want to stay right here. This poor man needs help." She turned as she spoke to look at both her brother and her sister. "And you two need not be so . . ." She broke off, and steadied herself. Andrew could see she was trembling. He fought the urge to go to her and put his arm about her. He had to laugh at himself. She probably had more strength than he did at the moment. Besides, she was the enemy. His eyes remained on her. God, how could he ever think of Anne McLeod as an enemy? He would have to be very careful. Sir Andrew Craighton could not afford such a mistake. His life, and a whole lot more, depended upon him not being careless.

"I will introduce myself," Andrew said. "My name is Andrew, and Lord Eric has employed me to stay here in the event that he is made prisoner. I shall be soldier, secretary, anything you wish."

"Are you daft, Eric!" Kathryn said fiercely.

"Hold your tongue, Kathryn! Pay no attention to her, Andrew, she's a shrew." He tried to smile, but Andrew was really not listening. He was again looking at Anne, in fact he was absorbing her as if he was memorizing every line of her face. He had the strongest feeling that he could actually inhale her loveliness and hold it inside him.

"Kathryn," her brother said, "instead of being so unpleasant, can you bring us some food and some more wine? I think the both of us are exhausted."

Before she could answer, a heavy pounding on the front door reverberated through the house. The others may have been surprised, but Andrew had expected it.

42

When the order came to open in the king's name, Kathryn recognized the voice that had given it. She walked to the door like an avenging goddess to face the man she knew stood on the opposite side.

She opened the door and they stood face to face again, the mark of her whip vivid on his lip.

Andrew studied the intruder carefully, memorizing the tanned face and taking note of the sharpest gray eyes he had ever seen. A new kind of excitement filled him. Here was a foe to sharpen the wit. A formidable enemy, one he would have to be wary of. He was conscious of all things, the most important being the way the stranger's and Kathryn's eyes met and held.

Kathryn faced Donovan; anger and emotion turned her eyes to glittering emeralds. Her eyes never left him. "This is Donovan McAdam." Her voice shook a little.

Eric bowed. There was a current of tension in the air. Donovan seemed to forcefully drag his eyes from Kathryn to look at her brother. "Lord Eric McLeod, you are under arrest."

Eric rose slowly to his feet, filled his wine cup again, and drank after toasting Donovan with a cool arrogance. Andrew wasn't too sure he didn't see a touch of admiration in Donovan's eyes. Then Eric drew his sword from its sheath and proffered it. Donovan accepted the sword wordlessly.

"Keep in mind that your victory is only today. We will never deny our position . . . or our king," Kathryn said.

"I shall do that, mistress," Donovan said softly. "I shall always keep your position in mind." Their eyes did battle again. Then again Donovan tore his eyes away and looked at Andrew. "Who is he?"

"This is Andrew, our secretary," Kathryn replied coldly.

Andrew was amazed that she had, in a way, stood to defend him.

"Stand, sir," Donovan said. Kathryn laughed again while Andrew struggled to his feet.

"Andrew is a servant," Kathryn said, amusement dripping in her voice.

Donovan's face flushed. She was trying to make him look foolish and lowbred. His anger was being tested with his control. "He is English," he said, ignoring her attitude as much as he could.

"Yes," she said, "he is English. He is also my secretary. Where do you plan to take my brother?" She added the last as if the subject of Andrew was dismissed.

"He will be held to await James's judgment," Donovan muttered angrily.

Donovan ordered his men to take Eric into their custody. He tried to keep his eyes from revealing his anger as Eric said a leisurely good-bye to his sisters, as proud and arrogant as if he were going on a short journey, even though this journey could very well be his last.

Donovan had turned to leave as well when Kathryn spoke his name sharply. He stopped in the doorway, but didn't turn around. His broad shoulders squared and stiffened, as if bracing for a blow.

"Tonight I will send my brother food."

"Aye," came the firm answer.

"And wine."

"Aye."

She had pressed defiantly, as if wanting to see how much strain he would accept. He turned and his face was harsh. But his eyes, holding hers, were more easily read by Andrew than by Kathryn, who could not seem to get past her own indignant rage. This woman could stir this man beyond what was normal, Andrew thought. This might be a useful thing to know. Every man had his weakness and Andrew meant to find any chinks in Donovan McAdam's armor.

"Do not think we are so easily beaten," Kathryn

grated.

"I do not deny that it was not easy, mistress. But whether you choose to believe it or not you are beaten. Now, it is up to me to choose what to do with you."

"Bastard!" Kathryn hissed. Her sister gasped and even Andrew was not sure Donovan wasn't going to strike her down where she stood. Men had been buried for saying less offensive words to this man. But instead he smiled a grim smile.

"Nay, mistress. I come from a family, mayhap not as high placed as yours, but equally honorable. Besides, stations have a way of changing rapidly. You should keep it in mind should you ever request mercy or forgiveness for your uncivilized attitude."

"Mercy! Forgiveness! Don't believe I would ever come to you for a favor!"

"Again you are hasty," he said smoothly. "Surely you have just asked for one." He smiled again. "Comfort for your brother," he reminded, "or had you forgotten?"

There was a swift intake of breath from her and had she tried her eyes could not have gleamed with a more murderous glow.

"You deny these things?"

"Are you asking for them?" he countered casually.

If she had held a broadsword surely she would have struck him dead. Andrew watched with deep interest as she struggled for control. She is a smart creature. She is sure of another day of battle, Andrew thought. It was true that sometimes strategic retreat gave one a victory in another battle.

"Yes," she said through gritted teeth.

"Ah, such an unladylike way to ask a gentleman for a favor. Surely you can be a bit more pleasant."

It took all the effort Andrew had not to laugh aloud. But in the next breath the laughter was turned in the other direction. Gracefully she moved toward Donovan and it was the first look of surprise seen in his eyes by anyone, although Kathryn didn't see it; but Andrew did.

She went to her knees before him, her hands folded in supplication. "My lord, I request your magnificent mercy and beg you to let me send aid to my brother."

He was not yet a lord and he very well knew she knew it. He contained his rage well but the hands he used to reach down and grasp her shoulders were shaking, a very rare thing for him. He nearly jerked her to her feet, and could see the scornful laughter in her eyes. "You may take to your brother what you choose, but it is not because of your gentle lady's request. 'Tis because I had no intention of doing him harm. He will stand before Parliament and answer for his crimes."

"Crimes! To fight for your king is now a crime?"

"You fought for the wrong king. When you lose you should be prepared to pay the price for it."

She knew most certainly his double-edged threat was made against her. She would have given anything to be able to anger him enough that he would tell her what her fate was meant to be. "We shall continue to fight to restore our king to his rightful throne," she taunted.

Now he released her and his eyes blazed with a desire to hurt her, hurt her pride as she had wanted to hurt his. "Mistress, James the Third is dead. Murdered. News was brought to me and we found him two hours ago near Beaton's Mill."

Kathryn's face had gone gray, and even Andrew rose slowly to his feet. His mind spun. He must see that this news got into the right hands at once. Once the word was spread situations would be changed.

He had been sent to see if there was some way to attain peace between England and Scotland and now things might shift. He had to know how and with whom he could deal. The man who stood in the doorway did not seem to be one of them. Dealing with this

46

man would be, to say the least, dangerous . . . maybe deadly.

Kathryn was silent. But now that Donovan's anger had surfaced he had a hard time bringing it under control.

"A reward has been set. Five thousand crowns for any information that will lead to the capture of the assassins. Do you ken where you stand now, mistress? Does it satisfy you? If not there be better news. After Parliament sets, honors will be distributed to those loyal to the king. My king! Land, titles, and wives. Do you understand yet, or must I make it clearer to you?"

If it were possible for Kathryn's face to grow whiter it did. For she understood quite well. But the shock passed as quickly as it had come and her own rage surfaced along with a deadly calm. "Do you think to aspire, do you dare? Well do not. I should die first."

Now he grinned broadly, knowing he had pricked her emotions. "Do not flatter yourself, mistress. No one said you were chosen for any honors yet. Good night."

He was gone and he left her gasping in his wake, angry at a force she could not reach.

"Damn you! Damn you!" she muttered.

Then again she became aware of Andrew's presence. She turned to face him, then her eyes moved to her pale-faced sister.

There was no doubt in the minds of the three of them. Young Jamie, the fourth James, was king of Scotland, and this news was going to have completely different effects on the three of them.

Chapter 4

Andrew settled into an extremely quiet, nervous, and unsettled house. He was given a room that adjoined both Anne's and Kathryn's rooms; the connecting doors were locked, of course. The first night that he spent beneath the McLeod roof he was surprised he managed to get any sleep at all, knowing she was in the room next to his. Anne, the beautiful Anne. How he wanted to bring her some comfort. He found it hard to believe himself. No woman had ever affected him this way.

That night he could hear her pacing the floor, just as he could hear almost the same movements from Kathryn's room.

All of them knew there was little for him to do now except guard Eric's sisters as best he could.

The king is dead, long live the king; It was a cry that had been heard down the centuries, mourning the old and heralding the new. There were none who did not know that soon the procession carrying the black draped litter that carried the coffin of James III would pass on its way to the Abbey of Cambuskenneth. There the king would be buried.

As if the mood of nature was the same as those who watched and waited, a heavy, dark rain fell. It beat against the walls and windows, and dripped off eaves and corners of buildings to run in rivulets to form puddles in the dirty streets. Bells tolled throughout the city.

The cortege bearing the dead king passed through the city to the muffled beat of drums.

With this entourage rode the King of Scotland, James IV. A few rode with him, among them, Donovan McAdam.

Kathryn stood at her window with Anne and Andrew and watched them ride through, not caring to hide her tears. As they passed below, Donovan looked up as if he expected to see her there. Without being able to see the tears on her face he knew she wept.

Fear gripped the city as lord after lord was brought to the great castle of Edinburgh to stand trial. They waited within the same walls where an uncrowned king had begun his reign in bloodshed.

It was in the dawn hours, and the guarded coffin lay in the center room of the abbey. A man walked in, his boots making a sharp sound on the stone floor. Guards drew to attention. He walked slowly toward the coffin, and his eyes seemed glued to it. Only when he was just three feet from the guards did he acknowledge their presence. "Leave us." He said the words with a deadness in his voice. The guards vanished silently.

He knelt by the coffin and lay his hand on it. For a moment he seemed frozen, stiff and cold as the stone pillars that surrounded him.

Behind one of these stood Donovan McAdam, for he knew his king well, and he had known those dark hours before dawn would be the bitterest of all. Just as he knew that that would be the time James would come here. He also knew what his king sought . . . but there was no power on earth that could give him what he desperately wanted. Still, the presence of a friend who knew and understood the force of ambi-

49

tion, power, and lust that had driven James to this pass, might be some comfort.

James did not acknowledge the presence of his friend as he knelt beside him, yet James knew he was there. It was dim and quiet and neither man spoke for long minutes. Then Donovan turned his head to find James's dark eyes fixed upon him.

"I need your counsel." The words were quietly spoken.

" 'Tis yours, my lord." The reply was just as quiet and in no way condemning.

James frowned. "How would you suggest I might be satisfied in my own mind and conscience . . . ," James hesitated. "My conscience," he repeated, "for my part in the cruel act which took my father's life?"

"You are in deep conflict. You need some comfort."

"If I suffer," James muttered, "it is right I suffer, for I am guilty of a terrible crime."

"But you are not guilty. Did I not stand beside you when you gave the order that your father was to be spared, to be brought to you alive?"

"Aye, but that does not relieve my guilt."

"You claim guilt, out of love. But it was not you who did the deed or ordered it done."

"I am guilty. Because it was I who set off the train of deeds which ended in a foul, traitorous, and bloody murder. I shall have to learn to live with my guilt."

"But you grieve, and you sorrow. You suffer, and when a man does that he wants forgiveness."

"Forgiveness! And who is there to forgive me?"

"God," came the blunt reply, "at least he has a full understanding of what is and was truly in your heart."

James closed his eyes for a moment, then turned again to look at Donovan. He did not see pity in his eyes, and for that he was grateful. What he saw was human understanding for the frailty of the human mind and heart.

"Mayhap you speak the truth, Donovan. I have

stepped in that direction this day."

Donovan waited. He had known the king had ridden out in the driving rain earlier, refusing to let anyone ride with him. It had sometimes been a relief to him to ride hard when something pressed his mind. Now, he felt, James was about to tell him where he had gone.

"I will wear a reminder of my guilt for the balance of my life."

Donovan still remained quiet as James turned fully toward him. Slowly he unfastened doublet and shirt. Beneath them, binding his body and already chafing it red, was an iron belt at least a half inch thick.

Donovan's brows drew together in a frown. "Sire."

"Nay, Donovan, 'tis to remain the balance of my life to remind me of a deed done in my name. To remind me of my guilt when I pray. I do not ever want to forget."

Donovan felt a deep pity, but there were no more words to be said. And James was again facing the coffin and seemed lost in thought. Donovan remained beside his king for over two hours. With the tolling of morning bells James seemed to regain his hold on the present. Both men rose and left the abbey together.

Two weeks later Andrew was called into Kathryn's presence. When he came he found her before the huge fireplace, reading a note. Kathryn crumpled the note in her hand and tossed it on the fire, watching it burn. For safety's sake she had to make sure all evidence of its presence was completely destroyed.

Andrew stood behind her and would have given a great deal to know what the note said. He hesitantly tried for a grain of information.

Kathryn rose from her knees by the fire and began to pace the room deep in thought.

"Is something wrong, mistress? Have you word of

51

your brother, mayhap?"

"Nay, Andrew, 'tis not that." She stopped pacing and looked at him. "I must have permission from the king, or that . . . damn McAdam, to leave the city."

"Impossible."

"Why?"

" 'For what reason,' they will ask. You and your family are not exactly in Jamie's or Donovan McAdam's good graces."

"Still, I must go."

"Where?"

"To Direlton."

Andrew had been in touch with all that was going on since the death of the king. He knew that small groups still fought, that uprisings had to be put down in multitudes of places. He suspected now that Kathryn knew of another, maybe was even involved in it. He felt a tinge of fear. Kathryn had the courage and strength to fight, but what of Anne? She would be left alone should Kathryn be caught. And Donovan McAdam, what would he do with Kathryn should he catch her involved?

Andrew also knew that McAdam had paid several visits to the house; each time Kathryn had refused to see him. Anne had been the one to entertain him and Andrew was not too happy about this either. He did not know that Donovan spent most of the time asking subtle questions about Kathryn.

"Why to Direlton?" he asked quietly.

"Scone is on the way and I choose to go to the coronation."

"Is your trip only to see Jamie crowned?" Again his question was soft.

Kathryn regarded him carefully and seemed to make a decision. It strummed Andrew's guilt a bit, but he remained still. "Eric trusted you and I shall do the same. There is to be an uprising at Direlton."

"And you are part of it?" Now Andrew was shaken.

"Nay! I'm not a fool! But those who are stirring it are. They are known, I'm sure of it. I would warn them and prevent more bloodshed."

"If 'tis known you knew and warned them you would be playing right into McAdam's hands. He would have you at his mercy."

" 'Tis a chance I shall have to take."

" 'Tis too dangerous."

"Andrew," her voice was cold now, "you will go to Donovan McAdam this day. You will tell him I . . . humbly," she added bitterly, "request his permission to go north for the coronation. After that his permission to go on to Direlton to . . . to visit friends."

"He's no fool."

"I don't care a whit for him! Andrew, do as I say."

"Yes, Mistress Kathryn," Andrew said. Reluctantly, he left her.

As Andrew rode to the castle the rain began to fall again. He rode swiftly, and when he reached the castle door and stated his business he was ushered into a corner room whose windows gave a wonderful view. He stood for several minutes before he realized the best view from the window was the McLeod home. And these rooms belonged to Donovan McAdam. Andrew began to wonder if he had chosen them for this purpose.

In the next and larger room, through a curtained doorway, he could hear Donovan McAdam's voice.

When he was told to come in, Andrew turned from the window, crossed the room, and pushed open the curtains . . . and came face to face with Donovan McAdam. He smiled and was aware that Donovan's smile was just as sharpened by alert wit and deep suspicion as his was.

"Good morning, sir." Andrew tried for a humble tone of voice but he was certain Donovan didn't accept it for more than it was.

"Good morning." Donovan did not ask Andrew to sit. There was no reason why he should. Just the same Andrew was glad he didn't. To ask him to sit would be a clear claim that he knew Andrew belonged to a more elevated position. From their first meeting in the McLeod home Andrew had been sure Donovan was suspicious of him. Today, when he looked into those piercing gray eyes, he was still sure of it.

"My mistress sends her greetings, sir."

Donovan remained silent, as if he were surprised, but his shrewd gaze never left Andrew's, to the latter's extreme discomfort.

"Lady McLeod wishes me to tell you that she has received the heralds of the crown concerning the coronation of His Majesty at Scone on the twenty-fourth of this month, three days hence. My mistress would like permission to attend the ceremonies."

Donovan continued to watch Andrew closely and Andrew could feel his nerves grow taut; still he remained as submissive as a man of his build could manage to look.

"And that is all she wishes?" Donovan asked noncommittally.

"Yes sir . . . oh, except after the ceremony she would like permission to ride north and visit some friends."

"Where?"

"At Direlton."

Andrew's eyes met silver gray ones that seemed to be trying to pierce all his shields. He remained silent.

Donovan was trying to see beyond the seemingly innocent blue eyes to the man he firmly suspected existed behind them. Kathryn McLeod was not one to meekly request, nor was she one to surrender to his rules so easily. No, he didn't believe for one minute. . . . But he would listen to reason.

"I believe the trip to Direlton seems to be the most

54

important request of the two. Why did you save it for last? Why does she want to travel north?"

Andrew had to seem less than brilliant enough to have been devious. He asked innocently, "Why does my mistress want to travel north, sir? Why, to go to the coronation."

Donovan was momentarily angry. He started to say something, then stopped and his eyes narrowed. No, this man was far from stupid. He rose and moved away from his chair. Andrew remained immobile while Donovan walked behind him. This was a very uncomfortable position for Andrew, who was being appraised from the rear. He could feel Donovan's eyes like a piercing sword. His shoulders twitched. When Donovan spoke again it gave Andrew the opportunity to turn slightly to face him. When he did he found that another man had quietly entered the room and stood beside Donovan. Andrew did not recognize the man so he remained silent. But when Donovan turned to the man with every sign of deference Andrew knew with a burst of recognition that he faced James IV . . . the king.

For a moment he was taken completely off guard. He couldn't think clearly. It was not every day a man found himself in the presence of a man as electrifying as James, and even less often when you looked at the situation from Andrew's perspective. He returned Andrew's gaze with a faint frown.

"Sir," Donovan said, without identifying the king, "Lady Kathryn McLeod wishes to attend the coronation, and she wishes to proceed to Direlton after the ceremony."

Andrew added, "Of course Mistress Anne, if she is well enough, will accompany her to Scone."

"But she will not go on to Direlton?" James inquired softly.

Andrew looked at the floor, but not before he had seen a look exchanged between James and Donovan.

His hands began to sweat. Surely they knew, both of them. Was it a trap to catch more rebels? He was scared for Kathryn, who seemed oblivious to the danger.

"Lady Kathryn may go where she chooses," James answered casually. Andrew pretended to look to Donovan for confirmation of this and was prepared for the next words.

"You heard His Majesty."

To this point Andrew had not been told he was speaking to the king, so he tried his best to show his amazement at being told he was in the presence of James. But Donovan's eyes on him made him sure that at least one of them was unconvinced.

"Oh . . . ah . . . your grace . . ." He went down on one knee.

James watched Andrew closely for a few moments; then his eyes moved to Donovan, who was scowling darkly.

"You may leave," James said, and Andrew did, as rapidly as he could. Standing under Donovan's astute gaze was bad enough, but both James's and his together were too much for Andrew's nerves to bear.

When James and Donovan heard the outer door close it was Donovan who spoke first.

"If that was a play, it was a bad one."

"That was an English border accent, wasn't it?"

"It was, Your Grace. The man is Andrew Craighton and he has told many he was from Dorsetshire . . . mayhap too many. Anyway he is said to have served Richard the Third and fled England after his defeat. He fought with Eric McLeod at Sauchieburn under the McLeod banner and he's still wearing the McLeod livery. In fact he is protector of the household now that Eric McLeod is being held. I have no word of any kind of proof that he is more than he says he is. I would like your permission to watch him closely for a while."

"Obviously you do not trust him an inch to make such a request."

"Not an inch," Donovan agreed, "I cannot afford to."

James was weary, unmercifully so. He sat back in a chair and half closed his eyes. Andrew had raised the specter of England and those who would like to find the Scottish king vulnerable. He had to put that worry aside for the moment. There was nothing to do but, as Donovan said, watch Andrew closely.

"I have seen couriers arriving all day. Is something brewing?" Donovan questioned.

" 'Twas the couriers from the highlands."

"What news from there?"

James leaned back in his chair and sighed. Then for a few seconds he seemed caught in deep thought. "What do you think of Lord Drummond?" James, to Donovan's puzzlement, had changed the subject.

"He is loyal to you, there is no question about that." Donovan sought some way to ease James's weariness and his obvious black mood. "Besides, he has some very pretty daughters."

"And you," James laughed, "my celibate friend, consider it is time I sought something more frivolous to bide my time."

"It would do you no harm, Sire," Donovan grinned.

"Ah, my friend," James said softly, "since Jennie has wed you have not sought to link your name to another, albeit you have slept with enough wenches to tire a stallion."

Donovan's smile grew tight, as if he had to force it to remain on his face. He walked to the window and looked out. "I have been giving my life a great deal of thought."

James sat up in his chair and watched his favorite companion. This was a novel thing. Donovan had eluded marriage as if it were a torture. Now he spoke of a woman and James was more than curious. He was completely diverted from his mental weariness.

He remained silent, waiting for Donovan to tell him the thoughts he held. Donovan turned from the window to face him.

Donovan's thoughts were confused, unsettled. Marriage had been pushed from his mind quite brutally by the lovely Jennie. He had sworn he would be much older, and forced to marry for the sake of an heir, before he would resort to marriage. But now, he wanted someone . . . he did not love her, he just wanted, desired her. He wanted to read her eyes when he informed her they would wed. He wanted to hear her denials, fight the battle . . . and he wanted to subdue her, bend her to his will. He wanted. . . . He inhaled and spoke carefully.

"I think it is time . . . now . . . that I considered marriage."

James knew quite well what Donovan meant. He had stood beside his king and he knew this king meant to be generous in his rewards for loyalty. It was time to begin his future with holdings, new titles . . . and obviously, with a wife.

"And who," James asked softly, "are you considering asking my permission to wed?"

"Lady McLeod," Donovan replied.

James remained quiet and Donovan's brow arched in question of the silence.

"Which Lady McLeod?" James repeated the question he had asked Andrew . . . and received the same answer.

"Lady Kathryn."

"Ah . . . I see."

"I know the situation," Donovan said quietly.

"Do you now," James answered softly. "Then why do you choose a lady who is a sworn enemy, whose brother you have taken prisoner, and whose position is, to say the least, perilous?"

"She's a woman of courage and strength. If I am to begin a new future I would choose the best."

"Somewhat like choosing a brood mare to mate with the right stallion and produce prime stock?" The question was asked with amusement.

"Somewhat," Donovan tried to smile. He knew he lied, but he hoped his king didn't know, because he really had no answers . . . no logical reason for what he wanted to do . . . except he wanted Kathryn McLeod with every breath he took. He'd done his best to push her from his mind, but it seemed she was constantly right within his view — always at a distance, yet always out of reach. Every time he came to her home on one pretext or another he found her just gone . . . eluding him as expertly as a highland mist. By damn, with the king's word behind him he would soon teach her that he was . . . what? Her master? No, that was not what he wanted to be to her. But what he did want from her was so intangible that even he could not grasp it. Maybe it was, just once to see her submit of her own free will to someone or something else.

Without thinking he raised his hand to gently touch the scar on his cheek. It was almost as if she had branded him somehow. He had watched the fire in her eyes that day, and the night he had come to take her brother. The fire burnt with a searing touch and he wanted to capture that fire in his hands. Even if he was burnt in the doing of it.

"There are things you must know first, Donovan, before you make your request."

"Things, what things?"

"I said the highland couriers have arrived."

"Aye."

"They bring word of a planned uprising."

"Another?"

"Aye. There is open rebellion not far from Scone. I don't want the coronation interrupted by rebels. It would be a bad beginning," James added. Not that the beginning was not bloody enough, James thought.

"You have sure word, names?"

"Aye."

"Then we will put an end to it. Where is it to be?"

James rose and walked to the curtained door. There he stopped, his hand on the curtain, and turned to look again at Donovan. His face again showed his weariness and his reluctance to hurt a friend. "At Direlton," he said softly.

Then he was gone, leaving Donovan to digest the words he had just said. Could she be involved? Would she be so foolish as to place herself so neatly in his hands?

He gazed about him in the small room in which he stood. Opposite him a door opened into another equally small room. Obviously these two rooms had been part of the suite in which he now lived. And anyone in one of these two rooms would have to cross his suite to get out of them. He walked to the window. It was high and small. There was no possible escape from them except through the rooms he occupied. He called for a servant.

"Prepare these rooms," he gestured to the two small ones, "for a prisoner. I want them very comfortable."

"Aye, sir." The servant left to do his bidding.

Donovan pictured Kathryn there, caught in these two rooms. He would hold her here until she learned that there was no way to freedom except through him. He was well over thirty, and never in his life had he encountered a serious defeat. He did not even dream that he would ever encounter it from a woman.

Andrew returned to the McLeod home more than just a little shaken. He was certain that both Donovan and James knew about the planned uprising, just as certain as he was that Kathryn would try to warn the lords involved of their foolishness and their jeopardy.

He also was sure it was because Kathryn wanted no more bloodshed, no more to be locked away as her brother was, to await James's mercy. She would ride to protect them and Andrew wracked his brain for a way to stop her.

Kathryn had warned him not to be seen returning directly to her, to use caution and come up the back stairs. There were too many people who feared James enough to carry tales and Andrew was a strong and purposeful man, and most would know that it would be well within Andrew's realm to carry out whatever orders Kathryn would give. It would also endanger Andrew's life and his ability to conspire with Kathryn.

He climbed the narrow spiral stairs and found a door at the top. As he opened it and stepped out he suddenly faced a pretty young maid with her arms full of linens. He well knew that all gossip and rumors and sometimes truth could be found with the servants of a household. He smiled at her and she returned his smile with one of her own that was an open invitation. She had seen Andrew often and had had her own fantasies as far as the rugged and exciting-looking man was concerned.

"What are you doing up here?" She smiled invitingly.

"Why, looking for you of course," he said easily. He closed the door behind him. Her eyes warmed and he gazed at her with some interest. Who knew what bits of information she held that would be of interest to him. He reached out and took hold of her shoulders, drawing her to him.

"Do ye really want me to believe that?" she laughed.

"Why not? You need only to look in a mirror to see why any man would seek you out."

"Aye, any man in the household but you."

"Why so?"

"I don't know. You seem different than most. I mean you seem more . . ." She shrugged, unable to voice what was different between Andrew and other servants.

61

He moved to stand closer and watched her eyes dance both with pleasure and uncertainty. This man had attracted her from the moment he had arrived and she was quite willing to test out his abilities at close range. He was exciting and she was not the only one in the household who had looked longingly after him as he passed. When he drew her closer to him she came willingly and would have surrendered with little battle.

He was just about to kiss her when the door on the opposite end of the room opened and Anne McLeod stepped into the room.

He cursed himself for seven kinds of a fool. The one person he would never want to see him in this position was Anne. Anne, the only woman who had ever reached that well-guarded place within him.

Her great violet-hued eyes held his and no emotion crossed her face, yet her cheeks were flushed and her hands were gripped into fists at her sides. Maybe Anne felt more than she ever intended to put into words. This excited him beyond reason. He let the girl go and she hastily disappeared; then he smiled and bowed. "Lady Anne," he said softly, and watched with pleasure as her eyes lifted to his and her cheeks grew even pinker.

Chapter 5

The moment of silence while their eyes held each other grew . . . and grew. Then Andrew realized that his shy little rose was going to prove to have some thorns. He smiled.

She wore royal blue and it made her ebony hair seem to glow with life and her wide eyes an even deeper blue. He had no way of knowing she was summoning all her courage. He had had a traumatic effect on her from that first night when he had come wounded to her home. She had helped care for him, all the time praying he would not notice how her hands trembled.

There was something about Andrew's presence that Anne could not understand. He'd had an effect on her that made her question herself, a raw energy and an overwhelming maleness that made her first nervous, then excited.

This was not the kind of man to whom she was accustomed. Of course she had had little experience with any but her brother's closest friends, and none would have attempted to press her in any way.

Andrew had never pressed her either, but his presence was somehow overpowering. He had been kind, generous, and gentle, and Anne could not understand what more she sought from him.

The worst thing that had preyed on her mind was

that it would be scandalous to admit to a soul that she was so attracted to a servant. She was Lady Anne and this sort of thing could never be. Still, he was so . . . so magnetic.

Andrew, too, was caught in the same thoughts. How he wished she could see him at court, a knight in his own right, a man with a position equal to hers. Would her eyes change? Would she . . . ?

"Lady Anne," he questioned again as he took another step toward her. This was a mistake, for when he did the soft scent of her perfume entwined around him. He remained immobile. But now Anne was regaining her composure. Her lips curved in a soft smile.

"When my father was alive, he never would not tolerate dalliances with the maids. Do you know he once fined those who toyed with them?"

" 'Twas only one maid," he replied with a grin. He was pleased to hear her laugh softly.

"I'm afraid that doesn't matter."

"Then . . . I must pay my fine. What is it?"

"Sixpence."

He moved even closer, and she had to tip her head to look up at him. He reached into his pocket and drew out the coins. Then he reached out to take her hand and place the coins in it. He closed her fingers around them. Anne sucked in her breath at the tingle that seemed to flow from his hand to hers. He held her hand a moment or so longer than was necessary, for he was as reluctant to break the contact as she. He was startled only a second at the erotic effect just her touch had on him. Then slowly, as their eyes held, she withdrew her hand from his. She found it difficult to find something to say.

"Have you much money of your own?" she questioned.

"Very little, why? I haven't much need for money," he replied, "but you will."

"Why, Andrew?"

"I . . . can't explain now. I just . . . well, your brother has entrusted your safety to me."

"Mine and Kathryn's," she reminded.

"Yes, and that is another matter."

"I don't understand."

"Kathryn is . . . sometimes unpredictable and a little . . ."

"Uncontrollable," she offered with a smile. But this time he didn't return it. He was truly afraid for her, because he knew in his heart that Anne would always stand by her family and if what he thought was going to happen happened it might take every ounce of ingenuity to keep her safe and still serve his king. He denied the thought to himself that he would find it very hard if a choice had to be made.

"Anne . . . Lady Anne, please, listen to me."

He wanted to reach out and pull her into his arms, but he didn't dare. She was shaken because she could feel a strange flowing warmth fill her and a touch of panic, for she knew if he had reached for her, she would have stepped into the circle of those strong arms and been contented. It was forbidden by all she knew and held dear, yet she knew she would have done so and it frightened her.

She tried to look away and her downcast lashes were dark against her creamy skin. Then again she looked up. She reached out this time and surprised him by taking his hand. She replaced the coins in it.

"Why won't you take my money?"

"Because you have very little, and besides . . . you were entrusted to take care of me and I have every confidence that you will do just that."

"You know," he said softly, "that should you ever have need of me I would be here to serve you. Still you must remember what I said. You may need money. Please do this for me if for no other reason. Your welfare is important to . . . so many people."

It was a gallant speech hardly that of a commoner. Anne was puzzled by the contrast between what she heard, felt, and saw and what she was supposed to believe.

"All right. I will do as you say," she whispered.

By all the gods he wanted to hold her, and kiss her with an urgency that was driving him mad.

It was very dimly lit in the narrow hall. He felt her eyes on him and heard her soft drawn breath.

"I don't frighten you do I, Anne?" he questioned gently.

"No," she replied, completely oblivious to the fact that he had omitted her title and had said her name almost as a caress.

"Then listen to me. You are as important as your sister or your brother. But for once . . . maybe you have to step back from them."

"I could never do that. Their fortunes are mine. I love them. Andrew, why do you speak so?"

"Because I love you," he wanted to say, but he knew that was impossible. He sighed. He should have known. In her sweet and gentle way she was just as stubborn—and proud—as her sister. He could not hurt her by trying to tell her what her sister was planning. He thought he could spare her that, at least until he had done his best to convince Kathryn not to make this suicidal journey.

"Because these are dangerous times."

"And you would protect me."

"Any way that I can."

"From what?"

"Whatever threatens you, your peace of mind, your future . . . anything."

"You are a puzzle, Andrew."

"I. What puzzle, Anne? Your brother has hired me to do just that. It is my duty."

"Duty," she repeated. A soft smile touched her lips. "I feel there is more here than duty. Maybe that is why

I trust you so and feel so safe . . . and maybe that is why I feel you are so much more than just a servant."

"I am nothing more nor less than what you would wish me to be. I am your protector and you are my lady. Do not doubt me, Anne. I would do all for—," he paused, knowing he was only getting himself in deeper, "for your family. I have my honor and I choose to live by it."

"I see." She didn't know why she was disappointed in him for not saying it was she and she alone who held him. Again she realized how forbidden this was.

Andrew realized she was hurt and thought once he had regained his equilibrium he could convince her of his sincerity and ease her mind. "Will you let me come and talk to you later? Maybe I can make you understand more clearly."

"Of course."

He started to turn away from her. The last thing he wanted was her to be present when he told Kathryn what he believed. But again he did not take the gentle, quiet Anne seriously enough.

"You go to see Kathryn now?"

"Ah . . . well . . . yes, I do. But it is unimportant. Just a report of daily events."

Her eyes told him she didn't believe that for a minute. Her head lifted and she gazed at him, then said proudly, "Come, I will go with you."

Before he could resist she was walking away. He could do little but follow. " 'Twill be an honor, Lady Anne," Andrew said lamely . . . to her back.

Kathryn spun about when the door opened, dressed for riding and prepared to see Andrew alone. She was especially *not* prepared to see her sister lead a rather abashed Andrew into the room.

"What are you doing here, Anne?"

Andrew closed the door and watched with a half

smile as Anne stood her ground. He was somehow pleased despite the situation they were in.

"Kathryn, I have every right to know what is going on. Just where are you preparing to go?"

Kathryn's frown deepened, and her eyes flicked from Anne to Andrew and remained there, much to his discomfort.

"Kathryn," Anne demanded, "this does concern me as well as you."

"I know it does, Anne. But why do you have to know *everything* now when it is extremely dangerous to know *anything?* Why do you interfere!"

"I won't interfere. But I've a right to know. You are not the only one in the family who is interested in its welfare."

At that moment Andrew could have crushed her in his arms.

"I know that. You said you won't interfere."

"Yes. I only want to know the truth."

"Good. Andrew, I see no reason you shouldn't sit," Kathryn motioned him to a chair near the fireplace and drew one up beside him. Anne did the same and Andrew kept his pleasure to himself. "Now, Andrew, tell me everything."

Andrew had been watching Anne, but now his eyes turned to Kathryn. "I saw Donovan McAdam . . . I also saw the king," he began.

"Good God," Kathryn said, her voice heavy with aggravation. "I've seen the wretch many times. Is that all you have to report?"

"No . . . there is a good sight more." He bent forward to rest his arms on his knees. His huge body felt uncomfortable on the small, delicate chair. Before he could say more to Kathryn, Anne spoke.

"You have bought new boots," Anne said softly. Andrew glanced at her and for a moment they seemed to exist alone in the room; then he smiled. Anne had changed the subject to ease the tension.

"Aye, new boots. I needed them. Even though they left me with only a sixpence to my name." The humor was lost on Kathryn, who was annoyed that she felt something existed between these two she knew nothing about.

Kathryn made an impatient sound and Andrew restrained his laughter.

"Yes," Andrew chuckled. "Let's get on with it." Again he leaned forward on the chair. "Mistress Kathryn, you have both Donovan McAdam's permission . . . and the king's to go to the coronation. I believe that James wants as many there as he can get. You may even go to Direlton. But I wouldn't if I were you," he added quietly.

"I didn't ask for advice," Kathryn said. "What must be done must be. There is no other to warn them of the great mistake they are making. Would you have me let them hang?"

"James knows," Andrew said softly. "And that means they will hang anyway. I would not want you among them."

"I don't believe that. It is only what you feel. Besides, you do not take the rest of the country into consideration. They all stand against him."

"That is in your heart, in your head, but it just isn't true. You just want to believe it so desperately that you harbor the illusion. The border men are led by Patrick Hepburn and his friend McAdam. The Drummonds and the Douglases stand firm. Others will be joining them soon. Any more resistance is dangerous . . . and foolish. Why do you refuse to believe that the little plot at Direlton is known? Don't go and warn them."

"Andrew," she said, with the glimmer of another thought unveiled in her eyes.

"And I will not go," he added both quickly and firmly. "You endanger Anne's life as well as any chance your brother has of gaining his freedom. These

69

men are stupid fools and the royal wrath will take of them. You cannot warn them before it is too late."

"I will think about what you say," Kathryn said. But Andrew was far from sure that he had even made an impression on her. At the moment he was too frightened for Anne to even care. Maybe Donovan McAdam and Kathryn deserved to clash.

Kathryn stood, then smiled at Andrew. It was a kind and gentle smile, and that alone should have warned him.

"Good night, Andrew," she said, then turned and left.

Anne had not spoken for a while, but had watched Andrew's face as he almost pleaded with her sister. Anne may have been the quiet one, the gentle one, but she was far from a fool. There was so much more to this man than anyone knew. Somehow that frightened her. Andrew felt her eyes on him and when he looked at her he grew very still.

"Who are you, Andrew?" she whispered, almost afraid of his answer.

But Andrew had no intention of answering. He was frustrated and worried, but he was not going to lie to her. He rose from the uncomfortable seat.

"Good night . . . Lady Anne." He turned and left the room, feeling her eyes on him all the way to the door.

By Donovan's orders twenty men remained to be his escort. The rest took the narrow byroads, roads hardly used but bearing north . . . toward Scone and then to Direlton. He had given them plenty of time so that they would be camped nearby when he needed them.

He thought of Kathryn. She would have left, too. If he knew her as well as he thought he did she would have left early so the horse would have plenty of time for rest before the long trip to Direlton. She was an exceptional horsewoman and he knew she could handle the pressure of the ride as well as he could. He battled the feelings that only served to confuse him. This woman was enough to drive any man mad. A kind of excitement bubbled inside him that had nothing to do with the coronation of his king.

He waved a gauntleted hand at the men who guarded the gates. He controlled the military power; on his shoulders rested the security of his nation.

He was certain not many would be present at the coronation. Too much fear still stalked the land. One of his responsibilities was to help bring order to this chaos and establish James's rule with as little difficulty as possible.

Kathryn would be one of the few with noble blood to attend. He allowed her to linger in his mind during the course of the hard ride. Breathtakingly beautiful she was. But that was not all that he saw in her. She had struck a chord in him that had not been strummed for many years, and it angered, yet intrigued him that she had achieved this. Surrender was not in her vocabulary. . . . But it was not in his either. Yet he wasn't sure what he wanted from her. To bend her will was only a part. The rest stood in the shadows of his mind, refusing to be recognized no matter how he tried.

He remembered another long ride as well — the journey he'd taken when he left home to seek service that would aid him on his climb to where he now stood. He had risen by diligence, hard work, and loyalty to his king that could not be swayed.

On that first ride he had worn boots he had made for himself and he rode a stolen horse. Now he dressed magnificently and he was riding a great black stallion bred from the best stock. He was a match for Kathryn McLeod and he meant to prove it as he had proven his worth elsewhere.

He refused to acknowledge why he felt he had to

prove it.

Donovan reached Scone at ten o'clock. He dismounted in front of the chapel and his horse was led away. He prepared to wait for James's arrival. But Kathryn arrived first.

He saw her from a distance. Even from where he was he knew it could be no one but her. The glimmer of gold and white banners could be seen against the green of the trees and he felt strangely breathless as he awaited her. She was riding into the promised danger of his world as if she cared little for his thoughts or his power. It was defiance at its ultimate peak.

Her dress was trimmed in white ermine, and people cheered as she rode by. He knew she and her family were loved and respected and he let himself believe this was the main reason he meant to wed her. She would fight, but after he trapped her at Direlton she would have no choice.

In his shirt he carried a paper already signed by James that made it official. After the coronation Lady Kathryn McLeod would become his wife. She had no choices at all. This was the test, the way he meant to prove to her who was master and who was defeated.

His eyes never left her. The sun had created a miracle of lights in her hair and her skin seemed to glow. Although she refused to look in his direction he knew quite well she was aware of him. Her eyes seemed to be seeing something just above his head and they sparkled like sun-kissed emeralds. He fought the stir of emotions she roused in him. He felt a pulsing heat flow through him and as she drew her horse to a stop he strode toward her.

Kathryn's senses were alive with him, from the breathtaking width of his shoulders to the silver gray eyes that seemed to be absorbing everything about her. She could feel the tingle of awareness as his gaze raked over her. He purposefully strode toward her and she saw the determination on his face and in every move of his tall, masculine body. She didn't want his touch . . . in fact, she preferred to keep as much distance between them as she could. He exuded danger for her in every move, every breath.

Kathryn expected two of her men to aid her in dismounting so she deliberately refused to see Donovan. But no man had the courage to face down the steely glint in his gray eyes as he gazed at them, coldly daring them to interfere. Then he walked toward her.

When he stopped by her side he surprised her by not speaking first. Instead he reached up and took the whip from her hand.

"I never underestimate the opposing force, my lady," he smiled. He reached up and took her waist in his hands to lift her down.

"Mayhap you overestimate your own abilities," she said coldly.

"I think not," he said softly.

"Then don't aim too high in your reach or you might be returned to where you belong."

His patience was growing thin. But he restrained himself only by remembering where they were and why they were here. He offered his arm instead.

He was too close, too powerful, and Kathryn was more unsure than she thought she should be. She didn't like the unwelcome ability he had to stir something in her that she refused to recognize.

"I would rather wait and watch the king arrive."

She stood on the steps beside him and the scent of her perfume drifted to him on the breeze. Sun glinted in her hair and he could feel the pulsing life of her without even touching her. And he wanted to touch her.

Was she really fool enough to go on to Direlton? He hoped . . . God, the thought of her stirred his senses. In a way he respected her desire to warn the rebellious lords. But he blessed the day he had found out her intent, for he knew it was the only way to subdue her

73

. . . and claim her he would . . . no matter what kind of a battle she fought.

Although they both seemed to be waiting for the king's arrival they were completely aware of each other.

Then an ancient pageantry began. A new king was coming to be crowned at Scone. Traditionally the king must be the finest horseman in Scotland. His father had failed, but James rode like he was born to the saddle. He dismounted and as the bells began to toll, Donovan and Kathryn followed him into the chapel.

Border nobility filled the chapel, but conspicuously absent were the highlanders. There were only three that knew the brooding and plotting that kept the others away: only James, Donovan, and Kathryn knew the true meaning of the absent lords.

Just before James entered the chapel Kathryn looked at Donovan. Despite what she insisted she truly felt for him, she had to admire how he looked and the way he held himself. It was as if he was the master of all he surveyed. All but her, she cried silently. He may rule his world . . . but never hers! Never!

The fact was he looked startlingly handsome; he was better dressed than most other lords she had seen at any functions. He carried himself with pride and self-assurance. She forced herself to look away.

James, dressed in sables and velvet, was kneeling now in front of the altar, pledging his vow in low, measured tones. His voice was resonant, compelling, and fearless.

Over their heads the arched and vaulted roof echoed to the ancient ceremony and she watched as the crown, gold and glittering with rubies, emeralds, pearls, and diamonds, was placed on his head.

Then it was finished—James was king. The coronation was over. Donovan offered his arm to Kathryn and they followed James as he walked out of the chapel . . . as alone as he had been when he had entered.

Kathryn looked up at Donovan; above his lip the small white scar could be seen. She studied him and for a moment his gray eyes warmed . . . then they became wary.

"So," she said softly, "you and your king have achieved all the power you want."

"Yes," he agreed. His voice was as controlled as hers. "The power to grant any favor . . . or destroy any enemy." His words were a promise and a display of his power.

"Grant any favor? No matter what I would ask, James has given you the power to grant?"

"I can," he said softly, but with firm assurance in his voice. "What do you want?"

"Nothing," she smiled up at him now. He had carelessly offered her anything and she knew he sensed a trap, but too late. "I want nothing from you, Donovan McAdam . . . nothing."

"You speak hastily. That is a bargain you yourself will break." He was angry now and cursing the fact that she had this irritating ability to get to him as no others did. "You ride away so soon, Lady McLeod. Why is it you feel the need to hurry. Why not stay for the celebration?"

"Nay, I must go soon. I have friends who are awaiting me."

"But there is no need to hurry."

"I'm afraid I must. Will you help me mount?" Her expression was cool and mocking. He wanted to seize her now, but her men were armed and hot blooded. Besides, he had not the proof and without it she could easily slip between his fingers. Even so, for a minute he was tempted. His jaw set grimly and he lifted her to her saddle.

He stood for a minute holding her bridle and looking up at her, trying to match her attitude of calm. "You would be very wise, Lady McLeod, to return to

Edinburgh." It was the last time he would try to warn her.

"Perhaps I shall," she replied, for that moment she was uncertain, as if she sensed something. Then she remembered her duty was to her clan. Surely she would be in time to prevent the plot from being carried out. She spurred her horse and he stood and watched her ride away.

Kathryn rode like the wind, sure that no one would be following until the next day. They would celebrate until late, drinking heavily, she hoped, and most likely would not get a start until midday. By that time the renegade highlanders would be warned and the plot dissolved.

But it was not to be so easy. She was met by resistance so firm that she became distraught. She stood in Direlton castle and for the third time came close to begging John Fleming to put a stop to the rebellion.

"Can you not see that he has the power to destroy you! Are you fools! I watched the coronation. It is time to lay down your arms and bring peace."

"No!" Fleming said angrily. "We are the only ones with the courage. But once we've begun it others will follow."

"You cannot win, you fool!"

He meant to answer, but before he could say another word a man burst into the room. "The king! He is here!"

"Damnation!" Fleming cried. "I thought you said he could not possibly get here before morning."

"I told you he knew!" Kathryn cried.

"And how did he know?" Fleming said bitterly. "Did you betray us, Lady McLeod?"

"Now you are truly a fool," she said scornfully. "Would I betray you, then ride to warn you. Can your simple mind understand that I am caught as well as you?" The last words died as the sound of Donovan's warning echoed in her ears. He had her trapped.

Donovan knew by now that Kathryn had told them they were coming. He was so intent on her that it was difficult to even consider the fact that this was a rebellion they had to stop. It would be James's first act as crowned king. And Donovan knew he meant to make it one to be remembered.

It was swift, decisive, and bloody. Outnumbered and unprepared to meet the royal force, the rebels had come out with some courage to fight. But most of them were dead. In one hour, a white flag was fluttering from what remained of the ramparts, and the handful of men left surrendered.

Lord Campbell, who had ridden with Donovan came up to the king with Lord Fleming beside him. Fleming, as far as Donovan knew, had no way of knowing his brother was part of the traitors' group. As Campbell and Fleming were responding to the king's questions, Donovan rode into the castle yard. He dismounted. He had been to this castle more than one time before and he thought he knew where to find the one he sought. The stairs carved into the side of the tower were narrow, but he ran up them quickly, past the second floor, to the third.

She stood motionless by the window with her cloak drawn around her, waiting silently for him. Then he opened the door and stepped inside. The silence grew longer and deeper.

Now, in this small room, she would bide her time. Her head still held proudly. She would not plead for mercy. She expected the king to understand her reason for being there. Donovan watched her for a minute. Then he strode across the room and gripped her arm to draw her close to him.

"The game is over, Lady Kathryn, and you have lost. Let me remind you that I warned you once that a price would be paid and you should be prepared to pay it."

"Aye," she said sweetly, still defiant even in the face of capture. She showed no fear and he tried to resist a spark of admiration. She had no idea of the price she was going to pay, and he wondered what was going to happen when she found out.

He led her from the room to the top of the dangerously narrow steps. From their height she could look down on James, who sat on his horse watching them. She paused and he mistook it for fear of the steep and dangerous descent.

"Are you afraid?" He reached a hand to aid her.

"No," she said firmly, ignoring his hand; even though her insides twisted in fear she would never show it to the man who thought he was her conqueror. She walked down the stairs behind him, and he again offered his arm as they crossed the yard of the king. James sat with a deep frown on his face. This was the woman his best friend wanted to marry. He wondered if any man could tame this one without beating her senseless. Well, that would soon be discovered. She stopped before him and still he remained silent and frowning.

Then slowly she bent her head and curtsied very low. She knew she stood before the throne of justice. She would show respect, but she did not mean to plead.

"If you wanted to spend time with your brother in a cell you did not have to ride this far to do it," James said.

"Aye, Your Grace," she could only reply, having no words that would make a difference.

James half smiled. Then he turned his horse and rode away. Kathryn looked up into Donovan's eyes for some kind of answer. Donovan was watching Lord Fleming as he was being told of his brother. Fleming turned to look at him with a cold and murderous look. Donovan had never quite trusted any of the Flemings.

Then he became aware that Kathryn's eyes were on him.

"Does the king mean that I will be imprisoned in the castle as well?"

"Aye," came the cold reply. Then he turned to her and without another word he took her arm firmly and guided her toward her horse. There he lifted her into the saddle. Still her eyes looked coldly past him. Kathryn wore her pride like a shield and he had barely put a dent in it.

Chapter 6

It was a six-hour ride back to Edinburgh, a very long, strained, and silent six hours in which Kathryn sat her horse with grim resolve.

When they clattered over the stone court of the castle Kathryn was relieved, even though it meant imprisonment. At least she would be away from the glinting, silver gray gaze and the stern face of her captor. Surely he would no longer desire to link her name to his. Not with this fiasco hanging over her.

Her eyes were half-closed from fatigue and her whole body ached from exhaustion. Yet she had been determined to ride without complaint and the horse had been motionless for some minutes before she realized they had stopped.

Donovan dismounted and walked to her side and took hold of the bridle. He looked up at her and was confused by his own reactions, both mental and physical. One moment he wanted to shake her until her teeth rattled and the next he wanted to hold her and ease her fears and the exhaustion he saw clearly written on her face.

She tried to dismount, but her body seemed to resist all efforts to move. He half lifted her down and she hardly knew that he kept his arm about her as her horse was led away.

She looked in the direction she felt sure she would

be led: toward the cells, with their barred windows and their coldness. She turned in his arms to look up at him and gestured slightly toward it. "Is that where I am to go? Will I see Eric?" she said with a resigned sigh.

"No," he replied. The answer seemed to have to suffice for both questions.

Again she looked up at him in surprise. "No?" she repeated.

"You will go with me." His face was like carved stone.

She reached in desperation for some of the arrogant control she had always had. She needed some tangible thing to hold between them. She was too vulnerable . . . and she was afraid to admit it. Fear of anything was a rare thing for her to experience. It shattered her resolve.

He saw the minute cracks in the wall that stood between them. Now was the time to press his advantage, to prove he was the victor and always would be. Why couldn't he gloat over his victory? He could not seem to take his eyes off of her. His men had disappeared and the horses had been taken away. They stood alone in the darkness. Only torches placed at random lit the courtyard in pale light. She continued to mentally resist even though the hard strength of his arm was the only thing that supported her. Her legs felt weak. She attempted to move away, but he restrained her. He held her immobile and her tired mind and body could not understand nor cope with his closeness.

"I would prefer a cell to whatever you may choose."

"You have no say in the matter. Your chance to choose differently has long passed." He had the warmth of her close to him and reluctantly he could feel his every sense come alive.

"Why must we stand here?" The cry was one of despair. She hated to be weak before him.

"Because I choose to." His voice was cold and she

did not know that he had to force the coldness to be there.

He turned her to face him and she could feel his body pressed to hers. She had to fight; she could not lose this confrontation or he would destroy her. She could not find words and in her despair she struck out with doubled fists.

He was taken by surprise and more than one blow landed before he got her under control by sheer physical strength. He was as angry at himself as he was at her. He knew her exhaustion and what must be the bitter taste of fear. He could not blame her for fighting back. And, somewhere deep inside, was the desire to hold her gently. If he could have found some word of comfort, if he thought she might accept one, he would have spoken it at that second. But he recovered quickly. This weakness for her would never do.

He gripped her arm in an almost brutal grasp and jerked her after him. His apartments were on the second floor. They went up a flight of stairs, through an anteroom, and through another small room. He half pushed her through a doorway, then entered himself. He kicked the door shut, leaned against it, and hooked his large hands in his belt while he surveyed her. Kathryn looked at him, then turned to look around her at the massive, comfortable furniture and the huge bed that dominated the room. Then she looked back at Donovan again and inhaled deeply.

"I am not afraid of you." She held more control over her voice than she thought she had.

"I don't need your fear, mistress," he answered.

"You are as exhausted as I. Why did you not stop on the way?"

"With you?" he laughed softly, "Again you underestimate me. I'm not like some of the fools you've dangled on a string."

She turned away from him and walked to the fireplace that had already been laid. To keep her eyes from his she knelt before it to light it. She felt the heat of his regard. Then she rose and poured wine in two goblets. Only then did she turn to face him again.

Slowly she raised her goblet to her lips. Her eyes held his as she drank. He could have laughed. Even in the untenable position she found herself she stood defiant to the last. This contest was going to prove very stimulating indeed. He still held the final blow in his pocket—the official letter that made her his betrothed. But he didn't show it to her . . . not yet. This time he had to bend her to his will, or the battle would rage forever, and he was not looking forward to having a wife who waged eternal war.

But she was the most exciting challenge he had ever faced. He would teach her that she could not resist the life chosen for her and that doing battle against the king—or him—would be futile. Once she was tamed he could get on with his life, much the richer for possessing her.

"Mistress Kathryn, I desire to be served."

She stood stiffly. "Call a page to do it."

"Nay," he said quietly, "you shall do it. If you do not choose to remain here, there is always a nice, damp, and very uncomfortable cell to place you in."

As he said the last words he walked to a table, drew out a chair, and sighed as he sat down. Then he rested his elbows on the table and smiled at her.

"There is a tray of food beside the wine. I'll take some of that as well. You must be as hungry as I and I'm famished."

"Be damned to you!" she cried.

He started to rise, his face calm. "Then a cell it is. Very foolish, mistress."

"Wait," she glared at him. Then she turned and picked up a knife and began to slice some meat. He smiled at her stiff back, knowing she envisioned the meat was his neck. She cut off thick slices from a joint of meat, then lifted the plate in one hand, still carrying the knife in the other.

"Hold!" His voice was still cool and controlled. "Don't be foolish, Kathryn. The knife will do you little good and I think you are too tired to do battle with me knowing I will subdue you. Lay the knife aside and bring me something to drink instead."

Again she obeyed with a glint in her eyes that promised there would be another time and that thoughts of revenge were going to be close to the surface.

She placed the goblet and plate before him, wondering if he was going to find some perverse pleasure in eating first before he gave her permission. God, she hated him. She would not bend her pride before him. In time he would grow tired of this game and forget she was a prisoner at all.

He watched her, knew her thoughts, and for one minute felt a surge of gentleness. Yet he knew he could not allow her to see it. She was much too quick, too clever, and he would pay dearly for such a mistake.

"Get yourself some food and sit with me." He kept his voice even and steady.

"I won't eat with you," she replied, her jaw set and her eyes cold.

He shrugged and smiled, "So be it. I favor a slim woman anyway."

She wanted to scream at him, throw something at him, anything. She braced both hands on the table and glared at him. "I refuse to play your little games. What are you going to do with me?"

"Keep you here," he said with lazy calmness. "You are not the king's prisoner . . . you are mine."

Her face was pale and she drew on every ounce of dignity she had. She stood erect and looked down on him with an icy stare.

"Then as a prisoner I have a right to be left in peace. Why am I forced to suffer your presence?"

He smiled. "You have a sharp tongue. I shall have

to cure you of that . . . among some other things." He stood up and she had to catch her breath as he seemed to tower over her. But she refused to back up a step. He took hold of her shoulders and drew her stiff, resisting body close to him. A battle raged, will against will, flame against flame.

"I," he said in a voice that was firm and brooked no interference, "am your jailer. You are my prisoner for as long as I see fit to hold you. Should you make it too difficult your only recourse is James's mercy and a very cold cell. I stand between you and disaster for your whole family. Listen to me well, Kathryn. It would be best to please me, for the alternative is not so pleasant."

"Please you?" she half groaned. "Is this my punishment for loyalty to my king? I will never exist to please you."

He chuckled, "No, no cell for you. I have other plans." He drew her closer and his mouth hovered near hers. All effort she made to resist was useless. She had only time to moan "no" before his mouth took hers in an experienced kiss meant to assault her senses. Her lips had been half parted in the almost inarticulate sound of resistance and anything else she might have said was lost when he kissed her. With one arm he held her bound against a body that felt like steel, while the other went to the back of her head to lace into her hair and force her still.

She could feel the pounding of his heart and hers seemed to strive to match the rhythm. She was aware of everything about him, as if every nerve in her body was being touched by fingers of flame.

Somewhere in the deepest recesses of her being a spark was ignited and it flared to life. It coursed through her limbs, awakening a force that destroyed her will.

At first the kiss was hurting, searching, demanding. Then it softened and the gentleness of it swirled around her will like a misty cloud, dissolving it, draining it. But the moment he felt that smallest moment of surrender he released her.

Her inexperience was known to him the moment their lips touched and deep within he was glad for it because, he thought, it was a point of weakness. When he released her he looked down into the emerald glow of her eyes. "I will keep you here, close to my chambers."

"No." She looked truly panicked. "You will brand my name. You cannot do this!"

"Ah, Kathryn . . . I can, and I will."

He let go of her then and started toward the door. For a stricken moment she wanted to plead with him, to beg him to let her go. Then her pride interfered.

At the door he turned to look at her. "I warn you, Kathryn, enjoy your dinner tonight in peace. Tomorrow," he shrugged and his gaze was truly wicked, "who knows."

In a moment he was gone, the door closed behind him. She heard the key turn in the lock.

A wild realization came to her. He was a man without wealth and she was a woman with a great deal. She also held a prestigious name and he wanted that as well. So he would force her to submit to a relationship that would destroy any other prospects for a good marriage in the future.

She would give him cause to regret his course of action. She was a blood relative to the Stuarts. No one was going to force her to choose him as husband, especially a lowborn such as he.

She walked to the table, took up a piece of meat and some bread, and walked to the bed to sit and eat. She would force him to let her stand before the king with her brother. She would put herself at James's mercy . . . because she wasn't too sure of Donovan McAdam's.

Outside her door, Donovan paced his own room,

trying to convince himself he was doing the right thing. He had her in his power. Why didn't he tell her that the date of their wedding was already set? Six weeks from this night she would be his bride, willing or no. So why didn't he just tell her so and end it all?

He'd seen her anger in her eyes, he'd seen her denial, her resistance, her pride. . . . What was it he *wanted* to see before he could bring an end to this?

For a moment he looked at the door and fought the urge that filled him. He could go and take her now. What could she do to stop him? He crossed the room and his hand actually trembled as he reached for the door handle.

No, that would put him on the defensive. Besides, he'd never had to force a woman and he wasn't about to start now. No, he thought, better he broke her will and made her submit willingly to him. . . . Willingly—the thought intrigued him. Before he told her she would be his bride she would come to him and admit that she wanted him as much as he wanted her. She was a sensual woman, he had known that from one kiss. And she was inexperienced as well. He had successfully seduced more than one beautiful lady within the court and elsewhere. He would tame her, he would make her come to him, and then, when he had her where he wanted her, he would make her his wife. A very noble future was his and he knew she would be the perfect woman to stand beside him. Pleased with his plan he began to prepare for bed.

Andrew, booted and spurred, waited outside a closed door. Behind that door was Anne, a surprisingly different Anne. When word had come of Kathryn's capture and subsequent imprisonment, Anne had displayed more reserve and courage than he had expected.

She had taken over the household and he knew she

87

was slowly selling some of her jewelry to do it. He hated that.

He waited outside impatiently. It had been ten days since that quiet day he had seen her and refused to answer her questions about his identity. Ten days. He knew she had been deliberately avoiding him.

He stood up and paced, slapping at his boots with his heavy, short whip. He had been announced and she knew he waited. He was growing annoyed when the door opened.

"Mistress Anne will see you now."

He strode through the door, then turned to look at the servant with a scowl that would frighten anyone.

Andrew's overpowering build and obvious strength, coupled with the appearance of a man who had battled often and successfully, made the servant bow quickly and leave. Andrew thought he heard Anne's soft laugh, but when he turned again to face her her countenance was sober.

All his anger seemed to drain away as he looked at her. She was dressed in blue, a color he would never see again without associating it with her. She sat on a high-backed chair, with a small footstool beneath her feet.

"Good morning, mistress." They were not the words he wanted to say, but it was all he was allowed.

"Andrew, you look quite capable of beating any belligerent borderers. But I have heard you are leaving and I would like to ask you why."

The last thing he could say was the truth: that he had been able to make the kinds of contacts he really wanted; that he had found those who would betray their king for the right promises; that he had to meet them. No, he could not say that to her and he was temporarily at a loss for words. This was odd for Andrew, who had always been in command of himself and master of a smooth tongue. He had also been proud of his ability to lie, and he couldn't even do that now.

"I shall be gone only the balance of the day and most of the night. I will still be home by morning," he said, knowing he had not answered her at all. When she remained silent, and just looked at him, he was aware she was not taken in for a minute.

"I want to see what's happening in the borderlands," he said. At least this would give credence to the fact that he rode toward England. "With Parliament meeting tomorrow it is imperative that we have an idea of how strong James is there now. It seems the border force is his greatest strength." Anne's face was pale and her eyes held his so strongly that he began to struggle for words. He wanted to tell her so much more.

She rose and walked to the window and stood with her back to him.

"Andrew . . . what of Eric . . . and Kathryn?"

"Donovan McAdam holds Kathryn and I'm told she's safe and comfortable. As for your brother, I will be back in time, before the Parliament sets. I may have . . ."

She spun about, her fear and worry written in her eyes.

"Good God, Anne, even James cannot hang every lord in Scotland." He regretted his words the moment he said them. She turned away from him, but not before he saw the tears glistening in her eyes.

"Are you afraid, Anne?" he asked gently.

"No, I am not afraid, but Andrew, why can my brother be tried for treason when he was fighting for the real king? He had sworn his oath to the king. He could not forswear himself. His honor would have been stained forever. And Kathryn, all she is guilty of is trying to prevent more bloodshed. Why is this happening to us?"

"Anne, according to law James can't. But," he added helplessly, "James is crowned king now. There are some who fought with the old king who now stand

89

with the new. Their honor did not seem such a barrier. They have found ways around it."

"I see."

"Maybe," he said softly as he came to stand behind her, "you don't see everything yet."

She turned so quickly that he was caught off guard. He was dangerously close. But he could not seem to gather the strength to step back.

Her eyes were like blue shadows and her skin seemed almost translucent. Below him, soft, inviting lips parted in question, questions he couldn't answer. His arms ached to gather her close and tell her that he could make everything in her world all right.

Would she still look at him with such hope and trust in her eyes if she knew who he really was and where he was going this night? His goal was to bring peace, and to try and find the path to that he had to deal with traitors.

"I must go . . . Lady Anne . . . ."

"Before you go, Andrew, you must know that I am not afraid when you are here. I trust you as all my family has trusted you. I do not know everything as you say, but I do know that I shall await your return most anxiously. Maybe . . . then, you can tell me of these things I do not know."

If anything, this made matters worse. He felt a pain stir within him, a pain he had never known or tasted before. It took every ounce of concentrated effort he could gather to step back a little safer distance from her.

"Take care and ride safely, Andrew."

"Would you have your knight leave without giving him some token?" He tried to make his smile teasing and his voice light, but it was more than difficult.

"Token?" she half whispered.

He reached to take the thin, blue scarf that had covered her head. He gathered it in his huge hand and pressed it to his lips, inhaling the scent of her on it.

Maybe he would never be able to tell her the truth, but he could not leave without some touch of her to carry with him.

Then he backed a few steps from her, and taking the vision of her with him, turned and left the room.

Anne stood for a long time watching the closed door. She had never been so engulfed in conflicting emotions in her life. It was wrong, all her training told her it was wrong. He was a servant and she . . . she was confused. She no longer knew where her family stood. Yet she had the responsibility of her family's pride now and she could not damage it. Yet she felt such overpowering things, unbelievable things, when he was near.

She pressed her hand to her chest and could feel the thudding of her heart as her pulse raced. She did not understand, but she knew denying what she felt was nearly impossible. She inhaled deeply. But she must deny it, to him and to anyone else.

Andrew took the road to the south, riding as hard and fast as he could. Before midnight he crossed the border into England. At a prearranged place he met with two men.

"Sir Andrew," one man said, "we are honored. I wasn't sure what time to expect you."

"I don't have much time. I have to be back before dawn."

Andrew stripped off his clothes quickly and dressed in a fine shirt and breeches and velvet doublet. The livery of the McLeods would be too easily recognized. Instantly he was Sir Andrew Craighton.

"We've kept the border pretty active for James," the man grinned.

"You've been raiding?" Andrew asked.

"We surely have. We expect some reprisals tonight. There's a full moon."

"Wonderful," Andrew grated, "that last thing I need is to run into a raid."

"Especially one led by Donovan McAdam, eh? He is the one who keeps order on the border isn't he?"

"That he is, and take my word for it you don't want to tangle with him unless you are forced to it."

"He is that good, eh?"

"No," Andrew grinned, "he is better."

Andrew handed him a sealed packet. "This is my report to the king. See that it gets to London by tomorrow night. It bears all the news, so be careful."

"I'll be careful. Sir Andrew, this was to be given to you." He handed him a gold ring on which a ruby gleamed. "The king wants to be certain there is no confusion. If necessary you can send that."

Andrew nodded his approval. "Now I have things to do and I have to hurry. I—"

"I know. You have promised someone you would be back by dawn. Tell me . . . is she pretty?"

Andrew smiled, lifted the piece of thin, blue silk, inhaled its scent, then put it inside his shirt. "She is what dreams are made of, my friend, and that is all you are going to be told. Now, get on your way."

They supplied Andrew with a fresh horse and he was again on his way. He complimented himself on picking a perfect night for his ride. He traveled now with one companion, a man he would use as a courier from this night on. He knew he could count on getting no sleep this night, but it didn't matter. He intended to be back in time.

Anne stood with a great deal of responsibility on her shoulders. He also knew she would be a target for an opportunist. He knew she didn't lack courage, but she deserved to be defended.

He could draw up a vision of her so completely that he could actually see the sheen of her skin and feel the texture of her ebony hair.

An hour later he was thinking longingly of his narrow, hard bed in the McLeod house and even more of the thick, feathered bed in his own home.

His companion did not talk. He sensed that Andrew was in no mood.

They had to be extremely careful. Because of English raids along the border he was not too certain Donovan McAdam was not in the vicinity somewhere.

They had been riding through a heavy forest, and now the trees had begun to thin. They cautiously slowed their horses before they left the shelter of the trees. Then they moved out. The moon was now high and clear and it seemed, to their astute eyes, that the clearing was empty and safe to cross.

There were only a few trees around them and Andrew was about to leave their shadows when he saw the three riders approaching him. He knew they had seen him, but not the man behind him. He also knew that one of the men coming toward him was Donovan McAdam.

"Hold," he whispered, "dismount quickly. Get up in one of those trees. Keep your crossbow on him. I may be forced to fight. I know he is a man of honor, but should I lose make sure your arrow flies straight."

"Yes, sir."

Andrew brought his horse to a halt. There was no doubt the three were closing in on him. He waited.

"Come no further," Andrew called out. Then he had another thought. Quickly he removed Anne's scarf from his shirt and tied it about the lower part of his face. Now he could very well be a bandit. Donovan McAdam might be able to be forced into a duel. If so the winner would have the right to ride, or walk, away.

"I want to be close enough to talk," Donovan called back. Andrew smiled. He wanted to identify him. It meant Donovan truly was suspicious.

"There is nothing to talk about. Either we go in peace, or we fight."

"Why are you here?"

"No questions."

"How much money do you carry?" Donovan was edging closer. Did he know this Englishman? The clothes were fine.

"I pay no ransom," Andrew called back. The time had come to make his stand. He could not afford to be identified and he knew the Scots following Donovan would honor the code. If Andrew won, he rode away safe. "Shall we elect single combat to decide this?" he taunted. The only insurance he had against being identified was the bowman who now had his arrow aimed at Donovan's heart. Andrew hoped he would not have to use it.

Donovan did not take more than a moment to make a decision. He wanted to unmask this man. He had to make his identity clear. "Done," he said.

But Andrew fought for more. He would not be responsible for Anne suffering the scandal of having an English spy in her house. Not here, not now, and not by this man.

Both men dismounted, drew their swords, and walked toward each other. In seconds they stood close enough and the battle was ready to begin.

Chapter 7

Andrew was certain Donovan couldn't really recognize him, but from the way his narrowed eyes watched Andrew, he knew the suspicion was strong. He could feel a quiver of something akin to excitement. Outnumbered or no, he would stand his ground. He wanted to cross swords with Donovan McAdam. It would compensate a little for all his past submissiveness. He smiled behind the scarf. Donovan would need to disarm and unmask Andrew to be certain.

On the border all pledges were kept. No man would have it linked to his name that he had made a vow and not kept it. His honor, and any man's trust in him, would be a worthless commodity from then on.

This is what Andrew needed to prod Donovan, and to keep himself unknown. Andrew noticed that Donovan had ordered his men to dismount.

"If I protect myself, my lord," he laughed softly, "will I find myself victim to more swords than is just?"

"Englishman," Donovan's laugh echoed Andrew's, "do you accuse me of dishonor?"

Andrew shrugged and Donovan's smile faded. With a grim and angry look in his eyes he called back over his shoulder. "The *gentleman* seems to doubt your honor, my friends." There was a low murmur of anger through the group. "Let him understand," again Donovan's smile reappeared, "that *if* he bests me he is free to go." He made it clear by stance and words that he was more than certain Andrew had no chance to achieve such an honor.

Andrew — tall, lithe, and elegant in black velvet — was a contrast to Donovan, who was dressed in tawny leather. His clothing was one thing that made Donovan wonder about Andrew's identity. Until this moment he had never seen Andrew in anything but McLeod livery. How and where had he changed? And what was the reason? Many thoughts about this swirled in Donovan's mind, but he would have to sort them and get answers when he had disarmed and unmasked him. Both men took off their cloaks, then their jackets. Donovan rolled his sleeves to the elbow. Then they faced each other. The sword tips met and the sound of steel striking steel cut the night air.

The first experimental thrust on Donovan's part was parried by Andrew just in time. Andrew meant to do his best to look slightly inept and maybe just a bit frightened. Donovan had a reputation and Andrew wanted him to think it had intimidated him. The men who surrounded them laughed and there was almost a holiday air about the affair as the Scots began making wagers between themselves. Andrew continued to back away from Donovan, who stalked him relentlessly. Andrew was wielding his sword as though it was only a clumsy barrier between them.

Donovan's eyes glittered with amusement. He moved gracefully, and yet purposefully. Despite his size he was stepping on the soft ground almost delicately. The men around them sensed a quick victory and their smiles broadened while wagers increased.

Andrew moved to one side clumsily to avoid one particularly clever feint. Now that Andrew seemed off balance, Donovan attacked with a vicious thrust. He was seeking the sword arm. He wanted to kill, but he wished to disarm him first. He needed the satisfaction of knowing who he was and if his suspicions were right.

But Andrew's expertise suddenly seemed to come alive; he caught Donovan's sword in a sudden, shattering blow that knocked it from his hand.

This was such a shock to everyone that for some seconds there was silence. Donovan was no less shocked as he stood disarmed before Andrew. He was not afraid, though he knew he could be near death; yet he stood for just a split second completely vulnerable. Why did this Englishman not run him through?

But Andrew knew that he had to prove that he understood in border law that it was a breach of honor to kill an unarmed man. His whole motive for being here was to negotiate peace, hopefully by marriage between James and England's Princess Margaret. If he killed Donovan he would be dishonored, and the Scots would take full toll. Any chance of a peace would die here with Donovan McAdam.

Andrew knew Donovan's gaze was filled with questions. He had no hold on Andrew, yet Andrew felt pinned down.

Andrew smiled behind the silk scarf, and he could see Donovan sensed the smile, and he knew Donovan's anger was growing. Good, he thought, an angry man was a careless man.

"English spy," Donovan whispered.

"I, my lord? I am only a raider making a fortune." Donovan could hear the amusement in Andrew's voice.

"I'm to believe that? Unmask."

" 'Tis I who have you at sword's point, my lord," Andrew chuckled. Then he took Donovan completely by surprise. Andrew's sword tipped and caught the hilt of Donovan's sword, flipping it neatly in the air. Donovan reflexively caught it by the handle. Even the Scots surrounding them gave a cheer at the bravery of this man, English or no. Any man who had Donovan McAdam at a disadvantage would be a fool to give him a second chance. Even Donovan felt a stir of respect.

"Mayhap, my lord," Andrew said softly, "there are more important things than our private battle. Maybe there is even a way to build bridges between English and Scot."

"Then unmask and talk."

"I can't do that."

"Then I cannot accept what you say as truth. You are a spy and you will die as one."

Donovan was uncertain and angry. He wanted nothing as badly as he wanted to unmask Andrew. Another thought had swept through him. If it was Andrew Craighton and he was an English spy, just how much of this did the McLeods know? Was the entire family involved in an English plot to bring down James? He had to know. But he was more cautious now. Andrew was not the novice with the sword he had pretended to be. He was an expert and the battle had grown deadly serious. Ancient hatreds were called on. English against Scot . . . England against Scotland. Both men cooled their savagery and settled into the battle.

"En garde," Donovan said. He wanted to think that he was merely about to kill an English spy. But his heart pounded with the realization that he was about to learn what this English spy meant to the McLeods . . . especially Kathyrn. The duel that followed was a cruel and grueling match.

No word came from the awed men who watched. Sweat poured from the antagonists and their shirts clung to their backs and shoulders and to their strong forearms. The clash of steel resounded across the meadow.

Andrew had ridden all night and was tiring faster than Donovan. He needed to finish this affair before he was spent. But Donovan was much too quick and just as filled with deadly intent.

They fought for half an hour and Andrew began to feel the strain. He could feel his heart pounding against his ribs. He moved with care, trying to recover breath and strength, retreating easily and gracefully, always sideways to Donovan, dancing back, out of his reach.

Seizing the offensive, Andrew slid his blade under Donovan's to force him back, then followed. He was using the last of his strength, and Donovan was beginning to sense it. He retreated easily, his thick hair hanging dripping wet over his forehead. He too was trying to save strength.

Then at last Donovan's sword pierced Andrew's shoulder with enough force to make his blade slip from his fingers. Donovan's sword point was touching Andrew's chest. He could kill him easily now. But he stopped. Andrew had returned his sword when it had been lost, an act of pure gallantry. In all honor Donovan could not kill him unarmed. His true desire was to unmask him and take him back to James. But . . . if he did, who would pay the greater price—the spy, Kathryn and the other McLeods . . . or him? He wanted proof for himself and promised to find a way to keep the spy ineffectual in the future.

"Remove that ring from your finger and drop it."

Andrew did as he was told, furious at himself for wearing the ring instead of putting it safely away.

"And now," Donovan said softly, as he took a step closer, "it is time I see who you are."

"I would not come any closer, my lord," Andrew said quietly, "there is a man in those trees behind me with a crossbow. An arrow is aimed at your heart. Kill me and you die. I think it is time we put off this battle for another day."

The words were so low spoken that they reached only Donovan, who froze. Then his eyes lifted to scan the trees to see if this might be a bluff. But somehow he was sure it wasn't.

The pain in Andrew's shoulder was irritating but not dangerous. He had overcome worse. Still, the blood was soaking his shirt. He watched Donovan's grim face.

"Use that sword and you will die where you stand."

Donovan knew he was a perfect target and he cursed. He held Andrew's eyes and stepped back.

"You look like a stuck pig," Donovan gibed. "You're full of tricks, aren't you. A sly and devious man, like all the English."

"And you sound like an uneducated, border free-booter," Andrew tossed back.

"You will have need for tricks."

"Maybe all the trickery is in your imagination. There are those who have ideas that should be listened to."

"English ideas."

"Think on them while you ride home. To kill James would only put his child brother on the throne. A child can be guided by lords who have much to gain."

Donovan sucked in his breath. He had not given thought to much but James's safety. But what Andrew said was true. James's brother was still a boy. James had entrusted him to Donovan's care for protection. If the English could kidnap him they would have a potential king. All that would be needed would be James's assassination. It also meant that traitors were in their own midst. He wanted names.

"And who are these lords who would profit?"

Andrew chuckled. "In time," he answered. He needed more knowledge for his own security. He needed enough leverage to make James listen to the offer of marriage.

"We will meet again," Donovan promised.

"I have hopes that it can be with a little more intelligence."

Donovan gritted his teeth at the insult, but he reined in his anger. "I have a feeling it will be sooner than you think." He saluted Andrew with his sword, and his gray eyes were like silver sparks. Then Donovan walked back to his men. As they started away Andrew moved back to his horse.

His archer came down from the tree to stand beside him. "You're hurt badly, sir?"

"No, 'tis nothing."

"I should not have liked to have shot him."

"He would have killed me if it had not been for you," Andrew reminded.

"Aye, it was something to watch, sir." There was a tinge of admiration in his tone. "There has never been a man who has bested Donovan McAdam. To see him disarmed was a shock."

Andrew realized just what effect McAdam had on the border. He was part legend, part authority, and he held a great deal of their honest affection.

"You have a love for this freebooter?"

" 'Tis not that, sir . . . he is one Scot that even the English can respect."

"Well, I have a long, hard ride. I have a feeling I must be where he can reach me by tomorrow. You must carry another message for me, I must return to Edinburgh at once."

He handed a packet of letters to the younger man and urged him toward his horse. In the packet were names of men — Lord Douglas, Lord Fleming, and others — who would give him the tools to make James consider the offer England made. Andrew had respect for men who stood and did battle for a cause. He also had no respect, or love, or even compassion, for men who betrayed behind the cover of night. He remembered well his meeting with them just the night before.

He had cultivated them from the moment he had become suspicious of them, and had been quickly rewarded. How quickly, he thought with distaste, they were ready to snatch for the power of the throne. Both men would be instrumental in the guidance of the boy-king should their plot come about. But Andrew had another plot in mind.

He had met them in a shadowed room, been offered wine and valuable news.

"Sir Andrew, while you enjoy your wine," Fleming said, "let us regale you with a little gossip. This is a tidbit sir, but it has possibilities. It seems our king has become involved in an affair of the heart."

Andrew had hid his shock well. They may have been pleased by this news, but he certainly was not. Kings had been known to do some very remarkable things when love struck them. If it was so then a political marriage would be far from James's mind. But Andrew, an accomplished deceiver of deceivers, smiled.

"And who might this fortunate lass be?"

"Maggie Drummond, my very lovely wife's sister," Fleming had answered.

"Maggie Drummond." Andrew looked sharply at Fleming.

"If Maggie is like her sister, and she does have the same beauty, this could prove to be interesting. I am wed to her sister, and she can accomplish more than what any feeble man's imagination can conjure. You know that the Drummonds have already given one queen to Scotland. It could be interesting if they were to give another."

"There is no question of marriage is there?"

"No . . . not now. But it could be a possibility. But we much prefer James's little brother. A woman's mind is devious, but a child can be . . . properly guided."

Andrew had felt contempt for the man then and he could still taste it on his tongue.

But now, since he had made all plans known to Jeffrey, he had to wait. Wait, and keep himself from Donovan McAdam's grasp. The latter might be the most difficult.

Andrew rode fast and hard. Donovan could not go

pounding on Anne's door looking for a servant in the middle of the night. James would have no such actions on the part of the crown. Things were too unsettled, and pressing a lady such as Anne could just cause all to rise to her aid. But Donovan would be at Anne's door in the morning and Andrew would have to be there.

He had never been in such a state of exhaustion, and Fleming's parting words sat on his conscience. "Sir Andrew, I know that England has been bled by the War of the Roses, and she is in no condition to fight. Secondly, Henry Tudor is obviously using the old method of spies and hired traitors such as you and I."

Andrew frowned murderously at the thought of being linked to men such as Fleming. This, he promised himself, was the last of such events in his life.

Andrew also remembered something that set his teeth on edge.

Fleming's man had entered while he and Fleming were talking. He carried a tray of food. He was a big man, with a long-handled knife in his belt. Fleming had glanced at the servant, but Andrew had kept his eyes on him. Alertness was why he caught the exchange of looks between Fleming and the servant when Fleming had stated, "James the Third is dead."

The thrill of a possible discovery coursed through Andrew. "We English do not hire assassins, Lord Fleming."

"Do not jest," Fleming said quietly.

"I'm not jesting." Andrew replied. Then he directed a question at the servant: "what is your name?"

"Stephen."

"You may leave us, Stephen," Fleming said. His command was quick and harsh and, Andrew felt, just a little nervous.

Stephen threw his master a look of warning, of threat, but he obeyed. Now Andrew suspected much;

that Fleming, through Stephen, was guilty of the murder of James III. It all fit together; someday he would have this information to use as well. He also realized that Donovan McAdam stood in Fleming's way, too. Donovan was an adversary who Andrew could respect. He didn't want him murdered. In fact, he wanted no murders on his soul.

His horse ate the miles in long, measured strides and Andrew now allowed his mind to focus on Anne. When McAdam came, would Anne tell him that Andrew had left her home the night before?

With her sister and brother held political prisoners, surely Anne would hold little affection for Donovan McAdam in her heart. Still, would she take the chance of being labeled a spy consorting with the English? It could prove the final loss for her and her family.

All she needed to do was to deliver him up to McAdam when he came. In gratitude she might be able to beg the king for her brother and sister's safety.

God, the possibilities were enormous. All he needed to do was to turn about and ride for home. He could wash his hands of James, Donovan McAdam, the McLeods, everyone . . . except Anne. He cursed himself as a vision of her came between him and rationality. He couldn't leave. He had to admit to himself that even though it could come to nothing he had to see her again, in fact had to remain and defend her until this had passed.

He reached the house and rode cautiously to the stables. It seemed that the entire world was asleep, but he took no chances. He cooled and rubbed his horse so it would show no sign of travel. Then he slipped through the predawn light toward the back of the house.

He came cautiously to a window he always left slightly open, just in case. He pushed it wide and climbed in. The exertion tired him more and the wound began to bleed again. In fact he was becoming a little dizzy from loss of blood.

Inside he stood for a minute; then he tossed his cloak aside and struck flint to light a candle. When he turned from the table he faced a huge wingbacked chair. As the light flooded the room he came face to face with Anne McLeod.

Donovan McAdam rode hard, but necessity made it imperative that he go to the castle first. No matter what he thought, the McLeods were a prestigious family who could gather many about them. Since the coronation, James had been plagued with uprisings. He did not need another, especially one that might prove hard to put down. Besides, he did not want to wage war against the family of the woman who was to be his wife. Then he thought of Kathryn and smiled. He might be able to use this to make her listen to reason. Of course, he would have to have some proof that Anne McLeod was involved. He would get permission from James to go to see her. He knew her, and her reputation was one of sensitive gentleness. He could make her believe he was a tyrant if it would open the door to Kathryn.

In the back of his mind were the blue eyes that had laughed at him above the scarf about that face. It had been Andrew Craighton, he was sure of it. But being sure was no proof. Anne McLeod had to give it to him. She could never stand up to him, and certainly not for the benefit of a man such as Andrew Craighton. He tried to villainize Andrew in his mind, but admiration got in his way. Admiration and respect, for despite all, he had shown a sense of honor that was strong and solid.

Andrew Craighton had more in his background than anyone knew. The ring in Donovan's pocket was unique and could be traced in time. Andrew was just as unique and Donovan thought he just might have a way to trace him as well.

He had his suspicions. Andrew had too much quality, too much education, and he was too damn good with a sword to be an English freebooter.

Within the castle was a book that listed all the English peerage. Maybe, with enough diligence, he could put a name and, he was reasonably sure, a title to this thorn in his side.

Thorn or no, he had to admit Andrew was one of the best swordsmen he had ever faced. The thought passed rapidly through his head that he would have been the kind of ally any man would want at his side in any confrontation.

Donovan and his men clattered into the court at Edinburgh, their horses making a racket that drew notice from the servants, who ran to care for the horses and for their masters.

Donovan dismounted and climbed the stone steps. He started first for his own apartments. Before he would go to the king he would set some other things in motion.

He would have Andrew's background searched for and he would have to change clothes and wash before he roused the king from his bed and tried to explain where his suspicions lay.

The McLeods, whatever else, were nobility, and James wanted them under control. He also didn't want the reputation of abusing defenseless women, though Donovan was not sure that description applied to Kathryn McLeod at all.

He was thinking of her as he walked down the long hall to his door. He was not prepared for the door to his apartment to open and he quickly stepped back into the shadows of another doorway to watch. If someone was entering and leaving his apartments at their leisure he wanted to know who he was. Assassins moved in the shadows of night and he knew his life was worth a great deal to many people.

The very last thing he expected, since he had left one of his most trusted knights to guard her, was for Kathryn McLeod to step out into the hall and look carefully about her.

He stood in a deep doorway and he knew that, since there was very little light, she would have to be right beside him before she saw him. He stood very still while she made her way toward him.

She was almost beside him when he reached out and grasped her wrist. She gave a muffled shriek of shock.

"Going somewhere, Lady Kathryn?"

Before she could answer, the door to his apartment was flung open and the young man he had left to guard her came dashing out into the hall.

He saw Donovan and Kathryn when he was only a few steps down the hall. His acute shame registered on his face when he saw Donovan standing there with a firm grip on the woman he had been sent to guard.

Kathryn looked up at Donovan without a whit of regret on her face. She even smiled at him. "Sir," the young man could barely gasp. He really didn't want to meet Donovan's eyes, but his pride wouldn't let him do anything less.

"You fell asleep mayhap?" Donovan questioned softly.

"Do not blame your guard," Kathryn said, "he was very watchful. In fact we even tossed dice for a while."

"Would someone care to explain to me just how this has come about?"

"Sir, I'm sorry. I thought . . ." His face reddened and he stammered to silence.

"He thought this night you would claim me for your mistress," Kathryn said coldly.

"So?"

"So," she said quietly, "I asked him if I could wait for you in your bedroom. That it would be so much more convenient for you. After all, your will and your commands are law here are they not?" Her voice dripped with honey, and that, he thought, should be enough to frighten any reasonable man to death.

"You are dismissed, Robert. Find your bed."

"Sir . . . I . . ."

"It's all right, Robert. Tomorrow you will guard her again."

"Thank you, sir." The young man could have choked in relief. He left, grateful that he had seemed to find his captain in one of his better moods. It made him shake to think of what could have happened.

Without speaking Donovan dragged Kathryn with him and returned to his room. Inside he let go of her to remove his cloak and sit wearily down in a chair. She stood watching him.

"You really weren't trying to escape, were you?"

"No."

"I thought not. There is no place you could go that I could not reach. But you knew that, too."

"Yes."

"Then what were you trying to prove?"

"I was trying to prove nothing."

He watched her for a while, then rose and came to stand beside her. She looked up at him with no fear in her eyes.

"Where were you going?"

"I thought, while you were gone, that I might be able to find my brother. I wanted only a word with him, to see him, to know he was all right."

"Why didn't you ask me?" His voice softened more than he wanted it to. He was tired, he thought, that was the only reason.

"Should I trust you?" she said quietly. Her stillness, the look in her eyes, made the words sting.

"Yes. I have been proud of my reputation. I have not broken a trust in my life. Royalty or no, a man's honor is sometimes all he has."

"And what of a woman's honor?"

108

"It is precious as well. Kathryn,"—neither of them noticed that he had said her name so familiarly—"there are some things that must be, some you can't control. It does no harm to your honor when you do not control the situation. It is time that you accepted that."

"Accept what?" she asked, but her eyes told him she was wary. He walked to the door and slid the bolt home. Then he turned to face her.

"There will be no need to return to your prison again today. You will stay here. At least for a while. Until I can find a guard that is not so susceptible to your charms."

He began to remove his doublet as he walked toward her.

Chapter 8

Kathryn sucked in her breath and backed away from Donovan. But he ignored her apparent fear, for he knew her too well now to believe it was an emotion she had ever felt.

He removed his doublet and tossed it on a chair, then sat down to remove his boots. Kathryn watched him warily. If he thought it was going to be a simple matter to bed her she was going to prove him mistaken. It would have to be rape, for she would never give him the satisfaction of yielding to him.

Donovan sat back in the chair with a sigh. He was tired, he admitted to himself. She could see the exhaustion in his eyes, mingled with an awareness she didn't understand. She didn't want to understand.

Kathryn clasped her hands behind her so he would not notice that they were shaking. "If it is your plan to shame me before my people then understand this: You will have to watch me every moment, every second, for I will find a way to pay you back."

"And so I will have to watch you every moment and every second. It means I am forced to keep you very close," he grinned aggravatingly.

"You are the victor," she said scathingly, "in the name of *your* king you are free to do as you choose."

"Ah, Kathryn," he laughed softly as he rose and began to remove his shirt. Now, even though she stood stiffly he could see the fear in her eyes. "There is an easier way, and I have found it." He removed his shirt and tossed it aside. Kathryn swallowed heavily. When he moved to stand closer she found him devastating to her peace of mind.

"And this is your 'easier way', to take what no one offers freely."

"Are you sure you would not offer freely?"

She could have choked on her anger, but her mind now was too involved in other things. His nearness was doing things . . . unwelcome things. He reached out and lightly touched her hair, feeling the silkiness of it.

"Don't," she said, and slapped his hand away. He laughed softly and put one arm about her, drawing her close.

"Listen to me, Kathryn. It is the law of life that the strongest — the victors as you put it — hold the power. It takes a strong man to wield that power justly. James wants no more of the revolts. It is best that he joins the strongest together."

"Meaning you are to subdue revolts by bedding me," she laughed.

"If bedding you was the answer I could have done that long ago. I'm afraid your position is going to be of a much more permanent measure."

Her eyes held his and he remained silent for the short seconds it took her to digest what he had just said.

"Marriage!" she gasped.

"Aye, marriage."

"No! Never. There is no love here. It would be the same as taking me without marriage. I do not want you!"

"No one has asked you what you want. It is a royal decree now. And as for love," he again laughed as he drew her resisting body closer, "pity the man who falls in love with you, Kathryn. You would rip heart and

111

soul to pieces. Nay, I will take you as you are and forget love. It will prove to be an exciting marriage to say the least."

"I will never be your wife!"

"Do not profess things you can't control. In a few weeks we will be married. I am not a man to leave my wife alone or her bed empty. We will have children and that will end the idea of revolt gathered around the McLeods."

"You have it all in your hands." Her voice was cold and her eyes filled with fury.

"Nay . . . in my arms."

"Well, hold fast and sleep lightly," she said through gritted teeth, "you will always spend sleepless nights. If you force me to this I shall either kill you . . . or I shall deceive you and all the children I bear will be bastards whose father you will never know."

Anger sparked in his gray eyes and they glistened like burnished silver. "Nay," he whispered as coldly as she, "you will take vows before God, standing at my side. From that moment on you will be mine and no man would dare. Believe me," now he smiled again, "I will not leave you with enough strength to offer another man, but should I find you with another it would mean his life. And I would not hesitate to punish you either if you betrayed me. You see my name and my honor are valuable to me." He wanted to add, just as he knew hers was to her. Once married she would never give herself to another man. It was her own honor he trusted.

"Let me go."

"Mayhap . . . later," he said softly. His arms had her bound to him and she was pressed so intimately to him that she could feel the beat of his heart and the heat of his body, which was growing warmer and warmer. "Now I would taste what has been promised me."

"No . . . no, let me go. I won't tumble into your

bed like some trollop."

"Make no mistake," he chuckled, "you will warm my bed. For now . . ."

She was certain he meant to take her then and she fought valiantly, but the battle was useless. With a strength beyond anything she could ever hope to cope with, he drew her closer and closer. His arms were around her in a merciless grip. She could not breathe, she could not think; then his mouth took hers in a passionate and heated kiss that swept up her senses and sent them spiraling.

Her mind and body seemed stripped of reserve. Her whole consciousness seemed stimulated by the feel, taste, and scent of him, all of them acutely arousing. It seemed as if there were only two of them in the entire universe.

As if with a will of their own she found her lips parting to accept his and her arms entwined about his neck. The thought of enemy was battered from her mind and she found herself yielding helplessly to a will greater than her own.

He released her as abruptly as he had taken her. It was a shattering experience and she felt shame at her own weakness, a weakness based on desire, not fear. Aghast at her own response she lashed out at him, but he caught her wrist before the blow could land. For a long moment they stood thus, eyes locked and wills clashing.

"I will never come to you."

"I told you, I don't need your willingness. Even though you deny what I felt, I know you are a woman of strong passion. I can awaken that. If you deny it then we can put it to the test here and now." He motioned to the bed some distance away and watched her eyes again grow brilliant with a fear she would never admit. She was afraid of herself, of her own passion and disobedient senses.

"I shall hate you till my dying breath."

"Your hate I can handle, Kathryn. Because in time I shall turn it into a much more tender emotion."

"Love," she spat.

"If not love, at least passion. That is enough."

"Is it you are afraid of love?" she threw at him. "Is that why you will settle for second best?"

"Love? It is a wasted dream, a thing for poets and dreamers. I do not need love to have all I desire. A fine castle, a wife who will give me strong sons. A future. If they are devoid of this thing you call love then why care, for I will have everything else. All that the sword and the arm of a strong man can hold. Believe me, Kathryn, I can hold what is mine."

"And that is all that it takes to hold a woman?"

"What else?"

"Don't force me to go through with this farce of a marriage."

"Farce? I promise you it will be a marriage in fact and that it will be consummated and held firm."

"You will regret this."

"Another threat, Kathryn. Please, spare me. It is as much a fact as the rising of the sun. The king will have it publicly announced soon and we will wed."

He kissed her slowly, leisurely, as if he were enjoying her capture immensely. He took no notice of the glow of her emerald eyes or the calculating look that fleeted quickly.

"Ah well, Kathryn," he chuckled, feeling certain the first step to mastering Kathryn McLeod had been made clear. "There is pressing business at the moment that must be taken care of, else I might just enjoy proving to you that your fate might not be so hard."

"Conceited jackass. Your absence will bring me a great deal of pleasure . . . where do you go?"

"Already missing me, my love?" he laughed.

"Hardly," she grated, "I had hoped you might be going to battle somewhere."

He laughed again and took the time to kiss her

again, running one hand down her curved form. She twisted helplessly in his arms, denying the stir of warmth this caused.

With a sigh he reluctantly released her and went to get clean clothes. Her eyes followed him as he dressed.

She watched as he drew on another shirt, its white more brilliant against the bronze of his skin. That he was handsome there was no doubt and that he had the body of a god was unmistakable, but, she thought with anguish, he had the heart of a stone.

Her mind sought every avenue of escape, but there was none. His relationship with the king gave him great power. If she ran she would be found and returned, and she wouldn't give him that satisfaction.

Dressed again he sat to pull on his boots, then rose to don his cloak.

"You will be quite safe here." His smile was devilish. "In fact you might get used to my bed. Don't think of leaving these rooms until I return or you might find yourself in that cold cell yet. My men will have orders to keep very close watch."

Her glare was murderous and the door closed on his satisfied chuckle.

Kathryn's fury rose and she paced like a trapped animal. She raged for nearly an hour, applying choice names to Donovan and to the king. But finally good sense prevailed. This was what he wanted. He had even said he could handle her anger.

Slowly Kathryn sat down on the bed and gave herself over to deeper thoughts. It was quite obvious someone or something had turned him away from the thought of loving anyone. She wondered why, and most important she wondered who.

It was then that the idea for her ultimate revenge came to her. He had underestimated her. Maybe he wore a shield because he was vulnerable. Maybe he was the one who was afraid, not she. The idea so intrigued her that she lay across the bed to give it some thought. An hour later she rose and undressed, then returned to the bed, where she fell into a satisfied sleep.

Donovan had lost his smile the moment he had closed the door behind him. His plans had been made long before, but he had not taken into consideration the effect Kathryn's exceptional beauty would have on him.

He cautioned himself to be very careful with her and wary of her intelligent mind. One mistake in his life had cost him much. He did not intend to make the same mistake again.

It was only her lush body that had set his pulses pounding and his nerves humming. It was because he desired her. Once she was his wife there would be no problems. He would get over the unique experience of having her and settle into a calm life in which passion was a tool, but love was an element to be ignored.

He never questioned the reason he had chosen Kathryn over Anne. He could have had either one. But he had not given the shy, gentle Anne a thought.

As he walked he absently touched the scar on his cheek. She had branded him, now it was his turn, and brand her he would. He would own her body and soul. Only then could he put her out of his thoughts where she seemed always to be like a ghost.

For now he had business that could no longer be put aside. His certainty that Andrew Craighton was the Englishman was enough to give him haste. Andrew was wounded, and surely could not have gotten back so easily. No one would give an English spy aid without jeopardizing everything. Anne McLeod was no fool. She knew what results could occur if she did. No, she was no fool, and she loved her brother and sister too much. Andrew Craighton was as good as in his hands, and he was another hold over Kathryn.

Satisfied, he ordered three men to go with him, then rode toward the McLeod's.

Andrew, who had never been shaken by his appearance before kings, who had stood toe-to-toe with the bitterest of enemies, who had always met head-on the most difficult of situations, found himself stunned to silence by a pair of deep purple-blue eyes.

"Lady Anne," he finally stammered. Then it finally occurred to him where she was. "What are you doing here?"

"I've been waiting for you for hours."

"Why?"

"Because, Andrew Craighton . . . or whatever your name is, we seem to have a great deal that needs to be brought out into the open."

"I'm afraid I . . ." He meant to deny what she had said, but his blood-soaked shirt had just caught her attention. She nearly leapt from the chair, her eyes wide with shock.

"You're hurt!"

"It's nothing, a minor scratch. I can take care of it, if you—"

"Will you please stop that!" Her anger made her eyes blaze and her cheeks grow pink. This was an Anne he had not seen. A fury lit her face and she came to him. "Sit down, and please don't make excuses that a child wouldn't believe. I have tended to my brother's wounds before. I know serious injuries when I see them. Now, I will fetch some water."

"Don't waken anyone."

"I had no intention of waking anyone," she said grimly as she left. He sagged into a chair. Now he had a serious problem. She would have a million questions he couldn't answer.

Anne returned within minutes with a basin of water and some cloths. She sat the basin down on a nearby table and began to tear the cloths into strips.

"Take off that bloody shirt so I can dispose of it. I take it that you don't want any other eyes to see it." Her voice would abide no arguments from him. Maybe she just felt he was one of her servants in some kind of trouble and her generous nature would not allow her to desert him. He would keep up the illusion if that was what she believed.

Andrew eased the shirt from his shoulders and dropped it on the floor. There was a heavy silence and he looked toward her in surprise.

She held a piece of torn cloth in her hand, but seemed frozen, her eyes on him.

There was not an ounce of fat on his muscular body. Small scars marred his flesh, and one lengthy one, as if a broadsword had breached his defenses. But the muscles beneath his sun-darkened skin gave evidence of a hard, rigorous life and of a great deal of time spent riding a horse and wielding a sword. His waist seemed slim because of the balance of his broad shoulders and heavy chest. He was so intensely male that she heard her own breath catch. Then her eyes raised to his and something volatile seemed to fill the room, drawing out all the air and leaving both breathless.

With almost an agony of effort she dragged her eyes from him and forced them to concentrate on the piece of cloth she had been folding into a pad. "Sit down . . . please." Her voice was still weak from the strange emotion.

Andrew sat, inhaling deeply and trying to fight what he knew so well. It was lust, he argued with himself, but he knew it was much more.

She came to stand beside him, and he had to grit his teeth to keep from uttering a sound when she began to wash the blood from his chest and back. Her touch was light and occasionally her hands brushed against his bare skin, making them both flinch.

"Lady Anne, I can do this for myself, it is nothing that you should have to bother with."

"Hush, Andrew," Anne said softly, "it pleases me to do this for you. Besides, it has you in a position where you cannot walk away from my questions."

"Questions?" he said innocently. "If 'tis about this little cut 'twas only a chance meeting with an old enemy."

"Then it was not over anything . . . or anyone special."

Andrew looked up at her, then wished he hadn't. A half-smile touched her lips.

"No, Mistress Anne, 'twas not a battle over a lady."

"I had suspected it was not."

Now he turned his whole body to look at her, but she pressed her hands to his shoulders to turn him back around. "Do sit still, I'm almost done. And I want you to be well taken care of so you have no more excuses not to answer my questions." Then she tied the last strip in place. "There, 'tis done."

He stood almost at once and moved away from her gentle touch and the delicate scent of her perfume . . . and the innocent-eyed questions that he knew could reach a place where a man with a broadsword could not tread. He went first to get a clean shirt, and as he donned it he tried to keep his voice level. "I appreciate your gentle ministrations, Lady Anne, but it would not be good for your reputation if you were found in a servant's room, alone at this late hour."

"Servant's room," she repeated. She walked away from him several feet then turned to look at him again. "I wonder if this is where you belong."

"I don't understand, Mistress Anne. I . . ."

"Stop, Andrew, don't . . . don't lie to me any more."

Her voice had become serious. Had he been so inept that she could read through him so easily?

"Lie about what?"

"Andrew . . . how did you acquire that wound to-

119

night?"

"I told you. . . ."

"Yes, I know you told me, but what you told me was not the truth, was it? Who are you, Andrew?"

"Some things . . . maybe it is better that you do not know."

"Will there be a problem over this?" she motioned to his shoulder. "Will someone be asking questions?"

"Yes," he said very reluctantly.

"Who?" The question was quiet . . . but firm.

"Donovan McAdam." He held her eyes with his now, trying to read what was going on behind them.

"And if I am to lie for you, Andrew, don't you think it fair to tell me why?"

"To say nothing would not be a lie."

"Don't you know Donovan McAdam well enough to know that he will not be satisfied with nothing."

"He is your enemy, Anne."

"I think not, Andrew. He wants peace, too. He wants his king to sit on the throne. The man has ambition and warring with women will not see him to what he wants. Is he your enemy, Andrew?" The last question was asked with enough conviction to tell him she had no illusions of what he was.

"Nay, he is not. But he stands between me and what I must do."

Anne sank slowly into a chair, as if she had lost all strength in her legs. Her eyes were filled with dismay.

"Then . . . you are . . . a spy, an English spy. My God, Kathryn . . . Eric."

She too knew the consequences of him being taken by Donovan McAdam. It would condemn the McLeods forever. There would be no recourse to Jamie or Donovan. It would mean death for Eric and God knows what fate for Kathryn and herself.

Andrew couldn't stand what he saw written on her face. He went to her, and kneeling on one knee beside her, took one of her small hands in his huge callused ones. "Anne, it is not like you think. Look at me."

Her eyes met his and he could read a real fear mingled with her pain.

"I would not bring you or your family harm, that I swear. I am not here to create problems but to try to end them. I swear by all I hold sacred, Anne, I do not come with deception or betrayal. I want more than that."

She was quiet and that cut him to the heart. For a long moment neither seemed able to breathe.

"It seems I continually ask you the same question, but I must know. Who are you, Andrew?"

"I am Sir William Frances Andrew Craighton. I am to Henry Tudor what your Donovan is to James. But I want to bring hope not war."

She wanted desperately to believe him, but if he lied her whole family would be forfeit.

"What is this 'hope' you bring?"

"Marriage."

"Marriage?"

"James needs a wife. All kings need a good marriage, preferably a strong political one. Why not the marriage of Margaret, Henry's sister, to James? It would unite our two countries. Anne, it could put an end to the strife that has existed between us all these years."

"But Andrew, it cannot happen. How are you trying to do this?"

He inhaled. If he told her all he knew and Donovan McAdam found out before he was ready to act everything would be for nothing.

"You ask me to trust you, Andrew," Anne said quietly, "you tell me to put the lives of my sister and brother in your hands. You ask me much, but you offer me little trust in return."

"My trust can cost you so much, Anne."

"And the lack of it could cost others much as well. Kathryn and Eric mean too much to me to give up their lives easily."

He sighed. She spoke the truth. If he expected trust he would have to give it. He rose and paced before her for several minutes. It was too near dawn. Donovan McAdam would be there soon. He had to decide.

Anne remained quiet, but her heart felt like lead and her nerves made her whole body seem to be afire.

"There are traitors who would open the doors of key cities all along the border if Henry chose to attack. When the time is right I will trade these traitors for a chance to make our position clear to James and strike an agreement with him."

"Why not make that claim now? When Donovan McAdam comes tell him the truth."

"And what proof have I? He will have me as a spy before I can move."

Anne wrapped her arms about herself as if she were suddenly very cold. All her instincts had told her Andrew was so much more than she knew, but she had hardly expected the dilemma in which she found herself.

Andrew stood by the window through which the first gray light of dawn could be seen. Time had wings. He couldn't go to her and demand anything. She had every right to help her brother and sister. He had put his life in her hands because . . . because it was more important to him than anything else for her to say she trusted him.

The light of day was growing brighter and still neither spoke. He knew she waged a battle with herself, but it was no bloodier a battle than the one within him. The clatter of hooves in the outer court told them both that the sands of time had run out. Anne rose from her chair and silently gathered the basin with its bloody water and the shirt Andrew had thrown aside. The she walked to the door.

"Anne?" he said softly. Her great, blue eyes met his. "Remain here," was all she said. Then she left and the door closed very softly behind her.

Andrew had never questioned his courage before, had never given it a second thought. But now he was shaken.

His life, the future of their two countries, lay in Anne's soft, small hands. He could easily escape, even now. If he rode for the border he could make it while Donovan questioned Anne. But that would mean leaving her to face whatever happened. It would be admitting to her that he had lied. He could not do it. Time that had flown so fast before now seemed to stand still. He waited for long, seemingly interminable minutes. Then he heard the approaching footsteps . . . and they were not Anne's.

Chapter 9

Quite sure of himself and what he knew he would find at the McLeod's, Donovan was prepared to have a wounded Andrew taken to the castle where he could imprison him and question him. The door was answered by a young girl who appeared somewhat caught between awe and fear.

"Yes, sir?"

"Tell Lady Anne McLeod that I must talk to her at once on the king's business."

Now her fear was even more acute. The king's business could only mean one thing for the McLeod family. Since this was the day James would set in judgment of the political prisoners, it was certain, in her mind, that this could only mean Anne was to be arrested too.

Before the shaken girl could answer, Anne's voice came calmly from the head of the stairs. "It's all right, Mary. Please go on with your duties," Anne spoke softly; then she walked with slow dignity down the stairs. Her face showed no sign that she was in the least upset with Donovan's presence.

Donovan watched her come toward him, unconsciously comparing her with Kathryn. There would be no problem with this one, he thought. Her delicate look and shy manner had him completely prepared to dominate her with little problem.

"You honor my home, sir," she smiled at Donovan, who smiled back without noticing. "I pray that it is to tell me that my brother and sister will be released soon."

"I'm afraid not, Lady Anne. I've come to put your secretary, Andrew Craighton, under arrest."

"Arrest? Why, what has Andrew done?"

"Is Andrew Craighton here?" Donovan ignored her question. He was certain Andrew Craighton was in no condition to be anywhere but in bed.

"Yes, he is. The household is not awake yet, and I'm very sure no one has disturbed Andrew."

"Disturb him now."

"You shall have to give me some reason, sir. You see . . . Kathryn has always handled our affairs. Since she is not here I have depended upon Andrew completely. So much that he sat with me over accounts until nearly three this morning."

"Are you trying to tell me, Lady Anne," Donovan laughed, "that Andrew Craighton was here in your home, until three this morning?"

"No."

"I thought not."

"He was here all night, we only worked until three."

Donovan scowled into her serene face, as if he could intimidate her by his presence alone. But Anne only smiled slightly, as if questioning the look.

"Do you realize your position, Lady Anne?"

"My position?" she questioned innocently. "But what is my position, sir? I do not raise arms against the king and would become a loyal subject. I pray the trials tomorrow, no, today, will give my family freedom." Anne blinked as if tears hovered near. "Why do you feel it necessary to come armed to a lone woman's home? Andrew has been the only protector this home has had since . . ."

"I must speak with Andrew Craighton," Donovan insisted. "Surely you can . . . ah . . . waken him for a short time?"

Anne rose and walked to the doorway. "If you gentlemen will be seated I will send for Andrew at once."

"We prefer to stand, Lady Anne," Donovan replied. He could not believe he felt so uncomfortable under her cool gaze.

"Very well." Anne turned her back to him and called for aid. The same young girl appeared. "Go up and wake Andrew. Tell him to please join us."

"Yes, my lady." The girl curtsied low and left. Again Anne turned and looked at Donovan.

"Can I get you something while you wait?"

"No, thank you."

"Tell me, sir," Anne questioned. "Is this persecution of my family a necessity for James? What have we done to single us out so that even the women and servants are condemned, even though we have never raised swords . . . or had any choice in the matter?"

Donovan flushed, annoyed that he had been so sweetly labeled a persecutor of the helpless. "There is no persecution, Lady Anne, and there will be no punishment where there is no guilt."

"But what could I or my secretary be guilty of?" She sounded as if she meant to laugh at his foolishness.

Donovan's annoyance was growing. "I have accused you of nothing, Lady Anne."

"And Andrew?" The question was softly asked and it was only then he realized that Lady Anne was much more clever than he had thought. The charges against Andrew, and how much proof he had, was what she wanted to know.

"Your Andrew Craighton is a spy, Lady Anne," he said quietly. "Tell me, did you or any of your family think of that before you accepted him into your home?" His question was just as softly put as hers. Their eyes held for several seconds.

"Andrew fought with my brother for *our* king. Tell me, if you had lost, would the women in your life,

126

your sisters and brothers or the people who worked for you, would they be as guilty as you?"

"That is not in question, Lady Anne."

"But if it were?"

"No," he said. "They would not."

"Then why come here?"

"Lady Anne, maybe Andrew Craighton was put here to betray you as well."

"I?"

"You, your family. How will it look to James should a spy be found here—it will not make your situation comfortable, to say the least."

"Andrew," she stated firmly, "will bring no harm to this family, nor to your king."

"You are so confident?"

Anne was about to answer when Andrew's voice came from the doorway. "Lady Anne has every reason to be confident. She knows I would bring no dishonor to this house . . . nor to the McLeods. I hold them in the greatest esteem."

Donovan turned to face Andrew, trying to envision his face covered by a blue silk scarf. If Andrew had been wounded he showed no sign of it. He was immaculately dressed and his attitude showed just enough deference to be believable.

"It seems you've had a tiring night, Andrew," Donovan said casually.

"Sir?"

"From what Lady Anne has told me, the two of you have been laboring over the accounts for long hours."

"Yes, sir," Andrew smiled, then his eyes went to Anne, who was watching him closely. "But to labor for Mistress Anne is no sacrifice, sir, it is a privilege." Andrew's eyes warmed.

"Very well put, Andrew, very gentlemanly. You seem to have had a great deal of education in your background," Donovan spoke casually. "It seems you are used to the better life."

"I have seen good and bad times. I am happy in what I'm doing now. It is my duty to defend Lady Anne . . . and Lady Kathryn, but it seems that is most unlikely now."

"Yes." Donovan walked close to Andrew, his eyes appraising. "You wield a sword quite well, too."

"Sir?"

"A sword, Andrew, you do know how to use a sword?"

"I have fought for two kings. I would not be alive today if I didn't know how to use a sword. I am sure Lord Eric would not have asked for my help had he not had faith in my ability."

"Yes, but I wonder . . ."

Andrew retained his calm exterior as he braced himself for what would happen next.

"Yes, I wonder," Donovan continued. He rested his hand on Andrew's wounded shoulder. The strength of his hold was purposely strong. He felt for bandages, but Andrew had removed them. He had put on two shirts, a velvet doublet, and a flat, heavy chain about his neck to prevent blood from seeping through.

The hand grew heavier and Donovan watched his expression closely. The pain was excruciating, but Andrew's face remained immobile. Andrew could see Anne's face grow pale and he willed her to silence.

Donovan was disappointed, but if Andrew had not had time to bandage his shoulder he would feel the pain. The contest lasted only minutes, but to Andrew it felt like hours. His hands began to sweat. But it was Anne who forced the issue.

"I have told you that Andrew was here all night last night. If you choose to arrest him then you must take me as well. This is past belief. Surely you and your king have more important things to do than to prey on the innocent, and without any proof. You have my word that Andrew will remain here. What more do you want? You have brought our family to its knees!

What more do you demand from us, our blood? Please, leave my house."

Donovan inhaled, caught in a vise. James had enough problems. This seemingly helpless and delicate creature could draw hotheaded Scots to her rescue. That was the last thing he needed.

"Know this, Englishman," his voice rasped softly in Andrew's ear. "My eyes are on you and there are ways of finding the truth. Your time is short, very short."

"Your eyes should be elsewhere if you work on James's behalf. Why have I drawn your antagonism, sir? As Lady Anne has said, I will remain here."

"See that you do."

Donovan motioned to his men to follow him and left. When Andrew heard the outer door close he sagged into a chair and Anne rushed to his side.

"Andrew," she half sobbed as she sank to her knees beside him. He turned his head to look down into eyes filled with much more than he wanted to see.

"I'm all right. I'm afraid I'll need to be bandaged again. The man has a grip like iron. I . . . I'm grateful, Anne, for your help . . . and for your trust."

Anne looked up at him and realized he had no intentions of saying more, that he knew too much still stood between them. Maybe someday . . . She rose slowly. "I'll go and get some fresh bandages. Go to your room. It's best no one sees."

He nodded and rose, aching with a need to find comfort in her arms. But he was still too much of a danger for her and he still had too much that had to be done. He remained silent and walked almost wearily to his room.

Donovan was furious! One slim girl had effectively brought him to a stop. If it were not such a crucial time, if James did not have such a fragile hold on the throne, if hot heads and strong swords could not rise and destroy so easily, he would have dragged them both to the castle. Why couldn't she have been like her sister, fire and brimstone? That he could have handled easily. But this woman was condensed fire hidden behind a silk screen of fragility. It was like fighting a mist.

But he would find a way to pin this elusive Englishman down. It became imperative now that he put a name to Andrew Craighton, freebooter or hired sword.

He sent for James's counsel as soon as he returned to the castle. When the man appeared Alexander was quick with the question.

"You have the book of English peerage?"

"Aye, sir."

"Get it. As quickly as you can trace it down I want the proper title for that English spy who calls himself Andrew Craighton." He nearly threw the ring at the startled man. "And find where this ring comes from and what value it is."

"Aye, sir, I'll do it as rapidly as I can."

"Make it fast. I need to know before this man can cause us a problem."

"Aye, sir." The counsel was most anxious to get out of the vicinity of this enraged man.

He exited quickly and Donovan was left with his anger.

Within hours the Parliament would be called and James would judge the men who had raised swords against him. Donovan was hoping the sentences would at the worst be exile. If it were so he would see to the care of Kathryn. But her sister would be completely alone. He contemplated this for long minutes while he paced the floor; then suddenly he stopped pacing. He stood quietly, then smiled. He should have thought of this sooner. Anne was alone; if her brother was sentenced today she would need protection. Who better to protect her than James . . . and himself. Where would she be safer than in their care. Yes, Anne McLeod would be under his care—and with her, he would make sure, would be her secretary . . . Andrew Craighton.

Satisfied that he could draw his enemy within reach, he removed his doublet and tossed it in a chair. He knew Kathryn slept in the next room, his prisoner, in his bed. The thought, once in his mind, refused to leave. He sat down, only to rise again and pace the floor. He ran his hand through his hair, in frustration. He didn't want to want her like he did. He understood the physical desire, he had surrendered to it with many a pretty lass, but not this. It was more than desire and he would be damned if he would ever again let any woman change the course of his life or interfere in what he planned for his future.

For the first time in two years he thought of Jennie, let her into his mind. Jennie, who had taught him first to make love, then to love . . . then to hate.

For a long time she had tortured him with her ability to linger in his mind and stir his senses until he could stand it no longer. Betrayal had been her name and she had marked him in a way Kathryn's whip never could.

He sat down and buried his face in his hands, fighting his weariness. It had been so long since he had slept. He reached again for Jennie and was shaken when he found the shadowed corners of his mind filled with another form, another pair of emerald eyes, another slim, gold body . . . Kathryn.

He removed his boots and walked across the anteroom to the bedroom door. Gently he opened the door. In the dim light of early day he could see her lying in his bed . . . his bed. He moved slowly across the room until he stood by the bed.

Kathryn was deep in sleep, her lips parted slightly by her deep breathing. Her hair had come loose from its pins and spilled across his pillow. God, but she was beautiful. A beautiful trap, his memory demanded. Wed her, bed her, have her when you choose . . . but never love her, for she would wield the power of that love like a two-edged sword.

He sighed, he was so weary that it was hard to find rational thought. If he allowed the irrational thoughts that filled his mind to gain control he would waken her and make love to her as he wanted to, but he thought of the night a few weeks ahead when she must come willingly to him. No, he wouldn't take by force what was his.

He removed the rest of his clothes and very gently got into bed beside her. She stirred, but didn't waken. Instead she nestled against his warmth. He put his arms about her and pressed his cheek to her hair. Then he too slept.

It was only two hours, two very short hours, before Donovan was jolted awake by a pillow being slammed in his face.

He slept with his sword on the floor beside him and he was out of bed, crouched with sword in hand, nearly naked, when her revengeful laughter made him grit his teeth.

"No one can say you are not always prepared, but the next time you climb into my bed you had best bring your sword with you."

"Don't worry, Kathryn," he grinned and stood erect, tossing the sword on the bed. Her smile faded as he walked the three steps to the bed. His eyes held hers and they promised his own brand of revenge. "Don't worry," he repeated calmly as he got back under the covers. "When the time comes that we share this bed I will come prepared. You may have complete faith in that."

She flung herself from the bed the moment he drew the covers over him. He folded his hands behind his head and watched her as she hastily grabbed a robe and put it on.

"You are not amusing," she stormed.

"I hadn't meant to be." His answer was calm.

"Why are you here?"

"Here?"

"In my bed," she snapped.

"My bed," he corrected pleasantly.

"Your bed," she repeated with a sneer.

"You talk in your sleep, you know." He grinned.

"Curses about you I hope."

"No, to be exact you said some very pleasant things about how warm I was and how comfortable—"

"Liar!" she interrupted, her cheeks aflame. He had intruded into dreams she had thought to be hers alone.

"No lie, Kathryn. You are much gentler and sweeter when you sleep."

She hated the deep smoothness of his voice, the way it seemed to reach across the room and caress her. She didn't like these terrible confusing feelings. She had to keep in her mind the thought that today was the day her brother would stand before James's justice . . . James's justice, and Donovan McAdam's. She realized again that not only was he watching her, but he seemed to be reading her thoughts, for his gaze had grown serious. She turned her head away and stood irresolute and shaken. Kathryn McLeod had never felt so helpless and miserable in her life.

Donovan rose from the bed and came to stand behind her.

"This imprisonment is your fault, you know," he said. "Had I your word you would not attempt to interfere again, I would give you your own rooms here and you would have more freedom. At least until we are wed."

"You would still insist on this wedding even though . . ."

"Even though you hate me?" he finished.

"I," she began, her arms wrapping tightly about herself, "had dreamed of the marriage I would make. 'Twould not be one of coercion, but mutual respect and affections."

"Again you speak of love." His soft laugh was chilled.

"You do not care how I feel about this marriage." She turned to face him. "All you seem to desire is a name, title, and wealth. Well, I cannot stop you. But I am not coming to you like a docile cow being bred with the strongest of bulls. I warned you once and I'll warn you again. You will regret this."

He took hold of her upper arms and drew her against him. "You deny too many things both to me and to yourself. This will be a better marriage than most because it is not wrapped in unattainable dreams and sweet words of love that are never meant. You are a woman of strong passions. I knew that from the first moment we touched. You can deny all you choose, but those passions will be awakened."

"Always so sure of yourself, but you will have your defeat."

"Now it is your surety that speaks. Beware, Kathryn, or I might take the challenge just to prove to you that I know and understand you better than you think." He held her gaze steadily. "I want chains of peace, Kathryn, and our marriage will tie your house irrevocably to James. You are beautiful and a man would be a blind fool not to desire you. But don't ever think to use that desire against me. No pretenses of love would be believed on either side. Make the best of it and we can find our own kind of peace."

"I am like chattel, like a whore, bought and sold."

"You punish your own self. As my wife you will be treated with the greatest honor and respect by the court and by me. If you choose to destroy this then so be it, you will be treated accordingly."

"You are so cold, so unfeeling."

He smiled a bitter smile. "Wary, Kathryn—a man would also be a fool to give you a weapon to use against him." Then he chuckled, "When the time comes I will be warm enough to satisfy you."

Before Kathryn could answer, the toll of bells echoed within the room. Donovan released her. "I must dress, James has called the Parliament."

"You judge today," Kathryn whispered softly, almost to herself. Donovan felt a touch of sympathy, but let no sign of it show.

"I do not judge."

"But you have influence with James."

"You bargain for a request, Kathryn?" he asked with seeming interest.

Kathryn licked her dry lips and returned his gaze. "Aye."

"And just what do you bargain?" Now the question was heavy with curiosity, as if he were considering this idea.

"I . . . I don't want my brother to die," she half whispered.

He shrugged. "Still you do not speak of terms."

Kathryn wanted to screech at him, to claw that infuriating smile from his face. But she steeled herself. This time her brother's life was the weight held in the balance.

"I . . . I will fight you no longer. I will do . . . as you choose. I offer . . . everything in return for his life."

Donovan seemed to be weighing the possibilities. Then he smiled at her and this time the smile made her heart begin to pound. "And how do I know that what I bargain for is worth the price? Surely I have a right to a small sample of what is offered."

Her face flushed with her rage, but she lifted her chin defiantly.

"Maybe," he added casually, "I should see just what

my reward will be. What say you, Kathryn, a small glimpse . . . a promise, mayhap?"

She clenched her teeth together and with trembling hands she reached to unfasten the robe, the only thing she wore. He watched her in silence. The robe loosened, then fell to a heap at her feet. Now her eyes fled his and only her stern control kept the tears from betraying the pain at her loss of pride.

Donovan could feel his heart pound rapidly God, she was cream and gold perfection. Enough to destroy the control of any man. An excitement stirred in him. Kathryn trembled under the heat of a gaze that seemed to be paralyzing her breath within her. Then he moved to stand close enough that only a breath existed between them. Then he reached to gently trace the line of her jaw, down the slender curve of her throat to her shoulder. His hand skimmed her flesh to rest lightly on one soft breast, then downward again to the curve of her hip, where it rested possessively.

"Now that you have examined my worth do you consider it fair trade?" she asked coldly.

"Aye," he said softly and bent to brush her lips with a light kiss, "and I'm grateful that you are bargaining with no other. I look forward to our wedding with great anticipation."

He turned to leave and Kathryn's eyes filled with shock. "My brother!"

"I have nothing to bargain with Kathryn. Your brother's life is in James's hands alone. He will tolerate no interference even from me. But consider this just a prelude to our future together. You will make a wife that all men will envy."

She was shaking uncontrollably until her teeth chattered. He had made a fool of her.

"You are a cheat and a liar!"

"I? But how did I cheat you? I only wanted to view what is already mine. And lie? I never told you I would accept your generous bargain. No, Kathryn, 'twas to prove a point. I know women as they are. Don't ever attempt to use yourself as leverage with me. Oh, I will have you, but there are no terms involved."

"I hate you."

"Even so you are still enough to entice a saint to your bed. I am no saint."

"A keen observation," she stated as she bent to pick up her robe and hold it before her. He watched her closely.

"You also hold your honor as a shield. Do you have enough to promise you will not interfere again? If so you will have some semblance of freedom in the castle."

"How generous of you."

"Do you want it?"

"Aye," she said reluctantly.

"Then I have your word?"

"Aye."

"Aye is not enough, Kathryn. My trust does not extend that far. Tell me."

"I will not interfere, I will not try to escape."

"Good." He turned to gather his clothes and begin dressing. She was silent until he finished and rose to leave.

"Can I ask one request only?" she asked. He turned and waited expectantly. "I . . . I would know of my brother's fate as quickly as I can . . . please," she added softly.

He studied her seeming helplessness. It was an act. She would turn on him like a tigress if he gave an inch. Still he saw the shadowed pain in her eyes and he could not help himself.

"Aye, I'll have word sent."

"Thank you." She turned her back to him.

How easy it would be to go to her, gather her into his arms, and assure her that he would do all in his power to keep her brother from death. But he couldn't. He could not hand her the whip that could flog him. It was better that it remained this way between them. Kathryn would be his and he would eventually rule her and wipe out everything else but their future. In time the battles would cease. He turned to leave and Kathryn heard the door close. Only then did she allow the tears. She would die before she ever let him see her cry.

Chapter 10

James Stuart convened his first Parliament on the twentieth of July in the Tolbott in Edinburgh. He sat on a curved, thronelike chair, raised on a dais with three steps that led up to it. He was magnificently dressed and wore his sables proudly. Beneath the fine linen of his embroidered shirt, the heavy iron belt chafed and pained him. Still he wore it day and night. Now as he sat in judgment, his own guilt seemed to press in on him from all sides and his face looked somber. This scene was familiar to him, except that this time he was king.

Just below him, to his right, sat the earl of Argyll, the chancellor. To his left sat Patrick Hepburn and next to Patrick sat Donovan McAdam. His council was full of border names. Home was chamberlain, and the vicar of Linlithgow held the office of clerk of the rolls and council. Whitelaw was secretary to the king and his papers were spread on the table in front of him and his hands were already ink stained.

The sword of state had been borne in and James held the scepter in his hand. He looked down at his subjects in the moment of quiet which preceded the chancellor's opening statements.

"My lords," the words rang out. "My lords, barons, and commissioners of boroughs, today the Parliament considers first the special summons against those who had partaken with the king's father against him to a number of twenty-eight lords and thirty-seven barons."

The accused men stood facing James and those who had not been brought over from the castle had obeyed his summons. They had obeyed their new king and James was sure his quick action at Direlton had brought them here. They might be afraid, but they were more afraid to disobey.

Donovan did not know his king's intent; in fact, no one knew. He watched James's impassive face as the chancellor continued.

David Lindsey was the first and he walked forward until he reached the bottom step, where he knelt on one knee. His eyes lifted to his king with a pride that could not be broken. Gray of head, but strong of body, he waited.

"Lord David, you are appearing in this court for coming against the king at Sauchieburn, what is your answer to these charges?"

Lord David looked up into James's dark face. Like the others, he was completely unable to read the thought behind his eyes. He looked about him at the other lords who sat in judgment with James, lords who at one time had been part of the old king's court. Within him an anger stirred. He had sworn an oath of fealty to his king and as a loyal knight had stood beside the man he had sworn to until the very last. He hated the men who would swear an oath to one and turn on him at the first sign that his power weakened. They were, to him, opportunists who could never be trusted. He looked at Fleming and Lord Douglas, but his eyes were not met.

"I would prove with my sword against any of those who call me traitor, especially against those who swung to a political breeze without understanding what an oath calls for. The oath they swear now is as useless as the old."

It was a cry of protest against injustice. Desperately

he searched for a way to drag the truth out in the open, to shame these former rebels who now sat in judgment. He had fought for James III because he was his king, *his* king. Could a man, who had given his oath, done any less?

"You," he pointed to Fleming and Lord Douglas, "you caused the king to rise against his father! You caused his father's cruel murder! If this king does not see the truth, if he does not punish you, you will someday murder him as well!" Again he turned to face James. "Sire, people whose oaths are given with so little care can never be true to you. I shall be truer to Your Grace then and now, than they shall be."

Donovan watched James. Had he been able he would have spoken for Lindsey, for he understood the man's honor well. An oath could not be broken. He, too, wondered what James was thinking. James regarded Lindsey solemnly. But Lindsey would say no more. His pride was more clear at this moment than it had ever been. More than one man held his admiration in silence.

Again Donovan was about to speak when another man stepped forward to stand beside Lindsey: Eric McLeod. Donovan studied him. How like his sister he was. The same coloring and attitude and the same unbendable pride.

"Sire, there is no man of the law who would dare to speak for us." He paused, then spoke again, his voice quiet and controlled. "If I die here there is no other to carry the McLeod name. It will be abolished from memory. I . . . and my remaining family are shattered at this thought. But better that than that I had broken a sworn oath of fealty to my king. I must speak for myself but I would like to ask Your Grace's permission to speak for my cousin, Lord Lindsey."

"Granted, my lord," James said. Still his face was impassive.

A murmur ran through the tiers of seats. Donovan

watched closely, thinking this might have been Kathryn. The eyes, the molding of the face, were so much alike. He watched Eric so intently that Eric sensed it and looked at Donovan with a puzzled frown. Neither man noticed that James did much the same.

But Eric's mind was not on his sister at this moment. He was recalling the mysterious note that had been smuggled to him. Whoever had sent it understood the finest detail of the law and had given Eric a weapon to use. But he hesitated, for if he did not know the origin of the note how could he be certain more betrayal was not in store for him and consequently for his friends. The hesitation seemed overlong to James, who frowned. His voice came laden with importance. "My lord, you were about to say something in your defense?"

Eric wet his lips. He did not lack courage. There were those present who had stood beside him in battle and knew the truth of that. And it did not go unnoticed that the rest of the accused stood quietly, their willingness to let Eric speak for them a sign of their high regard for him.

"Your Grace, I pose a question to you."

James arched a questioning brow and his lips twitched in a smile. He nodded.

"When you swore your oath of fealty, when you received the crown of Scotland, you made a vow which does not give you the right to set in judgment here."

There was a muted gasp throughout the hall, but James's eyes had not left Eric's.

"You swore, Sire, that you would never set in judgment against your lords on any occasion when you had been party to their deeds." The boldness of this truth hit hard.

The iron belt bit deep. It pained James, fretted him when he moved as he did now to stand and face his lords. But he savored the pain as a reminder both that this was the truth and that he was guilty.

"Aye," he said quietly, "you speak the truth. I have sworn so. Know you this, Eric McLeod. Never, while I live, will I ever be false to my oaths to my native land." He put one hand on a richly jeweled dagger and surveyed the faces before him. It was as if it pleased him to somehow announce his guilt, because guilty or not, he was still king. "I shall leave Parliament itself to set in the judgment here. I command them to adhere strictly to the law. I shall await the decisions." He was going to leave, for, he felt, Lindsey was wrong when he said Fleming and Lord Douglas and others had seduced him into rebellion. He had done it himself. He would not set in judgment, and only hours later would others realize how much he had done to make the decision be as he had wanted.

He was leaving. Slowly he went down the steps, down the narrow aisle, and into an anteroom.

Eric was shaken. The first step had been right and true, as the note had predicted. His respect for James and his justice leapt a notch or two.

Donovan watched, just as puzzled. It was as if James had somehow paved the way for this occurrence. Donovan had the distinct feeling he had missed something that his clever king had not, and this annoyed him. He regarded Eric with a dark frown. He would listen more carefully.

Eric's brow was beaded with sweat. He had only one more statement to make and he prayed silently that this one small and almost overlooked Scottish law would stand. "These summonses are invalid. By law, we were to appear before this court, this Parliament, within the space of eleven days. If the charges were not brought within eleven days then the time to bring them is past. Now, my lords, it is eleven and one days. The time has expired. We need answer nothing to this summons."

Donovan sat very still. He almost smiled, but restrained himself well. This was a small point of Scottish law, a very small point and often overlooked. But this time it was being invoked. He cast a look at the chancellor, who seemed quite aware of the law as well. A great hum filled the room of the Tolbott. James's secretary leapt to his feet and hurried out. Lindsey and the other lords standing trial surrounded Eric, clapping him on the shoulders and smiling.

There was an uproar now, and the door to the anteroom opened. James, followed by his secretary, reentered the room. The court criers shouted for silence. Donovan watched James closely, realizing now that this all had been a ploy designed and staged by James so he could have the ability to draw these wayward yet loyal lords back into his realm. He did not want to destroy men who had the courage to follow their king to the bitterest of ends. He needed that courage, and he meant to have it.

The chancellor was motioned toward the king and he went to him at once, bending close to hear over the pandemonium the words the king said. Then he smiled and turned to face the accused men.

"You have proved your loyalty to the king's grace, by obeying these summons. His Majesty will not judge you and, since the law finds you right and true, no new summons will be made."

There was a hail of joy and again the sounds of men's voices raised in jubilation. But when silence was again established the next words came like icy water.

"But by royal edict, you shall be deprived of your hereditary rights and offices for the space of three years."

This time Donovan could not retain his smile any longer. It was comfortless punishment. Not martyrdom, but plain poverty. The chancellor spoke again. "His Majesty gives you permission to leave, but the sentence of exile will begin in three days. Each will be served the papers to tell where his exile will be spent and each will go in separate ways so that you may never conspire against the king again."

Donovan knew that James now held Parliament in

144

the palm of his hand. Because of his justice there was little he could ask them for that they would not give, and he meant to ask them for a very great deal.

Donovan had always been aware of James's reckless conduct in battle, and his tremendous courage. He now revised his opinion of James as a politician. He was a magician. A canny Scot.

James mounted the steps to the chair again. Before he turned to face the gathering, his eyes met Donovan's . . . and he winked.

Whitelaw rose, papers in hand. He and James had planned every move to the second. It was incredible, for he was about to list all the things James wanted, knowing that Parliament would grant each request. Whitelaw began with laws on education. All sons of eight or older must be educated in mathematics, in languages, including Latin, and in art and law. The founding of a university at Aberdeen. The founding of a college of surgeons in Edinburgh. Legal reforms, abolishment of some taxes — the list went on and on.

Donovan's gray eyes met those of his king and he had never felt so proud in his life. As the formalities proceeded, Donovan's mind wandered. He thought of Kathryn and Anne. The exile of their brother would leave them poor, but in his own care for three years. By the time Eric could return, Kathryn would be his wife, a fine husband would be found for Anne, and Andrew Craighton would have been well taken care of. He was more than satisfied; he was elated.

Then Parliament was over for the day. The council would meet again the next day without the accused lords.

James held them only moments longer while he informed them that there would be a feast of celebration that night. When Donovan could finally break free he walked toward his rooms, knowing Kathryn must have been beside herself with fear by now. He didn't question why he was so pleased her brother was not to die. It was enough to know his problems were ended.

When he opened the door to his room Kathryn fairly leapt from the chair she had been sitting in. Her eyes were suspiciously red, but her gaze was level and questioning.

"There were no death sentences," he stated. He could see her visual relief. "But he has been exiled for three years."

"Exiled . . . where?"

"I don't know yet."

"Poor Eric," she said more to herself than to him, as she turned and walked to the window to look out.

He stood for a minute watching her. The majority of women, put in her circumstances, would have been worried about their future. She would be little short of destitute, for her wealth would be held by the king for her brother's return . . . or until she wed. Could she be wondering if he would continue with the thought of wedding her since she was now nearly penniless. Of course there were her land and her title. Her name alone was prestigious enough. He would have given anything to know what was going on in her mind at this moment.

As if their minds had somehow been atuned, she turned from the window and looked at him. "My sister Anne, what will happen to her?"

"The same as to you I imagine. A marriage—an advantageous marriage—will be arranged for her. Until then I'm returning you to your home." This thought had just occurred to him and he watched her eyes light with pleasure. "But with restrictions. You and your sister will have some extent of freedom. But I and several of my men will also be sharing your house with you. You will need protection and your affairs will be handled by me from now on."

"Why . . . why do you want to wed with me? I am penniless now, of no use to you. Being the opportunist that you are, surely if you request it your king can

146

make a more advantageous arrangement for you."

"You underestimate yourself. The McLeod name alone will draw lords under my banner. You have land and," he smiled, "a lot of assets that I look forward to sharing."

"I . . ." — she looked suddenly shaken — "I would ask one thing of you."

This was a surprise to him; Kathryn, who had vowed never to ask him for anything, now wanted something from him. It pleased him but still he was wary. "What do you want?"

"Anne."

"What of Anne?"

"She is . . . sensitive and gentle. It is wrong to force someone like Anne into a marriage with a man who is less than . . . kind or understanding. She would break. It would destroy her."

"But she must wed."

"Then let it be someone of her choice. Someone who could care for her and not use her brutally."

"I cannot promise that."

"Would it make a difference if I begged you?" she demanded. He could see she was trying to fight her own anger and get it under control.

"Maybe it would please me better if you pleaded for yourself."

Kathryn smiled, "I have been assured of my fate too often by you. I have had my pride cast in the dust by you. Never again will your soft-voiced traps catch me. No, I will not plead for myself. There is no gain in trying to make the stone wall of this castle bleed just as there is no gain in trying to breech the stone of your heart. I know by James's decree we will wed, and I cannot refuse you. But think carefully of what you own, Donovan McAdam. You will own my body . . . the rest of me is mine alone and you can never touch it."

"I have asked for nothing more," he replied. He walked to a table and poured a drink, then sat down in a chair. "Since I have your word I am going to let you return to your home for the three days before your brother must leave."

She looked at him in surprise but said nothing. She had been too neatly trapped before. But Donovan continued, "Tonight there is to be a feast of celebration. You will dress in your best gown and you will attend with me. There James will announce our betrothal. My men will escort you home when you are ready and wait there for you."

"As you wish."

Again he regarded her in silence; then he drank the last of his wine and set the goblet aside. For the first time in all the times they had faced each other she looked closely at him. Tired lines were etched in his face, and he sat as though he were weary. If she remembered well he had had very little sleep in the past days.

"You need to find your bed for a while or festivities and too much ale might put an end to you."

He chuckled, "Are you turning wifely suddenly? I should think you would want just that."

"No," she replied frigidly, "once you have linked your name to mine I take no pleasure in anything that damages it. It is my pride not yours that concerns me."

"You're right, I am tired, and your shrew's tongue annoys me. Go, you will find your escort waiting for you below."

Kathryn was uncertain. She had wanted to strike at him, to hurt him. Why then did she feel the unwelcome urge to go to him, to hold him close and offer comfort. It was another kind of trap and she struggled to avoid it. Without a word she walked to the door. In a moment she was gone.

Donovan rose from his seat and stood for a moment, realizing the room seemed so much emptier without her.

As he had said, two men waited patiently for her. Both were quite impressed with the fact that they were chosen by Donovan McAdam, a man they admired, to guard his woman.

"Lady Kathryn," one approached her as she came down the stairs, "your horse is saddled and ready. It is our pleasure, my lady, to escort you home."

"Where you are to guard me and make sure I do not run away," she snapped.

He was confused and embarrassed by the truth of the situation. "Aye my lady . . . to guard . . . and protect you."

"I'm sorry, I did not mean to take my frustration out on you. Come, I am anxious to ride again, and to see my brother."

It had been ten days, ten days since she had tasted such freedom, and she savored it. She rode at reckless speed and both guards were pressed to keep up with her. Both agreed their captain had chosen quite a woman for himself.

When they clattered into the courtyard, Kathryn dismounted before either man could get to her side. They could only follow her as she half ran into the house. It was then that they began to worry about whether this job was going to be quite as simple as they had originally thought.

When Kathryn entered the house Anne was just coming down the stairs. She had rebandaged Andrew's wound and forced him to promise he would try to get some sleep. Anne was so excited when she saw Kathryn that she ran down the balance of the stairs and the sisters enthusiastically embraced.

"Oh, Kathryn, I was so frightened. I didn't know if I would ever see you again. Do you know anything of Eric?"

"Aye, I know of Eric."

"Kathryn?"

"It's to be exile."

"Oh," Anne breathed dismally, "can we go with him? Kathryn, we could both go with him!"

"No, Anne, neither of us can go with him."

"But, what will become of us? With Eric gone what will we do?"

"First we are going upstairs. I am going to bathe and you are going to help me choose my very best and most enticing dress. Then, you will do the same for yourself. Tonight we go to a celebration and our host is the king."

Kathryn started up the steps with her arm linked with Anne's. But Anne was quite aware that there was a great deal Kathryn wasn't telling her. Annoyed with Kathryn's attitude, she abruptly came to a stop, and Kathryn turned to her in surprise.

"Anne?"

"Please stop hiding the truth from me, Kathryn. You know quite well what the king has planned for us. Since it concerns me so deeply why don't you just tell me the truth?"

"All right Anne. I didn't mean . . . I just didn't want . . . oh damn!"

"What, Kathryn, what?" Anne insisted.

At that moment Andrew came to the top of the steps and started down. He was just in time to hear Kathryn's answer.

"I am to wed with Donovan McAdam . . . and you . . ."

"I . . . ?"

"I have been told that a suitable match will be arranged for you. You will be wed as well. Donovan McAdam will take up residence here. After our wedding he will be lord of this house."

Andrew froze in his tracks and Anne's eyes lifted to him, filled with dismay. There was nothing he could do and this crushed his pride. To admit he loved her might cost the lives of hundreds, for peace between their two countries might depend on him.

Yet how could he stand it, how could he just let her

be handed to a man she didn't even know?

"And I shall have to go . . . God knows where with this man . . ." Her voice died as she seemed to be envisioning a fate she did not have the power to do anything about. Anne was much too smart not to know that it would be suicidal for Andrew to try to do anything about it either. She felt a hopeless weakness grip her for a moment, then she reached for control. The situation had not come yet. Maybe she could find a way out before it did.

"Kathryn, must I go to this celebration tonight?"

"Yes, Anne. There is no way out. If the king commands we go, then we go. The McLeods are not in a position to disobey. Remember Eric is not gone yet. Sentences can be changed."

Anne's face went pale. She could not do anything. She was hopelessly trapped.

Kathryn looked up to see Andrew standing on the stairs. At her glance he began to descend again.

"It is good to see you home again, Mistress Kathryn. I'm afraid I overheard your brother's sentence. I'm sorry you will be separated but it will only be for three years."

"It may as well be a lifetime, Andrew. When he returns he shall be forced to live in his own home on Donovan McAdam's charity."

" 'Tis not a good fate, mistress, but 'tis better than death. Sir Eric is a resourceful man. And . . . and decisions can be as quickly changed."

"What do you mean?" Kathryn grasped for any plan that might free them.

"Nay, mistress, I know of no way around it now. I try only to give you hope . . . and to urge you to think very carefully about any situation that presents itself."

"I shall," Kathryn replied. But Andrew knew her quick mind was assembling ideas at the moment. She regarded him with narrowed eyes, then her eyes leapt quickly from Andrew to Anne and back to Andrew. He could clearly see her thoughts moving.

"You have been a great help to Anne while I was prisoner, Andrew. I am grateful to you for that."

"It was my honor," he replied.

Anne had regained her composure now. She inhaled deeply. Andrew's words had given her hope as well. There had to be a way.

"Come, Kathryn, it is best we prepare for this celebration."

She started up the stairs and a surprised Kathryn followed. Andrew watched until they were out of sight, struggling with his rage. He had never had a place for a woman in his life before. He had been the eternal warrior, following an easy path and doing as he chose. Now there was something he wanted . . . and it was out of his grasp.

Still . . . he would, as he had advised Kathryn, watch for any opportunity that came.

Chapter 11

Andrew sat before a low-burning fire, a dark scowl on his face. He had never felt so helpless in his life. Above him Anne and Kathryn were making preparations to attend the celebration of the king's coronation. Anne . . . she was dressing carefully. It twisted inside him. Dressing carefully to be paraded before all of Jamie's lords. To be auctioned off to the most loyal and trusted of them. Given to a man she did not love. If only James would not confirm any agreement of marriage for a few more weeks, Andrew would have all he needed to go to Donovan and the king. Then he would be free to claim Anne himself.

Surely his claim could only firm the arrangement. An English bride for a Scottish king and a Scottish bride for an English lord. . . . If only he had the time . . . if only Donovan didn't catch him first . . . if only . . . His dark look deepened. He had never asked Anne, never held her, never kissed her. How could he plan his if onlys when he didn't even know what was in her heart.

Kathryn stood before a huge mirror, but her eyes were watching her sister's reflection. Anne sat before her own mirror brushing her hair. Kathryn could clearly see that her mind was elsewhere, and she was sure she knew where.

Anne drew the brush through her long, ebony hair without thought. She didn't want to go to this farce of a party. She knew its reasons. Ostensibly it was for James's coronation and the betrothal of one of his most valuable men to her sister. If that were not bad enough, she knew that she walked into that celebration as a sacrifice, an offering . . . a reward. The thought made her shake so badly that she lay the brush aside. She twisted her hair into a long coil and pinned it atop her head. Only then did her eyes catch Kathryn watching her. She tried to smile, but it was a poor effort. Kathryn came to stand behind her.

"Oh, Kathryn, how can you do it! How can you wed a man you do not love?"

"I do not see that I have much of a choice. Eric will be gone, our worldly goods will be in other hands . . . and it is the king's command."

"I can't," Anne's face was pale, "Kathryn, I can't. Why can you not just tell them that I've become suddenly ill."

Kathryn knelt down beside Anne, taking one of her hands. "Anne, listen to me. Until we wed there is hope. We are McLeods. Would you have them come for us and drag us there like conquered cowards. We have our pride and our hope. Smile at them, laugh with them, dance with them. Play their game for the time being. But remember, *until you are wed there is hope*. There is still the possibility that we can find our way free of these planned marriages. But it takes courage and I know you have an abundance of that. Now come on. Let's give them a battle before we give in."

Anne looked closely at Kathryn, "Kathryn . . . if . . . will you marry Donovan McAdam?"

"It seems he believes so," Kathryn said coldly. "But I have already made my warning clear. If I am forced to it I will, but he will regret every moment of it."

"Who do you suppose . . . ?"

"They will choose for you? I don't know," Kathryn stood and walked a few steps away. Her back to Anne, she spoke softly. "Anne . . . is there someone you would choose for yourself?"

154

Anne thought of Andrew. Yes, she thought, there is someone she would choose for herself if she could. But there was a world standing between them, and his life at stake should she confide her thoughts to anyone . . . even Kathryn.

"Why should you ask that?" she countered.

"It . . . would be more difficult for you I suppose. Anne . . . be very careful." She turned about and for a long moment they looked at each other.

Then Anne smiled. "I will."

Kathryn turned back to her mirror, and was satisfied with what she saw. She was wearing not only the most daring dress she had ever seen, but the most wickedly expensive. She chuckled when she thought of the look on Donovan's face when he found the dress had been charged to him. It was only one defiant blow, she thought, my dear Donovan. There are so many more in store for you. She vowed to prove more of a handful than Donovan wanted to cope with.

Some time before the battle she had ridden to Edinburgh for fittings, and this afternoon she had ridden out to get the dress. She had made a point of riding with Andrew at her side. She liked Andrew and she was certain he was more than fond of Anne and could be the protector she might need. Besides, she grinned, she was sure it would annoy Donovan.

She had confided to Andrew on the ride that she was sure she was constantly being watched by some of Donovan's men. Andrew had replied dryly, "I'm quite sure you are, Lady Kathryn . . . in fact, I'm quite sure we are all being watched very closely."

The dress would be worth it. It was made of black rustling silk, the bodice square, and deeply decolleté. Its skirt billowed out, but it was slit to the waist in an inverted V. The skirt beneath was scarlet. She wore no jewelry except one spray of diamonds that was pinned where the silk was cut away between her breasts. She had contrived this to draw eyes and it was effective.

James Stuart's court was gay, lightly immoral, and extravagant in true Stuart style. Jewelry gleamed on bright-gowned women. Donovan waited with tightly reined impatience for Kathryn's arrival. It would be a brilliant evening. Their betrothal would be announced, and when she returned home he and several of his men would be riding with her to take up residence there. He found his nerves growing taut with expectation.

Andrew rose to his feet as he heard Anne and Kathryn coming down the stairs. Kathryn was beautiful, all fire and brilliance, but Andrew could not take his eyes from Anne. The deep wine gown she wore made her eyes luminous and her ebony hair glisten like satin. Her eyes never met his and her cheeks were flushed. She's frightened, he thought bitterly. It was the closest Andrew came to betraying his country, and the closest he ever came to hating Jeffrey Sparrow.

"He has sent someone for us?" Kathryn questioned.

"Yes, Lady Kathryn," Andrew replied. "Would you like me to ride with you?"

"No," Anne's voice came whisper soft before Kathryn could answer. "I . . . I don't want you there. It would be safer for you to stay here."

He knew what she meant. She was unsure of his reactions and she didn't want him to jeopardize his position. She wanted him safe.

He would have given his soul to have taken her from here willing or no, and run as far as he could. His arms ached to hold her.

Time, precious time kept ticking away. Time when they could be together. If only he could tell her.

"All right," he rasped, feeling as if his breath was caught in his chest like a red hot piece of iron. "I shall wait here." His eyes held Anne's now. "I shall wait here," he repeated, "until I know you are safely home."

"That is a good idea," Kathryn said briskly. "Come,

Anne, we don't want to anger the king."

They left and the sound of the door closing after them sounded brutally final to Andrew.

He sank down into the chair before the fire with thoughts of murder in his mind. He gritted his teeth as the vision appeared before him of Anne in the arms of another man. He cursed and rose from the chair to pace the floor like a caged lion. He could not bear the silent hours that stretched before him.

Ambassadors had arrived four days before from all parts of the world. Danish and French could be heard vying with each other. Spanish women flirted from behind fans, their voices as soft as the music that came from the players on the balcony. Even so, among all the beauty and glitter, Kathryn and Anne caused a stir when they entered. Men were quick to notice the charms and beauty of the two; and quick to think that the sisters were there to be bargained for. Of course none knew yet that Kathryn was promised to Donovan. He was impatient to make it clear to all, without realizing he had become slightly possessive . . . and just a wee bit jealous.

The nearest men swung around to look, and soon Kathryn and Anne found themselves surrounded. The other women stared icily.

Donovan stood quite a distance away, beside some friends. He knew Kathryn had come, he actually sensed her presence. He shouldered his way through the crowd. But when he was close enough to get the full impact, he stopped and stared at her in disbelief.

Kathryn smiled and extended her hand to him. He saw the familiar tilt to the corners of her mouth, and the laughter — and challenge — in her eyes. But he took her hand without a word. Men around them dropped back a little, quite unprepared to stand between Donovan and anything he wanted.

"Your servant, my lord," Kathryn made a dramatic

curtsy. She had succeeded in shocking him. But now she read his face clearly and for a brief moment she was afraid he was going to drag her from the room. She could see the steel-like glitter in his eyes. Donovan was about to speak but he was prevented by the arrival of the king.

James entered, walking slowly. He enjoyed entrances. He spoke to a few people, then stopped beside Anne and Kathryn and Donovan. His eyes scanned Anne and Kathryn, glittering with a kind of amusement.

"What lovely creatures you are." James's gaze moved to Donovan, then back to Kathryn. "In truth, my dear Lady Kathryn, your charms are well displayed."

" 'Tis the latest style from Venice, Your Grace," Kathryn said.

"And you most certainly do the style justice, my lady."

"Thank you, sire."

"Lady Anne," James turned his attention to Anne, "you are a welcome addition to our court. You should find this evening . . . enlightening. It is our wish that you enjoy yourself, and that you spend more time here."

"I shall try, Your Majesty," Anne said softly. But James and Donovan were well aware of her reserve.

James tried for humor, but failed miserably. "Lady Kathryn, you and your sister are not vying for the eyes of his lordship?" He inclined his head toward Donovan.

"No, Your Majesty," Kathryn replied. Her chin tipped frigidly and Donovan could have choked his king.

James laughed, then moved on to speak to the French ambassador. Donovan stood close to Kathryn and would have spoken again but another of James's favored lords came to stand close to Anne, his eyes warming as he scanned her. He asked her to dance with him and Anne knew it would certainly not please the king if she refused. She tried to keep Kathryn's advice in mind. She was not wed yet, and there was still hope. She held Andrew in her mind while she smiled and placed her hand on his arm and they moved away.

This left a now slightly nervous Kathryn and a more

than angry Donovan temporarily alone. He smiled faintly and his nearness made her conscious of every pulse of her blood.

"It is time to eat, Kathryn, you will sit with me."

It was more of a command than a request and she resented it as she resented everything about Donovan McAdam. But she was engaged in a challenge that somehow excited her.

She might have argued just to torment him, but when he turned to look at her again she could sense a growing emotion that was threatening to be loosened at any moment.

"Of course," she said quietly. He took her arm in a grip of iron and they moved to the table, where they sat down side by side. They were silent while enormous platters of meat and fowl were being brought.

"I saw you talking with that delightful little blond creature when I came in," Kathryn said casually.

Donovan was surprised and pleased that in all the confusion she had taken notice of him.

"Lady Duncan? Yes, she is beautiful."

Kathryn drank her goblet of wine, then lifted her eyes to him. "Is Lady Duncan your latest whore?"

Donovan, angry, annoyed, and just a little guilty, muttered, "Madam, I have scarcely met Lady Duncan."

"Well," she replied coldly, "you are away often and when you come home you will most likely have a number of women besides your wife." Her smile was deadly. "So I think Anne and I should keep Andrew for protection, don't you?" Her eyes met his and he grinned. She must have been watching his every move. He didn't question why this should please him.

"Are you jealous, madam? You've no need to be."

"How you lie!"

His gaze lingered on her bare shoulders and Kathryn raised a newly filled goblet to her lips and looked at him over the brim. Donovan reached out and ran his fingers lightly across her shoulder. She could feel a trail of heat

159

that did little for her strained composure.

"Don't do that."

He raised an eyebrow. "You invited it, my sweet. I can hardly resist."

Kathryn's hand tightened around the goblet and it shook slightly. Donovan laughed softly and Kathryn drank the wine.

The wine goblets were larger than she had judged and the servant made certain they were kept filled. She began to feel pleasantly warm.

Donovan watched Kathryn and those about them watched the pair. Rumors were flowing that this was the woman who would wed Donovan McAdam. Was it true? Everyone questioned and a few felt certain that from the look in Donovan's eyes he was surely interested.

David Murray seemed utterly fascinated with Anne. At the end of the dance he was reluctant to let her go.

"Come, sit by me at the table and share the meal with me," he urged Anne. She cast her eyes quickly in Kathryn's direction and watched her laugh at something Donovan had said. She nodded her agreement and a pleased David led her to a seat, then sat as close to her as he could without pressing. He had the vague impression that Anne was like a white dove, likely to fly away. Aspirations began to grow in his mind. He had fought valiantly beside his king and his loyalty to James and Donovan ran deep. He also knew the situation with the McLeods. There would have to be advantageous marriages made, rewards for such loyalty, and a way to cement the reign of James IV. Why should he not be the one to have Anne McLeod? Because custom was so it never occurred to him to question Anne on any choices. She was a ward of the king and would do what he commanded.

He began to think of everything: his rise of position, marriage into a prestigious family, wealth, influence. In fact he thought of everything concerning himself, and nothing concerning Anne except what she could bring to him.

Her conversation was shy and mostly answers to his questions. He had no idea that she sensed at once his intentions. It angered her that he looked upon her as a just reward for doing battle for his king. In fact it was her helplessness that angered her. She looked at him and could not help comparing him to Andrew and the comparison was hardly flattering to the newly made lord. She was filled with an aching need she could hardly name. Andrew had never said a thing to her except in gentle kindness. She knew he trusted her . . . but was trust all he felt?

What disaster would befall her or Kathryn if she were to refuse the king's wishes? Worse, what would the result be if Andrew did say he cared? He was in no position to do anything about it. His life had become too precious to her for her to bring any more danger into it than what he already faced. She would keep his secret safe and hope for success. Yet with the rumors circulating about James and Maggie Drummond she wasn't too sure what success he might find.

She thought of how empty her life would be when Andrew was no longer part of it. Engrossed in her thought, she was taken by surprise when David lay his hand on her arm. She looked at him to find his gaze had swept past her. Turning, she followed his gaze.

James had risen and was holding his goblet aloft in one hand while the other raised to silence the assemblage. Anne's eyes went quickly to Kathryn, whose face had paled. She sat proudly erect, but her eyes were on the king, as were Donovan's.

"Come, one and all," James said. "Let us drink a toast together. We have more cause to celebrate. Tonight it gives us pleasure to announce the betrothal of our loyal friend, Donovan McAdam, and Lady Kathryn McLeod."

There were cheers as Donovan and Kathryn rose and the toast was drunk. Kathryn had steadily been drinking wine to numb the fury she knew she would feel when the announcement came. To say that she was more than slightly drunk would have been an understatement. It was only Donovan's firm hold on her arm that kept her from swaying dangerously as she drank down another full goblet as if in defiance of Donovan and his king.

Donovan knew quite well she was reaching for the condition in which she could say and do anything that might upset him. He wasn't about to let her get away with it.

Her brilliant beauty had drawn more than enough eyes to suit him. He was not jealous, he countered mentally, but he had both their positions to consider. She was a woman who had all the courage necessary to say what she felt in her heart and he was certain James would find her sentiments hard to accept. If she pressed him, James might be forced to do more than he wanted to do.

All this, combined with the fact that he could not let her get out of hand for his own peace of mind, forced him to get her out of there as fast as he could.

Any other time he might have been amused, and played the game with her. But in the back of his mind was the worrisome thought that James could change his mind about the marriage between them as easily as he had made up his mind.

"I think it is about time, my lady, that I take you home before you attempt to do something foolish that you will most certainly regret."

His anger was just below the surface as his hard grip on her arm clearly told her. "I choose not to go," she said arrogantly.

"I should hate to make a spectacle here," he said grimly, "but I shall beat your backside until you're black and blue. Now," he grated, "don't lean. Walk straight."

Kathryn made the effort only because the rapidly drunk wine had finally rendered her temporarily incapable of doing battle. She traversed the whole length carefully putting one foot before the other.

Finally they were outside the big doors. Kathryn put both hands to her temples. Her head had begun to pound and she swore feelingly. She stood unsteadily and looked up at Donovan with a satisfied look on her face.

"I imagine I disgraced myself a little and you a great deal, I hope." She smiled mockingly.

"You look like a drunken lady from the streets," he said, his fury erupting. "One I wouldn't bother to lie with." He seized her hand and started toward his room.

"Are you jealous, Lord McAdam?" she laughed. "Have you finally lost your temper or have you just realized what a mistake marrying me would really be?"

She was taunting him, tormenting him with the promised threat of disasters to come if he continued with his claims.

He came to a stop, still gripping her arm. The force of her forward movement brought her against him. His arms closed about her and she looked up into his eyes dark as gray storm clouds.

"You'll be sorry you chose me, m'lord," she jeered. "If it's in my power I'll ruin everything you touch. And if you touch me," she added, "I shall do my best to ruin that as well."

He smiled a smile made of ice. . . . He was wise enough to know that she was much too clever not to know precisely what she was doing.

"I'm taking you home." His voice was low and held a promise of its own. "Our wedding will be in less than two weeks. Until that day you will be confined there, forbidden to ride or to walk outside your gate. We shall see, madam, just who is in command." He took hold of her shoulders and drew her close.

Despite the cold fury that held him, another much more threatening emotion began to surface. She saw it replace the anger and for the first time his intent shook her.

Something deep inside her cried out for something she refused to recognize. All she wanted to see was a man she was being forced to marry. All she wanted to recognize was that he was heartless and cold. He had never spoken of love and never meant to. The despair of such a future filled her.

"Let me go."

He wanted to fling her from him, but instead he drew her closer so he could feel every lush, soft curve that seemed to fit so well against him. His body responded with a surge of desire that only increased his anger.

It was a contest of wills and if a small voice deep inside whispered of another emotion he forced himself to ignore it. He had loved before and the flame of it had singed his heart. He would never surrender to such an emotion again. But by God he would have her.

She affected him as no other woman had since Jennie and he had to control it or surrender to it, and that he vowed he would never do.

Kathryn could feel his desire, she could see the heat in his gray eyes and something in her responded with an unwelcome warmth.

He bent his head and took her mouth in a kiss first meant to be dominating. But the intent got lost when her soft mouth parted beneath the force of his. She moaned softly as the kiss deepened. A flame licked to life inside her, making her feel as if her bones had turned to water. The passion, once ignited, grew, and neither seemed to be able to control it.

With an effort that took all his concentration he held her away from him. Momentarily he had lost control. Now he lied to himself to protect the vulnerable place that still had an unhealed wound. He could control his desire for her until she was his. Then he would satisfy his lust for her whenever he chose. Then he would teach her that he could take and hold what he wanted.

If he denied a gentler emotion it was no stronger a denial than the one that raged in Kathryn.

"So you still find me fit to adorn your life like stolen booty, m'lord. I'm honored."

He grinned, calm now. "Aye, you will adorn my life, Kathryn. It will be a lusty marriage at least, one filled with continual interest."

"Continual interest! You lowbred barbarian," she hissed. "I am not a bauble you can play with. Is there nothing in your heart but rock?"

"You speak of love again," he laughed. "I told you before that love is a useless emotion. I would never give you that kind of weapon, Kathryn. I have a feeling you would wield it like a broadsword. Come, it's time I take you home."

He gripped her arm and forced her to move beside him. Within minutes they were on the way home.

Andrew leaned back wearily against the high trestle-seat. Only the light of one candle and a low-burning fire lit the room. To him it seemed the hours were endless. The curtains were drawn across the windows and the room had an oppressive silence.

He rose and walked to the window to draw back the curtain again. There was no sign of anyone. He let the curtain fall back and returned to the chair.

He thought of the meeting he was to have in less than a week, a meeting that would give him papers signed by each of the traitors involved. Papers that would be the proof he would need to gain access to the king. Papers that might ensure peace, but better still, might gain him Anne. Less than a week. But would Anne be promised to someone before he could accomplish what he had to do? He knew McAdam didn't trust him, thought he was a spy. Without the papers he would never be able to prove anything and his word would hardly be enough to sway the powerful men he would have to face.

Suddenly he heard the outer door open and the sound of voices. It brought an alert light to his blue eyes and he turned and waited impatiently. Again it grated on his pride not to be able to open the door and reach for the woman he loved.

But it was wise that he didn't, for when the door opened he was surprised to see Kathryn with Donovan McAdam behind her.

"Lady Kathryn," Andrew said, trying to ignore the narrow-eyed gaze Donovan cast him. "Where . . . where is Lady Anne?" He had to strain to control the fear that was rising in him. Donovan was watching too suspiciously for him to say or do more.

"Lady Anne will be brought safely home," Donovan said harshly. "Most likely by one of what will become her many suitors." He watched Andrew, hoping for some sign of betrayal. But Andrew kept his face as impassive and impersonal as he could manage. "You may find your way to bed now."

Kathryn's eyes begged Andrew to stay. "I'm sorry, m'lord, but Sir Eric has entrusted to me the safety of this household. It is my duty to see that all its occupants are safely inside and the doors are locked against . . . intruders or any who would threaten the peace of the house."

For a moment Donovan wanted to have Andrew dragged off to the castle dungeon, where he could extensively question him. But he had no way to justify this to James . . . not yet at least.

"After tonight there will be less need for your dedicated worry. I and two of my men will be staying here. And after Lady Kathryn is my wife and Lady Anne is safely married there will be no further need for your services at all." He had said the words hoping for some response, and he was rewarded by a massive struggle he could only sense by the glow of blazing wrath in Andrew's blue eyes. He was glad now that he had decided to hit Andrew with the news. He was almost certain now, and he would be close enough to watch Andrew's every move.

"I am safely home now," Kathryn said, still aggravated by the throbbing in her head and Donovan's unsettling presence. She too had seen the dangerous glint in Andrew's eyes, and she wanted no more confrontations this night. "It is quite all right to leave me here with Andrew. We will await my sister's arrival . . . soon."

"Then I bid you good night, Lady Kathryn." Donovan's voice was arrogant. "You are confined to this house. My men and I will be here from tonight on, to make sure you do not disobey me." He turned and left and Kathryn glared after him.

Kathryn again pressed her hand to her forehead, cursing at the ache in her head.

"You may retire, Andrew. I'll wait for Anne."

"My lady, if I may say so, you look a little ill. I think it would be wiser if I waited for Lady Anne's return and you found some sleep."

"Umm, maybe you are right," Kathryn replied. But she walked to the fire and extended her hands to the warmth. "Andrew?"

"Yes, Lady Kathryn."

"Who do you think the choice of a husband for my sister is likely to be?" She turned to look at him and saw his effort at control.

"I have no way of knowing," he said.

"I would like to see Anne happily wed," she said, watching him closer.

"Aye, my lady . . . happily," he repeated.

"Anne is . . . well she's different from me. She is somewhat delicate."

"Mayhap she is not quite as fragile as everyone thinks."

"Mayhap, but . . . I wouldn't want to see her hurt . . . or see her make a costly mistake."

"No, Lady Kathryn," his look was level, "I would not want to see her make a mistake. In fact I would protect her from any harm if I can."

Kathryn smiled. "Good night, Andrew," she said

softly. He watched her walk from the room, wondering how much he had revealed to the very clever woman who had just left.

He sighed. For a few minutes he paced the room. He tried to keep his mind from creating unwelcome images, and from wondering just who was going to bring Anne home.

Two more hours. Hours of frustrated waiting. Andrew's nerves were drawn as taut as a bowstring. Then the welcome sound came. He walked to the window and looked out. The moonlight was bright enough that he had little trouble recognizing Anne. But his eyes quickly went from her to the handsome man who was with her. They talked for a few minutes, then the man took Anne's hand and kissed it. A bitter blackness rose in Andrew and he tasted the tang of jealousy.

He raged at a fate that so casually could take the woman he wanted and make her the possession of another.

But he was again seated comfortably before the fire when Anne came in.

"Andrew." Her voice sounded pleased, but he wasn't sure he wasn't desperately reading something into it that wasn't there. "What are you doing up?"

"Waiting for you, Lady Anne," he replied as he rose. Her eyes searched his and his hold on his control wavered. "It is my duty. . . ." Those were words he didn't want to say.

"Oh . . . I see." She started to leave the room.

"Lady Anne, wait."

She turned to face him again.

"The gentleman who brought you home, was he a guard supplied by James?"

"No," she said softly. Her cheeks had flushed as his gaze held hers. "It was Lord David Murray."

"Ah," he said bitterly, "another newly made lord."

She walked to his side. There was so much she wanted to say to him, but their situation was impossible. She knew she could be the cause of his death, and that she could not bear. The scent of her perfume reached tenuous fingers to envelope him and Andrew had to struggle to keep from reaching for her.

For a long moment they stood close. Their eyes met and held, saying things they would be forbidden to put into words.

"You are very beautiful. Why should I not believe that every man at the celebration was at your feet?"

"That's really not true, Andrew," she smiled. "It is my sister who drew all the attention."

"Then they are all blind," he said, drowning in a violet sea. Within him a wave of desire rose that almost took his breath away. If he paid for it with his life he had to touch her. His hands were large and callused, yet he reached to lay his hand against her cheek so gently that he felt her breath catch. "Anne," he whispered.

For a moment time seemed suspended and they stood touching but knowing there could be little hope for anything more. Yet the magnitude of the white hot need in both made the battle impossible. Neither knew which one moved first but suddenly she was in his arms. Murmuring her name in a low groan, he crushed her to him. He kissed her with a growing hunger and she returned it with a willingness that set his mind spinning into oblivion and his body afire with a spiraling need.

Anne felt her heart soar and could have wept with joy. She could feel with sensuous pleasure his hard body and the heat of his desire. If all she could have would be this stolen moment then she intended to savor it and gather from it the strength she would need to face what she must.

Andrew was lost in her. He kissed her feverishly, drugged by her intoxicating taste and the softness of her pliant body. The passion grew until all resistance was being destroyed in a fiery volcanic explosion. She was his! his heart cried.

They were breathless and she looked up into his eyes

with her answer to his unasked question written clearly for him to see.

But the moment was shattered when a heavy fist pounded on the locked front door.

For a moment they could do little more than stare at each other in shock. For Andrew it was the sudden knowledge that he was about to do Anne the greatest harm he could do. It wounded him deeply and the frustrated desire became worse.

Anne too realized the truth, but it was with pleasure. At least she knew that Andrew's need for her matched hers for him.

"Wait," he said. "I'll see who it is. Then we must talk."

She nodded, knowing what his words would be. He would deny this for her benefit, maybe even claim it only a moment's passion. But she knew better.

Andrew walked to the door, hoping he could rid himself of the unwanted intruders quickly. He had almost destroyed Anne's future, and he meant to repair the situation.

He opened the door and gazed silently at Donovan McAdam and the two men who stood behind him.

Chapter 12

Donovan read Andrew's shock in the seconds before Andrew's face became closed again. But he felt the shock was more because Donovan might have discovered some truth about his purpose and was here to face him.

"M'lord?" Andrew questioned hesitantly.

"Have the ladies retired, Andrew?" Donovan questioned as he moved to enter. Andrew could do little but step back and let him do so.

"Lady Anne is still up, m'lord, but Lady Kathryn has retired."

"I imagined she would." Donovan's mouth twitched in a half smile. "She was in condition to do little more. You can help my men bring our things inside."

At that moment Anne stepped into the entranceway. "Andrew what . . . Lord McAdam." She too fought to retain her shock and the quick wave of fear that washed through her. Was Andrew discovered! Was he in danger? "It is too late for visitors, sir."

"I am not a visitor, Lady Anne. We will be taking up residence here. I was sure Kathryn would have informed you of my plans."

"I have not spoken to my sister since earlier this evening when we were preparing to attend the celebration." Anne had regained her composure. "I was just telling Andrew that the king has announced your betrothal to Kathryn."

Andrew said nothing; he was busy watching Donovan, who had not taken his eyes from Andrew as well. There was an air of challenge surrounding the two men that emanated from them like a radiant heat.

"Andrew?"

"Yes, Lady Anne?"

"There will be no more need for you to keep such a late hour. You may retire now."

Andrew could have smiled at her attempt to protect him but he knew Donovan's suspicions were already too deep to sway.

"Aye, Lady Anne." He tried for his most subservient attitude. "Good night," he bowed slightly toward Donovan and started for the stairs.

"Wait," Donovan's voice made him freeze. "Where are your chambers?"

Andrew had to relax his clenched jaw to speak. "My room lies between Lady Anne's and Lady Kathryn's . . . should either of them need me during the night."

"Find another room." Donovan was pushing him to resistance. "That will be my room." Andrew could see Anne's cheeks grow pink and rebellion growing in her eyes.

"Aye, sir," he said quickly, before she could voice her anger. "There is an empty room across the hall that will serve as well. It will leave me close enough to call," Andrew smiled coldly, "should I be needed. I will move my things at once."

"That won't be necessary."

"Sir?"

"Tomorrow is soon enough." Donovan's cold smile matched Andrew's.

Of course Andrew knew that his things and the room would be most thoroughly searched, but he had been too cautious to leave anything where it might be found.

"As you wish, sir." Again he started for the stairs. He was reluctant to leave Anne alone with Donovan, but he had no choice. Donovan was watching as he climbed a few steps then turned to look at them. Beyond Donovan, Anne's face was pale and her eyes full of fear, yet she smiled. He continued his climb.

"Come, Lady Anne. I shall escort you to your room." Donovan offered his arm.

Anne walked up the stairs beside him. She had never been more frightened. This man could destroy Andrew with a word. He was too powerful and too dangerous to cross.

"Lord Murray was very impressed with you tonight, Lady Anne." Donovan kept his voice casual. "In fact he and James were discussing you when I left."

If he expected a battle from Anne he was disappointed. She remained calm.

"I am flattered that James chose to discuss me," she replied.

"You find David appealing?"

"He was quite . . . entertaining."

"I see." They stopped before the door that was obviously to be Donovan's. "And which is your room?"

Anne pointed and Donovan nodded as he glanced toward the other door. "And that one is Kathryn's?"

"Yes."

"There are adjoining doors?"

"Are you insinuating . . ." Anne's anger was growing.

"I am insinuating nothing, Lady Anne, merely asking a question."

"Yes," she said, "and both are locked."

Donovan cast her an amused glance. "And if you had needed help just how was Andrew . . . your . . . ah . . . protector, supposed to reach you?"

"I . . ." She was left wordless.

"Or were the doors to be unlocked . . . at night."

Anne was enraged at his open innuendo and with scarlet cheeks she whirled from him and walked to her door, which she slammed very firmly between them. Then he heard the bolt slide home. He chuckled. Lady Anne was not quite as gentle as most supposed.

The smile died as he again turned to face the two doors. One his . . . and the other Kathryn's. There was a question to which he needed an answer. He walked into the room that had once been Andrew's and looked across it to the door that led to Kathryn's. In a few quick strides he crossed the room and stood by the door. He hesitated . . . but he had to know. He reached for the handle and turned. The door swung quietly open.

Kathryn had entered her room in a state of combined mental exhaustion and inebriation. It was not Kathryn's way to weep, but to do battle. In this case she had been pushed nearly beyond endurance. Tears formed in her eyes and escaped to run down her cheeks. For a time she did not even realize they were there. Then she felt their warmth and tasted the salt of them on her lips.

She brushed them away. He had reduced her to this! Weeping because he was not quoting love sonnets to her. The thought swept through her like a forest fire.

Maybe she would have to bend to the king's demand, maybe she would have to wed Donovan McAdam, but she would never have to surrender the part of her that told her there was more to marriage than what Donovan McAdam offered.

Her parents had been happy with each other. She had seen the affectionate bond that had existed between them. Had it been too much to expect?

She thought of Anne and worried that Anne would break under the heavy hand of a careless man. If only she would find a way to get Anne free. The thoughts tangled in her mind and her head throbbed miserably. Taking up a decanter from a nearby table, she poured another glass of wine. At least for tonight she could blunt the effects of the evening.

She drank it down and set the goblet aside. Then she loosened her hair and ran her fingers through its thick fiery strands until it flowed about her. She took off her clothes and cast them on a nearby chair. It was warm in the room. This, combined with the wine heating her blood, made her too uncomfortable for the nightgown that lay at the foot of the bed. She climbed into the huge four-poster and in a matter of minutes drifted into a deep sleep.

She never knew when the door swung open, never heard the soft tread as Donovan entered the room.

The vision that met his eyes almost made him give an audible gasp. The pale amber glow of the slowly dying fire mingled with a mist of moonlight and fell across the bed, lighting Kathryn's body in a gold-white glow. Her hair, its auburn fire reflecting the flame, seemed to shimmer about her. Strands of it lay across her breasts and swirled about her arms and shoulders. Her legs were long and slender and tapered up to the soft curve of her hip, across which one hand limply lay. The other arm was bent above her head.

Her mouth, sensual and full, was parted as she breathed lightly. Dark lashes lay against cheeks soft and smooth. He could not take his eyes from her as he slowly walked across the room to stand by the bed.

He could feel the fire of desire leap through his veins and his loins tightened in response to the need. What held him? Who could stop him? She was his by the king's decree. Why did he not wake her and take her now? But he couldn't and he sought a logical reason. He wanted her as a wife and would not use her as a harlot before. He was a man of honor and the thought of rape was distasteful. When they were wed she would come to him. It did not enter his mind that this also was a form of rape. He knew she was unwilling, that she spoke of love. But he could not afford any breach in his defenses.

Yet, when he looked at her, a warmth filled him that he did not try to explain. It made his heart throb heavily to know that in a matter of days they would share this bed.

His mind told him to leave now, before he was totally lost in unwelcome thoughts. But he couldn't seem to control another part of him: the part that said he must

175

touch.

He sat gently on the edge of the bed. He didn't want to wake her. He knew it was the amount of wine she had drunk that kept her asleep. So gently that it was like the touch of a breeze, he lightly touched her flesh, laying his hand on her waist and letting it drift slowly up to cup her breast. He bent forward and just as lightly touched her lips with his. She tasted of wine and the sweet softness of woman. The urge to drink heavily of the nectar was almost too much for him. His body was crying out for so much more .

He taunted himself with the feel and the taste of her until he could bear no more. Then, like a shadow he rose and left the room without looking back, for one more look, one more touch would have been too much. On the other side of the door he leaned against it and realized his hands were shaking and he was sweating.

The danger that she could reach a place within him was prevalent in his mind. He rebuilt his barriers. One whisper of love to a creature like this would be devastating, for she would rule him ever after. He could not afford that. He needed a weapon of defense.

It was only then he thought of the unlocked door . . . and that he stood in a room that had belonged to Andrew Craighton. The fury of it hit him like a bolt of lightning. Did something exist between Kathryn and the English spy? The thought of it was like a blackness. He could not yet prove what he suspected. Yet it was unthinkable that Kathryn would make good her threat to deceive him. Somehow he must find a way to the truth about Andrew Craighton and if there was any hint that he had put a hand on Kathryn . . . Donovan was determined to destroy him.

In the depth of sleep Kathryn drifted in a mist-filled world. She walked through the veil of mist as if she were lost and seeking something. Then he was there. A tall, broad-shouldered form whose face she could not see, and yet, with a sense of warmth and peace she knew him.

He wore a dark cloak that fell to his ankles and they stood only inches apart. She heard her name whispered. Then he extended one arm, opening the cape so that she could be enfolded in it. She took the two steps and felt his warmth surround her. She could feel his hand on her skin, touching lightly. She sensed the strength that held her. Her mouth was raised to his kiss and she felt his mouth against hers hard, yet so gentle. Still she could not see him. Yet she knew. This was the promise of love. This was all she sought and this was where she would always belong. Again she felt the kiss deepen, then the softly whispered words: "Kathryn, I love you . . . I love you." In her sleep Kathryn moaned softly as the dream slipped away and she was left alone.

Andrew found sleep an impossibility. He was trapped. He could not . . . no . . . would not leave Anne. Yet he had to find a way to get in and out of the house without the knowledge of Donovan and the men obviously set to watch his every move.

Too much conversation with either Kathryn or Anne would only make Donovan's suspicions worse. He paced the floor. Jeffrey had placed him in an impossible situation. It was like chasing himself in circles. He needed the signatures of the traitors or a treaty with Henry to use as leverage, and he could have them in a matter of days . . . if he could get out.

He was actually laboring on behalf of Donovan and James as much as on behalf of Henry. Peace would be good for all. But he'd never convince Donovan McAdam of that and James's mercy could only be judged on what he saw and all he would be able to see in Andrew would be a hated English spy.

Andrew removed his clothes and extinguished the candle, leaving the room almost dark. He lay on the bed, his hands behind his head, and pushed all other thoughts from his mind but Anne. In the solitude of his room he could allow himself this luxury. But only for now. That fleeting moment in the room below might be all he ever had, so he warmed his heart in the heat of the memory.

For Anne the night was just as difficult and just as long. After only a few hours of sleep she rose and dressed and left her room. Work was always distracting.

Downstairs she gave orders to the cook for breakfast. It would be quite different today than any other day. Today instead of three there would be six . . . all of them would be playing the same dangerous game.

Kathryn woke up with a wretched taste in her mouth and other discomforts that made her feel in less than the most pleasant of moods. She ordered her bath at once, with no intention of lingering over it. Anne should not have to face the day alone. But when she left her room and walked down the stairs it was to the sound of voices coming from below.

The laughter of men was new in her home since her brother had been among the defeated. She stood quietly for a moment as the familiar sound stirred painful memories. She missed Eric so.

She was still standing motionless and listening when Andrew's voice came from behind her.

"Good morning, Lady Kathryn."

She turned and smiled at him. "Good morning, Andrew. It seems our guests rise early."

"Yes," he replied as he stopped beside her. "Is Lady Anne awake yet?" He tried to make his voice impersonal.

"If I'm not mistaken, and if you will listen closely, I think that is Anne's voice I hear." Kathryn laughed, "Don't try to hide your surprise, Andrew, and you'd better stop underestimating Anne."

"Yes," he grinned, "I guess I had better. Shall we join them?"

"Yes, let's walk into the lion's den and see if well-fed lions are less dangerous."

Anne had disarmed the men who had come to share her home with her shy charm and sweet disposition. Relaxed, they found it very easy to talk to the beautiful woman who was the sister of their leader's betrothed.

When Kathryn and Andrew came into the room the guards both rose to their feet.

"Do sit down, gentlemen," Kathryn said while Andrew drew out her chair so she could sit down. Andrew was about to leave the room until Anne's voice stopped him.

"Join us at the table, Andrew, I have already explained to these gentlemen that you are considered more a part of the family than as a secretary."

He was grateful, because he fully intended to remain within hearing distance anyhow. He silently moved to a chair opposite Anne, where he could enjoy watching her.

"Where is our other . . . guest?" Andrew asked Anne.

"He said he had something to do and would return in time for breakfast."

This made Andrew's nerves jump. Had Donovan found some kind of evidence in his room after all? Was he careless? He thought very carefully, but was sure he had not been.

The conversation went on around him and he ate very little while he worried about where McAdam could have gone so early.

At that moment Donovan walked into the room. Andrew held his breath for a minute, but when nothing happened he began to breathe again.

Donovan said a brisk good-morning to every one, then took the only vacant seat left, next to Kathryn. She perceptibly stiffened and her smile grew a little weaker. She could not believe that she allowed him to have any affect on her at all.

"How is your head this morning, Lady Kathryn?" His grin was enough to aggravate her more.

"I'm fine, thank you."

"Good, I hope it won't take you too long to change into your riding habit."

"And why should I?"

"Because we're going riding."

"I'm in no mood to ride."

"Then I suggest that you get into the mood, for we are going riding whether you will or not. I'd hate to see you on a horse with that dress. Although it is quite beautiful it would be, to say the least, uncomfortable and revealing."

Although he smiled there was no one at the table that did not accept what he said as an order. But Kathryn was more than ready to do battle . . . until she saw Anne's face. Then she looked at Andrew. Maybe it would be better to go. Who knew what she might find out.

"You wage battle on a helpless woman quite well, sir. Have you had a great deal of practice?"

Donovan laughed. "Helpless, Lady Kathryn? I would challenge any man to call you helpless. As far as my practice with helpless women, I don't know because I've never run across one yet."

Kathryn rose to her feet, biting back the words that she wanted to throw at him. With great effort she restrained the words but the look in her eyes would have withered a lesser man. She walked slowly and deliberately from the room.

There was a strained silence around the table for several moments. Then Donovan spoke.

"Lady Anne, I meant to inform you at once but I'm afraid my thoughts were diverted. James is having a dinner tomorrow night to welcome . . . a friend. He requests your presence."

Andrew kept his eyes from Anne. Both knew that James's plans for Anne would not be so easily stopped.

"And Kathryn?"

"As my betrothed she will attend."

"I shall be honored," Anne said quietly. Then she rose. "If you will excuse me." She left the room, and Donovan's attention returned to Andrew.

"I would suggest . . . very firmly . . . that you do not leave the premises until I return."

Andrew looked from Donovan to the two men who still sat at the table with them. Then he smiled. "My duty lies here, m'lord, why should I leave?"

"I was just reminding you, in case you should be thinking about it."

"As I said, sir, there is no need for me to leave."

"You puzzle me, Englishman," Donovan said.

"I, sir? Why should I be a puzzle? There are many freebooters who use their swords to live by. I fought with Eric McLeod, and it is at his request that I remain as secretary . . . to protect his sisters."

"Speaking of swords, the one in your room is one of the best blades I have ever seen. It is a fit blade for a king."

Andrew remained outwardly calm, but he fervently wished he had not left the sword for Donovan to find and examine. "It is a find blade. But if a man is going to live by the sword then it is important that he have the best. Would you not agree?"

"Mayhap we will have an opportunity to cross swords while I am here. I have a feeling the exercise could be very enlightening."

Andrew's mouth was tight and his eyes never wavered from Donovan's piercing gaze. "It would be a pleasure, I assure you. I will look forward to it."

The open threat hung between them and both the young men were well aware of it and spoke no word of interference lest the wrath of Donovan McAdam should turn on them.

At that moment Kathryn returned wearing a riding habit that was, to say the least, stunning. She did not speak at once but looked from Donovan to Andrew and sensed Andrew was in the midst of a dangerous situation.

"I'm ready, m'lord," she said. She held her short whip in her hand and tapped it lightly against the palm of the other hand.

Donovan grinned and stood up. He walked to her side and took the whip from her hand and tossed it to one of his men.

"I don't think you'll have need of this today." He took her arm and propelled her with him toward the door. At the doorway he turned to look at Andrew again. "I won't forget that we have an appointment one day soon. Until then remember you are not to leave."

Kathryn had no time for questions before the firm grip on her arm urged her on.

Outside Kathryn found their horses already saddled and standing. She looked up at Donovan with a taunting smile.

"You are so sure of yourself."

"Why should I not be?" he said amiably. "I have what I want."

"Not yet you don't, and maybe you should not count on it." She wanted to strike the arrogance from his face and he read it well and laughed.

"And that, my love, is why I took your whip from you."

"Insufferable wretch," she grated. He helped her mount and they rode out through the gates toward the town.

As they rode side by side he could not help but admire her horsemanship. Her back was rigid and he could actually taste her resentment. He cursed silently to himself as another memory filled his mind.

"Where are we going?" she inquired.

"I have an appointment to keep. It will only take a few minutes. Then, if you like we can ride anywhere you choose."

"An appointment?"

"Yes." With the one word he told her he had no intention of telling her where the appointment was. Her curiosity was piqued.

They continued the ride in silence as they clattered through the city streets. He reined in his horse before a small shop and was helping her to dismount before she took notice of the sign. It was a jeweler's shop.

She was more than curious now, but she had no intention of asking him again. They entered the small shop together and were quickly greeted by an old man with white hair and eyes that missed little.

"Ah, m'lord, you honor my shop again."

"I've brought the lady in question." Donovan smiled. "You can see that her hands are rather small and her fingers very slender. Can you do what I have asked?"

"But of course, sir."

"Kathryn, come over here."

Kathryn came to stand beside him. The old man reached a withered hand toward her. "May I?" he said gently.

She placed her hand in his for a moment and he seemed to be examining it closely. Then he looked up at Donovan.

"You are right, sir. Her fingers are very slender. The ring itself is huge. It will take considerable cutting."

"But you can do it in time? There are less than ten days."

Instantly Kathryn knew the reason for the trip and she knew why he had refused to tell her. Here is where he meant to purchase the ring for their wedding. She jerked her hand away and looked coldly up into Donovan's eyes.

He reached out and took hold of her wrist in a brutal grip, forcing her to extend her hand to the old man again.

From a small bag he took a ring. It was large, obviously made for a very large man. It boasted a small crest surrounded by several glittering green emeralds. Donovan held her eyes as the old man fit the ring on her finger. His voice was calm.

"The ring has been part of my family for a long time. I choose to have it cut down to your size. When we are married I will place it on your finger. From that day on there is no man in the whole of Scotland who will not know to whom you belong."

"You mean to brand me," she whispered.

He touched his other hand to the small scar on his lip and smiled. "Turnabout is fair play, don't you think?"

She did not speak again, but held her hand steady while her finger was measured. After his assurances that the ring would be ready in time Donovan flipped the old man a coin. "See that it is." Then he took Kathryn's arm and they left the shop.

Outside she jerked her arm from his grip and walked to her horse. But he was undaunted as he came to help her mount. She was filled with an overpowering emotion. It was so strong it nearly brought the tears to her eyes.

They rode along in the same heavy silence. All her intimate dreams seemed to be shattered. There was no hope for love in a marriage such as this one would be.

Donovan knew what she thought. He had chosen to do what he had done on purpose, and he refused to acknowledge the touch of guilt that plagued him.

What he did not tell her was that the ring had been his father's and his mother had held it for him. From the time of her death he had worn it. He had planned to give it to the woman he had wanted to marry . . . to . . . he refused to acknowledge Jennie's lingering presence or to remember the scorn he had felt when she had returned it.

Now he need not swear to love, he had only to brand this woman his and the ring would be enough. He had effectively proven his intent. Why then did the bitter taste of it linger on his tongue? Why was he plagued by one tender moment in the stillness of the night when he had reached to touch.

It was safer this way. There would be no questions between them about the basis on which this marriage was made. It was advantageous to both so there need not be the pretense of romantic love. Let them meet in passion, he thought. That was all he would demand, and that was all he intended to give.

Andrew wanted desperately to go to Anne and talk to her, to somehow lend her his strength. But the eyes of Donovan's two men missed very little.

He became pleasant and companionable and soon they were involved in conversation. He learned a great deal about Donovan McAdam, none of which was much of a secret. He also learned that Donovan's men respected him. At least Andrew had the hope that if he did get the proof he wanted and he could get Donovan in a position where he could force him to listen. Donovan was a man with enough intelligence and courage to take advantage of the situation.

By midmorning Donovan and Kathryn had not yet returned. Anne came downstairs and Andrew kept a close eye on her movements until he ran across an opportune moment to get her aside and speak to her. They walked in the garden. Both knew they were being watched.

"You're upset, Anne. What did he say to you?"

"Kathryn and I have been invited to dinner at the castle tomorrow night."

"Does that distress you?"

"Do you have any idea why the dinner is being given?"

"No, why?"

"To welcome James's mistress, Maggie Drummond."

"Kings have had mistresses before."

"I think, Andrew, that Maggie Drummond is more than that."

"He cannot marry her."

"Why not?"

"She is not of royal blood. . . . It's . . . it's not advantageous to him."

"Andrew," — she turned to face him — "do you still believe that love respects titles or royal blood? If he chooses to marry her, who is to stop him?"

"I should hope someone or something could."

"I'm afraid."

"Anne, don't be. What if you just didn't go?" He said the words, but he knew the answer.

"One does not defy the king," she said quietly.

He looked down into her eyes and longed to put his arms about her. Eyes were on them so all he could do was try to make her understand that all hope was not gone. Only what could he say? What could he promise her? Nothing.

"Anne."

"No, don't say anything, Andrew. Don't try to soothe me with promises that are out of reach."

"What if he proclaims a husband for you at this dinner?"

"I don't know. There is little that can be done. If it must be . . . then it must. And you must leave and forget me, as I will try to forget you."

"Can you?" he questioned; the hope was like a flame dancing in the depths of his eyes.

"No," she whispered, "but I must try to accept and so must you."

"Let us hold on to hope as long as we can, Anne. It is too hard to let you go like this."

She reached out a hand and lay it on his arm only for an instant. Her eyes spoke words forbidden to them. Then she turned and left him, and he watched her walk back into the house.

Andrew had just reentered the house when the door opened and Donovan and Kathryn came in. One look at their faces and Andrew was sure the ride had been traumatic for them both.

Kathryn did not say a word of farewell to Donovan. She simply walked up the stairs and in seconds the sound of her door closing came to them.

This was going to be the stormiest marriage Scotland had ever seen. Andrew smiled, pleased with the thought. As far as he was concerned Donovan McAdam deserved every bit of upheaval he could get. Andrew's only worry was the things he had seen in Kathryn's eyes.

Love and hate, he had learned, were often two sides to the same coin. If he could be successful in his mission it might just be amusing to stay around and watch the explosion occur.

Chapter 13

Long before dawn had touched the horizon James had risen from his bed. He walked to the window and leaned against its wide frame to draw the curtains aside and look out.

It was moments such as this when James faced the loneliness that was part of being a king. Oh, he had many around him, but few he could really talk to and receive complete honesty.

Today Maggie would come. Beautiful fair-haired Maggie. It was still difficult to believe the way he felt, the depth of his love for her. He had bedded many women, all seeking the king's favor for herself or for family. But Maggie asked for nothing. In fact she had resisted him as far as her abilities could go. No, Maggie asked for nothing but his happiness, yet he would have given her all. He remembered so well how they had met.

He had ridden toward Drummond Castle with the assurance from Lord Drummond, who would eventually join them there, that they would be royally welcomed. He had not expected the warmth of the welcome he had gotten.

No one had taken into consideration the panic in Maggie, who was alone at Drummond Castle. She knew its defense was always important and kept in mind her father's orders should any sign of attack appear. When a huge body of men approached, arms and armor glittering, she was immediately on the defensive. The last thing she had expected was for the king to arrive without her father.

The castle, very old, was a great square. From its architecture James could picture its inner court, with huge flagstones and pillared arches.

Then James became conscious that the gates were closed and he frowned, but he kept the pace of his approach. He waited for the gates to open and for sounds of greeting. Instead a hail of arrows came from the castle.

It was at that moment when those in the castle recognized the standards of the king. Maggie was more frightened than she had ever been in her life. She had raised arms against the king. This alone could bring death to her entire family.

James checked his horse so suddenly the animal reared. For a moment James was so angry he could hardly think. If Lord Drummond had been in his hands then he would have hanged him. But Drummond was not there.

The men around him gazed at the castle in sheer amazement. Then the force around him prepared for a battle. They had their king to defend.

At that moment the unexpected happened again. Suddenly the gates were thrown open. With the protests of his men in his ears James clattered over the drawbridge. He was too angry to think of anything else but getting his hands on whoever was responsible. The small court was deserted. Still mounted, he entered through the wide doors of the castle itself, his horses hooves sounding loudly on the square flagstones of the hall. He reined in—then he saw her.

She was coming toward him, not running, but on light, quick feet, her skirts held up a little. She came close and saw clearly the dark tanned face under the gold plumed helmet. She picked up her skirts and ran the last few feet and stood poised before him. In the few seconds it had taken her to cross the hall his men had entered.

Margaret Drummond spread her skirts in a deep, graceful curtsy and spoke clearly. "I am Margaret Drummond, if it please Your Grace. Welcome to Drummond."

There was a silence while James wrestled with anger and the pleasure of her beauty. Her full yellow skirt was like the petals of a flower and her eyes were flecked with green and gold and she wore a small satin cap over a wealth of shiny blond hair.

"You have a strange way of welcoming your king, mistress."

Maggie drew a deep breath and put out a hand in an appealing gesture that reached James in a way she could not imagine. "Your Grace will you forgive me. I am alone . . . ."

"Did you give the order to shoot arrows at your king, mistress?"

Her eyes were enormous. "Aye, my lord."

James grinned as he took off his helmet and handed it to one of his men.

"Art thou warlike, mistress?"

"I am alone," Maggie answered bravely. "I was in the kitchen when you came and had to decide quickly. I am not used to military things. My father has always protected us. I have been trained by my father to take certain steps to protect the castle should a troop of unidentified men approach. I did but heed my father's training, my lord."

"You did not see our banners?"

"They were not identified at once and I"—her head bowed in shame—"I was frightened."

He was both amused and captivated by her beauty and her reaction. For despite the words she spoke he didn't really believe she had been afraid. Her eyes again raised to his. He was shaken by the realization that he did not want her ever to be afraid of him.

He imagined her in a dark kitchen. "What were you doing in the kitchen? That is for servants."

"Making perfume from the roses."

He smiled. Involuntarily he inhaled to see if he could smell the scent of roses. She held up a hand and he took it in his gauntleted one and raised it to his lips. This is what Lord Drummond saw when he stomped into his own castle.

The scent of roses stayed with James, as did the beauty of Maggie. Several hours later he found himself away from the others in a corner with Lord Drummond.

"M'lord," James began. Over by the empty fireplace was Maggie Drummond. James fastened his eyes on her and did not look at her father as he spoke. "Your daughter, the Lady Margaret, finds favor with me."

At this Lord Drummond too cast a quick look at Maggie. He clasped and unclasped his gnarled hands. "Maggie?"

"Maggie," repeated James, smiling a little as he said her name.

Drummond was not unsensible of the honor that interest bestowed on his house, an honor that might blossom into financial reward and royal grants. "Your Grace," Drummond said reluctantly, "Maggie is betrothed."

James's brows drew together. His voice was like the crack of a whip. "To whom?"

"Maggie is betrothed to Ian Crieff. He is a fine lad, fought well at Sauchieburn, and today. Your Majesty knows him. He is there, there next to Maggie."

James could see the back of Crieff's broad shoulders and his thick, light hair. Crieff's obvious suitability was an annoyance to James. At that moment Crieff turned toward them and James stood up. Then he spoke harshly. "We shall find a suitable bride for him."

He walked away leaving a stunned Lord Drummond, who could only gasp, " 'Tis an honor sire."

During the evening Maggie felt the whole fabric of her life was suddenly changing. It had been taken out of her hands and yet she was not ready to relinquish it. Seeing James from only a few feet away she knew well enough he was a formidable adversary, king or not.

She knew now she would never marry Ian Crieff. She looked at him in sudden desperation and knew with fatalism he could not help her, and she could not ask him because it could mean his life. The only one who could help her was James himself. He had to let her go. She knew the time would come soon when she would have to face the king. She knew this just as she knew what he and everyone else would expect from her.

Was he a man who could accept honesty? Could one tell the king without drastic repercussions that one chose not to accept his attention? Maggie had never loved anyone, including Ian, yet she would have been contented with her life had not James walked into it.

An hour after the supper she was sent for. Her heart beat rapidly as she left her room and walked slowly toward the meeting with James. She meant to plead her cause, to make him understand that once he walked through her life it would be forever changed. When he tired of her he could go on with his, but hers would never be the same. She entered a small anteroom on the ground floor, formerly used as a bedroom. The candles had been lit and the curtains drawn over the doorway. Maggie was alone with James.

He was standing. His request for her presence had swept away the need for formality and Maggie, taking advantage of this, made a small curtsy such as she would to any other man.

"M'lord," she said.

He kissed her hand and Maggie quickly withdrew it. Maggie, who played chess well, went instantly on the offensive. "M'lord, although I am not unknowing of the honor you do me, and regardless of the love and loyalty

I bear Your Majesty, I would like leave to speak truly."

This was hardly what James had expected. "You have my leave," was all his surprise could manage.

"It is not long. It is simply that I must decline this honor."

This hit James squarely between the eyes, but as always, James rose to the battle. She should have known this was his nature. When James wanted something he was not one to let anything stand in his way, much less a woman's will. He could only think of her betrothed and try to understand her temporary resistance.

"You love another man?"

"I have known Ian Crieff all my life and we planned to wed."

He took her by the shoulders. "And you deem that love? You know nothing about love." Her face was pale but she looked up at him wordlessly . . . but bravely. He was the king and this took a man's courage. He made no motion to caress her. He held her so she must look at him. "It is not our will that you should marry Crieff. What is more, mistress, never speak to me again of loving him. It pleases me not." Her silence deepened while he studied her face. "My attentions displease you." He said the last as the reality touched him. Women fell at his feet, offering themselves freely. Yet this shy beauty was bluntly telling him that, king or no, she didn't want him.

Desperately Maggie came back at him with the only hurt she could inflict. "Aye Your Majesty, they displease me."

Roughly he took hold of her, binding her to him. She tried to twist away but his hold only tightened. She could not move. Then he kissed her.

Maggie Drummond had been kissed before, but never like this. Something happened that she could never put words to. This was not the same. His mouth was gentle, yet firm, and sensation after sensation, all new and overpowering, flowed through her. She broke away from him and backed away, her lips parted and her eyes luminous.

They looked at each other for a long time, recognizing what had leapt between them, James elated and Maggie frightened as she had never been before. He came to her, towering over her.

"And still you deny me?" he asked softly.

"I do," she whispered. "To you it is a game, another conquest. For me it is my life."

He sought one logical reason why a woman would deny. "Are you a virgin?"

Her lashes lowered and her cheeks grew pink. "Aye, my lord."

"So that is your reason," he smiled. "Young Crieff has been more patient than I will be."

"He did not demand, Your Grace. He was kind and good." Now James frowned. "That was not intended to hurt you, my lord. You are different. You are the king."

"Unhappily so," he muttered. "But I am also a man, mistress. Do not forget. I—." He broke off sharply and turned away.

"M'lord, how could I possibly forget you are a man."

He swung back to her, to make sure whether he had heard a hint of laughter in her voice. When he saw her smile he grinned boyishly. Suddenly he was filled with an irrational happiness. She was sweet as honey and warm as summer sun.

"It pleases me you have known no other man."

"You flatter me. But is it not fortunate that I am too shy to ask you questions like the ones you ask me. Is't not, James Stuart?"

He truly laughed.

"You are six and twenty and surely you have—"

"Cease, mistress."

"I jest but a wee bit."

"And I relent . . . a wee bit. How old are you?"

"Nineteen."

"Will you sit with me, Maggie?"

James sat down in a large chair and tossed a pillow on the floor beside him. Maggie sat down close to his knee. He reached down with ease and turned her so her shoulder was against his legs and her head near his knee. She made no protest when he removed the silk cap and laid his hands on the spun gold of her hair.

There was a quietness about Maggie, a peacefulness like a lake on a warm summer day. He could feel it seep through him. He needed this peace. He needed someone to touch his life who made no demands, who wanted nothing. Someone to whom he could talk freely, knowing that the words would not be carried elsewhere and wrung like a wet cloth to discharge all that could be used to manipulate him.

There was peace in the room. The candlelight was dimmer than the flood of moonlight that made a radiant shimmering path from the long window across the room.

The night air from the plowed fields was sweet and clean and from outside came the hum of creatures of the night, a singing sound. Maggie bit her lip to keep back the stinging tears, because the beauty of the night had indefinably engulfed them.

She knew the passions of this strong man had been awakened. She wanted to understand and to forgive him, but that did not mean she would surrender.

She would stand in a dangerous place. She knew quite well it would be almost impossible for James to marry her. Kings had to marry advantageously. What had she to bring to a king? Little wealth, no property, no kingdom. No, James had to marry elsewhere, and the pain of being his mistress, loving him, then losing him one day to someone else would be too brutal for her to bear.

"Tomorrow I leave," he said quietly, as if he hoped that she would protest and ask him to stay.

"I know," she whispered.

"I want you to come with me." He waited long seconds, realizing his breath was caught in his chest and he longed for an answer that would end this new and brilliant need.

Maggie didn't move; in fact she could not look at him. "I cannot, my lord."

He couldn't believe he had heard her, so he continued, "It is my desire to have part of my court with me."

Maggie stood up. "I am desolate that I shall have to decline." She stood straight as if she braced herself for a blow.

James looked at her for a moment before he seemed to realize he had been refused. "Lord God, Madam, do I hear right?"

Maggie spoke stiffly, "May I have my cap back, Your Grace?"

"No!" His dark eyes swept her. "You came here to me. . . ."

"You commanded me!" Her eyes blazed at his injustice.

"Aye, mistress. I am accustomed to it, nor do I like interruptions. You came here acting as if I were a pirate and telling me you would have none of me." He was frowning. "I would give you all the time you need."

"I want no week, no month, no year. May I have your leave to retire, Your Grace?"

He took a step toward her.

"I am tired, my lord," she said quietly. If she had retreated he might have stalked her with more force. But she stood her ground. Only the look in her eyes stopped him.

"Leave then!"

She drew a long breath. "May I have my cap?"

"No!" He crushed it in his hand.

"Good night, my lord."

She was gone and James, who had never been thwarted, who never had to ask or beg for anything, stared at the empty door.

Then he sat down. After a while a slight smile touched his lips. James had been a master campaigner. Now he sat to plan a campaign that had somehow become ultimately important to him.

James sighed and stepped back from the window to return to his bed. He smiled again as he thought of the battle he had waged to win Maggie Drummond . . . and the day he had won. Crieff had been sent away and eventually promised a wealthy bride. He knew the futility of fighting his king.

Maggie and James had waged a war and as the battle had gone on he had fallen more and more deeply in love with her.

The last time he had come he had swept into her room unannounced. Her shocked maids had been ordered to leave. Then he had snatched her up in his arms and kissed her until all protests died and she returned the kiss.

Locked in his embrace, it was as though she had lost separate identity, had none except with him. Her arms slipped around his neck and held him close. She felt her body yield and mold itself against his. As he reached for the hooks to her gown she closed her eyes and heard his soft whisper: "I love you, lass . . . I love you."

And love her he did, he thought. Even though the world would be against a king making such a marriage, in his heart that was his strongest desire. Today she would come, his heart sang, and the lonely hours of dawn would be swept away.

James drifted again into sleep and wakened with the stirring of the castle. Soon he was surrounded and his privacy destroyed. He was caught up in the day's endeavors.

One of the first items of business was an interview with the Sieur de Montcressault representing the duchess of Burgundy.

The audience lasted an hour. It was a private audience. After it was over Donovan was sent for and he came quickly, filled with curiosity.

When Donovan came in James was alone and pacing the room. But Donovan was more surprised when James attacked a piece of business first that he had intended for some time.

James removed a sword from an honored place on the wall. It was the sword of Bruce. He ordered Donovan to kneel.

"You have been a loyal friend, standing with me in battle and to claim the peace." He touched Donovan's shoulders, "Rise, my lord."

Donovan was warmed with the new honor and James poured two goblets of wine.

"We'll drink a toast . . . to Scotland."

"To Scotland," Donovan echoed.

James then pointed to a letter that lay open on his desk. Donovan picked it up and read slowly and carefully. While he read his mind superimposed this letter and its information over the history of England, and more particularly of the English royal succession.

The letter came from the duchess of Burgundy, a Yorkist, and a woman who hated Henry Tudor. She felt Henry had her throne. Henry's throne was Lancastrian through the blood of John of Gaunt.

"The strength of Henry's claim to the English throne lies in the fact that everyone else was either beheaded, murdered, or slain in battle."

"But now his claim is unopposed," Donovan offered, still puzzled.

"Maybe."

"Maybe?"

"When Edward, the fourth Edward, a Yorkist, climbed back on the throne he had two sons, nine and twelve or thereabouts. Edward also had a brother, Richard. A rather unscrupulous character. It is said that Richard had his nephews murdered and he succeeded to the throne. Richard the Third."

"And Henry killed Richard at Bosworth. A very suggestive tale," Donovan said thoughtfully.

"Henry holds his throne through the marriage to the Princess Elizabeth. It's all quite sinister." James grinned and Donovan knew he was inordinately pleased about something. "Especially since Richard's murder of his nephews has never been proven. No trace of either prince has been found."

"I understand the history lesson, Your Grace, but hardly the point you are making."

"Donovan, think of this. If you were Henry, would it disturb you that a man who calls himself the prince of York was still alive and that the duchess of Burgundy has found him?"

"Aye, my lord. It would upset me a great deal." Donovan smiled now too. "And it wouldn't really matter if it was true or not."

"It would prick like a huge thorn. It may not bleed Henry to death, but it would sting."

"Could it be true?"

James shrugged. "Since the bodies of the two princes were never found. After all, they were the true heirs to the English throne. How can we . . . or anyone else, say for sure one of them has not been found?"

"And Your Grace is going to support this man's claim."

"Aye."

"Prince or no?"

"Aye, my lord," James chuckled. "It will sting our Henry, won't it?"

"You want to fight him?"

"Aye," James repeated.

"There is a better way, less bloodshed, less chances."

"No." James's dark eyes were narrowed.

"Give me leave to say it."

"Say what you want. I'll have none of it."

"Tomorrow the council will recommend your marriage. There are two princesses of England. A child by you and one of these princesses could have everything."

"Put it out of your head, Donovan. I do not marry an English princess."

Donovan heard a note in James's voice he had never heard before. James had voiced something from the depths of him, a curse against those who would force him to a marriage to ease the political situation when the woman he loved was on her way to him at this very moment.

"Jesus God," James half whispered, "Donovan, can I not take a bit of life for my own? Can I not have a marriage of my own choosing?"

"Can you?" Donovan questioned softly. He could feel James's loneliness and desire.

"Would you not?"

"I put little stock in love, Your Grace. A convenient marriage is the better one. In such a marriage each knows where the other stands and there is no false sentiment to mar the pleasures one takes."

James looked at Donovan closely. He was one of the few who knew the source of Donovan's hardened heart. But James would not mention Jennie's name to his friend again.

"Mayhap that is not all I would settle for. Mayhap 'twould be better should we change places, for I seek what cannot be bought. Truth, warmth, and some affection from the woman who shares my bed."

"And it could be these things are nonexistent," Donovan countered.

James laughed. He would not press his friend any further, but Donovan knew he was not going to be pressed any further either. James was in love and Donovan knew well how blind that emotion could render a man.

Yet Donovan worried. There would be repercussions from James's position when the council tried to force a political marriage.

"Ah well, my friend. That is not our worry at the moment. But this Perkin Warbeck, this man who calls himself Richard, the prince of York, is. We will bring this prince of York to Scotland from where he can so easily put his foot on English soil."

"Aye, Your Grace." Donovan was defeated for now. But many things could happen between the knowledge of the duke of York's presence and taking up arms to defend him. As far as marriage . . . he was afraid for James and his position with Maggie Drummond.

James nodded. To be king at least gave him the power to temporarily silence objections.

They discussed a few more things of lesser importance, then Donovan left. He was halfway down the hall when it struck him that he was actually a lord. His success had reached great heights. Soon he would have a wife men would envy. Wealth and power . . . why then did he feel a nagging emptiness? What more was there for a man to ask for? He tried to shrug aside the feeling and succeeded in putting it in the back of his mind . . . at least for now.

Maggie Drummond looked hesitantly around the room in which she stood. Men were carrying in her boxes, and her two sisters, Eufemia and Sybilla, were telling them where to put each article.

Maggie still studied the room, paying little attention to any of them. It was a small room of uneven shape, about fifteen by thirteen feet. A plaster frieze ran around the corner; there was a small fireplace and an elaborately carved mantel. The bed took up most of the room.

Eufemia and Sybilla would have rooms not far from hers and both were already enjoying the fact that they were in the castle and in favor with the king.

Her brother-in-law, Lord Fleming, Eufemia's husband, was already enjoying the fact that James had already bestowed a land grant on Maggie's father and Fleming had already received the wine concessions for Edinburgh. Fleming was also nursing a secret that gave a great deal of pleasure. Within the entourage Maggie had arrived with was another woman. Fleming had personally seen she had the opportunity to be placed there. He kept her presence a secret from Jamie and Donovan. He wanted this woman's presence to be a complete shock to both men at the dinner that would be held in honor of Maggie's arrival. And she would be a shock that was aimed more at McAdam than at any other. It was sure to damage McAdam's plans.

Maggie liked the room because it seemed so separate from the hustle and bustle of the castle, so private, so completely hers and James's.

Somewhere in the vast palace was James Stuart. She knew there was no doubt he would come to her as soon as he was free. She felt the knot of warmth in the depths of her waiting only for James's touch to expand into the brilliance they shared.

When things were settled Maggie urged her sisters to see to their own rooms or to explore the castle and its fascinating people, anything to get them from her room. If James came she wanted to greet him alone.

When they were gone Maggie bathed and did her hair in a way she knew pleased James. The dress she wore was thin, white silk, with long, trailing sleeves and a square neck.

She paused and stood quietly. It was Jamie himself she waited for. Jamie . . . the king.

She went to her mirror and alone she stood before the large square of glass. Her white shoulders and the curve of her breasts gleamed in the candlelight. She touched her flesh lightly with the scent of roses James loved so well.

She watched her reflection, seeing a sadness in her eyes. If she loved Jamie so, and he loved her, what could be found wrong in that, she questioned herself. She could not answer her own question, for a feeling of fear rose up in her until she almost cried out.

Then she heard his footsteps in the hall. Suddenly he stood in the doorway. She turned and paused. Then he stepped inside and closed the door behind him.

He seemed larger, stronger, and more tanned since the last time she had seen him. He took her breath by the way his eyes seemed to scan her with heat, missing nothing.

"Maggie, Maggie," he breathed. She took a step or two, feeling her legs go weak. Then he was beside her, snatching her up in his arms and crushing her to him until she could hardly breathe.

"It has been too long since I've seen you, Maggie," he breathed as he kissed her fiercely and passionately, "too long."

She tried to drown her fear in the scent and feel and touch of him. She molded her body to the hard form she now knew so well. He had awakened her heart and her body and she gave with a matching passion. But why could she not completely destroy the dark fear of something she could not name. She held James closer, hoping he and the love she felt for him could destroy this terror.

The castle was brilliantly lit; from her room Kathryn could see the glow. She and Anne were both dressing and preparing for the small dinner where they would meet Maggie Drummond for the first time.

Kathryn did not know Maggie, but had heard many of the whispers. It seemed no matter how prepared everyone was to dislike her and call her opportunist and other, more pointed names, they had come away with a different emotion. Maggie won hearts with a shy honesty and an obvious love for James that swayed people.

Kathryn felt a strange rapport with this woman who had not asked for the king's love. She thought of how it must be for Maggie to know that no one wanted a marriage between her and James.

At least, Kathryn thought bitterly, even if Maggie would only remain James's mistress, he loved her. About that all of the rumors were the same. He loved her. That was more than Kathryn would ever have.

She was curious about Maggie and wondered if they could be friends. She felt she would need a friend once she and Anne were separated by their forced marriages. A friend near the king might be able to help should the situation grow too difficult for her to bear.

In the room next to hers, Donovan was also aware that the dinner was being held in Maggie's behalf. It would be small, since there was no way for James to make it more at the moment. Donovan still had great reservations about James and Maggie, but he could find no room in his heart to condemn either. He was only worried that it was going to create an incident that would cause James more trouble than he knew. He too felt the touch of apprehension that tore at Maggie's thoughts.

Again it justified his very logical reasoning that love created havoc in a man's life and it would be best to stay as far away from it as possible.

Would he have married Kathryn if it had not been for all the material benefits that came with her? He most likely would have taken her as mistress. He smiled at this. If it was a battle to wed her, he hated to think of the war he would have had to wage if he had decided to just take her. He thought impatiently of their wedding day. When the door that stood between he and Kathryn would be removed and the two rooms would belong to them both.

Donovan was downstairs first and waited for

Kathryn and Anne to appear. He sipped a goblet of wine and for a moment gave himself over to thoughts of Andrew.

The man had shown every sign of the obedient servant. But Donovan watched for the first mistake. When Andrew made it he was going to find Donovan quick to take the advantage.

The man grated on his nerves and as far as he was concerned Anne and Kathryn confided in Andrew much too much. He could taste it in the silence that met him when he came upon them together.

If the man thought to reach for Kathryn, Donovan would have to teach him that with James's power behind him his arm stretched far. He would make sure Andrew was taught more than one hard lesson.

He rose when he heard footsteps on the stairs, and walked to the doorway. Kathryn descended slowly. No matter what else he thought, there was no doubt in his mind that Kathryn was the most beautiful woman he had ever seen. Despite his need for control around her, just the sight of her — and the memories she awakened could render him somewhat breathless with desire.

She paused only a moment when she saw him, then approached slowly.

"You're very beautiful, Kathryn."

"Thank you . . . m'lord."

She said the words formally and pointedly, acknowledging his new title as if she refused to believe he had earned it. It was enough to prick his annoyance, but he refused to rise to her bait. She wanted a battle, she wanted to continually make clear to him that her resistance was still firm. He consoled himself again by thinking that the time was growing short during which he would allow her to nurse her antagonism. He would be the lord in his house and she would have that lesson to swallow. It should tame her arrogance a great deal.

Anne joined them at that moment. Both restrained the words they might have slung at each other had she not.

They rode slowly to the castle and Anne could feel the tension between Kathryn and Donovan. She tried to ease the situation with questions.

"You have met Maggie Drummond, Lord McAdam," she smiled at Donovan, "what is she like?"

Donovan's humor was touched. He looked at Kathryn as he spoke. "She is a lovely creature, sweet of nature and amiable. James finds her presence soothing as would most men with a woman who was not a shrew."

Kathryn was stung by the innuendo but she struggled to retain her control. " 'Tis different with Jamie. As a king he must wed for the good of his country. Because of that I would hope Maggie can give him some comfort. She can afford to be gentle and kind. She is his mistress, that is far from being a forced bride. She had a choice."

Donovan chuckled. "If given the choice to be my wife or my mistress I wonder which you would choose."

"Neither," Kathryn said coldly. "I do not doubt you have had many mistresses in the past and undoubtedly will have many more even after you have wed. After all," she said as sweetly as she could, "the vows were to acquire land and title, weren't they?"

Donovan laughed. "Maybe I'll let you choose my mistress for me. After all you will know first hand what pleases me most by then . . . won't you?"

If they had not reached the castle by then Anne was sure a battle would have followed.

Inside they were informed that the dinner was being held in a small room more conducive to intimacy. They were led there and Donovan extended his arm to Kathryn, who lay her hand on it reluctantly. Donovan was smiling and more than proud of Kathryn's beauty as they entered.

But the smile faded and Kathryn could feel his arm go rigid. When she looked at him she could see his face had paled and his jaw had grown firm with clenched teeth.

James's and Donovan's eyes met and again Kathryn sensed a strong emotion. There were many unspoken words between James and Donovan. Kathryn returned her astute gaze to the group surrounding the king.

She followed his gaze across the room and saw James standing with two women. One of them was obviously the fair-haired Maggie whom Kathryn had heard so much about. The other woman stood with her back to them.

When James saw Donovan he spoke a few words to Maggie, who turned to look at them. Kathryn's eyes were on the other woman, who slowly turned.

She was exquisitely beautiful: ivory skin, flame-colored hair, green eyes, and a flawless figure.

Again Kathryn looked up at Donovan and realized the two knew each other and this meeting was having a traumatic effect on Donovan, one he was doing his best to control.

Chapter 14

James watched Donovan's face as the three approached. He was filled with regret that he had not been able to warn Donovan of Jennie's presence, but he had only discovered it himself a short time before dinner. How she had got herself part of Maggie's entourage was a question he meant to find the answer to at the first possible moment.

"Your Grace," Donovan said as the trio approached the king. But his voice was slightly unsteady. He had been staring before, but now he studiously avoided Jennie's eyes.

"Donovan, I was just telling Maggie that you would be bringing your promised bride shortly."

Donovan was aware that he had made this point for Jennie's benefit, but she seemed little impressed with it. Her emerald gaze was on Donovan.

"Maggie, this is Lady Kathryn McLeod and her sister, Anne."

Both Kathryn and Anne, still a little unsure of how they were to welcome Maggie, tried to be as warm as possible, and Maggie responded in kind. James was pleased about this, for the king's mistress was in a very sensitive position.

"And this, Lady Kathryn, Lady Anne, is Lady Jennie Gray. She is one of Maggie's ladies."

Both Anne and Kathryn acknowledged Jennie as

politely as they could, but Kathryn's mind was filled with questions.

"We have not seen you in Edinburgh before, Lady Gray," Kathryn said.

"No, I'm afraid it has been some time since I have been here."

"And your husband, *Lady Gray?*" Donovan's voice was as sharp as a honed blade. "Is he well?"

"My husband is dead, *Lord* McAdam." Her velvet voice contrasted his. "I have been a widow for nearly a year. Maggie has been good enough to take pity on my solitude and offer me the excitement of the court."

When she had said her husband was dead Kathryn sensed something in Donovan that was puzzling. No one had said it, but she was more than certain Jennie Gray and Donovan had met before. Even James seemed a little uncomfortable with the situation.

It shouldn't make any difference to her, she chided herself. What if he had known her before? His past, present, and even his future meant little to her. She would not say anything about it because she didn't want to give him the ammunition to laugh at her or accuse her of jealousy . . . although she would have to admit Jennie Gray overshadowed other women when it came to her beauty.

Others joined them at this point and soon the group was disassembled and caught up in conversations with others. This was how Kathryn found herself standing next to Lord Fleming.

He had not missed anything that had occurred in the room. He knew that Kathryn had no idea who Jennie Gray really was or what position she had held in Donovan's life. He fully intended to enlighten her. After some light conversation he found the opportunity.

"What think you of Maggie Drummond?"

"She is quite beautiful," Kathryn smiled. "It seems

James is very happy."

"Yes, he seems to be. She surrounds herself with others who are beautiful."

"You find that hard to believe?"

"To keep the king's eyes on you I would think a woman would surround herself with ladies not quite as pretty. For example the Lady Jennie. She is exquisite. Do you think James's eye will roam?"

"Do you?" she countered.

"Ah, I doubt it in this case. He has too much regard for Donovan McAdam."

"What has his regard for Donovan have to do with it?"

Fleming winked. "He would not want to tread on his toes."

"You do not make yourself clear, Lord Fleming. Donovan has only just met her," Kathryn said with calculated innocence.

"What makes you think that?" Fleming laughed.

"Is't not true?"

"You have been sheltered, Lady Kathryn. The . . . affair between Jennie and Donovan was . . . to say the least the talk of the year some time ago. He was completely in love with her. Rumor even had it that they would wed. Then she wed Lord Gray. He was, it was told, quite devastated. Now she has returned . . . a widow and a very wealthy and beautiful one. Who could not look at her with deep appreciation?" He swept his eyes past her and chuckled. She turned to follow his gaze, and saw Donovan and Jennie walking to the door together. "In fact," he continued, "it looks as if the two are planning on renewing their acquaintance."

Something within her seemed to tear, and deny it as she would, there was a feeling of shock followed by an anger that seemed to consume her.

Fleming was quite satisfied with the look he saw in Kathryn's eyes before she controlled it. He hated

McAdam and would stir the pot of jealousy at every opportunity.

Conversation was broken at the announcement of dinner and Kathryn's fury rose to a boiling point when neither Jennie nor Donovan appeared. The dinner seemed to go on for hours with gaiety and effervescent conversation . . . and still Jennie and Donovan did not reappear. Kathryn smiled until she felt her face would crack. She would give no one the satisfaction of knowing she was upset. She tried to keep her thoughts away from the pictures that tried to fill her mind. Donovan and Jennie . . . did he still love her? If so why would he demand their marriage? Did he think she would be played for a fool, to be wed and find her husband sleeping with another woman? Dear God, did he think to flaunt a mistress before her? He would have to answer these questions before she would relent an inch.

It was during the entertainment that Donovan and Jennie returned. He wore a stiff and cold look, but it was Jennie who held Kathryn's attention. She looked like a contented cat that had just lapped up the last of the cream.

When Donovan had first seen Jennie, old memories flooded his mind. It took every ounce of control he had not to react. He had seen Kathryn look at him with a puzzled frown. But there was nothing he could say to her that she would understand or accept.

His second thought was how and why Jennie was here. The first shock had left him shaken but now the question filled his mind.

She had not changed, she was still as perfect in her beauty as she had always been, and despite his efforts it was difficult to forget the passion they had shared. But with that he remembered the nights of loneliness, the bitterness, the anger. He was tied in an emotional

211

knot and meant to do something about it.

It did not occur to Donovan then not to go through with his marriage to Kathryn. He had been hurt and he had healed. He was not going to let anything alter his plans now. Yet he was not sure just how to handle the situation while Kathryn's eyes were piercing him.

Then, among the bustle when dinner was announced, Donovan was given an answer. Jennie bent close to him.

"I must talk to you alone, please, Donovan, it's important." Her voice was softly pleading, but it was not this that drew him. He was now immune to her expert wiles . . . he thought. He nodded, took her arm, and they left the room. Now they stood in a small anteroom, facing each other for the first time in years.

"You look well, Donovan," her voice was huskily sensual. It could have, combined with her beauty and the intoxicating perfume, roused a stone, but Donovan had been stung before.

"And you are as beautiful as ever, Lady Gray."

"Must you be so heartless and cold, Donovan?" Her eyes misted.

"What did you expect?"

"At least that you would be kind and try to understand." One tear, like a miniature crystal, ran down her cheek. "Donovan, all was not as you think it was. I have never forgotten what we meant to each other."

"Don't you think it's a little late for that?"

"Donovan . . . please . . ."

"Damnit, it was you who left without a word and wed a man twice your age. Do you think I didn't know that it was because he was wealthy and I was only . . . God, Jennie, did your pretty clothes and your jewels mean that much to you? Obviously they did."

"It wasn't that. I loved you, Donovan."

"You had a poor way of showing it. All of this doesn't matter at all. We are different and there is nothing that can be done about the past. In fact there is nothing I want to do about it. As a widow you must have all the wealth you bargained for. I hope you enjoy it."

"Why do you want to punish me? Can't we talk as we did before. Can't you at least let me explain? Maybe you will not be so angry with me when you know. Maybe you will . . . let me back into your life."

"That door is closed, Jennie, closed a long time ago. I wed within a matter of days."

She made a low sound, almost a cry of pain, and turned from him. He heard the cry and it touched him, but he didn't see the narrowed eyes or the clenched teeth. He didn't see the anger yield to a look of cold determination. "Who . . . who will you wed?"

"Lady Kathryn McLeod."

This answer was not news to Jennie. She had come with the knowledge of Kathryn and her family and that they had been loyal to the late king and had fought James. But she hadn't known there was to be a wedding so soon.

"And you condemn me for marrying wealth," she said softly. "Is't not the same with you?"

"I have finally learned that an advantageous marriage is the best."

Jennie's heart leapt. At least he did not profess love back. She was sure she could rekindle the flame in Donovan. Had she not tasted the fierceness of his passion before?

"Then, if you do not love her why not claim her a mistress. You can possess all, I have heard that James is generous. Then . . . one day you could wed for love, one you would choose. A wife who is taken by force can never be a faithful one."

Donovan laughed as if these words had no effect on him at all. But they did. Kathryn herself had threatened with the same thing. "Do you doubt for a minute I will not see that my wife remains loyal to me?"

"And what of you, Donovan?" she questioned in a sultry whisper as she turned about. She came to him and put her arms about him. "Will you be loyal to her? Will you not want the passion a loving woman could give you instead of a cold and loveless person to share your bed?"

Old and familiar emotions reached with misty fingers to tangle his thoughts. His body responded against his will. It too remembered.

At that moment he hated her and yet was caught in a remembered desire that stormed his senses. He wanted to hurt her and yet he was astounded that he wanted to make love to her with a violence that would in some way punish her.

He tried to think of Kathryn, but logic told him she would never surrender to him. Maybe a mistress would teach Kathryn a lesson or two. But he knew the dangers of Jennie's charms. Perhaps just the threat of a mistress might be enough. It was a dangerous game but if it brought Kathryn to the realization that she could make their marriage acceptable it might work. Her pride and her name meant a great deal to her.

"As for me, Jennie, maybe you should remember a younger and more foolish man who begged you to marry him. I'm not that foolish young man any more. There will never be a woman that I will trust that way again. I've learned to take what I want and what pleases me." He gripped her shoulders and jerked her against him, making her gasp. Then he took her mouth in a punishing kiss that left her weak and shaken.

What happened then shook them both in separate

ways. Jennie realized the boy she had maneuvered so well was a man who could make her pulses race. The latent power she felt in him exploded in the depths of her, stirring a white hot passion.

But Donovan realized something totally different.

The kiss was different and the woman was different. No longer was the wild need stirred beyond control. Instead a softer, more pliant mouth, a more hesitant and gentle kiss, and a sweeter taste intruded. Kathryn walked in his senses. With unexplained pleasure he realized he had finally defeated the memories that had torn his life until now. He was free of Jennie and the thought was almost overwhelming.

Jennie, too sure of her power, broke the kiss and turned away from him. She walked a little distance away and with her back to him, she never saw the look in his eyes that could have told her her hold over him existed no more.

"Donovan, the choice of marriage to a man of wealth was forced on me by my father. You knew his ambitions. My husband could give him what he wanted so he was willing to give me."

He saw her through clearer vision than he'd possessed before and realized what a fool he had been. What she said now was a lie and he knew it, but it matched all the others she had told him before. He remembered her father as doting and loving, apt to give her anything her heart desired. No, it had been Jennie who wanted all a rich man could give her, and now it was Jennie who so accurately knew his position at the right hand of James. Jennie was greedy. She wanted it all.

"It was horrible, giving myself to him when I knew I didn't love him . . . that I loved you."

Donovan made his decision. Jennie might be very useful in the taming of his wife-to-be. And he now had no compunctions about using her when he knew it was exactly what she meant to do to him.

"Did you have any children?" he asked with seeming interest.

"No, I was careful to see to that."

"You didn't even give him that much?"

"Why should I? I was given to him, I never loved him."

"And now you choose to live at court."

"Maggie and I have been friends for some time now."

"By accident or on purpose?"

"Why must you twist everything I say?" She spun about, but the knowing smile he had worn was quickly changed to one of near sympathetic interest. She smiled. "Well, maybe it was not quite the accident it appears. Maggie is . . . sweet."

"And usable. Take warning, Jennie, don't do anything to harm Maggie. For the first time I believe James truly loves her."

"I have no interest in James, Maggie is welcome to him. It is you I have come here to see. Don't turn me away, Donovan."

Donovan admired her acting ability and was wondering why he had never seen it before. She would use him until something more attractive came along, something like being the mistress of the king.

As long as he knew her completely he could allow her to play her games. If the little charade kept Kathryn off stride all the better.

Her eyes were wide and full of pleading and one hand was outstretched to him. It was a most effective pose.

"I have no intention of turning you away," he grinned. "I think at court is exactly where you belong." Where I can keep my eye on what you're up to, he thought. "It is lively and full of fun and laughter. You will enjoy it."

Jennie came to him and reached to touch his face lightly. "And what of you, Donovan? Do you welcome me back?"

The invitation in her eyes was so clear he could not miss it. Before a few weeks ago he would have taken full advantage of it. But now . . . now a something in him had changed.

If one moment, one breathless heartbeat of a moment when he had reached to touch Kathryn had changed him in any way he refused to admit it. He would take Kathryn and Jennie the way they were. Kathryn, as a bride who would bring him a great deal and Jennie as a promise of what he could have if he chose. But he would not give an ounce of love to either of them, for underneath they were the same, each looking for a weapon to wield. He had no intention of handing them one.

"Of course, Jennie. I'm sure . . . eventually, we can be friends."

"Friends? Is that all?"

He shrugged, and smiled a smile that could be interpreted as she chose. Sure of her beauty and sure that she could regain the hold she had once had over him, Jennie felt a surge of pleasure. She melted against him. But he did not seem inclined to take advantage of the situation. He took hold of her shoulders and moved her gently but firmly back from him.

"It's best we remember where we are. James would not be amused should someone come in here and find us in a . . . compromising position."

"Not to mention your future bride," she said with cautious sarcasm.

"No," he chuckled, "with Kathryn's temper I don't think I'd want that to happen either. Besides she might take an obstinate position and I don't need to renew a war with my future bride."

"Renew?" she questioned.

Donovan could have bitten his tongue. He had, with a slip, given Jennie the insight into his situation with Kathryn. Jennie was ambitious and might take the notion that she could maneuver a more stable place for herself.

"You must remember the McLeods were loyal to the late king. We have effectively brought them all together under James. We don't want to jeopardize that. James would not look favorably on it."

Jennie outwardly accepted this, but within, plans began to swirl in her mind. She would play a cat-and-mouse game until she found allies, and knew where everyone in James's court stood. Born with the cat-like ability to always land on her feet, Jennie was prepared to wait. But if there was war between Donovan and his future bride she intended to add all the ammunition to it that she could.

"You have risen high, Donovan," — her eyes glowed with admiration — "and I'm sure you richly deserve all you have acquired. 'Tis said you and Patrick Hepburn are the two the king trusts most."

"I value his trust. Betrayal is not in my ability to understand," he said, subtly warning her he would never be betrayed again.

Jennie's eyes warmed as they looked up into his. "I was young and foolish, Donovan, and I never had it in my heart to betray you. If my father had not wed me to another we would be married now. It was a terrible mistake, and I must pay for it. But I want you to know, that I never stopped loving and wanting you." Her voice grew sultry as she moved against him. "If ever you need me . . . in any way . . . I want you to know that I will be here. What we had can never be forgotten."

Deliberately misinterpreting her words, Donovan smiled. "It's good to know I'll have a friend that I can count on. Don't you think we'd best get back? We don't want any more gossip than we can help, do we?"

Jennie smiled sweetly, her thoughts in a whirl. If a

scandal would bring Donovan to her she would happily arrange one. She intended to find out all she could about Kathryn McLeod. After all, she reasoned, the McLeods had been loyal to the old king . . . and treason was still punishable by death.

They left the small anteroom with thoughts that were worlds apart.

Jennie was forming schemes in her mind and sharpening her wits to listen carefully to what transpired around her.

Donovan was just as involved in the subtle idea that Jennie had maneuvered herself into the court with more motive than a chance at being reunited with him.

Donovan watched Kathryn across the crowded room and despite her smile and her laughter he could sense a rage that lingered behind her eyes. She resolutely refused to look at him, so to keep a minor explosion from occurring he kept his distance for a while.

Kathryn, he hoped, was jealous. Her pride had been stung when he had left with Jennie. It satisfied him. He'd made it very clear that he was in command of their situation.

Though both made an effort to keep space between them it was inevitable that they would fail.

Fleming, who sensed what was building between the two, and knowing as much about Donovan and Jennie as he did, insidiously fed the flames of distrust in Kathryn with subtle innuendos and risqué stories of what had been between Jennie and Donovan.

Kathryn didn't want to care. Donovan was only marrying her for what she could bring him. She had no choice in the matter. Oh, she had threatened that she would deceive him, ruin his name and do a multitude of other things. But deep within, Kathryn knew she could not do that. Not as much because of him but because of her own pride.

She would not have her own honor in the dust because of him. She would still do everything in her power to dissuade him from carrying out their wedding. But if she could not then she would be committed to bring to his home all she was.

She knew all this just as she knew there was a part of her she could never allow him to reach. He held no love and trust toward her so she would be forced to find some other basis on which they could exist together.

She watched Jennie cross the room and spitefully thought that it did not seem hard for her to bring Donovan McAdam to heel again. Obviously Jennie Gray was an exceptional bedmate, she thought viciously. Well, let him go to her. Let him share Jennie's bed, it would keep him from hers. Kathryn would be glad for that. At least she would not have to endure his touch. She raised her shields, ignoring a hurt voice inside her. She had wanted so much more and now her dreams had been snatched away by a man who felt nothing for her at all. Nothing except that she was a convenience . . . a necessity.

When the dinner was over, the ride home was a cold and silent affair for Anne, Kathryn, and Donovan. Anne could sense the hostility and knew the reason. But there was little she could do to ease it. Exhausted, she excused herself quickly and went to her room, leaving Donovan and Kathryn alone.

Kathryn took her cloak from her shoulders and draped it across a chair, aware that Donovan watched her closely. A servant appeared and Donovan curtly ordered her to bring a decanter of wine and then retire.

Obediently the servant brought the wine and gladly fled the room. She shook her head when she was out of sight.

"Them two are either going to kill one another or have the unhappiest marriage in Scotland." She smiled to herself. "But Lady Kathryn is being stubborn. If a man like Donovan McAdam wanted me I would be more than willing."

Donovan poured two glasses of wine and handed one to Kathryn, who shook her head. She started for the stairs. "You will wait, mistress." She spun about to face him and he could see she was spoiling for a fight. "I do not like to drink alone, and I have something to tell you."

"If it is to explain to me the relationship between you and Lady Gray don't bother. I already know all I care to know."

"Court gossip is not always reliable," he laughed as he leaned against the huge fireplace and took a sip of wine. "Who may I ask, was the source of your . . . ah . . . enlightenment?"

"That's of no consequence."

"No, I suppose it's not. It was not Lady Gray I planned to talk about."

"I suppose it would be uncomfortable to discuss your planned mistress with your planned wife."

Now he laughed aloud, "Does the green monster sit on your lovely shoulders, my lady? Your tongue has barbs. Maybe you are a wee bit jealous."

"Arrogant fool. Jealousy has naught to do with it. Why wed me when it is so very obvious your blood runs hot for that pasty-faced wench? Why do you not bed her and let me be?"

"Pasty-faced wench," his mirth was ill concealed. "With beauty such as yours you have no cause to malign her."

"Beauty is not the point. Tread carefully, Lord McAdam. My position and my name mean a great deal to me and I will not have them dragged in the mud because you choose to dally with a . . . a . . ." She breathed deeply, holding the word with effort.

"And yet," he said calmly, " 'tis you who claimed you would deceive me at the first opportunity. Were your words not that all of the children our marriage produced would be bastards? Do you think I fought long hard years to gain what I have to allow *you* to drag it in the mud?"

"And so I must become and remain the dutiful and obedient wife while my husband flaunts his mistress."

"Jennie is not my mistress . . . yet."

"If that is a threat, my lord, be careful."

He walked to a table and set the goblet of wine down. Then he came to her slowly. She stood immobile, her eyes holding his in defiance.

He stood close enough that the overpowering size and aura about him almost overwhelmed her. But if he meant to intimidate her he failed, and in a way this pleased him, too. She was not a woman whose courage and strength would vanish easily.

"Your family, your name, and your pride. They mean everything to you."

"You have stripped us of everything else. Our wealth and even our homes are yours. You leave us with little except those qualities you so casually name."

"I would bargain with you, Kathryn."

"Bargain. I tried to bargain with you once before and was humiliated for my efforts. Why should I trust you now?"

"Because there has to be peace in this house. Neither of us has to be content with what has to be, but there is too much at stake for me to allow this war to go on."

She turned her back to him and caught her lip between her teeth. Neither of us has to be content with what has to be, he said. He was telling her that this marriage was an inconvenience to him as well as to her. Why shouldn't it be, he had Jennie Gray waiting for him.

She felt as if she were caught in a velvet trap. James ruled, and power lay in the hands of the man who stood so close behind her.

Donovan knew his power, and he knew he had to bend Kathryn to it, yet he didn't like what he was feeling.

He took hold of her shoulders and felt her stiffen. It angered him, and it stirred desire in him. He drew her back against him and bent to kiss the soft curve of her shoulders.

"James would have us wed in the castle's chapel. It is small and beautiful, you will like it. You will go to the castle tomorrow and begin the preparations. Maggie will help you. Everything is to be the way you choose."

She tried to remain cold, but his touch was doing something to her that she could not explain, something that was unwelcome.

She couldn't surrender and just be used. She could see the span of days ahead. Days when she would belong to him, but he would be sharing the bed of another woman.

"It is very generous of you and your king to allow me to have our . . . celebration one of my choosing. I will do my best to bring it to your standards."

She felt his hands tighten on her shoulders; then he turned her to face him. Their eyes met.

She had declared war, now he intended to draw the lines of battle. He watched that awareness leap into her eyes.

His arms were around her now and she was caught against him, her body molded so intimately to his that she could not move.

His mouth lowered to catch hers and she uttered a muffled sound of protest. It was not a punishing or brutal kiss. In fact it was gentle and sensitive. He tasted her mouth again and again until she wanted to scream at him to stop. But he did not intend to stop.

He was caught in her, letting himself be caught in her, savoring every second.

His body seemed to leap to life as the warmth spread through him. There was no mistaking the desire that was building in him. They were too closely bound and he didn't try to hide it; instead one hand slid down the curve of her hips to pull her body even closer.

Kathryn was aflame and the fire was consuming every ounce of resistance she was battling to retain. Her lips parted beneath his assault. Every sense she had seemed to have come alive with a vital need. She had to be free! But he refused to let her go. The kiss deepened until she sagged against him, feeling her bones turn to water.

Only then did he release her; again they looked at each other, each breathless, and each aware of being vulnerable.

The last thing he wanted was to carry this beyond recall and if she were in his arms too much longer he knew he would do just that, even if it were against her will. Yet he wanted one more taste. He drew her close.

"Let me go," she whispered.

"No."

"You don't love me."

"But I want you."

"I will never love you."

"I have not asked for your love. That is too dangerous a thing to ask any woman for. But in a few days you will belong to me. I will not tolerate betrayal, Kathryn. Let me warn you now."

"And let me warn you that you are making a grave mistake."

"Then I shall just have to pay the price for it. But what I pay for . . . I get."

"Damn you."

"Good night, Kathryn." He kissed her lightly,

turned her about, and gave her a gentle push toward the stairs. Her fury lent wings to her feet and in a few seconds he heard her door slam.

Only then did his smile fade. He took up his wine and sat slowly down in a chair. His pulses still beat rapidly and the feel and taste of her lingered to strum his senses and forbid any idea of sleep.

But sleep was just as elusive for Kathryn. She paced her floor, her arms wrapped about herself to still the trembling of her body. For the first time in her life Kathryn was frightened of an emotion she could not control, and angry at the man who seemed able to awaken it with just a touch.

Chapter 15

Andrew had tested his imprisonment less than an hour after Donovan, Kathryn, and Anne had left for the castle. It took him only a few minutes to find that he was as securely kept as if he had been in one of the castle's dungeons. It was, to say the least, frustrating. It left him with nothing but time to think. And all he could think of was Anne and his helplessness.

He had to get his hands on the treaties between the traitorous lords and England. Documents that would free him to deal with Donovan McAdam and James. Documents that would give him Anne . . . he hoped. One way or another, if he had to create an incident that led to war, he was not going to let Anne be sacrificed to smooth James's path.

He left his door open just enough to be able to hear their return. But it was long hours before he did. He heard Anne come up the stairs and the sound of her door when it closed. Some time later he heard the loud slam of Kathryn's and smiled to himself. McAdam had his hands more than full.

He waited for the heavier footsteps and the closing of another door before he would attempt to move. But minutes passed and he heard nothing. He let the minutes stretch and still there was no sign that Donovan intended to climb the stairs.

Andrew smiled to himself. No doubt Donovan had already asked his well-placed guards if Andrew had tried to escape. It was good that Andrew was the expert he was and had spotted the guards before they had spotted him. Donovan was going to be disappointed. Of course he knew this would never put a stop to Donovan's suspicions. He had a feeling he and McAdam were going to cross paths violently again one day.

Andrew had wanted to say at least a word to Anne before she slept, to see how she was and maybe to find a word to reassure her. But with Donovan still awake and the time going by he realized Anne must be asleep by now. Reluctantly he gave up the wait and tried to sleep.

At breakfast the next morning Andrew was pleased in one moment and dismayed in the next. His pleasure came first when Donovan announced that Kathryn would be moving into the castle until at least a week after the wedding.

To Andrew it meant that, outside of the servants, he and Anne would be alone in the house. Maybe they would at least get a chance to talk. But that was not to be the case.

"Of course," Donovan said casually, his eyes on Andrew, "Lady Anne will accompany her sister, since she is to be part of the ceremony." He seemed so arrogantly satisfied that Andrew could have wiped the smile from his face with his fist.

"Am I to accompany the ladies to the castle, m'lord?"

"I don't see that that is necessary."

"It is my duty, sir. It is the order left me by Lord McLeod. I would hate to disappoint him."

"Are you saying that you don't think they would be safe in the castle?" Donovan raised an inquisitive brow.

"I did not say that, sir, only that I have my obligations and I take them quite seriously."

"I imagine you do," Donovan mused. "But I hardly think . . ."

"M'lord?" Anne interrupted.

"Yes, Lady Anne?"

"I would consider it a very special favor if you would allow Andrew to accompany me. Of course I shall help Kathryn in every way, but I will be quite alone since Kathryn will have many obligations. Andrew is a friend, one of the very few we have."

"A friend," Donovan repeated. He was sure Andrew was much more than that, and he had no intentions of putting Andrew in a place where he could thwart his plans, especially since he had to be away until at least two days before the wedding. Besides, he was nearly ready to put a permanent stop to Andrew. "I'm afraid, Lady Anne, I must deny you your trusted servant for a time. He will be riding with me."

Andrew was alert at once. There was no way to argue and he was more than curious to see what Donovan had planned.

"And where might you be going?" Anne was first to speak because of her worry for Andrew.

"We fight tomorrow night," Donovan said contemptuously, "and I believe you are more than adequate with a sword and would be part of James's defenses, since you claim to be the protector of this household. And since this household will be mine soon you will bear my livery."

"Aye, my lord," Andrew said as he rose.

"M'lord," Anne too rose and her voice was almost pleading. Andrew cast her a look that nearly begged for silence.

"I shall prepare at once, sir. Good day, Mistress Anne," he said. "I shall return well, rest assured." It

228

was all he could do both to comfort her and to assure her he would be all right.

Without another word Donovan left and Andrew followed. In minutes the room was silent. Then Anne whispered, "God speed you, Andrew."

Anne and Kathryn left for the castle only hours after Donovan and Andrew had gone. They were given very comfortable rooms and Maggie joined them as soon as she could, and she brought with her a warmth and enthusiasm that at least helped Anne and Kathryn to deal with their thoughts.

It might have surprised Maggie to know where Anne's thoughts were. Surprised her, but not alarmed her. She understood dreams much too well.

They set about their work preparing for the wedding, Kathryn with gritted teeth and failing hopes that some miracle would change Donovan's mind. And Anne with failing hopes as well. She was certain Donovan's anger and suspicions had reached a peak and that on those suspicions Andrew might soon find himself caught. She just wondered if Donovan would have him killed on some moor or bring him back to the castle to face imprisonment.

Andrew's eyes were almost shut. He could feel the dust ingrained on his face. Each jolt of his horse jerked him awake, then he settled back into his doze again.

Donovan's treatment of Andrew had been diabolically simple. He had served Donovan most of a week and Donovan had kept him in attendance every minute of the night and day.

The night surprise raid on the rebel forces of Lennox and Lyle had been successful.

The road they were on now was fairly good and

since Andrew's horse moved with a slow, rolling gait it was easy for an experienced man like Andrew to sleep in the saddle.

It was rolling, rich country, with carefully tilled fields. There were vast orchards, threaded with silver streams. The villages were enclosed; mansion houses abounded.

"It reminds me of England," Andrew said, half to himself.

Andrew had watched the king and Donovan closely. Both were formidable. Both were clever. Both were antagonists who would bring peace to Scotland and . . . maybe war to England. The thought brought him more awake than anything else. They were nearing the castle. If he ever saw England again he would be grateful.

He knew that the eyes on him missed nothing. They were waiting for the first overt sign that would give him away. They had tested him every minute of the day and night, often rousing him from sleep. He was sure that if he had not learned to sleep in the saddle he would have been at someone's throat by now.

But he wasn't. He answered their questions and obeyed their orders. He kept himself clean shaven and neat. No matter how tired he was, he never neglected his horse and he did his best not to rise to the bait Donovan dangled with every word.

But for the last few hours, as they grew closer and closer to the castle, Andrew felt he had somehow failed. Donovan had made a decision and the decision worried Andrew.

"There's the castle towers," a voice broke in on Andrew's thoughts. His companion smiled at him. The men had no idea why Donovan didn't like the English borderer. They liked him. He was assured, and unassuming, dependable, and witty.

The troop came to a halt and Andrew heard Captain Scott call his name.

"Aye, sir," he answered, with just enough pause to show Captain Scott that they were all playing his game. Scott had been riding beside Donovan and Andrew knew they had been talking about him.

"Dismount." Andrew dismounted and tossed the reins of his horse to his partner. He waited, trying to show none of his annoyance. "His lordship's horse wants its girth tightened."

Andrew moved to Donovan's side. "Which girth, m'lord?" he asked, looking up.

"The left," Donovan replied.

Andrew reached for the strap. It was loose. He tightened it while Donovan watched his hands. Then he checked the other side. Satisfied that it was tight he looked up. "Is that all you're wanting, my lord?" he asked softly, his blue eyes glittering.

Donovan half smiled in acceptance of the challenge. "For the moment."

"Aye, m'lord." Andrew patted the horse and walked away, taking his time, but not enough time to be obviously insolent. He swung into the saddle. Scott glared, and Andrew smiled.

Scott's hand tightened about his whip, and Andrew wondered how close he was to using it. Andrew smiled again. Scott was no match for him. After a while his smile changed to a grin and he rode on with the troop. He dozed again and when he awoke they had nearly reached the castle.

Andrew came instantly and fully awake. He stared ahead hungrily, sitting straight in the saddle. For some reason he seemed filled with immense energy.

The entrance toward which they were riding was to the north. They rode through the gate and entered the court.

Andrew watched Donovan closely now. If he had slipped, or Donovan had made a decision, now would be when he would take action . . . Then he

231

saw Anne.

He inhaled sharply then sighed deeply. Muffled in her cloak, she had a filmy scarf about her throat that fluttered in the wind. Her face, touched by the cold, glowed. She was less than fifteen feet away. Suddenly he was sure she had been waiting there for him. He was sure her eyes had searched each rider in the distance until she had found him so near. He knew then that she loved him too and the thought warmed him as no other could.

She had taken only one step toward him and he smiled as reassuringly as he could. She looked pale suddenly, as though she feared for him . . . feared and would be too proud to tell even her sister.

He knew how nerve-racking the days and nights must have been, but there was no way to get word to her that would not be dangerous for them both. He could not go and take her in his arms as he wanted to and again he deeply resented being a servant.

He had no intention of allowing his temper to rise. There was too much at stake. Tonight or tomorrow he would try and see her. He held his reins and walked past her. But her soft voice stopped him. "How are you, Andrew? I hope you have enjoyed his lordship's service. You look well."

"I am well, your ladyship." He could feel his heart beating fast. For a single breathless moment time halted. He searched her face. "You look well, too. I'm happy to see that."

The few words they could exchange were over, for Donovan was now standing close. She smiled as she spoke to Donovan. "My south tower rooms are more than comfortable and I'm sure Kathryn's rooms across the hall from me are more than satisfying to her. We thank you for your consideration."

Andrew knew the words were for him and he was grateful. He bowed slightly and continued on his duties, feeling Donovan's eyes burning into him. But he felt Anne's gentle gaze as well. His time was growing shorter by the minute, yet he would continue on with the game. He hoped to bring a chance of peace between England and Scotland. But more than that he wanted Anne and he would not go without her no matter what the danger.

Kathryn had battled valiantly to keep from going down to meet the returning men. They had fought rebels somewhere, and it was possible that Donovan was hurt . . . maybe even dead. That would free her, and yet the vision of it had destroyed her sleep for several nights. Now she refused to be there to submissively greet him as if she were impatient for his return knowing it meant their marriage within days.

She knew that invitations had gone far and wide. Huge as the castle was, it was filled to overflowing. The stables could hardly accommodate all the horses and the lesser nobility were actually sharing rooms.

There was no doubt that every move she made was watched. If she went to greet him it would be noted that Donovan McAdam had effectively brought her to understand that he was the master in their relationship. Since she did not go it was just as obvious the opposite was true. This, she knew, could do little less than annoy Donovan.

"Well let it annoy him," she thought wickedly. "Let him go on understanding that he cannot buy what should be freely given."

She walked to the window and stood so that it would be difficult to see her from below. Her eyes scanned the men quickly. Then the familiar broad-shouldered form was there and she felt something quicken inside. He stood in conversation with another man, his large hand holding the bridle of a magnificent black stallion and his helmet cradled in the crook of his other arm. There was an aura of confidence and power about him that set him away from the rest.

Her nerves, frayed already, were stretched taut by his apparent interest in everything about him. Any other man would have rushed to see his expected bride. But not him, she thought miserably. To him she was just a part of everything else he possessed and he knew she would be there when he wanted her.

She moved back from the window at the same moment Donovan looked up. The window was empty. Somehow this stung him. Surely she could have come part way, at least to acknowledge that his arrival was now an important part of her life.

Of course, he realized, this had been done on purpose and it would not serve him well to let her know it had affected him.

He strode into the hall and took his time to admire the changes Kathryn had wrought. He went to the chapel and again saw her touch in the placement of candles and rich clothes for the altar. Kathryn had done well and he found himself growing impatient to see her.

As he walked to Kathryn's rooms he renewed his self-control. He didn't want to admit to himself that a desire to be with her radiated through him like a pulsing heat. He convinced himself that he only went to see her to make sure she had not encountered any last-minute problems with the wedding arrangements.

He strode down the hall with a purposeful step and knocked on her door with a heavy fist. He was surprised when Kathryn herself opened the door for him.

He had forgotten how beautiful she really was. Nothing in the thoughts and memories he carried of her was as overpowering as her actual presence. She was a vision that momentarily took his breath.

The deep forest green she wore lent flame to her

hair and dancing gold flecks to her eyes. He fought his own desire, for he wanted to be welcomed with a kiss, he wanted to take her in his arms and hold her, kiss her until she met his will and his passion with a matching one.

"Are not your maids in attendance, my lady?" he questioned gruffly as he moved past her. The scent of her perfume was delicate and remained with him as he moved to a safer distance.

"There is much to do, my lord, and there is very little time left."

"Aye, we'll be wed soon. You look well, Kathryn."

"I am fine, my lord." Her voice seemed to him to be cold. Kathryn was thinking for the moment of her sister. "Might I inquire about Andrew's welfare? Is he well also?"

If she had struck him with a broadsword she could not have been more effective. For one moment a wild and uncontrolled jealousy raged through him like a fire. He was on the edge of arresting Andrew any-way, but this sealed his intent. Whatever Andrew was, Donovan knew a servant was not it. Andrew was not going to be a specter between him and his wife.

"Do not interest yourself with him any longer. He is in my service and you need not worry. I will see that he gets exactly what he deserves."

"Thank you, my lord."

He could see she intended to keep formality be-tween them, refusing to use his name as he had used hers. She was grateful to hear of Andrew's welfare, but cared little for his.

"Do not thank me. I have not returned him to your service. He will remain with me for a time longer."

"Why?" Kathryn asked. Andrew had always made Anne more secure and it was Anne that Kathryn thought of. She would be very nearly alone once

235

Kathryn was wed and would need Andrew's protection.

"Why does he interest you so much, Kathryn?" She heard suspicion in his voice. Another step, another word might bring Donovan's wrath down on Andrew's head. The thought that he was jealous pleased her. Let him worry. The only problem was she didn't want to hurt Andrew.

"It is just that Eric left him as an important part of our household. I would just like to know that he is well. It is our obligation."

"And your interest ends there?"

"Of course. Why should it go further?"

Their eyes met and held and a tempest seemed to swirl between them. Then he sighed. "I must be about my duties as well. The next time I see you will be on our wedding day. I meant to compliment you. The chapel and the great hall are well prepared."

"Thank you, my lord."

He wanted to tell her more, to break the icy wall between them. But the time was not right. He would wait as patiently as he could. Soon enough the battleground would be his. Without another word he spun on his heel and left.

Kathryn glared after him. No word of pleasure to be with her, no kindness. Nothing. "Barbarian," she muttered. But she forced her mind to other things to keep the tears in check. Never would she weep for such a man. A man with a stone where his heart should be.

Kathryn woke very early on the day of her wedding. She lay in her bed in the silence and watched the darkness through her windows begin to fade in the first gray streaks of dawn.

Kathryn's rooms were high in the tower. There was a morning room and in the next flight of several steps her servants slept. High above this, reached by a short flight of thickly carpeted stairs, was her bedroom.

The tower walls were over eight feet thick, but paneling kept out the drafts. A fireplace was installed in every room and every day sandalwood was brought and each fire was kept burning. The windows were seven feet high and tiny paned. Long drapes fell to the floor.

She rolled onto her stomach. In only a few hours she and Donovan would be wed. She wanted to hold the time away and at the same time she felt a strange excitement fill her.

In her mind she went over the provisions for the wedding. At least this could make her smile, for it cost Donovan close to a thousand pounds. She meant to show the king—and Donovan McAdam—that the McLeods knew how to be lavish and present an almost royal affair.

She frowned as she remembered the list. But she was sure she had forgotten nothing. Three hundred quarters of wheat for the finest bread. Three hundred tuns of ale from the castle brewery; one hundred tuns of wine, one hundred oxen, six wild bulls, one thousand sheep, three hundred porkers and calves, four hundred swans, two thousand geese, one thousand capons. In addition stags, fifteen hundred pasties of venison, fish and oysters; thirteen thousand dishes of jelly; cold baked tarts; hot and cold custards; sugared delicacies and wafers.

"He will choke on the expense," she giggled. "Let him pay dearly for his position."

The thought of Donovan being furious at the money it cost to wed her brightened her day. She thought of the chapel. The candles were of the purest wax and outside the fountains would flow wine. There would be entertainment for all the guests and the villagers. He would surely gaze with some astonishment at the bills he would soon receive from Edinburgh. Even her clothes had cost him nearly two thousand pounds.

She would have dwelt with more glee on her chance to torment Donovan, but a maid approached the bed to see if she was awake.

"I'm awake. What time is it?"

"It is nearly eleven, mistress. Your bath is ready."

Kathryn left her bed, walked to the tub of steaming, scented water, and sank into it with a sigh. But with the bustling maids around her she knew she could not take her leisure here. She stepped out of the tub and dried.

When she was dry, a satin petticoat and a low-cut blouse, both white, were put on. She sat down in front of her mirror to brush her hair dry. It shone like the satin undergarments she wore. Her hair was worn loose and free, as was the custom. Perfume was dabbed on her, then she stood up and her dress was slipped over her head.

It was white velvet and because of her rank she was entitled to wear the white ermine that trimmed it. The gown fitted tightly to below her waist, then fell in soft folds. The sleeves were long, partly covering her hands. The neckline was square and deep and she wore only a thin gold pendant with a pearl that hung between her breasts.

"I am ready," she said, and the realization held her momentarily still as she faced the fact that from now there would be no turning back.

It was like a dream. She walked slowly down the stairs with her maids lifting her long train behind her.

The chapel was ancient and beautiful and completely hushed. The afternoon sun filtered through the windows to mingle with the candlelight. Near the altar, Donovan waited.

He too had bathed and dressed carefully, caught in

an excitement that he could hardly believe. He, who had vowed to never take a wife, was waiting in a candlelit chapel . . . for a woman who did not want him. He had to smile at the unusual situation. But, it was expedient, he thought. It was opportune and right and convenient. Then he turned and saw Kathryn coming toward him. In the space of a second something seemed to happen to his breath. It was caught like a lump pressing on his heart, forcing it to beat with a solid thud. She was so very beautiful that he could hardly accept what his eyes were seeing.

He took her hand in his, feeling the coolness of her touch. But as he looked in her eyes he realized she was not afraid of him. He was pleased about that. He wanted a bride, not a terrified woman.

Both of them were surprised at how little time it took to be married. The priest was blessing them, then she was slowly turned to face him when he took her lightly into his arms and kissed her. He set her back from him gently and Kathryn looked up at him. The spark of arrogance was gone and his gaze was intent and serious. Then he smiled, took her hand in his, and they turned to leave the chapel and begin the festivities.

The dream continued. It didn't seem possible. Yet the great hall was just as Kathryn had planned for it to be.

The center table was raised slightly on a dais, covered by a white linen cloth that hung to the floor. Kathryn and Donovan stood while the guests drank toasts to their health and happiness.

Kathryn had orchestrated procedures that pleasantly surprised James and Maggie, and made Donovan feel suddenly quite proud of his choice in a wife.

She had arranged a special table for James and Maggie and, even though the first goblets of wine were for Donovan and Kathryn, she had them filled and carried them to James and Maggie. They toasted her and the feeling of communal enjoyment filled the room.

When they finally sat down, Donovan drew his chair close to Kathryn. They sat shoulder to shoulder and she was as acutely aware of him as he was of her. He looked down at the table where her smooth white hand lay next to his dark one. He reached to lay his hand on hers and felt hers tremble for a minute before she turned to face him. Her eyes were enormous and for a second he thought he saw a spark of fear, then it was gone. She smiled and he returned it. She had done her job well and silently both wondered if she had done it for him. He had no doubts that Kathryn's pride had carried her through it all. Still he distinctly felt there was a lot more in store for him. Her smile assured him he had best be careful. Kathryn had not surrendered; she had just defined the battle by not fighting where it was useless.

Kathryn looked away from him to scan her surroundings. She had fought him and lost. Today she became another of his possessions like his servants. Today . . . tonight . . . her body suddenly felt cold and lifeless. She closed her eyes for a minute and swallowed heavily. Then she opened her eyes. He was leaning back in his chair and she became aware that he had been watching her, somehow knowing what she was thinking . . . she flushed.

But she looked at him steadily. His wide shoulders were correctly covered in velvet that lay smooth over his heavy chest and arms. His face was tanned, the mouth mobile and sensuous. The whole face was stamped with a ruthless kind of strength, yet the smile, when he used it, could be forthright and full of humor, and the gray eyes were honest. Those eyes watched her now.

She tore her gaze from him and concentrated on

the entertainment. Between well-wishers and entertainment the hours seemed to her to rush by.

The dancing began and the celebration grew more boisterous. Wine flowed like water but it was some time before Kathryn reached for hers, only to find his hand on hers preventing her from lifting it. She looked at him.

"Not tonight, my lady," he said softly. He raised a hand and gently pushed a strand of hair from her cheek, and his strong fingers lay lightly against her throat. He could feel her pulses begin to race. "Or do you run and hide like a little girl?"

He could feel her stiffen. There was no time left. There were no games to be played. There was no way out and she refused to run.

She could feel her hands begin to sweat and the whole room began to spin. "I shall never plead with you. I . . . I imagine it is time. . . ." She couldn't finish.

"Yes, it is time."

"Please . . . I . . ."

"An hour. That should be long enough."

"Aye, my lord," she said stiffly.

She stood up and he stood, too, and a sudden cry went up as everyone saw her. James raised his cup in a toast to the bride.

Donovan put his arm about her and she managed a brilliant smile, a courtesy to James. She gave one last look at Donovan, almost hoping to see him relent. But he had no intention of doing that. Then she was gone.

He watched her disappear through the huge arched doorway. He eased back into his chair, trying to keep his mind from the preparations she would be making. It almost made him laugh to realize his hands were shaking. He reached for the goblet of wine. It would never do to let her know she could have such an effect on him. He drank the entire goblet in one smooth motion.

Kathryn stood in her bedroom while Anne and the maids divested her of her long gown Then the thin black silk gown for her wedding night was slipped over her head and she tied the narrow ribbons at her waist and another across its deep V of the neck.

The maids carried away the wedding dress and petticoats and fresh logs were put on the fire, although Kathryn felt more than warm enough.

Anne stood alone with her for a minute. Then she kissed Kathryn's cheek. "Kathryn . . ."

"Shhh . . . Anne. It is done, and I will make the best of it."

"Maybe it will be more than you think. He . . ."

"He thinks of me as a possession," Kathryn finished. "Don't worry, Anne. I'm not afraid of him. Maybe this will at least help get the king to forget you a little."

"I doubt it. Kathryn, this wasn't because of me? I just couldn't bear that."

"No. It wasn't. It was his decision and you had naught to do with it. You must go, Anne."

"Are you afraid?"

"No."

Anne wasn't sure she believed her, but she had little choice. She kissed Kathryn's cheek and left. Kathryn was alone, alone with a fear she would admit to no one but herself. Then she heard the footsteps in the hall.

Chapter 16

Donovan watched Kathryn leave the hall. She was reluctant, there was no doubt. She was also the most beautiful creature he had ever seen and he wanted her. His impatience made him caution himself. Tonight was too important to rush.

Kathryn had battled their marriage too long and he had to prove to her that professions of undying love were not really necessary for a relationship. Passion lay dormant in her and he knew it; passion was what he wanted to awaken.

He was brought out of his thoughts by his boisterous friends. Their impatience was even more obvious than his. It began with ribald jokes and more wine, drunk by James and his guests. It ended an hour later with James, and a group of half-intoxicated friends, deciding to undress him and toss him into his wife's bedroom naked! Donovan had drunk very little. This was one night when sobriety was important.

By the time the men got him to the door all were laughing and unable to do more than fumble at his clothes.

The door burst open and Donovan was pushed into the room by a dozen pairs of hands. He was laughing, his doublet was gone, and his shirt was open to the waist. He was breathing hard with his exertions and his bare chest rose and fell as he tried to catch his breath.

James and several of his lords were all laughing until they saw Kathryn framed by the light of the fire.

That she took their breath away was obvious by the sudden silence. A faint tingle of annoyance touched Donovan. He had no intention of sharing his bride and he didn't like the way she was being ogled. Yet she did not move. He was the one who pushed the group from the doorway and swung the door shut. "Good night, Your Grace," he called through the door and he heard laughter in response.

Donovan turned to look at Kathryn and a room that had been full became suddenly empty. Then he slid the bolt home. At her look of surprise he smiled.

"I don't trust any of them." He took a step or two toward her, then stopped. He had seen her stiffen in preparation and the last thing he wanted this night was for it to be a situation of attack and defense. There was too much to be gained and much too much to lose. "Since I've been so abstinent tonight, mistress, you might pour some wine."

Kathryn's mouth was dry and she was grateful for a chance to have something to drink, and something to occupy her attention at least for the moment. She poured the wine with unsteady fingers and brought a goblet to him. Their fingers brushed briefly and the warmth of his hand sent a shiver down her spine. She hated being so aware of him. Concentrating on her wine she took several sips before he spoke again.

"The wedding preparations were beautifully done. Kathryn, I doubt if the king would enjoy better."

"Thank you, m'lord."

"Even though," his eyes glittered with humor, "it

cost a king's ransom to do it." He was pleased with the twitch of her mouth as she struggled not to smile. "Of course you knew that, but were you aware that I was kept informed of what you were spending? The money matters naught, Kathryn. If you intended it to, you failed. It was worth every pound you spent."

She was pleased, angry, and puzzled at the same moment. Donovan meant to give her nothing behind which to hide. She was his wife and he meant it to be more than a game.

"I'm glad you were pleased, my lord," she responded.

Donovan set his goblet down in a nearby table and came to her, standing only inches away. She held her goblet with both hands between them as if it could be some kind of a shield.

"You seldom smile at me, and you do your best not to call me by name. Is that so difficult?"

"No, my lord," she said stiffly.

He smiled, and she tried not to respond to its warmth. "Would it cost me another ten pounds to hear you say it?" he said, his voice growing husky and intimate enough to awaken her senses. "Say it, Kathryn."

"Donovan," she half whispered.

"Was that so hard?" He reached out and lightly touched her hair, feeling the silk of it slip through his fingers. As if to learn the lines and planes of her face he traced her cheekbone, then let his fingers drift down her cheek to the line of her jaw. Then he traced to her ear and skimmed down the slender throat to rest lightly on her bare shoulder.

If he had come to her as a conqueror or with force, if he had demanded what was rightfully his, she could have retained her shields. But he came in gentleness, with a sensitivity that stormed her defenses until she found it hard to breathe.

A strange and unwelcome warmth seemed to flood her body, leaving her weak and filled with the desire to lean into the strength of those hard arms. She fought the feeling in a kind of desperation. But his nearness and the clean masculine smell of him, coupled with the intent gaze that held hers, played havoc with her battle.

If he would only say one word of love, one word that would tell her this was more than just convenient passion, she would be able to fully respond. But he wouldn't, because it was no less and no more than that. She wanted to cry, maybe even to ask . . . No! No! That she would never do. Because he might respond with words that meant nothing and that would be worse.

Donovan sighed, for he could not read whatever it was she seemed to want. He stepped back from her and then she noticed the jeweled dagger he wore at his belt.

"Is that customary?"

"I forgot it. I've learned that danger lurks everywhere. I've had to sleep with a weapon close most of my life. Of course," he said quietly, "there is no need of it tonight." He reached to remove the dagger and its sheath and lay it aside.

Kathryn's eyes fastened on his and he could see the pulse throbbing at her throat. He reached for her hand and slowly drew her to him. Then he raised her hand to his lips and kissed the palm softly. She felt a piercing shock at the feel of his mouth. She could deny him no longer, yet the ache filled her.

His other arm came about her waist and drew her body close to his. There was no denying that his passion was growing. What shattered her was that she could feel a responding glow growing in the center of her and this she fought.

His mouth was only a breath from hers and he

246

kissed the corner of her mouth with a light, sensual touch that struck her like a lightning bolt. She had never faced anything like this. The shock left her breathless, but it was nothing compared to the effect he was creating as his mouth continued to caress hers.

Slowly, slowly he seemed to be drawing on something hidden in the depths of her. A soft, inarticulate sound came involuntarily and the kiss grew deeper and deeper. Her lips parted under the insistent demand and she shivered as he delved deeper to taste more fully.

She felt as if she were drifting, sinking into a warm pool of growing desire. Her arms were now about his waist and she could feel the entire length of him molded to her. Then he released her lips and her eyes fluttered open to look up into his.

His eyes were filled with a warmth that would no longer be denied. They moved down to the wisp of ribbon tied over the soft swell of her breasts. She could actually feel the warmth as if he were touching her flesh.

Then his fingers moved to the ribbon and he pulled gently until it came undone. Lean, brown fingers pushed the filmy silk from her shoulders. Her skin was like ivory touched with firelight, and her breasts were firm. He cupped one in his hand, feeling her tremble. The softness excited him and let his thumb circle the taut nipple until he could read in her eyes the smoldering emotions he knew lay below the surface.

He continued the gentle assault while his other hand reached for the last tie that stood between them. She did not try to stop him, but he knew she did not mean to help him . . . not yet. He tugged at the second tie and the wisp of silk fell in a soft puddle at her feet.

Donovan felt his own blood race heatedly through

him. His memory had not lied. She was so breath-taking that he could only stand for a moment absorbing her.

Then he reached out and took her hand and very slowly backed toward the bed, drawing her with him, enjoying the sensuous movement of her body as the light kissed the shadows and hollows.

He sat on the edge of the bed. Then he placed his hands on her waist and drew her to him. She closed her eyes as his mouth caressed her skin. She gasped as his lips tasted, sucking gently, and his tongue circled a nipple, sending streaks of heat through her limbs.

Awakening passions swirled through her and she was lost before the storm of it like a rudderless ship. And Donovan knew when she lost control, for he hovered on the edge of it himself, resisting the temptation to give in to his desire. He wanted this time to be perfect for them both. He did not question his reason for this. She was his wife and he could take her as he chose and there was little she could do to prevent it. But he was just proud enough not to want it that way.

He heard her breathing grow ragged and saw her half-closed eyes and passion-parted lips. Then he rose and lifted her in his arms to turn and lay her against the pillows.

His loosened clothes were easily discarded and in minutes he was molding her body to his again.

Kathryn's emotions soared to the heavens and swept to the darkest shadows. Her body cried for his at the same moment her faltering will told her it was passion and no more. Passion he could as easily find with any other woman . . . maybe even his lost love, Jennie. But he was claiming her mouth again and his hands were doing wondrous things in the exploration of her body and soon she was unable to think of anything but this.

248

Kathryn felt cool to his heated skin, and Donovan closed his eyes for a moment to savor the sweet softness of her as she rested confidently against him. He felt the texture of her skin under his gentle touch and marveled at the creamy glow. His lips touched the silken fragrant hair, and wandered in slow lingering kisses to her forehead, her closed eyes, her cheeks. He then found the soft, half-parted lips that awaited his.

He felt the blood begin to surge through him as his heart picked up the pounding beat of his desire. He drank in her rare beauty as if he were a man dying of thirst. His hands reached again to caress her with a feather-light touch. His fingers touched her lips then drifted down her slender throat to a soft shoulder, down to caress one taut breast, then the slim curve of her waist. It rested gently on her hip, then slowly he bent to taste her upturned mouth again.

Tenderly and with exquisite patience he teased her mouth with soft kisses, nibbling gently, touching her lips' sweetness with his tongue as if he were tasting the nectar of the gods. She moaned softly as the flame of need burst within her and sent shivers of ecstatic pleasure to every nerve in her body.

Slowly, his lips traced a flaming path over skin. He pressed his lips to the valley between her breasts, then moved slowly from one delicious peak to the other. His hands slid about her and held her tightly to him as he covered her smooth skin with the flame of his need.

She gasped with the sweet pain as gently he nibbled her sensitive skin and her hands twined in his thick hair to press him closer . . . even closer yet.

Patiently he lifted her senses until she existed in a world that held only Donovan and the flame of their lovemaking.

His hands caressed, followed by seeking lips that drove her to a frantic desire. He heard her call out in passion and felt the joy surge through him. It was only when the need drove him to the brink of insanity did he give himself the pleasure of his all-consuming desire.

He captured her mouth with his to silence the passionate sounds she was making unknowingly.

Then he filled her with the power of his demanding possession.

She was wild with unleashed passion and he released all hold on reality and surrendered completely to the fire that branded his soul forever.

They tumbled together into the depths of the blazing inferno and lost themselves in a completion that left them weak and trembling and clinging to each other as if to hold on to something solid amidst a blinding violent storm.

Both were silent as reality, like a tidal wave, washed over them.

For her it was bitter as she realized what he had said had been true. He could awaken her body's response. It had betrayed her completely and she could have wept with the combined emotions of sated passion and the realization that it was nothing more than that. How he must be gloating inside to know he could unleash her passion as he had just done. God, she wanted to hurt him as he was hurting her. Why was he so brutal that he could take as he had done with no giving at all?

She denied the fact that his touch had not been brutal. He had taken her with care, had lifted her senses until she had physically desired him and had returned the wild, delicious passion.

She could not look into those all-knowing gray eyes and see the satisfaction, the arrogance she knew would be there. She turned her head from him and closed her eyes, reaching desperately for the control she would need.

For Donovan it was completely unbelievable. He lay holding her, sensing her withdrawal, and feeling a kind of tearing, as if she were ripping away a part of him and carrying it with her to a place he could not follow.

This was what he had wanted. He had had his way and made her understand that she could be a victim to her own passion. He had never tasted such physical satisfaction as he had in that wild moment when he had poured himself within her and felt her body shake with her response.

Yet there was more, should be more, and he was filled with a momentary longing for this elusive thing. It was only the echo of the tumultuous thing they had just shared, he answered the longing with logic. He needed more of her, to take his fill of her. Then it would be satisfied once and for all. He had found the pleasure he knew he would find and that was enough.

He was aware of her closed eyes and the way her face was turned from him. He was also aware of a subtle chill and the drawing back of her entire body. The contest had met only the first skirmish. The war would yet prove to be a long fight.

He knew she had reached the same heights as he. He had heard her uncontrolled sounds and he had known from the trembling of her body as she arched against him the moment she had met the fiery pinnacle. Why was it so hard for her to face the obvious truth? They were well matched in passion and they could enjoy each other completely if she would give up her deceiving dreams and know what they had was better than false words and promises.

"Kathryn," he whispered her name softly against the curve of her throat. She refused to respond. With one large hand he gripped her chin and turned her head to face him. Still she refused to look at him. "Look at me," he demanded.

Her eyes opened wide in defiance and even though they glittered suspiciously she would never give him the satisfaction of seeing her surrender to tears.

"You still choose to lie to yourself," he said. "But I'm not going to let it stand. You felt what I felt and you can't deny it."

There was no denying that he knew the effect he had on her. She bit her lip as her face flooded with shame. God! That he should know how desire had leapt to life in her body. That she could still feel the taste of his mouth as it had possessed hers. She knew that he had known she had wanted him. The horrible truth was that some part of her still did. Some savage thing deep inside her clung to the memory of his touch and wanted more. It was an insatiable beast hungry to be fed more of the delicious fire. This savage thing had responded to him in a way she could not control.

"I could feel your heart pound as mine did. Do you think I could not feel your body tremble?"

"Yes," she cried in misery. "Yes, you did what you had threatened! Yes, my body did respond to you. I'm sure your experience with any wench who would lift her skirts has made you an expert. But I do not want you, Donovan McAdam! I will hate you till my dying breath. Take as you choose, as your right. But you will never really have me, only this shell you must use!"

Donovan gazed down on her as a new hunger blossomed. Here was a woman worth having. She had fought him every inch of the way using the only tool she had: her pride. Here was a woman that could give him all he had ever desired. She did not want him . . . not yet. But he meant to make her want him.

"You're a fool to cling to whispered words of love that mean nothing. This is what there is, Kathryn. This is the truth, the rest is dreams and little to make a life out of."

Before she could verbalize any kind of defense he was kissing her again. He gripped her hands that had forced themselves between them and pinioned them over her head.

She was ashamed of the burst of hot desire that flooded her body from the center of her to the tips of her extremities. His tongue teased and tormented, ravaging her mouth, drawing on her will, on and on until she felt dizzy and her will began to crumble before a force more powerful. A slow ache began to build and every inch of her was completely aware of the hard length of him pressed against her.

With his free hand he stroked her body, caressing her breasts, cupping one in his hand and circling the nipple with his thumb until they hardened into excited peaks. The soft sounds she heard could not have come from her . . . but they did.

He bent his head to her breasts and let his tongue swirl over them, sucking lightly first one hardened tip and then the other.

His hand moved down her body, caressing with only fingertips, yet the touch echoed through her body like the brilliance of lightning. Then long, searching fingers nestled between her thighs and began to stroke rhythmically until she could feel the heated moistness and the mounting flame of urgency his hand evoked.

He caressed the sweet satin pulse of her and felt the response inside her quiver and build.

She shivered before the onslaught of her spiraling senses. His mouth felt like a hot flame against her sensitive skin as he found her breasts once more, his tongue laving and lingering until sparks of anticipation tingled down her spine.

Then his mouth moved down her body until it was pressing nibbling kisses on her belly and hips. She had long ago forgotten that his hand no longer held her prisoner, because his restless discovering lips and fingers held her prisoner in a totally different way.

He held her hips now and she gasped as he moved closer to that pulsing fiery hollow. She wanted to stop him, but hands meant to push him away tangled of their own volition in his thick dark hair.

His mouth found the throbbing wetness and probed eagerly, tasting the clean musky essence of her, bringing her new and unexpected sensations. Like ripples in a pond the tremors began to spread through her; her blood seethed and the sensations grew and grew until she felt as if she would explode.

She could hear her own panting and ragged breathing, and also the inarticulate sounds she was making. Yet she seemed to have no control. Her body was on fire and all else was melting before the flame. He had roused every sense, every nerve to a feverish pitch. She ached to feel his hard body fill her, arching in instinct to meet him, knowing that the flame would reduce her to ashes if she did not find the completion she knew he could give. There would be no satisfaction until then and her body was a furnace of desire seeking the final rapture that would subdue the flames.

Then suddenly the brilliant torture was gone and she felt the cold emptiness as he retreated from her. Only then could she open her eyes. Languorously they rose to meet the heated quicksilver of his, and in their depths she saw his purpose. Her heart pounded against her ribs as she faced the knowledge that despite all her words she wanted him . . . and he knew it.

"Say it, Kathryn, say what we both know is true. Say it or so help me I'll leave you like this. I can find another for relief, but you can't. Say it!"

"Damn you!" she half sobbed through gritted teeth.

"Aye, damn me all you please, but you want me as well." He moved his body against her and she could feel the hardness of him, intimately brushing the throbbing center of her need. "Say it, Kathryn! Say it. Say you want as I want, that you feel as I feel. Tell me what you need."

"Donovan! Don't . . ."

"Yield," he groaned against her lips. "Say you want me!"

He had aroused her to a frenzied pitch of desire and he knew it. Instinctively her body moved in search of that final desire and she would never know the agony it was costing him to restrain himself. But he would not lose this one battle. Retreat meant the loss of the war and he would not do it.

"I yield," she whispered.

"Say it!"

"I want you!" she cried. "Aye, I want you! Damn you, I want you!"

She gasped as he filled her with such force that it left her breathless. Then he began to move within her, sliding in and out of the velvet softness. Slowly, slowly at first, then harder and deeper and the rhythmic plunges lifted her again until she moved to a matching rhythm, clinging to him as he towered above her, one powerful arm braced on each side of her so he could look down into her eyes and know that moment when she was totally his, abandoned.

The spasms struck her with cataclysmic force. A brilliant explosion seemed to burst within her like a million suns and she felt the trembling in his powerful body. A ghostly, invisible chain seemed to lock about them forever, binding them with or without their will.

He kissed her slowly, draining a sigh from her, and his lips roamed to her throat. His huge hands tangled in her hair and he buried his face in the scented strands. He turned so that his lean, dark body lay beside hers. Yet his arms kept her possessively close. They were as one in that silent moment and no words were needed to express it.

Both remained quiet in this interlude while their pounding hearts slowed to a normal pace.

Kathryn wanted to cry, but no tears would come. Her betrayed body felt no loss and no need to weep.

She had wanted him and she could clearly recall now the wild wanton fury and the breathless words. She would have begged him to take her if she had had to. Her cheeks grew hot with the realization.

Only then did he grip her chin in his hand and lift her face so their eyes met. In the candlelight he could easily read the tangled emotions she was feeling. Despite all the others he read, the one most welcome was the sated passion he saw there. Whatever her battle had been he knew she had found pleasure in his arms. He would go no further than that. It was enough.

She struggled to regain the control she knew she would need.

"And so you have won, my lord," her voice was tremulous. "You have proven you are my conqueror."

"Nay, Kathryn, not your conqueror—your husband. You have stopped denying the fact to me. One day soon you will have to stop denying the fact to yourself. You are my wife. Now, and for the rest of our lives."

"The rest of our lives," she repeated in a broken whisper. The thought of a lifetime of yielding to passion with no word of care or love was enough to shake her to the core. He would use her as his wife to beget the sons he wanted. Yet she wondered if he would do as a lot of lords had done. When she had quickened with his seed and carried his child would he leave her bed and go to another to ease his passion? Would the other be Jennie Gray, a woman he had loved before?

"Aye, the rest of our lives." He tightened his arms about her as if he was annoyed at her resistance to this. He fought the sudden need to say something else, something that might heal her misery. He also faced a battle from a darker side of his mind that warned him with a subtle, insidious voice that one word of weakness might give her a weapon she would use to slay him. "And it will be a long fruitful life. We'll have children and build a fine future."

For the first time she truly wanted to weep. The frustration was bitter. She tried to move out of his arms. "Please let me go, my lord . . . if you're finished with me."

This stung his pride and his obstinance. He raised on one elbow and glared at her.

"You are a little ungrateful. You could have been the wife of another who would have taken less care, been less gentle with you."

"Ungrateful! I should be grateful that you took what was not freely offered."

Now he grinned and the gray eyes sparkled. "Was it not?"

She looked away from his all-knowing eyes and his smile died when he saw the glisten of tears that escaped beneath her lashes. Something in the deep shadows of his heart began to ache for something he could not put a name to.

"It was," he concluded firmly. He lay back and drew her tight against him. "And you will stay here

257

in my arms because it pleases me, and because it will be part of our life from now on . . . and because you must face the fact that I'm not going to let you go on lying to yourself."

He enjoyed her nearness, as he gently breathed in the scent of her hair. He could still taste her and wondered if the taste and feel of her would linger as long as his desire for her had. He was startled to realize that he was not filled with her as he'd hoped to be, that he wanted her yet. But his confidence soothed him. In time she would realize their positions could be comfortable and unique. After a while he decided that time would convince her and he drifted into sleep.

But for Kathryn sleep was not so easy to find. She delved into her thoughts, plumbed their depths and sought the answers that lay hidden in the shadows.

For a moment she hated her own traitorous body, but after this she was flooded with the surety that more than that had responded to his touch. Some parts of her that she could no longer control had been wakened. She fought it valiantly, using every weapon she could raise, he was her enemy . . . but he was her husband. He was a conqueror . . . yet he did not take her as a victim but more as a . . . wife . . . a cherished wife. He refused the idea of love . . . yet she had to war with the emotions he roused in her.

She felt the strength of the hard, muscled arms that held her and heard the solid beat of his heart . . . and realized she had to face something that had been growing. She faced it reluctantly, remembering the day he had taken her prisoner and had told her coldly that she would wed him. She had sworn then that she would reach beneath his shields and find why they were so strongly in place, why lust could take the place of love in his heart. Yet now she was afraid, for if she unleashed love in him she might be devoured by it.

Kathryn stirred gently awake. One candle was still burning, but it was low and shed very little light. She felt cold and realized then that Donovan was not in the bed with her.

She turned her head and let her eyes scan the room. Then she saw him standing by the window, gazing out at the star-studded night. He seemed lost in thought so she made no sound.

Candlelight flickered across his bronzed body. He had not bothered to dress, thinking she would not be awake. She inhaled deeply, shocked at the effect he had on her.

He stood with one shoulder braced against the stone frame of the window. The light glazed his skin, heightening shadows and gleaming on the long, sinuous muscles. He looked so powerful even in repose. She wondered where his thoughts drifted.

Donovan had wakened from a dream he could not understand. It was a tangled thing with nothing being as it appeared to be. He had lain holding Kathryn for some time and even when she stirred he was reluctant to let her go. He had breathed in the scent of her until his body began to urge him to remember their lovemaking of a few hours past.

He had been gentle with her and was pleased that he'd had enough sense to be so, for it had rewarded him with a passion he had never tasted before.

How is it, he wondered, that she can set my body and soul spinning? Has she some power, some charm that has cast me under its spell?

The old anguish returned, reminding him of betrayal. No, he could not trust the sweet taste of her lips, nor could he let her know she had pierced his

259

shields by the very emotion he had demanded.

But she was his wife and he had made it clear where their future would be. He would not love her . . . but God, he still wanted her.

What really stirred him was the fact that he could have her when he chose. It excited him. She would learn that he was right, that it was best not to rely on the fragility of love. No, he thought in satisfaction, they would have the kind of life that would not demand such things.

He had placed everything in the right perspective and the sooner she understood that the better life would be for both of them. When his thoughts drifted to her again he found her hard to dismiss. She was like an ethereal mist that he could not capture with his hands or his passion.

As if some force he could not name had caught him he turned suddenly and he heard the soft involuntary sound she made as their eyes met.

He read awareness in her expression and a more powerful excitement seemed to fill him. She rose on one elbow, clinging to the sheet, using it as a defense. Her eyes were enormous, as if she could not believe the shattering emotion that seemed to fill the room.

For a long moment their eyes held. She wanted him! She refused this. He wanted her . . . and no refusal would make a difference.

Slowly he pushed himself away from the window and walked toward her like an arrogant god. He stopped by the bed and reached down to tangle his hand in her hair.

"No . . . ," she half whispered. The cry caught in her throat and he would never forget the look in her eyes as he bent to kiss her.

Chapter 17

Andrew was beside himself with anxiety. He'd heard the reverie in the castle and knew that the wedding had been a huge, boisterous success. But then the silence of the days and nights seemed to go on and on and there was no sign of Anne returning home.

Even though he could not leave the house without being followed he had managed to send and receive some very satisfactory messages. Papers were ready to be signed and delivered to him. All he need do was get to them.

He sighed and set his goblet of wine aside. Then he rose and paced the floor, something he had been doing night after night. There was no reason for Anne to remain at the castle. The wedding was over. His mind conjured up reasons, the worst of which was that she had met another . . . and maybe an arrangement was being made at this very moment. The thought tortured his nerves and was responsible for more than one sleepless night.

He stopped pacing and dropped back into the chair.

The candles and firelight made shadows dance across the walls. They also made the room seem even emptier than it was.

He sat in silence, contemplating spending the rest

of his life without Anne. Even the glitter of the English court would hold no interest for him. He wondered if Donovan McAdam were not holding Anne longer than necessary on purpose. If what he suspicioned were true he owed Donovan something for the misery he was feeling now.

"Anne." He said her name aloud, realizing he was sitting in the very same chair he'd sat in the first moment he had seen her.

He could remember it as if it were just the day before. Even now he could envision her standing before the fire, turning to look at him with her purple blue eyes . . . taking his heart between one breath and the next. It would take a neat piece of dancing to make all that he planned work out. If he were dealing with any ordinary men he would have laughed at the situation, but James and Donovan were not to be played with.

He already knew of Donovan's suspicions and he knew something else. For some reason beyond his knowledge Donovan had an especial hate for him and it was not because he was English. No, it was something much more volatile and he would have given anything to know what it was. For some reason he felt it made Donovan more dangerous than even James.

He allowed himself a moment to dream. Dreams that the plans moved as he wished, dreams that his success had brought Anne to him . . . and dreams that traveled beyond that.

Caught in his reverie, he took a few moments before he heard the knocking on the door. He opened it to find a young man who wore the king's livery.

"I seek Andrew Craighton."

"I am he."

"I have a message for you." He handed the folded piece of parchment to Andrew.

"From the king?" Andrew was surprised. There was no reason James would have to contact Andrew.

"No."

"Then from who, lad?"

"Lady Anne McLeod. 'Twas a favor for her. I . . . I would not want the king to . . ."

"Have no fear," Andrew replied quickly. He fairly snatched the parchment from the boy's grasp and had enough gratitude not only to toss the boy a coin, but to actually wish it had been a bigger one. He closed the door quickly and tore the seal open. He knew there was little that she could say that could be personal so he searched for the unwritten words and the hidden meanings that could be there.

Andrew:

I am aware that I have been remiss in my duties to my home. I do hope you are managing everything well and that all is safe and secure. Be advised that I shall be returning home within the week. I am most anxious to discuss the events that have transpired since I have been gone. The wedding went well and the king seems to be taken with the idea of weddings for he has questioned me often about my desires to be wed. I'm sure his mind is already turning toward such plans. But I have had enough of weddings for now and am most anxious to be home. We will go over the accounts when I arrive and discuss future plans.

Anne

The simple signature actually made him feel her

presence. In all of her problems at the castle she was still thinking of him. His heart grew warm, and then chilled at the idea that the king was seriously giving thought to Anne's wedding. She had had enough weddings . . . obviously she did not agree with the one whose arms she was being pushed into. She was anxious to get home. He had to laugh. She couldn't be half as anxious as he was to have her here.

He wondered what "within the week" might mean. Anytime within the next seven days. God! That was like a lifetime.

It proved to be three more days. Three more days of tedious, nerve-racking hours for Andrew.

Anne had stayed on at the castle for the sole purpose of watching Kathryn. She knew that Kathryn and Donovan had never been anything but enemies, and was frightened at what their being married would mean. They were like fire and water, hardly able to mix.

She also knew Donovan McAdam could be a hard and demanding man. Would he break Kathryn before he bent her to his will?

The morning after the wedding Anne waited for Kathryn's appearance at the morning meal. She had to look into her sister's eyes and know she was all right before she could go home.

But neither Kathryn nor Donovan appeared and Anne was told that Donovan had sent for breakfast in their room.

The enthusiasm of the court surrounded her then, and she found herself riding with the king, Maggie, and several others that afternoon. But she soon became aware over the next few days that she was being consistently thrown into the company of Lord Murray.

She had no way of knowing that the infatuated young lord had already approached the king, and that negotiations were in full swing.

She found herself thinking of Andrew often and dreaming about him at night. She was confused, and torn between love of her sister, loyalty to her country, and a longing for Andrew's gentle strength, even though he was a spy, and this made her waking hours a personal hell.

It was two days after the wedding that she had the first real opportunity to talk to Kathryn. Donovan had been summoned by the king and Kathryn had gone to Anne's apartments.

She was relieved to see that Kathryn seemed well, although she seemed quieter and much more controlled. But Anne was reminded of a calm body of water with an undercurrent that could be fatally forceful.

But Kathryn was filled with worry and questions. She too had heard the rumors about an impending marriage for Anne. They had chatted for some time, circling the problems they both faced. But it was Anne who broached the subjects first.

"How very different our lives have become. Since Eric has been exiled nothing has been the same."

"No," Kathryn agreed. "And I suppose it never will be again. We must make the best of what we have, you and I."

"Kathryn . . . are you so . . . unhappy?"

" 'Tis not unhappiness, Anne. I suppose it is just the longing for what might have been."

"He is not cruel? He has not hurt you?"

"No," Kathryn lied. Physically she had not been hurt. She had been treated with gentleness and

265

care. But mentally the stress was dragging at her nerves and her will. "He is . . . is not unkind."

She had walked to the window to look out as she spoke. Now she turned to face Anne again.

"Anne, it would be best if you returned home as quickly as you can. I have heard so many rumors concerning you. Maybe once you are away from the court the king's interest will wane."

"I am not frightened of James," Anne said calmly.

"I do not want you forced into a marriage not of your choosing!" Kathryn cried. "You should be frightened of James. He is a powerful man and his mercy does not run as deep as his father's did. He will have his will obeyed, no matter what stands in his way . . . or who."

The sisters looked at each other for a long moment and Anne knew that Kathryn understood what she was feeling. As if to confirm this, Kathryn spoke again softly. "Have you any word from Andrew at all?"

Before she could answer, the door opened and both women sank in deep curtsies to the king, who entered just ahead of Donovan.

Anne, as she rose, cast a quick look at Kathryn. Her eyes had locked on Donovan and her lips were slightly parted as if her breath had been caught in her throat and her cheeks grew flushed at the warmth in Donovan's steady gaze. She loves him! Anne knew in that one breathless moment. She loves him and does not know it. She felt torn with pity. Kathryn was strong willed. She had been forced to do something she had not chosen to do. This drew her stubborn resistance and Kathryn, Anne knew from past experience, could not see a forest if trees were in the way. Maybe, she thought, it is better that I leave. Only two can fight this battle and Kathryn and Donovan must find some ground, one which they could stand if either were ever to find peace.

James bade them rise and smiled warmly on both women. To him they were beautiful pawns and he was pleased that Kathryn had been an obedient subject. He now expected the same from Anne.

"I have been told by Maggie, Lady Anne, that you have planned to leave us. We will miss you at court."

"Thank you, Your Grace, and I must thank Maggie for her kindness as well. But I have duties to my household."

" 'Twill not be long that you will have to face those duties alone."

"Sire?" Anne's heart began to pound in fear.

"Well, I'm sure Donovan and Kathryn will be returning home soon. Then you will be free to embrace a new part of your life. In fact that is what I wish to speak to you about, if Donovan and Kathryn will forgive us."

"Of course," Donovan agreed quickly, aborting the rebellious and protective look he saw in Kathryn's eyes. Kathryn did not want to leave a pale-faced Anne, who was looking at the king as if she were stricken. Donovan took Kathryn's arm and nearly propelled her from the room. In the hall she turned on him.

"You know of the king's plans," she stated.

"The king does not ask my advice for his every move," Donovan protested. But the guilt he felt made his eyes shift from hers.

"But you know of his plans. Why do you deny it? Why can you not tell me the truth? He has already chosen a husband for Anne, hasn't he?"

"That is for him and Anne to discuss."

"Discuss," she snarled, "as you and I discussed our wedding?"

"The king will choose well for her."

"What if . . . what if she loves another?"

As you do, was the first thought that stung his mind. Andrew! The bubbling hate for him swirled through him, stirred by his jealousy. He would put an end to Andrew soon enough. "Have I not made it clear to you that love has little to do with what is politically good?"

She felt the jolt of pain that set her teeth on edge. She would not mourn his lack of ability to love anything but himself and his well-planned future. Yet her worry for Anne drew her to a halt. She could not agitate him and expect to do anything to help Anne.

"Donovan . . . please."

Donovan was instantly wary. It was impossible to tell her that for her sake he would like to intervene for Anne. But he was as powerless as she in this instance. James made political marriages for the benefit of his reign. He would do what needed to be done despite protests. He expected Donovan to understand this and to support him as he had supported him throughout the entire war. Donovan knew the futility of trying to intervene when James had made up his mind.

Yet the look in Kathryn's eyes was one of genuine fear. That she loved her sister there was no doubt, and that she would do everything in her power to help her was clear as well. He found it hard to fight the look in her eyes. He wanted to replace it with another. If nothing better, gratitude. But he was not even to have that.

"I would beg you if that would please you. Can you not do something. Anne is too delicate, too fragile . . ."

"She is neither delicate nor fragile. Her strength of mind and body would match yours. You just cannot see her in any light than the one you must have placed her in all of your lives. Marriage has not harmed you in any way."

"Physically no . . . but it is not Anne's body of which I speak. A harsh man, a brutal man, will break her spirit."

"Save your arguments, Kathryn, there is naught I can do. Plans have been made and the king has already made his decision."

Kathryn's face lost its defiance and Donovan was really shaken when tears glistened in her eyes as she turned away from him. That she was truly frightened for her sister was clear to him. For a moment he wished there was something he could do about it.

But his logical control took hold. She meant to use tears of sympathy to gain her own ends. Well, it would not work. James had to have things in order and Kathryn and Anne would have to make the best of it. It would all work out fine once Anne adjusted to it and Kathryn could see that her life and peace of mind were not in jeopardy. It would all work out. . . . He meant to say so to Kathryn, but she was already walking away from him toward their apartments. He followed her, unsure of what he would do about it, quite unprepared as what to say . . . yet somehow wanting to do something.

Kathryn floundered in desperation. She had to have someone who understood, someone who cared for Anne almost as much as she did. Then she thought of Andrew. If he and Anne cared for each other maybe he could help her escape to some safe place. She racked her brain to think of where.

In her sitting room she went immediately to her desk. At least she could contact Andrew and have him come to the castle. Once here, they could plan an escape for Anne. She dipped a quill into the ink and began to write. Andrew . . .

Donovan stood just inside the door, closing it softly after him. Words died on his lips when he saw she was hastily penning a letter to someone. He walked up behind her on silent feet. The name leapt off the page at him and was followed by a wild fury. That in need she would turn to another man enraged him. That the man was Andrew Craighton made it worse. A black jealousy made him reach out and crumple the paper in his hand. Kathryn looked up in shock and her eyes met his wrath-filled ones.

Anne gazed at James in utter silence. Somehow she knew it surprised her that she was calm. Her initial fright had given away to a strange kind of control. She knew the futility of loving someone like Andrew and she knew the danger of standing against James. He would have his will done and anything that Andrew tried to do would only endanger him.

She stood very erect, her hands clasped before her to halt their trembling.

"There is something you wish to speak to me about, sire?"

James became aware of a singular type of courage and for a moment his eyes couldn't meet hers. He clasped his hands behind his back and walked to a window.

"It has occurred to us, Mistress Anne, that since your sister has wed and your brother is in exile that

270

you are somewhat alone."

"Alone, sire? If Kathryn and Donovan make their home with me I shall hardly be alone."

"Mayhap I choose that Donovan and Kathryn stay at the castle longer."

"Then I shall manage until they do return home."

He spun about to face her. He was somewhat surprised at her cool and almost detached attitude.

"That does not please us at all, madam, not at all."

Anne sighed. For a woman there was no other course to take. She had no one to turn to and she had to obey her king. Her chin lifted and the violet eyes were clear and unafraid.

"I am sorry if I have displeased you, Your Grace. What is it that you would have me do?"

He wasn't too sure he liked this calm understanding attitude either; besides, he felt a little guilty and he didn't like that at all.

"You must wed, my lady," he said firmly.

"And who would you choose for me to wed, sire?"

"Lord Murray," he replied.

"And when?"

"I do not see why there should be much wasted time."

"Might I at least have enough time to prepare, sire?" She asked softly. "The pride of the McLeods means a great deal to me." Her voice was soft, yet cut like a blade. "Even though I am a woman and have no man to bear arms for me. I would not choose to come to any man with only the clothes on my back."

"Then you do not deny this."

"No, sire . . . I have no choice, have I? I will do as you command."

"Then you may leave the castle and remain in

271

your home until you have gathered what you will need. But do not prolong this, Lady Anne. I would not like to send for you. It would displease me and make life difficult for . . . everyone."

"One month, sire . . . one month," she breathed.

"Aye . . . one month," James nodded.

There was a moment of silence filled with unspoken words. Then James turned and left. For several minutes Anne stood immobile. Then she buried her face in her hands and wept.

Donovan crushed the parchment into a ball and threw it into the fireplace.

"And why would you be sending a message to your secretary, Kathryn? You have no need of him. Your worries do not include him any longer."

"I was only telling him to . . . to prepare some things at home to make sure your transition is . . . made easy."

"Consideration for me . . . how touching." He had the distinct urge to slap her, shake her . . . and make love to her until he had wiped all memories but those of him from her mind. "Well your concern is not necessary. When we return home I have my own plans for your . . . secretary. . . ."

"Plans?" She rose and walked to him. "What do you intend to do?"

He shrugged. He had said more than he intended to. The last thing he wanted to do was give Kathryn information on his plans and have her go to Andrew to warn him. No, he wanted Andrew in his grasp. He would strike soon. Once Anne McLeod was wed he would make sure that Andrew Craighton vanished from their lives . . . and fell into his net, where he could take the time to

272

question him until he got satisfactory answers.

"I told you, Kathryn, Andrew Craighton is no longer your worry."

"What *is* my worry!" she demanded. "You use people, Donovan McAdam, use them and discard them. My sister means nothing to you! You would see her wed to a man she does not know or love! You would see me — ." She stopped as both were aware of what she meant to say.

"Wed to a man you do not love," he finished. "As I told you, Kathryn, you're letting false emotions destroy your logic. Your sister will resign herself as you must." Donovan walked to the door. He put his hand on the handle, then turned again to look at her. "And your precious Andrew will definitely not be a problem any more . . . for any of us." He opened the door and left.

Kathryn sagged into a chair. She was powerless and for the first time in her life the truth of this struck her a deadly blow. She could do nothing to help Anne . . . and she had clearly heard the threat to Andrew in Donovan's voice.

Donovan was angry enough that he was crossing the courtyard of the castle before he realized where he was going. Andrew Craighton! She had been sending some kind of letter to Andrew Craighton! Why? What did this thorn in his side mean to her?

The thought that he meant anything at all burned in his mind until if Andrew had been standing before him he would have run him through.

His suspicions of Andrew had grown and grown, and along with them, was the increasing certainty that something existed between Kathryn and Andrew. He meant to prove Andrew Craighton was a spy and have him executed as one. His reasons he held at bay. He didn't want to really face them, for it meant he would have to admit to himself that his feelings for Kathryn were more than he'd planned.

Three days! Three sleepless nights and Anne still had not come. Andrew had risen early mostly because his frustrations and his dreams would not allow him sleep.

After he ate breakfast he made a decision. He was going to the castle on one pretext or another. He would think of a reason as he rode, and find out for himself if Anne was well. It was still hard for him to believe how much he missed her. Her presence was everywhere, every shadowed corner held her ghosts and every room her scent.

He walked to the stables and was saddling his horse when a young maid ran across the courtyard.

"Andrew! Andrew!"

"Aye, lass, what's wrong?" His hand automatically reached for his sword.

"Nothing. Lady Anne is home!"

Andrew's reaction shocked even him. His hands were shaking and he could feel his breath deepen and his chest grow tight. He snapped an order for the horse to be unsaddled and was running across the courtyard before the words were finished.

He entered through the back door and moved quickly down the hall to the large entrance hall. At the doorway he stopped: she stood there, more beautiful than he remembered. For a moment he stood in silence, absorbing her beauty and knowing it would be all he would ever have. He had to control himself and it took a tremendous effort. Finally he spoke but his voice was hoarse and filled with emotion.

"Anne . . . it . . . it's good to see you home."

Anne smiled and walked to him, placing her hand on his arm, "I have missed you, Andrew. I'm pleased to see you are well. You received my letter?"

He knew other ears were listening and other eyes were watching, but he wanted to touch her even if it was only for a second. He took her hand in his and felt it tremble. She was as aware of him as he was of her. Then she withdrew her hand.

"Yes."

"Good. Will you join me at the table for dinner tonight? Bring the household accounts; we have a great deal to discuss."

"Yes," he repeated. Something about Anne had changed and he didn't know what. "Anne . . ."

"I'm fine, Andrew . . . really. I must go to my room and change, then we can go over the household accounts."

She turned from him and he watched her climb the stairs. Something was drastically wrong and a fear churned inside of him. There was something dark preying on her, and he grew grimly determined to pry it from her. He realized she would keep her own secrets if it meant protecting him. But he wanted to protect her, and he wasn't going to let her gentle heart make her a sacrifice.

In her room Anne was still calm. She had made her decision and knew exactly what she intended to do.

She sat by her window a long time, thinking of Kathryn. In one swift moment of understanding she had realized Kathryn was in love with Donovan, despite her protestations. She felt that even though they battled, the time would come when both of

275

them would realize it, especially since no one stood between them . . . no one and nothing but their own stubbornness.

For her and Andrew it was different story. A world stood between them, a world she could not fight, for the battle would mean tragedy for Andrew.

She was certain that one word from her and Andrew would raise his sword in her defense and that she would not allow. He would be fighting against impossible odds.

No she would make it clear to Andrew that he was to do nothing about their situation, that it was futile to raise a sword against the king.

But she had to find a way to keep Andrew safe. She had sensed Donovan's animosity toward Andrew, knew of his suspicions. Andrew trod a very dangerous thin line, and she was terrified of the possible consequences.

Tonight she had to find out why Andrew did not complete his plans and go to safety.

. . . But she had a month. Did she dare share a small amount of time with him? Time to create a memory that she could have to hold in the bleak days of her future. It was unfair to Andrew and she knew it, but she had to have something to support her strength.

For a while she allowed her dreams to reign unrestrained. In those minutes she belonged to Andrew and they were happy. Then she sighed and stood, putting the dreams aside. The one moment they had touched was vibrantly alive in her heart. This was what she would cling to in the dark hours.

She sent for a bath in the early afternoon and enjoyed it leisurely. She washed her ebony hair and brushed it dry. Then she coiled it in a long rope and twined it about her head, holding it by three huge wooden pins.

She touched her throat and wrists with perfume and dressed carefully.

Andrew worried and fretted the rest of the day. He was miserable and just about everyone around him knew it even if they had no idea of the cause. He growled at the stable boy for a minor mistake and snapped at a young maid, leaving her in tears.

By the time dinner came around he had clenched his teeth so much his jaws ached. But he too made preparations. The excitement of just being with Anne was alive in him. He too allowed himself to dream of possibilities. He saw visions of he and Anne together for the rest of their lives. He thought of children . . . God, the ideas were enough to turn his bones to jelly, and he damn well meant to do everything in his power to bring them to fruition.

The table was set so carefully that Andrew was taken by surprise when he walked into the room. Obviously it was done with great care . . . and at Anne's direction. He could sense her delicate touch. But she was not there yet.

A young maid lit the candles, then left Andrew alone. He walked around to the table where a wine decanter sat with two goblets beside it. He poured himself a hefty amount and drank it down quickly. Then he poured another and carried it with him to the table, where he sat and sipped it slowly.

He heard the soft sound of her step on the stairs and rose slowly to face the door.

He sucked in his breath, but stood immobile as she paused in the doorway, then moved across the room toward him. She was so beautiful that he could do little but drink in her beauty until she stood beside him.

"You look so elegant, Andrew." Her laugh was soft. "I have known all the time that you were so much more than you had professed to be. For tonight let us be ourselves."

"For tonight," he repeated. "You speak as if it will be the last night . . . the only night."

"We have so much to talk about." Her eyes held his. "So much to share. I've waited for so long. Tonight at least, we will both be free of the doubts. Tonight is ours."

Chapter 18

Andrew was struck with terror at her words. Despite the fact that he wanted her more than he had ever wanted anything in his life, he knew she could not be his. He would not let her sacrifice herself for him.

If Anne came to her husband on their wedding night and was not a virgin, the husband was free to do three things: continue to live with her and make her life a living hell, kill her, or banish her forever. And no law could protect her. She was, from her wedding day, his property.

He could read in her eyes that Anne knew all this, yet she felt it worth the sacrifice. But he could not let her. He drew on every ounce of will and courage. He would need it not to reach for the passion and beauty he knew lay behind her eyes.

They sat at the table and enjoyed a long, leisurely meal. It was the first time he could engage her in conversation without the threat of others. He found her witty and intelligent and as they laughed together his will slipped backward a notch.

Anne watched him, knowing his thoughts as well as he did. Anne the fragile, Anne the gentle, became a woman who had faced the bitterness and chosen her path, became a woman who knew what she wanted and meant to have it even if it was not meant to last.

"Andrew, it is too dangerous for you to remain here. Donovan McAdam is too clever a man not to push his suspicions until he decides to put you in the castle dungeon. Once there you can imagine what lengths he could go to to get the answers he wants."

"It is impossible for me to leave yet," he protested. Although he knew he had a chance of escaping long enough to gather what evidence he needed, he was not about to try. Not until he knew Anne would be safe while he was gone, and that she would not be wed to another by the time he got back.

"Why impossible?"

"Because," he lied with the hope he could make her believe, "I do not have all the evidence within my grasp and I cannot move until then. My entire mission here would be useless."

Anne rose from her chair swiftly, as if she were trying to control a burst of anger. She stood with her back to him for several moments. Then she spoke softly.

"Andrew, you must go. Please, for me, go."

Andrew heard the restrained tears in her voice and the urgency beneath them. It was real fear that twisted within her.

He walked to her, standing behind her. What he wanted was to put his arms about her, to let her know he could be strong enough for two. But if he held her, just how strong could he be? He hesitated. "Anne, it's only a matter of time. Don't you see that I can't go now."

She turned to look up at him. Again he felt himself dissolving in the depths of her eyes. "And if Donovan McAdam has you arrested, before you get

280

the evidence you want, what will you do then? You'll be tortured, you'll tell him what he wants to know, or what he suspects, that you are an English spy. Andrew, he will kill you."

"No, the man is not a fool."

"I don't understand."

"He wants to know a great deal, and when I tell him my suspicions he will have enough sense and care enough for his king to keep me alive."

"I don't believe you. It's because of me that you choose to remain. Don't you see that we are helpless. There is nothing we can do to prevent my marriage. I will wed Lord Murray in a month."

Andrew's "no" was harshly spoken through gritted teeth before he could control it.

"I wanted . . . Andrew we must part, but I don't want it to be like this."

Now he gripped her shoulders and drew her to him. His eyes blazed with anger and passion.

"And what think you of me, Anne? That I will run like a frightened rabbit and leave you to face the consequences? Do you think I could go to safety while you face first the king, then Donovan McAdam, to be followed by that pretty-faced bastard who would call you wife? Never, by God! I would die in a dungeon before I let him lay one hand on you!"

Tears welled in her eyes and her soft mouth trembled. "Can't you see that that is what I could not bear? If you die my heart dies with you. If I am to bear my future at all I must know that you are safe and well." The tears rolled down her face and Andrew was lost. All his command could not stop him from having this one moment to hold her.

She felt small and fragile as he enclosed her in his arms. The salt of her tears was on his tongue as her pliant mouth parted beneath his. Then the world whirled beyond his control.

He suddenly felt vibrantly and totally alive, more alive than he'd ever been. His blood sang through his veins and his heart pounded fiercely.

Anne was crushed against a hard massive chest, but she didn't care. The hard arms that held her filled her with a welcome warmth and as his mouth plundered hers she lifted her arms and put them about him, one hand tangled in his hair to encourage the magic he was creating.

Her feet were nearly lifted from the floor and her body was molded to the length of his.

When the kiss ended both were silent, stilled by the power of what existed between them.

"Ah, Anne. There is naught that has been more difficult than this. It will tear my heart apart to leave you, and worse to know . . ."

"Please listen to me. You must understand that there is something for which we both must set aside our honor. Will you hear me, Andrew, will you try to believe?"

"What, Anne?"

"I . . . I know I must wed another, that our lives will never be together. Even if you carried out your plans it would be too late to help me."

"Not if I kill the bastard," Andrew growled.

"I would have no blood on your hands for me."

"There is no other way."

"And if you kill him? Do you think James will let us be together then? Lord Murray is not an evil man, Andrew. He must do as James commands as well as I."

"Don't proclaim his innocence to me! What man would wed a woman who did not want him?" His smile was bitter. "Outside of that blasted McAdam."

Anne moved from his arms and walked to the

282

low-burning fire. She held her hands to the warmth.

"I know that he forced Kathryn into this marriage, but I am not sure that Kathryn is feeling so regretful."

"What does that mean?"

Anne turned to look at him. "I think Kathryn is in love with him and refuses to see it . . . or is afraid to voice it."

"How do you know this?"

Anne's eyes grew warm and a half-smile played about her lips. "Should I not recognize an emotion that I have felt? Can I not equate what I see in her eyes when she looks at him with what I feel in my own heart when I look at you? Should I not know love, Andrew, when I'm filled with it?"

Andrew was stricken to his soul by her gentle profession. The torture of it carried him across the room in a few quick strides to gather her into his arms.

"I never thought I could love any woman the way I love you, Anne. And I feel so helpless, so beaten."

"There are some people who never taste or feel what we have, and I want to carry it with me to keep forever. I can face tomorrow if I have tonight to wear as a shield."

"Anne . . ." He hesitated.

"If I must go to another man, if I must wed him, then at least give me this. I don't want him to be the first. I want to be with you. Give me tonight, Andrew, so I can have something to cling to when the days are dark . . . when we're apart."

"God," he groaned, "Anne, what would I condemn you to?"

"Nothing worse than losing you. After that little else matters."

"But if I could escape, find a way to get free. I

might be able to get back before the month is out."

"What will that change? James will still have me wed."

"I shall make it part of the bargain. He will have no names if he can't offer you freedom."

"But . . . your mission."

"Is not worth your sacrifice."

"James would be furious as would your king."

"Aye. But no one has forced James to give up the Maggie he loves. Maybe he will find one grain of understanding."

"Do you believe . . . ?" For the first time there was hope in her eyes.

"I believe that I love you beyond all else, lass, and I'll move heaven and hell to keep you. Even a king can remember he's a man. It might take a little persuasion but we'll force James."

"If."

"If?"

"If you can find a way to escape. If you can accomplish your mission. If you can make your bargain in time. Oh, Andrew, the whole world seems to be set against us."

"Then we'll fight the world, Anne, or anything else that stands in our way. Do you think I could have you for a minute, than let that minute go forever. I can't."

"Then we will trust our love to be strong enough. Hold me," she whispered, "let's share this promise. Give me tonight to hold."

Her soft tremulous mouth was inches from his. Her tear-glazed eyes were filled with her need for him and her pliant body was pressed to him. Any resistance he could muster melted like spring snow. They had this night, and visions of any punishment he might face dissolved. His determination took its place. Andrew never took defeat well and now he made a silent promise. Anne would never belong to another if he had to sacrifice his life to prevent it one way or the other, even if it meant the death of Lord Murray. He would see to it.

He bent his head and touched her soft mouth with his. The kiss was very gentle and when he released her lips he continued to hold her close to him. He could feel her body relax against him and he held her quietly, his arm about her waist and the other hand stroking gently.

"I . . . I don't know what . . . what I'm supposed to do," she breathed.

"Shhh, there's nothing you're supposed to do. I want to kiss you, that's all. Kiss me, Anne."

Eyes closed, she raised her lips to his, and he kissed her deeply, letting the kiss linger for a long time, until he felt the undulating warmth within him penetrate her, and she began to kiss him back. Very gently, as the kiss deepened, she felt him take the pins from her hair and let the shiny ebony mass fall about her.

His mouth moved slowly and lingeringly from her mouth to her cheek and for a moment she could feel him bury his face in her hair.

She knew a fear of the unknown, but his mouth was covering hers again and the fear slipped away to be replaced by an emotion she understood even less.

She felt as if she had only the solidity of him in her world and clung to him when she felt herself lifted and carried in his strong arms. She let her head rest against his shoulders until she felt the softness of the bed beneath her.

He lay beside her, cradling her in his arms, and his hands moved over her breasts and down the length of her body, exploring the curves and hollows through her dress. Then his fingers began to unfasten the hooks and buttons. She trembled, but could no more move to resist him than he, at that moment, could have stopped himself.

She felt the coolness of the air on her body, then the welcome warmth of his hands. It amazed her, for she had noticed his hard callused hands and was surprised at the gentleness of their touch. He seemed to know exactly what to do to still her fears and lift her senses.

She felt his mouth brush against the flesh of her breasts, then seek out the nipple. Lips and tongue teased until she groaned. It was a muted incoherent sound and his heart increased its beat when he knew he was pleasing her. He kissed her hair and eyes and the pulse that beat at the hollow of her throat. Then she was swept up in a wild and thoughtless emotion as he suckled first one breast then the other until he felt her quiver and seek more of the overwhelming sensations.

Then his hands were between her thighs, stroking the soft inner flesh, and she uttered a soft inarticulate sound deep in her throat as his hand found her. She gasped, but he was speaking softly now, easing her fears again while he created a magic that seemed to blossom from the center of her.

He spoke softly and gently and after a while she seemed to be losing any fragile control on who she was or where she was. There was only him. Her body writhed and strained to seek more, aching for something she couldn't recognize until she found it.

Her arms were about him, straining to draw him closer while his hands continued to their will. Then she shuddered and floated back to reality. He kissed her tenderly, cradling her against him.

Then he rose and stood by the bed and began to disrobe. He'd wanted her to help but realized she was insecure yet and not prepared to participate, in fact did not know how. Even her inexperience brought him pleasure. He wanted to teach her, wanted her to be his alone forever.

But he was to receive his first shock when he dropped the last of his clothes aside. Anne rose on her knees and reached both hands to him. She wanted to touch him, explore him, know him as he knew her. He sucked in his breath at the touch of her hand but remained still.

Her fingers traced the breadth of his shoulders and chest, stopping to let a finger caress a scar. There were many on his hard body. She wanted to become as familiar with his body as he was with hers.

The muscles moved as her hands seemed to be bringing his body to singing life. As her hands drifted down, caressing the flat belly and lean hips, she felt him stiffen and utter a ragged gasp. The knowledge that she could excite him excited her.

Then he moved toward her, gently pushing her back against the pillows, and the heat of his long body was again pressed to the length of hers, and he was stroking her flesh. He moved down slowly as his tongue began tracing patterns on her flesh, making it tingle. He moved lower and lower and then he felt her body stiffen. It was hard not to hold her, but he knew he must have been going too fast for her. He soothed her with his hands and mouth until she relaxed again.

"I won't hurt you, Anne," he whispered. "Trust me, yield to me," he coaxed until she lost her rigidity. Again he laced delicate swirls across her belly and inner thighs, glorying in the complete trust she had given him. Then his mouth sought the moist heated pulsing core and tasted deeply, his tongue probing and caressing the delicate spot. He heard her gasp his name, felt her body tremble, but in the same moment sensed her total surrender.

But caution was always uppermost in his mind. Anne was so delicate that his immense size would be too much for her. Just hovering over her filled him with trepidation. He could crush her so easily.

But Anne wanted him, was lost in the need he had created. When he rose above her he hesitated, but Anne arched up in urgency, her arms drawing him to her.

His knees were between her thighs and his hands clasped with hers above her head. When he began to penetrate he bent forward to catch his mouth with hers, knowing he would hurt her and aching for that moment of pain he would cause. Her moan was muffled against his lips and for a long moment he remained still, embedded in her, his body a part of hers. Then when he felt her response ease he began to move slowly, steadily.

Then his heart bounded and relief flooded him as he felt her moving against him. She was matching his pace and rhythm and the urgency flooded them both as he took her with him.

Gradually Anne felt his movements increase to match their ragged breathing. She felt again the wondrous familiarity of the pulsing deep in her loins and she matched her movements to his. Their bodies moved in one blending surge as he lifted her to forgetfulness and back.

The pinnacle was reached by them both. Anne cried out his name. Ripple after ripple of pleasure coursed through her, leaving her weakly clinging to him, eyes closed, gasping for breath.

Andrew removed his weight from her almost at once and lay beside her, but he never left go. He cradled her against him, kissing her again and again while he murmured breathless endearments. His hands still gently stroked and soothed her. For a long time they lay wordless and still. But the tormenting shadow lingered in the backs of both their minds. They had found this wondrous thing, but had they found it only to have it snatched away?

Anne sighed deeply, and Andrew was completely aware of her thoughts, for he knew they must match his.

Then he rose on one elbow and looked down into Anne's eyes. They were aglow with a warmth that pierced him. He wanted to be able to offer her so much and all he could promise right now was that he would struggle with every ounce of energy he had to keep them from being separated.

She raised her hands and caught his face between them, drawing his head down to hers. The kiss was so shattering and sensitive and trusting that Andrew groaned as he gathered her to him.

"I love you, Andrew. That is a truth no one can take from me. And if I never love again I will have the perfect night with you to remember."

"Don't! Don't talk like that. We'll . . . I'll find a way, Anne. Don't lose your trust in me. I love you too much to ever bear the thought of you in another's arms. I'll find a way."

"I will never lose faith in you. But we do not know what God has planned for us. I have stolen these few hours from time. Maybe it will make it easier to face."

"Aye . . . have your trust in God. But I'll put some trust in my sword and my right arm as well.

If I cannot change James's plans then I will come for you. Will you run with me, Anne? Mayhap to the end of the world to keep out of James's and Henry's reach."

"I would go to the end of the world or any place you chose beloved. But the danger is so black and so close. Outrunning James and Henry's powerful arm might not be so easy."

"No, 'twill not be easy. And . . . it would be just us, Anne. You would have to forsake so much."

"Balanced against all else, Andrew, it is you I cannot forsake. Maybe"—her eyes glittered with new hope—"we could find and join my brother."

"Maybe. What of Kathryn?" he asked.

"Kathryn. Andrew . . . Kathryn reminds me somewhat of you."

"Me?"

"She is strong, and when I read her eyes . . . I truly believe she had fallen in love with Donovan. Maybe she needs to think of herself and her situation more than me."

Andrew knew how deep the love between the sisters ran, just as he knew how great a sacrifice running with him would be. A well of love surged up in him and he kissed her almost fiercely and crushed her to him until he heard her muffled gasp.

"One month, Anne, one month. I shall find a way to get out of here. Once I do it can only be a matter of days until I've gotten all I need. I'll present it to McAdam first and then the king. After that . . ."

"After that do you think he'll change his mind?"

"Whether he does or not. We will go before he can do anything else. At least that way we might find some peace at home."

"And if not?"

"We'll find it someplace. But we'll be together."

"Then . . . you will be giving up so much for me as well."

"I would give up my life for you," he breathed as he kissed her again.

"Don't say that! I could not bear it!"

"Hush, Anne, sweet, it will not come to that."

But she was clinging to him and trembling as if a premonitory fear held her. His intent was reassurance, but passion grew like a fire in a dry forest.

The night was to be theirs and they spent it in complete sharing. They lay together and talked of the future that was still veiled in a mist. Still, as lovers do, they dwelt in their own magic world.

Anne was fascinated by Andrew and wanted to know all of him both mentally and physically. The soft touch of her knowledge-seeking hands drove him wild. He had loved many before, but never could he remember a fire that burned as brightly as this, or a woman who reached a depth of him untouched by any other.

It was in the wee hours of the morning that they finally slept the exhausted sleep of the sated.

The heavy fist that pounded on the door just before dawn jerked Andrew up from sleep. He was out of the bed and on his feet at once, searching for his sword before realizing that a very vulnerable Anne was sitting up in the bed, sleepy-eyed and surprised.

"Andrew . . ."

"Shhh." He waited only seconds before the pounding reverberated through the house again. Andrew cursed. There could be only one answer. Donovan McAdam had made a decision. There had only been a few hours before Andrew had planned to try his escape. Now he would have to face Donovan

McAdam and try to outsmart him long enough to find the time he needed. He could hardly face Anne's eyes.

"I'll go down and see who it is. In the meantime go to your room, strip the bed as though you had slept in it."

"Andrew!" Her alarm was building as the pounding came again.

"No questions now, lass, just hurry and do as I say. If that is who I think it is we do not have much time. Hurry, Anne."

She scooted from the bed, grabbing for her clothes, quite unaware of her nakedness and the long ebony hair that swirled about her slim white body. But Andrew was more than aware. His eyes feasted on her as if he were never to see her again. She was gone in a minute. Then Andrew inhaled and started for the stairs. As he reached the top step he heard the voices and recognized Donovan McAdam's at once.

"But Lady Anne is asleep, sir."

"No need to wake her. 'Tis Andrew Craighton we want, girl." Andrew was certain of his arrest.

He moved down a step or two and now he could see the men. There were five of them, including Scott, along with Donovan McAdam, who stood with his feet braced apart and his hands hooked in his belt. Andrew was not sure that the look on his face was one of some kind of angry frustration or of satisfaction. Andrew came down another step and drew the men's attention. But his eyes were on Donovan. There again was the look he could not understand. It was a hatred beyond what one enemy felt for another, especially one who was captured. Andrew would have given anything to know the motive that seemed to be eating at Donovan.

"English." Hatred was in the one word Donovan spoke, hatred and much more. "You are under arrest."

Andrew had read him right. The waiting was over. Minutes before he would have slipped through Donovan's fingers he was caught.

Andrew continued on down the stairs. Scott stood before him with a whip in one hand and a smug, gloating look on his face. Andrew let his pent-up frustration and anger free.

With one hand he seized the whip, and the other, clenched into a fist, caught Scott under his ribs in the pit of his stomach. As Scott fell Andrew jerked the whip from his fingers and brought the handle down across Scott's head, knocking him into a senseless heap on the floor. Then Andrew broke the whip over his knee and tossed it down beside an inert Scott. Then he turned to face Donovan with a half-smile on his lips.

The action had momentarily stunned everyone. It had taken Andrew only seconds to fell Scott.

"You think to escape, Andrew?" Donovan asked mildly.

"Hardly," Andrew chuckled mirthlessly.

Before Donovan could speak again the sound of running feet drew their attention to the stairs. Anne appeared, fully dressed, her hair hastily bound. She was breathless and her eyes were wide with fear.

"Andrew! Lord McAdam, what has happened?"

There was little Andrew could say without revealing the emotions that tore through him. He could not reveal a thing or Anne would suffer. He remained silent as Donovan spoke.

"I warned you once, Lady Anne, that the king was suspicious of your . . . servant. Now there are some very pertinent questions we would ask him.

293

Take him away," Donovan ordered. Andrew had only the time to cast Anne a warning glance. The last he saw as he was dragged out was Anne's fear-filled eyes and her pale face. Then the door closed between them.

"What . . . what are you going to do with him?"

"You need not worry, Lady Anne. James would question him."

"If you believe him a spy, James will as well. You mean for him to die," Anne stated breathlessly. The pain of this thought was nearly unbearable.

"He will not die if he gives us the information we want."

"And if he knows naught what you want?"

"He does."

"But if he doesn't?"

"Then it will be the worse for him. At least an English spy will be removed from court. That should not distress you overmuch. He is only a servant . . . isn't he?"

Anne took a deep breath. One word could mean Andrew's death.

"Of course he is a servant, but he is trusted by my brother and has come to mean a great deal to this household . . . and to myself and Kathryn."

Anne had no way of knowing that she had done Andrew more harm with her last two words than if she had condemned him an English spy. What Donovan heard was that Andrew in some way had become very dear to Kathryn . . . too dear.

His face grew cold and his jaw was clenched. He would remove Andrew from Kathryn's life if he had to kill him to do it.

"It should be best to put him from your mind, Lady Anne. There are more servants to be had. It would be best you concentrate on your own family's welfare."

He turned and left, closing the door behind him with a solid thud that to Anne sounded so harsh and final that it echoed in her mind like a death knell. Her promise of a future with Andrew was gone and she surrendered it before a much harsher reality. Andrew might die . . . she had to do something and there was only one person to whom she could turn who could have any influence on Donovan McAdam. Who else could she get to plead for Andrew's life with her . . . but Kathryn?

Kathryn was Donovan's wife. Surely he might listen to her if she asked for Andrew's life. It was the only ray of light Anne could see.

She bathed and dressed quickly and almost ran to the stable. Her horse was saddled quickly by a very shocked groom who had never seen Anne in this state of agitation before. Lady Anne spoke harshly to no one, yet she snapped at him when he did not seem quick enough.

Anne rode like the wind. The sun was well over the horizon when she clattered into the courtyard. She prayed that Kathryn was alone and that Donovan McAdam was occupied while she explained what had brought her.

Chapter 19

Andrew's cell was a damp, semidark, and dismal place but, he grimly thought, it was most likely he wouldn't be there long. He cursed at his timing. One more day and he would have been gone. Yet he wouldn't have traded the night he had spent with Anne . . . even for his freedom.

Anne. The thought of her both excited and frightened him. He was frightened of what she might do, for he knew for certain there was no limit to her courage.

He knew that any efforts on his behalf by Anne would only be dangerous for her. James would certainly not smile on someone he thought had harbored a spy. He was grateful for one point. Anne's sister, Kathryn, was Donovan's wife. Surely that could keep Anne from any severe penalties.

One month, one month and Anne would be wed. He had to find a way out of this predicament, but he had no idea how. Opportunist that he was, any minute chance was one he would grasp.

The cell was devoid of all but a pile of straw and Andrew was amazed to find it was reasonably clean. Clearly this was not the worst of the cells. He spread his cloak and lay down.

His head throbbed with tension and after a while his exhaustion caught up with him. He would need his wits about him if he were going to face Donovan again. He sighed, curled the cloak about him, and after a while he slept.

Kathryn sat before a crisply burning fire. In the days since she had been married her whole world seemed to have changed. She was confused by the man who called himself her husband.

She flushed when she thought of the nights they had spent together, for despite her continual resistance, and any protests she might make, he had an ability to touch the senses within her that had been touched by no other.

She was mending one of his shirts. She had more than enough servants to do that, but Donovan had been gone for hours and she was bored.

She snapped the thread when she was finished and lay her needle aside. She looked down at the shirt in her lap, then slowly lifted it and buried her face in it. It still carried his scent.

Tears sprang unbidden to her eyes as she thought of the futility of her situation. She hated the tears, and used his shirt to brush them from her cheeks.

She didn't want to face the insidious question that kept everything in her mind like a poisonous viper, but she could not force away the vision that filled her head.

Donovan and Jennie. It was very late—and very obvious that he did not plan to share their room this night—but whom was he sharing a bed with? The fabulously beautiful and very willing Jennie.

"Damn him! Damn him!" she whispered in rage

to herself. Try as she might she could not force the vision or the rage away and this only made the matter worse. She would not allow him . . .

She bit her lip, tossed the shirt aside, and rose to pace the floor. She meant to prove to Donovan McAdam that she would not let her pride be dragged in the mud. In the morning she would leave. She would visit her cousins in Stirling, and leave behind a note that would make it clear to him that she could stay out of his reach forever if she chose, moving from place to place. Let him play his little games, but she did not mean to be part of them.

A knock on her bedroom door made her spin about in surprise. She had dismissed her servants hours before. She walked to the door.

"Who is it?"

"Kathryn, it's Anne . . . please open the door. I must talk to you."

Surprise, and the sound of Anne's voice, made her rush to the door and swing it open. "Anne," was all she had time to say before the look on Anne's face made her hold out her arms, "What is it?"

"Kathryn, I need your help. You must help me!"

"Of course I'll help you. What is it? You're distraught. Come, sit down by the fire."

Kathryn could feel Anne shaking and she put an arm about her to lead her to a chair. Then she knelt beside her. "Now, calm down and tell me what's happened."

Anne inhaled deeply, reaching for control. Then she began to talk and Kathryn listened — listened to much more than Anne was really saying in words. When she finally ceased talking Kathryn spoke quietly.

"You're in love with Andrew . . . even though

298

you know what he is and what harm he can bring?"

"No, Kathryn, he will bring us no harm." She went on to explain what Andrew was trying to do. "He is a gentle man, a peaceful man, and I do love him, with my whole being I love him. I cannot bear to see Donovan kill him."

"Oh, Anne." Kathryn rose to pace again. "I do not know what help I can be."

"You're his wife!"

"Yes . . . his wife. When it is convenient for him."

"But you could try, you could ask him."

"Yes. But . . . maybe it would be better if we were to find out his plans first, and to see what steps he means to take."

"I'm afraid! He'll torture Andrew, force him to say things that are not true! I can't bear it."

"All right, Anne, all right," Kathryn soothed. "He won't do anything tonight or most likely for a few days until he wears Andrew's nerves down for a while. It will give us time to make some plans as well." She walked to Anne's side. "Now, come and lie down and rest. We'll be able to talk better in the morning."

"But, Kathryn . . ."

"Please. I know Andrew will be safe for a few days and I know Donovan won't be questioning him tonight."

"How do you know?"

"Because," Kathryn answered bitterly, "even though we have only been married a matter of days, he has already chosen his first mistress and I imagine there will be many more. He is with her."

"I'm sorry, Kathryn."

"Don't be. You have to love someone to be damaged by his infidelity. It does not cost me one moment of lost sleep. Now, come on. You've got to rest."

Anne obediently went to the bed and lay down. She kept her thoughts to herself. But she heard the tone and inflection in Kathryn's voice that Kathryn was hardly aware of. She was in love with Donovan McAdam. Anne wished that Kathryn were not so blind that she could not see it.

Anne was exhausted and she drifted into a dream-filled sleep. Kathryn returned to the fire to sit and gaze into its depth and begin to formulate a plan.

Donovan was both exhausted and half drunk. He had waited until word came to him that Andrew was locked safely in a cell. Then he went to the nearest bottle of whiskey.

It was rare for him to be caught in the state of confusion he was in. He could go to Kathryn and gloat at Andrew's capture. But he was the one who could not face the look he might see in her eyes. Would she be frightened for her precious Andrew? Would she be in tears for her servant? Another question pounded in his brain. What was Andrew to Kathryn? He knew they had never been lovers, their wedding night had made it clear to him, but did she love Andrew?

He drank deeply and slumped into a chair to prod these torturing ideas more. Already his churning mind was filled with pictures he, in his inebriated state, was finding very hard to handle.

It never occurred to him that Kathryn had visions of where he might be. He propped his feet on a stool and continued to assault the bottle in the hopes of wiping thoughts from his mind that he refused to label truth. After a while he slept.

James had been away from the castle several days. As always, on his return, he sought out Maggie.

He walked into her chambers to find her alone. She rose and held out her hand to him. "M'lord."

He came to her and kissed her. "You should not worry when I'm away." He held her a little away from him and looked at her. She looked extremely beautiful. "My absence seems to have done you good . . . or are you happy that I have returned?"

She flushed, but was silent, and this drew James's attention at once. "Have you been ill, sweetheart?" he asked as she moved away from him.

"No, m'lord, I am well."

"But something is amiss?"

"Nay, not amiss, sire. I am going to have a child," she said simply. She watched his face, trying to read his expression, trying to think all the thoughts that must plague him. Had he been a commoner instead of a king he would marry her; this she knew. But now . . .

He rose and came to her; taking both her hands in his he kissed one, then the other. What thoughts he had of tenderness, of pleasure, of the child, were revealed when his dark eyes fixed on her.

"When do you expect the child?"

"Is that important?"

"Very."

"In August."

"So you've known for a while. Why didn't you tell me before?"

"I saw no need."

"I shall judge the need," he said angrily.

"I know this raises a problem, m'lord, and I will willingly leave. But remember the wee one knows naught of the problems."

James walked to a chair and sat down. She knew his struggle and she loved him enough to truly want to ease it.

She lifted a pillow from a couch and walked to him, dropping the pillow at his feet. She sat and leaned back against his knee, taking one strong hand in both of hers. She did not need the physical contact to reassure her. She sat there quietly holding his hand and taking pleasure in his nearness. At this moment she did not even think of the child she carried. It was this man, this king, who was her life.

Looking up at his face, dark and lean, she sensed his troubled mind. She knew that the thought of an English war would occupy all his thoughts.

James slowly slid from the chair until he was seated beside her. His hands were clumsy as he reached for the laces of her gown and she knew he needed comfort as much as she. He needed the peace he could only seem to find in her arms.

"You are beautiful," he whispered.

"I am full of you," she replied as she drew him to her.

The next morning Donovan rose from his uncomfortable bed early, since the night had been a torture of unbelievable dreams. He rode from the castle before dawn, unaware that Fleming watched him ride away alone and smiled before he went quickly to Jennie Gray's door and knocked.

He knocked several times before a disheveled and sleepy-eyed Jennie opened it. She did not allow a maid to sleep in her chambers at night. It curtailed her freedom and she chose not to have unwanted gossip spread. She already had begun to circulate the whispers she wanted heard in Donovan's quarters.

It had not taken long for Jennie and Fleming to find they were compatible spirits and that their goals were somewhat the same. Both were well prepared to use each other if necessary.

"Fleming! What are you doing here at this hour?"

"I have come to bring you welcome news."

"What welcome news?"

"Donovan McAdam rides out alone."

"Alone . . . where?"

"I would say mayhap to Bothworth Castle. He and Patrick Hepburn are fast friends."

"What should this mean to me?"

"He meets with the king this night, so it is clear he will return home."

"I see . . . and if he should run across another traveler . . . why, they could ride home together."

"It might be an interesting ride."

"Aye . . . and an interesting arrival."

"Especially," he smiled, "if his new bride were waiting for him. It might prove . . . ah . . . enlightening to her."

"Yes, it might. Thank you, m'lord."

"You are more than welcome," he chuckled as she shut the door. Jennie washed and dressed hastily and was riding away from the castle when Kathryn awoke.

Stiff from falling asleep in the chair before the fire, Kathryn sent at once for hot water to bathe in. Anne still slept soundly, so she left her and went down to breakfast.

She had set her mind. Despite all her vows that she would never ask Donovan for anything, she was too worried about her sister's well-being to consider herself. She would go to Donovan at once and plead for Andrew's release. If at least Andrew and Anne were happy it would be well worth it.

She would have to swallow her pride a bit, but if it led to Andrew's freedom then at least he and Anne could search for a way to escape. With Eric in exile and Anne safe she could face her battle with Donovan.

Her battle, she laughed harshly to herself. What battle? Her resistance was nothing to him. She flushed to think of the effect he had on her. Night after night she raised her defenses and night after night he succeeded in turning her resistance to desire. Still, desire was all it was and never would she hear the words from him that meant he cared.

Downstairs she asked for Donovan, only to be told he had ridden to Bothworth Castle to discuss matters of state with Patrick Hepburn.

"He rode out alone?" she questioned.

"Aye, my lady," the stablehand replied, but his eyes shifted from hers and she instinctively knew that even though he had left alone, the woman with whom he had spent the night had found a way to be with him. She told herself she merely felt hatred for his callous treatment of her. They had been married such a short time. Did he want to make her look ineffectual and amusing to the court? Did he want to punish her for her resistance by taking a mistress so soon? Or . . . did he truly still love his flame-haired Jennie? Again this stirred an emotion that took all her will to deny.

"Tell me," she said casually, "has Lady Gray gone

304

riding this morning?"

"Aye, my lady," he added reluctantly. He had an immense respect and admiration for Donovan and a matching affection for Kathryn. He could not see what Donovan McAdam would want with the gold-eyed Lady Gray when he had a woman like Kathryn for his wife.

"Thank you, Will," she said, and smiled warmly to ease his nerves. He was not to blame because her husband chose to flaunt his mistress in her face.

He watched her walk away and spat fiercely. "The man is a bloody fool," he muttered as he returned to his work.

Donovan and Patrick Hepburn were of an age, and found many other similarities in their lives. They had been friends for many years and had fought side by side for James.

But the similarity did not end there, for Patrick had asked his king for Lady Jane Gorden in the same manner as Donovan had asked for Kathryn.

Donovan watched . . . and realized that Jane and Patrick were happy with each other. Maybe in time, Kathryn would see the futility of her continual battle with him and would settle into being his wife.

He thought of something else as well, something he could hardly understand. Jennie had given him every opportunity to claim her as mistress, and still he felt no desire for her. He found himself wanting Kathryn even when he was away from her. He could taste the sweet earthy taste of her and the scent of her lingered with him even now . . . and her hatred and resistance to his touch lingered as well. He knew he could raise her to a passion that matched his, but after he had possessed her there

305

was a dark void in her eyes he could not understand or fill. He didn't want to see it, yet he didn't know what he wanted. He just didn't understand Kathryn and he had no intention of giving her any hold over his emotions. It was too deadly a weapon to put into the hands of a strong woman like Kathryn.

When his business was finished with Patrick it was late afternoon.

"Stay the night and ride out in the morning," Patrick suggested.

"Nay, I will be home before the dinner meal is over. Besides I need the ride to clear my mind."

Patrick and Jane watched Donovan ride away. "He is an unhappy man for some reason," Patrick said.

"Aye," Jane agreed. "For some reason."

Patrick looked down into the eyes of the woman he loved. What a battle they had had until he had seen his love for her and admitted it to himself. Now she was the glow of light in his life. He felt a little sorry for Donovan's blindness.

Jane laughed softly and Patrick echoed the laugh. There was no way to make Donovan understand love unless he could see and admit it to himself.

"I only hope he doesn't come too close to losing her before he develops some wisdom."

"Aye," Jane agreed quietly.

Donovan rode slowly, deep in thought. He seemed to be standing on the edge of understanding something, yet . . . it was elusive, like a shadow he could see but could not touch . . . somewhat like Kathryn.

He was so deep in thought that he did not see

the figure at the side of the road until he was almost upon her.

"Jennie," he said in surprise as he reined in sharply.

Jennie had prepared herself well. She had dismounted, loosened her hair and torn her jacket. Then she had scooped some dust from the road and dirtied her clothes.

When she saw Donovan coming she had begun to limp and at the sound of his voice she had looked up at him with teary eyes and a look of pain and helplessness.

"Oh, Donovan, I'm so glad someone has finally come. I was thrown and I'm afraid I have injured my ankle."

"Where is your horse?"

"There," she pointed some distance away where her horse grazed contentedly, "But I cannot get him."

Donovan kicked his horse into motion and in a few minutes returned with her horse in tow.

He dismounted and lifted her gently to place her in the saddle, surprised that all he really felt was doubt about her tale, and annoyance. She must have been meeting someone and his appearance had sent her lover scurrying away. He really didn't care, and that surprised him, too.

"Must we hurry?" Jennie asked, promise deep in her voice.

"Yes, even at a good pace it will still be late when we return."

"There was a time, m'lord," she smiled, "when you did not care about the hour."

"And that time was over when you chose to wed another."

"But I am no longer wed," she responded.

307

"Aye," he said softly, "but I am."

He slapped her horse's rump to set it into motion and rode just far enough behind her so conversation was impossible. Her eyes glittered with rage, but Donovan's mind was already gone from her.

As time had fled Kathryn's rage had grown. For a while she forgot Andrew and Anne, and could only seethe with fury.

That they would make their affair so public, so blatant, enraged her. She sought some method of revenge, slight though it might be. . . . Then she pounced on the idea and issued commands that set those ideas into motion. If he wanted Jennie Gray he could damn well have her, but she would be damned if he would have both.

When all her preparations were done she set herself to watch for Donovan's approach.

The candles and torches in and about the great hall were lit by the time they arrived. Kathryn watched with a calm exterior. Inside the black emotions swirled.

Donovan rode through the gates with Jennie beside him and the first thing he saw was Kathryn awaiting him. His heart leapt at the sight of her. Hope that she had finally come to her senses filled him. Had he turned her into an obedient wife at last?

Kathryn stood on the broad stone step in the court of the castle and her face was unreadable as they rode up to her.

But Donovan's hopes vanished when he saw the chill of her smile. Then he finally realized how it must look to her. He smiled; a little jealousy might be beneficial. He was hardly prepared for what was to take place.

"Welcome home, m'lord," Kathryn said.

She did not remember what he said in reply. It was a polite answer. But the sound of his voice and his warm gaze that moved over her made the warm blood rise to her cheeks.

Yet she also felt cold, for it was now very clear that what she had suspicioned for so long was true. Kathryn did not have to look into the eyes of the woman who rode beside him to know of her smug smile of satisfaction. She saw the disheveled clothes and her unbound hair and broiled with the anger it brought. She could envision them rolling together in a hidden glade somewhere.

"And you, Lady Gray, have you had some mishap perhaps . . . or maybe the stallion you have chosen was overly enthusiastic."

The words and their reality crashed on Donovan. He frowned.

"Lord McAdam was kind enough to escort me home. I'm afraid I did have a small mishap. But,"— Jennie's eyes glittered—"there is no stallion I cannot handle."

"I do not doubt it," Kathryn murmured. Then her eyes returned to Donovan, who was helping Jennie dismount and fighting his own anger. The words Kathryn had spoken and their unsaid meaning were more than clear to him.

"It makes me happy to know you had such charming company, my lord," Kathryn said sweetly. Donovan was instantly on the defensive. He'd heard her voice drip with honey before and it was enough to chill the strongest of men.

Jennie and Donovan followed Kathryn into the hall. Once inside she swung around to face them again. "You look so . . . dusty," she smiled at Jen-

309

nie. "I have made some new arrangements for you. I have moved my quarters to another suite of rooms. There is a new room prepared for you, Lady Gray. Right next to Lord McAdam's chambers. I'm sure he will be glad to show you the way."

She gazed at Donovan's shocked face for a minute. Then she turned on her heel and walked away as slowly and regally as a queen. She did not look back.

Donovan was stunned, and for a moment he just stood immobile and didn't react at all. Then his own fury erupted. He paid no heed to Jennie's satisfied look, but nearly stormed in his wife's wake.

Jennie was satisfied. She went immediately to the room Kathryn had indicated. It was right next to Donovan's . . . with an adjoining door. She walked across the room and slid the bolt open.

Kathryn had made it clear to Donovan and to her that she no longer wanted Donovan. The unlocked door would soon make clear that she did and he need only take a few steps to take advantage of it.

Donovan stopped by the door that was now Kathryn's. It was then that he caught himself. He would not beg her to return to his room, he would simply make her room his when it was time for bed. If she wanted to play games with him then he would teach her that he could win even if she set the rules. He turned and walked away.

Donovan returned to his rooms to bide his time, patiently designing the steps he meant to take. Kathryn belonged to him and even her own stubbornness was not going to be a barrier between them.

He sat down at his desk. He would go over his accounts until he decided enough time had passed. The ink pots were full, the quills plentiful. Heavy curtains hung at the windows. All were new. Kathryn must have bought them. As he looked around he found the whole room seemed to speak of Kathryn's touch. He wanted her back here, where she belonged. He swore softly when a soft knock sounded on the door, then he smiled. Kathryn had come to her senses. He walked to the door and was more than surprised to find Anne there.

"M'lord, might I speak with you?"

"Certainly." He stood aside and let her pass, then closed the door.

"I didn't want to disturb you so late, m'lord. But the truth is I have waited as long as I can bear."

He didn't know what she meant. He took her hand and led her to a seat by the fireplace. "Sit down, please," he said. When she did, he sat opposite. She was so intent and so tense that he guessed she didn't want to waste time on inconsequential preliminaries. "Proceed," he urged.

She looked beautiful, and as the firelight played on her face he sensed something very different about her.

"I want to know the truth from you," she said quickly. "What happened to our secretary? What happened to Andrew?"

He was a trifle surprised, and he frowned a little, but since she asked for it he could tell her the truth. "Andrew is an English spy."

She didn't say that she didn't believe it, or even that she didn't know. "An English spy," she echoed his words.

"Aye mistress, a knight from Dorsetshire. Sir William Frances Andrew Craighton. He was with Henry Tudor in exile. He preceded Henry to England as an advance agent. In fact he participated in Henry's first abortive attempt to seize the crown. He was captured and escaped. God knows how, for few men escaped Richard the Third. That, so far, is what we know of him."

Her eyes were almost purple, then her lashes fell. Again he frowned. He did not understand. She was stunned, but there was a kind of pride in hearing what he said.

"An enviable record . . . in its way," he said, to see what her response would be. "A very clever man. No doubt he deceived you well."

She looked squarely at him. "I don't know, m'lord." There was the faintest hint of a smile. "Where is he then?"

"Imprisoned below."

She caught her lip between her teeth. He was alive . . . and near. She had to get out of this room because she was suddenly afraid she might reveal too much. If it were suspected she loved Andrew . . . she shivered and spoke.

"I am again sorry I disturbed you. But I wanted to know. You can understand, m'lord. He was most kind, and served our interests well." She rose.

He rose and walked to the door with her. "Lady Anne."

"Yes?"

"Did . . . did Kathryn send you for this information?"

Anne was surprised. "No, I asked for myself." She extended her hand and he kissed it. "Good night, m'lord."

She was gone, and painful doubts tore at him. Could Anne have lied? Did Kathryn really want to know what had happened? Did she love Andrew Craighton?

He drank down a glass of whiskey and poured another. One way or the other he would find the answer. He turned and left the room.

Chapter 20

Andrew stood before Donovan in his study. Because of being locked in darkness for some time his eyes were unaccustomed to the bright light, so he kept them half-closed for protection. Yet he watched Donovan closely as he leaned back on the fireplace seat while the flames roared up the chimney. Andrew had not been able to look at the fire at all.

He was standing only a few feet from Donovan. At Donovan's nod one of the men had ordered him to remove his shirt and livery. He did and he was well aware of Donovan's scrutiny. He knew Donovan only wanted to see his left shoulder. He smiled in grim satisfaction. The scar was very plain to see. Then Donovan spoke curtly. "Dress."

Andrew did with a grimace of distaste. He took time because he needed time; he was beginning to see more clearly.

The two men were waved out of the room, then Donovan settled back to his comfortable position and contemplated Andrew.

As he finished buckling his belt Andrew raised his eyes and looked steadily at Donovan.

Though he looked extremely tired, he was immaculately dressed, richly attired with a gold-hilted, jeweled dagger. He was freshly shaven. Andrew felt the contrast to himself. He was wearing the same clothes, and was unshaven, for he had been allowed no water.

"Sir Andrew Craighton," Donovan said mockingly.

"Aye, m'lord," Andrew replied. He bowed.

"You may sit."

"I prefer to stand," Andrew replied. He could prove as obstinate as Donovan McAdam. He could also play the cat-and-mouse game. Donovan wanted some answers and he was not about to give them. Andrew did not fool himself about the extent to which Donovan might go to get them. He pushed aside the image of Anne. There was no way he could ask questions that would endanger her.

Andrew, who had daringly escaped from Richard III, continued to gather his wits. Andrew knew his only advantage was Donovan's badly controlled temper. It was being held on short rein even now. He was curious about what seemed to be an overdone anger, and he wanted to find the reason for it.

"Proceed, my lord," he said lazily.

Donovan frowned. Andrew rubbed his hand over his bearded chin. He hated the position he was in only a little less than he hated the fact that he was powerless to help Anne.

Donovan was about six feet away. He was leaning against the fireplace, so that he faced Andrew. To the left of his large hand rested the blackened, heavy iron poker. Andrew felt every nerve in his body tingling. He forced himself to relax. The weapon he wanted was twelve feet away, with Donovan McAdam between him and it.

Andrew examined his fingernails nonchalantly,

315

then yawned, aggravating Donovan even further.

Donovan's voice was like a sharp blade. "There's no reason why I should not hang you, sir, except that I want information from you."

Andrew opened his eyes. "I don't have what you want. But if I did I would tell you nothing. You are not the caliber of man to whom I would give information even if I were about to die."

Donovan rose, his anger barely controlled. "Tomorrow I am giving you into James's personal custody. Do you know what that means?"

When the single sentence was spoken, Andrew realized that he was now a political prisoner. It must mean that James Stuart had decided on a course of action, most likely one that was hostile to England.

"I cannot say that I have enjoyed your hospitality," Andrew replied.

"James's hospitality might be less pleasant. Why don't you tell me what I wish to know?"

Andrew still didn't move. "Are you threatening me with torture?"

"Aye," Donovan replied. "And greater men than you have been broken."

"The role of torturer seems to suit you," Andrew replied as he slowly rose. But he knew that what he had just said was not true. He didn't need to bait Donovan. Donovan wanted nothing more than to get his hands around Andrew's throat. He didn't try to analyze the reason for this, he just knew it was so.

The luxury of anger had been denied Andrew too long. The blood pounded in his chest. He didn't need wits, he needed action.

"Whoreson Scot! I could fight you man to man

and beat you."

"You used to kneel to me," Donovan taunted. But he stood and took a step toward him.

Now only two feet separated them and, as if both were anticipating with brutal relish the violence that was to come, they measured each other. Huge fists and tempers hung by bare threads of control. Donovan wanted the physical and emotional satisfaction of pounding Andrew's taunting face. He wanted to wipe him from Kathryn's mind. Deep in his mind was a glimmer of admiration that made it worse. For if he felt it, Kathryn must have felt it, too.

Donovan moved slowly. He knew he risked being sent backward into the fireplace. He started to move sideways, out of the alcove, and as he moved he lashed out with his left fist in a whistling blow that grazed Andrew's shoulder. Andrew spun with it, to take the force from it, and came up with his right hand.

The blow landed high on Donovan's chest and a lesser man would have fallen. They were parallel with the alcove and Donovan was free of the bench before the fireplace.

Neither underestimated the other.

Andrew ducked Donovan's blow to the jaw, then drove his fist into Donovan's ribs, feeling at the same time the impact of Donovan's knuckles against his cheekbone. Andrew swayed back and hit with both fists. One caught Donovan's eye and the other struck harmlessly on his chest.

Strategy was forgotten. Both men were already wiping blood from their faces. Andrew licked blood off his lips, but he refused to back away from Donovan's murderous fists. Neither Donovan nor

Andrew would attempt any evasion of the blows. They preferred to take the punishment for the joy of giving it back. Andrew wanted to crush the man who had injured Anne and been responsible for so much distress. Donovan had Kathryn in his mind with each blow.

Eyes slit, teeth bared slightly, they fought with animal anger that lasted until Andrew was driven back by a blow to the jaw. He almost stumbled over a stool, but recovered. He flung himself forward and caught Donovan on the side of the face with a crashing right that sent Donovan to the floor.

Andrew stood unmoving, waiting, breathing heavily, blood dripping from a cut on his lip. Donovan had fallen against a heavy chair that had crashed to the floor with him. He got up slowly, his eyes never leaving Andrew's face, fists already knotted to resume battle, when sanity suddenly returned to Andrew.

In one brief moment Andrew realized that he could have leapt on Donovan and seized the dagger he wore. He had not done so. The poker was too far away. He could never reach it now. He had forgotten it completely while he might have succeeded. And now in a clear moment he saw what he deemed his only chance, for he knew they were evenly matched and he could not beat Donovan into insensibility before he himself succumbed. He saw his chance and seized it. He took the next blow from Donovan full on and fell backward onto the floor.

The blow had been to the mouth and he could feel his lips swell and the pain. His whole head pounded. The sudden draining of his anger left him limp. He remained motionless.

Donovan walked over to him and looked down. He felt at the dagger in his belt and realized he had not even thought of using it. But he was furious at his own self for he had knocked Andrew senseless before he had gotten the answer he wanted.

One of Donovan's eyes was almost closed. He touched his cheek, then looked at his bloody palm. Then he wiped it off on his leg, walked to the door and opened it.

The two guards outside the door had heard the noise, but knew they did not dare interrupt. Donovan paid no attention to their stares.

"Fetch me some water," he muttered, and went back into the room, standing over Andrew like a lion over fallen prey.

The water arrived and after Donovan washed the blood from himself he waited for Andrew to recover.

He waited for five minutes before his patience came to an end. "Fetch more water."

When the second bucket of water arrived Donovan tossed it on Andrew. Andrew struggled up. Deliberately he swayed. He put his hand to his temple, then appeared to struggle to again open his eyes.

Donovan's head throbbed. He had had too little sleep, and he had drunk much too much the day before. While he watched, Andrew tried to take a step and stumbled, catching himself on the table and clinging to it. He hoped his acting was good enough to temporarily fool a very astute Donovan.

Donovan made a gesture to the guards. "Take him back to his cell." He walked back to the fallen chair, set it back in place, and sat down wearily.

The guards obeyed. But it seemed plain to them that the Englishman couldn't walk. One of them put an arm about his waist and laid Andrew's arm across his shoulder. The other guard opened the door. The three of them moved out into the wide hall, walking abreast.

Andrew felt secure. They thought him helpless. It was possibly the only opportunity he would have to escape. He felt the strength gather in him. Then he cursed to himself as two young maids appeared giggling together. The moment was lost and a few minutes later he was tossed back into his cell, muttering some very obscene words as the darkness closed about him again.

Donovan was more than weary, he was momentarily overpowered by despair.

He sat for a long time, deep in thought. He was assured of the fact that James would break Andrew. But he was still less than satisfied. He wanted to kill him himself. But first he wanted to hear one of them admit what he already knew. If it could not be Andrew . . . then it must be Kathryn.

He returned to his bedroom, more than aware that Jennie was on the other side of a door he was sure was unlocked. But he was too angry to consider going to her. He washed carefully, wincing at the sting from the cuts on his face. Then he dressed just as carefully.

From a drawer he took a small box. Then he left the room and walked with a determined stride toward Kathryn's.

But again things were not to go quite the way

Donovan had planned. As he reached for the handle of Kathryn's door it was opened from inside and Kathryn and he faced each other so suddenly that neither could move or speak.

It was Kathryn who found her voice first. "My lord," she smiled, " 'tis unnecessary to roam the halls, sir. Surely what you seek is close enough. Or," she paused thoughtfully, "mayhap I should have put her in your bed so you could find her easier."

He gritted his teeth, grasped her arm in almost a brutal grip, and reached behind her to open the door. Then he thrust her inside, entered, and closed the door behind him.

She was wearing the same gown she had worn at dinner. It was graceful and she looked like a tempting witch. In her arms she carried what looked like white linen. He wondered vaguely what it was and where she was taking it.

Only when she laid it aside did he realize it was a shirt. It almost made him choke to think of where she might have been taking it.

Kathryn was watching the flickering emotions in his eyes without understanding. "My lord?" she questioned hesitantly. Her eyes were riveted on his face. "It seems you have been in a battle since I have seen you last. You were not . . . severely injured."

He flushed with annoyance. Be damned if he would tell her about his confrontation with Andrew. Let her believe what she wanted, he thought, but the sparkle of challenging laughter in her eyes and the thoughts and unspoken words were enough to make him grit his teeth.

She had been leaving the room when he had

come and his vital imagination was forming pictures that plucked his nerves raw. Visioning her in Andrew's semidark cell, her body pressed to his and her lips accepting his kiss willingly, was pushing his control.

"Where were you going? It's late. Were you returning to where you belong?"

"I'm afraid three would make it crowded, my lord."

"Then where were you going?" he insisted.

She lifted her chin in defiance, refusing to give him the satisfaction of knowing she was attempting to find out for certain if Jennie shared his bed or not. But her stubbornness let him believe what he would, and he believed the shirt and her visit were for Andrew Craighton.

"You should return to your mistress before your bed grows cold."

"I do not let someone else choose with whom I share a bed. I choose to share my bed with my wife," he said casually as he moved from her and began to remove his doublet.

"Why?"

"Why?" He arched a brow as if he didn't understand her question.

"Yes, why? Why not stay where you are welcome?"

Each word stung, but he would never allow her to know it.

He walked to her and it took all her will not to back away. "Learn well, Kathryn. No one dictates to me and especially," he chuckled, "I will not have my wife 'arranging' my liaison with a mistress. 'Tis unseemly, madam. Oh, by the way, I brought you a small gift. I had it brought from Paris."

He handed her the box and for a moment their hands touched and the contact affected them both. Kathryn opened the lid slowly.

She was surprised, to say the least, and a little unsettled. He was the most perplexing of men. Just when she thought she understood him well he did something that entirely upset her equilibrium.

She gasped softly as she gazed at the gleaming collar of emeralds.

"I brought it so you could wear it at your sister's wedding."

"Oh."

He looked at her steadily. For the first time he asked her honestly what she was thinking. "Why do you say 'oh' like that? You sound displeased."

She shrugged away his question. "A long time ago, my lord, you will probably not remember, 'twas in the chapel at Scone, I said I would never ask a favor. You replied I would break that bargain."

He replied curtly, "I remember. I shouldn't have said it."

"No, you were right. I am a supplicant . . . for two favors. Still you sound like you are showing that you are . . . that I am . . . I don't know what I mean!"

"I don't think you do either. But what you are trying to say is that 'tis only my male vanity that prompts me to give you a rather lovely piece of jewelry. But in that, madam, am I a villainous rogue, or am I just like any other man?"

"You are not like any other man," she said definitely.

At this he smiled a little. "I fear I am," he sighed, and moved a little away from her. "What

323

favor is it you wish of me?"

"Sit down, my lord."

He shook his head, "I have a notion I must hear this standing."

He drew a long breath, trying to keep calm. "I cannot give it unless you ask for it." He paused. "Kathryn?"

"I want you to stop Anne's wedding."

Again he shook his head wearily. "You could not ask for something I could give, could you? Not a jewel, or a title, or an appointment for one of your kin." He raised his hands, then dropped them. "It is completely impossible to stop the wedding. Impossible."

"Why?"

Again he paused and regarded her. "Why in the name of God didn't you ask me this weeks ago?"

"Because," her answer came softly but steadily, "it took me a long time, and I had to steel myself to ask you for anything."

"Well, now it's too late. At least for that favor. Now, what is the other favor you're so reluctant to ask for?"

She was silent, but he knew. He knew and suddenly he wanted to strike her, to hurt her somehow.

"Andrew Craighton," he snarled.

"Where is he . . . how is he?"

"So you were completely unamazed when I spoke his name. Did you think that would escape me, madam?"

"I knew his name."

"I've no doubt you do."

"What have you done to him! What? You—."
She broke off. There was no need to ask exactly

324

where Andrew was, she could guess, and she was completely helpless to aid him even though he was so near. Donovan appeared calm as he turned his back to her. Maybe he could have controlled himself if she had not asked the next question.

"Will he die?"

"Almost certainly," he turned quickly, wanting to see the effect his words had. He felt his breath grow shallow as he read pain in her eyes, never knowing the pain was for Anne and Andrew and not for herself.

"You may keep your gift, I shall never wear it."

"You will wear it," he said. "I want to see it around your neck. Perhaps to satisfy my vanity, perhaps as a badge of ownership . . ."

"I won't," she whispered.

"You will," he said, "or so help me I will have your Andrew beaten."

She moved to take the box from the table. She was aware of his eyes on her even when she refused to look at him. Fierce rage gripped her. She wanted to hurl the box at him. With an effort of will she kept her hands clenched on it.

"He has done nothing," she whispered. "Don't kill him, m'lord, have mercy."

When she looked at him, bitter, merciless anger was what she saw. He refused to understand the blackness that filled him. Instead he instinctively reacted to a pain he could not believe. Once and for all he would wipe Andrew from her mind and her heart. Once and for all she must know that she belonged to him and that he would never let her go. Not to Andrew Craighton or any other man.

She had only time to gasp his name in shock as

in two long strides he was beside her, catching her
up in his arms and kissing her until the room spun
and she could only cling to him dizzily.

With one sweep he lifted her and strode to the
bed. Kathryn knew the impossibility of fighting
him. He had a power over her senses that she
could not deny. And very deep inside, so deep that
she could not see it, was the knowledge that if he
was with her . . . he couldn't be in Jennie Gray's
bed.

It seemed to him as if he had never kissed her
before. The green-eyed enchantress, she always
contrived to stir his anger and make him forget all
his self-control, even when she wasn't aware of it.
She was a seductress, teasing, tempting, then drawing away the next minute. Fighting, showing her
contempt, then turning into a hungry tigress, a
witch leaving her mark on a man.

I will never be able to tame her, was his quick
thought. Just when I think I've reached her she'll
turn on me. Be very careful, his mind screeched,
but already he was caught in the brilliance of her
heated, half-parted lips. He was losing his detach-
ment, all the rationality he had ever possessed.
What he really found hardest to face was the
knowledge that slowly, without his realizing it, she
was becoming necessary to him.

He took possession of her mouth in a way that
drove everything else from her mind. She was
aware of the great need in him, a need that
matched the one building in her. It was something
different from what she had ever experienced before.

There was a deep, all-encompassing hunger that
pulled at her body and soul. It was almost as if he

might consume her, as if she might disappear into him forever. She felt the edges of her being soften and dissolve. Time bled into eternity.

She felt his hands moving slowly and caressingly over her then up to pull the pins from her hair, loosening it.

His mouth found the hollow at the base of her throat and she made a small helpless sound; she felt his hands push aside the gown she wore. Then she felt his fingers burn against her breasts.

He held her close against him, while his lips covered her open mouth, taking possession of it, stifling any protests she might utter.

He was kissing her breasts, his tongue tracing light teasing patterns over their taut, sensitive peaks. She began to whimper in the back of her throat as she was drained of all thought and will.

She struggled, but only halfheartedly; his arms imprisoned her again. She closed her eyes and let him have his way, feeling the desire to struggle or even to protest slipping away from her, to be replaced by something else . . . something that grew like a tight, hard knot inside her belly, spreading like a burning flush over her whole body.

He must have sensed her sudden abject surrender. From somewhere far away she heard him laugh softly and then he was catching her roughly against him.

Now she arched up against him, half sobbing and completely unable to understand the emotions that he could awaken in her body. She was all too conscious of the pressure of his long, hard-muscled legs against hers, of the feel of skin against her bare tingling breasts and the crisp feeling of his thick hair under her clutching fingers.

Somewhere in the recesses of her mind was the thought that he was like a fever, like a coiled snake in her belly, growing, spreading heat like honey in her loins, rendering her incapable of everything but feeling, needing.

One hand stroked her thighs gently, slowly, teasingly, moving her legs apart until his fingers found the warm, moist, and most sensitive place. He moved his fingers in tormenting caress, sliding within her then away, over and over, until she gasped and arched her hips to meet him.

Before she could find any release he moved down and his lips again created a fiery path. He sought the heated, throbbing place and found it. He gripped her buttocks, lifting her to meet his seeking tongue. She moaned and tried to escape the torment, but he held her, teasing, nibbling, and thrusting until she was wild and beyond reason.

Now his mouth was demanding, almost brutal, and she gasped and moaned. Her hands pressed against his broad shoulders but he was immovable. He tormented her, drew from her every ounce of passion.

He pushed himself a little way inside her and withdrew again, and again, until she wept and begged with the need for release. When he could see that she was far beyond reality . . . when she cried out and begged for him, his mouth came crashing down on hers. At the same time he thrust himself within her. He heard her anguished half-pleasure, half-agony groan. He was a large and very strong man and he drove himself to the depths of her. Harder and harder, until her body was quivering like a leaf in a hurricane and she clung to him like a rudderless ship in a storm.

The fiery strokes increased in depth and sureness until the delightful sensations made the gathering heat expand and she was moaning softly. Her legs had entwined about him, and her hands clung in wild desperation, as if she were drowning and he was the only solidity. Suddenly the fiery center exploded in one contraction after another. An explosive and fulfilling shudder rippled through her.

She had her eyes closed and she clung to him. Her world was out of control and she had never been a victim to unbridled, unbelievable possession as she was now.

She was taken to the heights, flung to the depths, and risen again to fly beyond reason . . . she had never been so exalted or so frightened in her life.

But the reality that chilled both her mind and her body was painful. Again he had proven that his mastery of her body was complete. But this time she sensed something new, something almost brutal. He had wanted somehow to hurt her and in a way he had. But it was more than that.

Within him was a deep burning anger and she didn't understand why it was directed at her. She could see annoyance at her, but not this deep and ugly thing that seemed to be festering within him. Why should he be the one who was so furious when it was he who was the unfaithful one, he who flaunted his mistress in her face?

The frustration was so strong that for the first time it brought Kathryn to tears. She turned away from him and muffled the sobs against her pillow.

Donovan sat up and looked at her. In the candlelight the soft curve of her back gleamed like ivory satin and he could have cursed with the knowledge that he wanted to reach out to her, to touch her gently, to feel the satin of her skin beneath his hands.

He knew she wept silently, and he should have felt the satisfaction he was reaching for. Instead he felt hollow, empty. It infuriated him. He who had never had to ask for any woman was shaken by the knowledge that not only could he not breach her defenses and bend her to his will . . . she was in love with another man. That was the poison that swirled through his blood. That was what he wanted to kill. She was a self-willed, independent woman and seemed to be able to withstand his cruelest taunts, his most calculated thrusts, retreating behind a closed look or silence. She had become unreachable . . . yet she was his wife.

He stood up and began to dress, his eyes on her motionless form. She had retreated from him again. It seemed that, despite his superior strength, his ability to overpower her senses and to force her to bend, he had not reached her at all.

He walked around the bed and sat down beside her. She knew his every move, felt the bed sag beneath his weight; still she refused to look at him. Angrily she brushed the tears away. She hated her moment of weakness.

She alone has power to defeat me, Donovan thought suddenly. She means trouble, she alone, of all the women I've known, has found a way to creep beneath my skin. She is an enemy . . . she loves another man . . . she has resisted me in every way and will probably continue to do so . . . but at this moment she is mine.

He could still feel her caressing hands, the spontaneous movements of her supple body, and the way she blotted out everything but the fact of his own insatiable, unsatisfied need for her, for this particular woman above all others. This wild, bold, sensual creature who could give herself with such complete abandonment that it was hard to believe that anything had ever existed but their desire.

"Look at me, Kathryn," he said.

He felt her body tense, but she refused to obey.

"Damnit, look at me."

Her eyes flew open and she glared at him in brilliant defiance.

"Tomorrow you will have all your things moved back into *our* room. You are my wife. That is where you belong and that is where you will go."

"And if I don't?"

"Then I shall give the orders to have your things moved and I shall personally drag you there. I would save you some embarrassment, but don't doubt that I will do exactly as I say. How shall I be, Kathryn? Will you do it with some pride or must I do it for you?"

Why, her mind screamed, why did he still have the power to do this to her. Is it because I love him, she thought helplessly. Is it because I can't stop myself from loving him in spite of the fact that he has never once told me that he loves me?

"Why do you feel you need to do this to me? Is it not enough to flaunt your mistress before me . . . before everyone?"

"I'm flaunting no one. You were the one to make the arrangements, not I. Nor did I request that any changes be made." He grinned aggravatingly. "When I choose to make changes I'll let you know."

"Perhaps when I'm with child," she snapped bitterly.

She refused to recognize the light of hopeful pleasure that danced in his eyes. "Do you think you are?"

"We've only been married a matter of days."

"But eventful days . . . and nights."

"Perhaps it would be best that I am. Then you could concentrate less on me and more on your other 'ladies'."

He reached out and caught her chin in one huge hand. His eyes glowed and his face was now unsmiling. "We will settle one thing here and now. You are my wife and I intend it to stay that way. Don't make any foolish mistakes, Kathryn. I do not give up easily what belongs to me."

She blinked and her brow drew together in a frown. What mistake was he talking about? It was he who made their marriage a farce.

"You can make the best of it or you can continue this battle. But mark me well, I will win. I will win, not because I have the power of the throne behind me, but because I have what I want and I have the strength and determination to hold it. You make your decisions . . . but expect no quarter from me . . . because I don't intend to let you go. Not for anything . . . or anybody."

He bent his head and kissed her savagely before she could do more than let out an angry gasp at the brutality of his attack. Then he rose and walked to the door. With a hand on the handle he turned again to face her.

"Tomorrow, Kathryn . . . and that is no idle threat." He opened the door and left, closing it softly behind him.

Kathryn glared at the door, a helpless rage swirling in her. Then she reached out to the table close to the bed, grasped a book that lay there, and tossed it with all the force she had against the closed door.

Outside the door Donovan smiled . . . and walked away. She was angry, but she had no choice. She would do what he had said. He felt quite pleased . . . and was quite unaware that pride often went before a fall.

Chapter 21

Kathryn rose very early the next morning and gave the orders at once that all her personal effects should be returned to her husband's room. It served to confuse everyone and temporarily silence the gossips before it set them buzzing again with questions of what next exciting thing would take place between two such willful people. The whole castle was firmly divided between the two.

Kathryn told Anne of her inability to move the granite wall of Donovan McAdam in the situation concerning Andrew.

"I don't understand him. It's more than catching an English spy. It's as if he truly hates Andrew for some other reason."

"But what reason?"

"I don't know."

"I've got to do something!" Anne cried. Kathryn looked at her in sympathy.

"There is naught you can do, Anne."

"But I cannot let him die! I cannot."

"We have hope. No sentence has been passed yet. We can petition James."

"And you believe his heart will be less cold than Donovan McAdam's?"

"I don't know," Kathryn said quietly.

They had been walking together in the garden

and as others were approaching they turned their words to another subject. It would not do to feed any information to whatever curious ears might be listening.

But almost two weeks passed by and there was no sign that Andrew was even to be tried. Anne could wait no longer. Silent as a wraith she slipped down the last flight of twisting stairs. She knocked softly on the big barred door.

After a moment it was opened. By torchlight she saw the startled face of the guard. She held up a gold coin where the torchlight could make it glitter. "Please, I must enter. Just for a few minutes."

The guard stepped away from the door. He took the money with a quick, furtive gesture. He knew instantly whom she had come to see.

"Down here," he whispered. He shut the door carefully and bolted it again, first looking up the narrow stairs to be sure they had been unobserved. Then he hastened ahead of her down the corridor.

A few feet down the hall Andrew was lying on the straw in his cell. He heard the approaching footsteps. Instantly he leapt to his feet. He stood by his door, his huge hands hooked around the heavy bars. Accustomed to the half-dark, he could see like a cat. What he saw shocked him into a muttered oath.

Anne picked up her skirts and ran toward him. "Andrew," his name burst from her lips, low yet compelling. She stood before him, face upturned to him through the bars. He tore his eyes from her and looked at the guard. "Don't breathe a word of this . . . on your life."

"Aye." The guard backed away from Andrew's fierce gaze. "But ye need not tell me such a thing. I would do nothing to distress Lady Anne . . . or to bring her any danger."

Andrew returned his gaze to Anne. "You should not have come here! You should know better! A good deal better!" His gaze was hungry as he absorbed her, but fear for her lent him anger.

Anne reached out with one hand and touched his fingers. "Should I, Andrew?"

"Stay only a moment. For God's sake, Anne, it's too dangerous for you."

"No, no," she contradicted. Then she cried. "I had to see you, Andrew, I had to!"

Now both of her hands were clasped over his. With a movement of his wrists, he took her hands in his. He was conscious now of his appearance; he was unshaven, unwashed, a captive in this dark and dirty place, a political captive whose death was most likely. Yet he was Sir Andrew Craighton and he was pleased there was no need for any more subterfuge.

"Beloved," he said softly, "somehow you understood. Don't be afraid for me."

She cried low, like a moan, "I cannot help you."

He smiled reassuringly. All the days had been swept away now, and it was as though they were alone and free to speak of their love. Yet he was more than unprepared for her next whispered words.

"I have come to help you escape."

"Good God above," he whispered, "there is no hope of that. Anne, love, it is just good to see you again, to have you here even for a moment." He crushed her fingers in his.

But Anne was already turning toward the guard. Her great purple eyes were full of pleading. "Might I just have a moment with him in his cell . . . please, I only want to say good-bye. Surely you are kind enough to understand."

"Aye my lady," he smiled. Had it been anyone else but Anne he might have said no. But he had known Lady Anne all her life and knew what a kind and gentle creature she was.

Andrew, who was watching his face, smiled as he saw and understood his thoughts. Anne had a definite weapon in her reputation for being so sweet and kind—and was clever enough to use it.

The guard forced him to back away, for he had a great deal of respect both for Andrew's size and his ability. Then he unlocked the door. Anne slipped inside and he drew the door closed and locked it. They heard his footsteps move away. Then they were alone together . . . maybe for the last time.

"Andrew," she said. Then she stopped. She could not tell him the words he must already know: that there was no escape for her. "I want you to be free."

"And you are to wed in two weeks."

"Even if you escape there is no way to stop that now. But I must know you are safe."

There was silence. The grip of his hands was even stronger. "I'll kill him," Andrew said matter-of-factly.

"No," she breathed, "I would not have the blood of an innocent man on your hands. I just want you to know that whatever else happens, I love you."

Andrew, his face bitterly grim, repeated, "I shall kill him." He dropped her hands and paced across the cell. Then he swung back to her. His words rushed out. "You said you came to help me escape. What did you mean?"

She reached between the heavy folds of her skirt to a pocket and withdrew a slender-bladed, jewel-hilted dagger. He stared at it in surprise, then laughed softly. Leave it to his beautiful, not so

337

timid, not so shy, and very courageous Anne to do something so totally unexpected. He went to her and took the dagger from her hand and it vanished quickly inside his shirt. Then he grasped her hands in his again.

"Listen, as soon as I can, as soon as I'm free I will find him, and I will kill him."

Anne only smiled. "And Sir Andrew Craighton would commit murder? I hardly think so. He is no match for you, Andrew. And his death would be murder. Fair battle is you . . . but not murder, never. If you do that neither you nor I could live with it."

"Anne," he said urgently, "is there naught you can do?"

"There is nothing. I have tried, Kathryn has tried. You do not understand." He did not understand that the real reason she had come was to say a final good-bye. "Andrew, I do not love him. I love you. I am here and we are together, even if it is only for a little while." Bright tears stood in her eyes.

Despite how dirty he felt he had to hold her. Anne sobbed as he reached for her and stepped willingly into the circle of his arms.

He rocked her gently. "I will get free. I promise you. I vow it."

She could say nothing. Suppose he did and she ran away from the marriage. They would send an entire force for them and they would be caught. There would be no one to speak for Andrew.

"Wait for me, Anne."

She clung to him and spoke through her tears, "You must think of me no longer, Andrew."

"What! Ask me not to breathe. Jesus God, how can you love me and say that?"

338

"I cannot help it," she cried. She buried her face in her hands.

"Forgive me," he muttered, the anguish tearing at him.

"I love you and you don't listen. It is true. Because I love you no one can ever touch me, really touch me."

"But I shall be free," he repeated strongly. "Never forget it. In the days to come be sure that one day I will be there, with you." He stopped. He heard the footsteps of the guard. "There is no more time now. But remember that each day that passes will bring me closer to you."

"Andrew!"

"Good-bye, my darling." He kissed her feverishly and passionately, then turned her about and gave her a light push toward the door.

Anne remembered to smile at the guard and thank him as he let her out. She was out on the steps again, leaving Andrew. Step by step she was leaving him, and hours and days and months . . . maybe years might elapse before she would ever see him again and there was nothing to do save one thing. While she went to another man she would pray every day and every night that Andrew was safe, well . . . and maybe finding some happiness.

Andrew spent the next day and a half trying to figure out how he would get the guard to come inside the cell and a route to get out of the castle. If he did manage to escape the cell, the castle would be like a formidable maze.

It was Donovan's black thoughts that gave Andrew the opportunity he wanted. Donovan wanted nothing more than another confrontation with Andrew Craighton.

Unable to contain it any longer and still chafing over the need to hear the truth about Kathryn, Donovan sent two guards for Andrew.

When they came for him, Andrew pretended stiffness and weakness from his confinement.

It was early evening and the whole castle seemed half-asleep. Andrew and the two guards turned to go down a hall. Here the hall was thirty feet long. Andrew managed it slowly. Then they neared a turn, where to go past the kitchen they had to enter a narrow winding hall.

Andrew moved slowly around the turn.

The action came so swiftly that later neither guard remembered it. Andrew's one hand had rested on a guard's shoulder as if he needed help. The other came suddenly upward, as though to clutch at support. But instead he seized the guard's head and knocked it into the stone wall with vicious strength. The guard slumped to the floor as Andrew turned on the other and drove his fist into his jaw.

The second guard had no time to cry out. Andrew looked as though he meant to kill. He reached for his knife, and in that split second Andrew struck him on the temple with a brutal blow that had all his weight behind it.

Both guards lay at his feet. He knew he had to get to the south tower. But he had to get there without being seen.

No one was in sight. He started down the hall in long strides. He heard movement at some distance behind him . . . but they were at too great a distance to worry about. He also knew he was very near Kathryn's rooms.

Outside he heard the gates closing and from that he could judge the time to be somewhere near five.

He also realized that if the outside gates were closed he was trapped inside the rosy stones of the castle walls.

He went up the carpeted stairs and stopped at the door. He pressed his ear against it but heard no sound from within. He opened the door and stepped inside. The room was empty. He crossed to the window. It was high, but he was sure he could manage to escape. He reached for the latch, but noticed only then that there were criss-crossed bars on the outside.

He cursed, then turned and crossed again to the door and stepped out. Then he started up the next flight of stairs . . . to Kathryn's room.

Then he heard her. The sound of her voice floated down. He heard her steps. She was moving about the room and humming. He hoped this meant she was alone.

Andrew climbed quietly and rapped as softly as he could. Kathryn opened the door herself. He stepped inside quickly and closed and bolted the door behind him. Kathryn and Andrew looked at each other.

"Andrew . . . are you all right? How . . . ?"

"I'm fine. I have but a moment. I only wanted to leave a message. That is why I came. I—if I succeed in my escape—will be at Hermitage. If Anne should need me, if she's in any danger, send for me."

Kathryn nodded her head.

"I must go," he whispered.

"How did you escape?"

"There's no time to explain," he muttered as he reached for the bolt.

"Don't unbolt it."

He looked at her in surprise. "Every minute I am

here endangers you as well. I must leave now."

Kathryn knew better than he what Donovan was capable of should he find Andrew in her room.

"No! Listen —," she cried.

"I can't," he said. He unbolted the door.

"No," Kathryn flung herself between him and the door. "There is a better way." She was trembling as she bolted the door again. He looked a little angry. "Andrew, there is a secret entrance to this tower. Anne and I used to use them for games when we were children."

He could hardly believe it as she showed him. His blue eyes sparkled and she saw his twisted grin. She raced across the room and was standing at the paneling and turning a cluster of roses that was carved into the wood. Then she seized it and pulled hard. A four-foot-high section of wall moved outward on a hinge.

"I used it only last week." She could hardly speak because of her excitement.

"What a wench you are," he chuckled as he bent to peer into the darkness.

"There are steps to your right," Kathryn said. "Hurry."

There was a hooded candle in a brass holder. She ran to the fire to light it and brought it to him. By its light Andrew could see the narrow steps cut into the stone walls. Kathryn continued to speak.

"This passage goes all the way under the river. It emerges in the priory, which you can see from my window. I'll meet you there in an hour with a horse."

Andrew took the candle.

"Go carefully," Kathryn cautioned.

"I will. I'm grateful, Lady Kathryn. You court danger helping me."

Kathryn smiled. "Could I see the man my sister loves taken to his death and not help? You will enter the chapel. There will be no one there. I shall come to the clump of trees you can see from the back door of the chapel. I'll close the panel after you."

He bent and kissed her cheek. "Remember," he said softly, "I'll be at Hermitage. If she needs me . . ."

"Yes, yes, go now," she urged.

"I will tell you that whatever else I feel for Donovan McAdam . . . he is a fortunate man to have you."

He heard the squeak of the hinges as he descended. The air was foul; it would probably be worse under the river, and now the light from above was gone and he had only the single glow of a candle. But now he had hope. He had two weeks before Anne wed and he might be able to accomplish a great deal in two weeks.

Kathryn reached the stable a few minutes later. The stableman was, to say the least, shocked.

"I want my horse!" Her voice was sharp and taut. The head groom stared at her.

"The gates are closed, your ladyship."

"I know it, dolt. Does the closing of a gate keep me from riding out when I wish? Bring my horse!"

He walked away and returned, leading the huge black stallion.

"He's not been ridden today," Kathryn said as she noticed the energy and spirit of the animal. She was satisfied that Andrew could have a long safe ride with him.

"He's been run this morning," the groom said

quickly.

"I meant he is fresh. I want to enjoy my ride." The great horse pawed the ground with his forelegs, as if in anticipation of a leg-stretching run. In a minute Kathryn was up in the saddle and clattering through the flagged court.

The groom watched her in apprehension. But Kathryn rode as if the devil was after her and reined in just at the gates.

"Open them," she cried.

They obeyed . . . and obeyed quickly. The iron gates swung open. As soon as there was enough room for her and the horse she spurred forward, cloak flying, almost upsetting the man next to her. Then they heard the noise of the flying hooves gradually become a faint beat in the distance.

Kathryn crossed the river over an old but solid bridge. Then she left the road, picking her way carefully down the sloping ground to the group of pines behind the chapel.

From behind one of the pines Andrew appeared when he saw her. Kathryn even had difficulty believing they were actually there together. At the same time she realized neither she nor Anne might ever see him again.

She looked at him. He was strong and tough and reliable and he was leaving them. For a long while, she thought, she had been able to depend on him.

"I don't want to keep you, Andrew, it's unsafe. Go. God speed you."

He swung up into the saddle. "Tell them you were thrown. Get down on your hands and knees and crawl. I'll abandon the horse as soon as I can and he'll find his way back. That way your story will have credence. Good-bye, Kathryn. God be with you too. Remember your promise."

"I will. Good-bye, Andrew."

He wheeled and the hooves dug into the hard ground. She watched him raise his hand in farewell.

She waved until the trees came between them and she could see him no longer.

She did not forget his instructions. Going down on her knees she crawled fast through the trees. Her knees hurt, and she got scratched. Only then did she feel some measure of safety. After she had crawled fifty feet she felt she could walk. A long branch pulled her cap loose and several strands of her hair. She rose, aware that she was coated with dust. Then she walked rapidly toward the bridge.

As she crossed it she looked down. The river was quiet and gleamed like silver in the darkening day. The gray skies were patched with clouds.

It was uphill walking and the castle, always beautiful, looked ephemeral against the cloudy sky. Inside those walls she knew Donovan was waiting.

She was not conscious of cold. In fact the long trudge had warmed her. She let the wind blow the cloak away from her body.

She tried to think of Donovan clearly, but she could not. Emotion filled her, and she knew when she faced him she would try only to protect herself . . . and Andrew.

She reached the castle doors and pounded on them with the handle of her whip. From inside the baying of hounds could be heard, mingling with the sounds of horses and men. The gates opened, but not because of her. The search was on for Andrew and when they opened the gates Kathryn stood before them. She walked inside and the first eyes she met were Donovan McAdam's.

She stood very straight, the wind whipping her cloak about her. He turned from the man to whom he had been giving orders and started toward her with long strides.

Kathryn raised her hand to push back a long lock of thick hair that had fallen across her face.

She looked up at him with an expression he knew so well, a mocking expression that taunted him.

"Was this for me?" She pointed to the hounds and the mounted men.

"No. But why are you outside the gates . . . on foot?"

"I was thrown."

"Thrown! Are you—." He broke off and his gray eyes narrowed.

"My mount will return when he runs out of bad temper."

She smiled and drew her cloak about her. Instead of looking at him she kept her eyes on the front of his jacket and on his broad shoulders. Her heart was pounding. These men were going after Andrew.

Desperately, to gain time, she bent to pet one of the hounds that had clustered about her. The mounted men waited . . . and Donovan stood blocking the path.

"I wanted to ride," she said calmly, "it was a wild day."

He took her arm and she had little choice but to move with him. Inside, he closed the door of his study and looked across the room at her.

Kathryn sat down quickly only because her legs would no longer hold her. The room was very still. Only the crackle of the fire broke the silence.

"You rode that damn black stallion," he said finally. "Suppose you'd been with child. You'd have lost it."

She placed her hand on her flat stomach.

"I've no child, and if I had I wouldn't lose it. Not

346

by riding. Not my son." Then she said recklessly. "Go to your damn whore! Get your brats from her. But remember, they will never bear your name."

He took a step toward her and she tipped her head back to look up at him. Then he turned and walked back to the fireplace and sat down on a bench.

Kathryn rose. "Go back to your Jennie. Get comfort. Go to your woman, your love."

"Get out of here," he snarled.

"What?"

"Get out, go! Leave me."

She stood immobile and Donovan was aware of everything about her. Everything he wanted. He knew then. He did not even bother to ask if she had helped Andrew. He knew she had. It tore at him, with a pain that set him mentally gasping. He wanted to crush her between his bare hands. He wanted to slaughter Andrew Craighton . . . and he wanted her, more than he ever had before. He fought a battle more fierce than he had ever faced: the combat of hate and love.

Kathryn watched him. There was a cut on the side of his face and a black bruise under one eye. The hand that hung down over the bench was split across the knuckles.

"My lord," she whispered.

"I warned you before." He looked up, but didn't move. Kathryn backed away a step.

Very slowly he rose and walked toward her, and Kathryn, her legs shaking, waited. He came to her and gripped her shoulders in a rough grasp.

"There will be a time, Kathryn, when you will push me too far. I may treat you as you are begging to be treated."

Her coldness matched his. "You'll tire of your

347

whore."

He said nothing.

"You'll tire of every woman save me . . . and me you will never have. Never!"

"Get out." He pushed her roughly from him. The gulf between them had grown very wide and very deep. Yet only a few words, a shard of the truth, would have set them both free.

In her room Kathryn closed the door behind her and leaned against it, weak and shaking. What a farce her marriage was. She hated him! she cried, but she knew now that wasn't so. She hated what he could do to her. That he could make her body sing with pleasure, yet speak no word of love. That he could go from her to that red-haired witch and be with her . . . make love to her. . . . The thoughts tore a sound of anguish from her and she crossed the room to throw herself across the bed and give way to the tears.

Donovan sat before the fire for quite some time before he realized his men were still waiting. He sent word to dismiss them.

There was no sense in chasing that huge black stallion of Kathryn's with Andrew mounted on it. He was gone . . . but would he ever be gone from Kathryn's heart or mind? Would he always be between them in his bed?

If he had had Andrew in the room he would have slain him where he stood. But he could not slay him . . . he could not slay Kathryn . . . and he could not slay the desire he had for her.

It was like an evil, two-headed monster. One head was Kathryn's smiling, inviting beauty. The other was her contempt and the black jealousy he felt. It seemed he could not slay one without killing the other.

She had accused him of keeping Jennie. Well, maybe Jennie was an answer. Maybe he could find some sense of peace in her arms. Maybe taking Jennie would somehow release him from whatever spell Kathryn had over him.

He rose and left the study. Grim determination moved him toward Jennie's room. As he walked down the hall he was doing his best to convince his body and his senses that Jennie was what he really wanted.

That her room was next to his rekindled his anger at Kathryn. How she battled him . . . yet he could remember her in his arms, her body hot and passionate, moving with his, molding with his until he had felt as if they were one heartbeat, one breath. What in God's name did she demand? Why could she not see that they could have the very best of everything? Why the hell did she have to confuse everything? Demanding without demanding. Taking but never giving.

Well he would wipe her from his mind, wipe her from his senses, destroy this senseless obsession once and for all.

He stopped before Jennie's door. It should be so easy. Jennie was beautiful and hungry for the position he could offer her as his mistress.

He reached for the door handle, but his hand hovered without touching it. He glared at the door, cursed his own reactions—but he could not turn the handle and enter.

Instead he went to his own door. He flung it open, expecting to find Kathryn there. But the room was empty. He closed the door behind him, realizing how completely empty the room felt. He looked around. Touches of Kathryn could be seen all over the room. It felt like her, and the scent of her lingered.

Her words lingered with him as well as everything else: "You will tire of every woman save me . . . and me you will never have." Well, he had her, and he would hold her, no matter what. No English bastard was going to . . . he paused.

It was like a white heat . . . the thought of Andrew and Kathryn together. The thought of her helping him to escape. The thought of . . .

He walked very slowly to the door that joined his and Jennie's rooms. Very slowly he reached out and slid the bolt home. Then he walked to a nearby table and picked up a flagon of whiskey. Strong, rich, smoked whiskey with a power to end the kind of thoughts in which his mind was embroiled.

He sat down near a fire that was already dying and propped his feet on the bench before it. He poured a glass and sipped.

He had intentions of getting very very drunk. For a short time he would wipe Kathryn from his mind. He drank again.

Somewhere around midnight Kathryn returned to their room. Her first quick glance was toward Jennie's door. It was a surprise to find the door bolted . . . on their side. Her second surprise was to see Donovan asleep in the chair. At least she thought it was sleep until she saw the empty bottle.

She smiled as she prepared for bed. As she climbed beneath the covers she allowed herself a twinge of satisfaction. Then she slept a peaceful sleep.

Chapter 22

Hermitage would not be a place Donovan would look for Andrew, and it was the prearranged place where the coveted papers were to be signed. But Andrew had waited a whole week for the gathering of the men, the signing, and the moment the papers would be handed to him. A week! And he knew it left him very little time before Anne's wedding would take place.

He sat in the quiet, semidark room and tried to remain patient. Candlelight made the shadows of the men dance erratically on the pale walls.

Lord Fleming put the tips of his fingers together. His black eyes gleamed.

Andrew drank some ale.

"All is different," Fleming said. "Jamie is king now, and besides he belongs to a new age. He is romantic, full of passion, hotheaded. He can ride and also he can read. Great deeds of Homeric heroes, the discourses of philosophers. He knows Froissart, Virgil, reads history, intones the scriptures. He is fascinated by the theories of Columbus, the argument of a new world. He has endowed the printers of Edinburgh. Nevertheless," Fleming bent forward and spoke slyly, "he is not a king to be led. He is human. Mortal." He abruptly stopped, as if he had said too much. "Now I think it best we consider the business at hand."

Andrew was digesting everything.

"We are prepared to grant your wishes, Sir Andrew."

Andrew nodded. He looked at the papers Lord Douglas was taking out of a case. Douglas was the last man to pick up a quill, dip it, spread out the paper and sign it.

"These walls will be yours, in the event you need them. Hermitage will be yours."

Andrew smiled and nodded his head. "That is well, my lords. You will be amply repaid, I assure you. The treaty will go to London."

Lord Douglas looked uncertain, fearful. Suddenly he rose. "I must leave. I am dining with James." There was an ink spot on his finger. He rubbed it and stared at the stain, as though it must proclaim his guilt and his treason. Then he left.

"He is a wee mite afraid, sir. His is an old quarrel with the Stuarts. Two Douglas heirs were murdered in Edinburgh Castle, some years ago, after being served a black bull's head on a silver platter. Douglas blood ran into the platter they say. Then Jamie's grandfather killed our Douglas's grandfather, whom he had drawn aside to speak with after supper, and in a rage at some impudence of Douglas's, drew his dagger and killed him on the spot. The struggle between the Douglas power and the crown on the border had been great, and the Douglas power is waning with this present struggle. So Hermitage is yours, and 'twill be of enormous use . . . but secretly. A feather in the cap of England not to be flaunted."

Fleming was pleased with the way he had put that, and Andrew found his dislike of the man rising.

"Most Scots," said Andrew slowly, "would rather die than bow a neck to England."

"True," said Fleming, "but we do not need to consider what most Scots want."

"The Scottish people did not like the foreign policies of James the Third," Andrew said.

"James the Third is dead."

"And death is an easy accomplishment. Anyone can die at any time. Only God knows how much time each of us has left. Even a king."

Fleming shrugged. "A king, his mistress, who knows."

"I see," Andrew replied, seeing very well. Fleming wanted no harm to come to the king's brother, he wanted it to come to the king.

It was so simple and standard a plot that Andrew felt cheated. To dominate, to hold a young king, a boy-king hostage, was the ambition of unscrupulous men. Through the boy they'd hold a country in their palm, and Andrew knew this could come true. He reminded himself that Fleming had already disposed of one monarch. It also occurred to him that Fleming would soon dispose of Maggie if he felt it expedient.

"Much may happen to Jamie, after all," Fleming said, "he is reckless. And I hear of the stirring of witch's brew, of bitter revolts. He might be killed . . . or for that matter his friends, Patrick Hepburn and Donovan McAdam." He did not have to say that these men stood in his way.

Andrew stood up. "I, too, must leave."

"We can help each other."

"I am sure," Andrew replied, "that we shall help each other toward the destinies designed for us."

Andrew paced his room. The excitement made his heart pound. He had all he needed. All he had to do now was to form a plan to get to Donovan without being killed before he could explain what he had. He pressed his hand against the papers in his doublet.

He faced a long ride. But he had to get the word to England . . . and he had to make Anne a part of the bargain before he dealt with Donovan.

Andrew had had enough rest. He waited only until he knew the castle slept. He moved stealthily to the stable, saddled his horse, and rode toward the border.

He rode at a steady, mile-eating pace, but the first light of dawn was touching the sky when he sighted his destination.

Everything was moving well, he thought. But he had no way of knowing that the events that were fermenting at that moment were to affect him and his entire mission.

The sun was rising, and Maggie's cook lifted the poached eggs onto a platter. Then he tasted the sauce. He licked his lips and looked up at the ceiling for inspiration.

"A little ginger?" his assistant said hopefully.

"Dolt." The cook raised the spoon threateningly. "Instead of just ginger," he said grandly, "ginger, cinnamon, and nutmeg." He poured the sauce over the eggs. "The wine," he reminded as he picked up the platter and bore it from the room.

Maggie and her sisters, Eufemia and Sybilla, were accompanied by Kathryn and Anne. When they were seated the cook began to serve.

"The eggs are delicious," Maggie said. The cook beamed. He wished this woman could be queen. She was a lady.

The golden goblets were tall and heavy. The wine gurgled into them. It had been touched with a shark's tooth. Eufemia lifted hers first, and drank

354

deeply.

Maggie took hers. "Let us drink a toast to James."

The women raised the goblets to their lips. They drank. The only exceptions were Anne and Kathryn, who took a light sip, then another.

Suddenly Maggie gave a cry, rose unsteadily to her feet, and threw the goblet from her onto the table, so that red wine stained the white cloth. Then she leaned across the table and struck the goblets from Anne and Kathryn's hands.

One of the servants screamed. Eufemia's goblet was empty. It fell from her hands as she doubled up, then collapsed.

Both Anne and Kathryn forgot her as they ran to Maggie.

"Fetch His Grace," Kathryn cried.

Her hands were trembling. The shark's tooth had been passed over the wine. It could not be poisoned.

"A doctor!" Anne cried. Her voice was filled with terror. Maggie was still standing, clutching the table, and Kathryn supported her from the side with both arms.

"Are you in pain?" Kathryn said.

She barely heard the answer. "Aye," said Maggie. Suddenly the curtains were torn aside and James rushed in. The fear was for Maggie and at this point few remembered that James and Maggie most often ate breakfast together.

James knocked a chair out of his path, not heeding Eufemia's still body, Sybilla's short quick gasps, or the heavy sound of men running in from outside. James took Maggie in his arms. Lifting her, he carried her away from the room in which her sister already lay . . . dead.

"My darling, my darling," he whispered. He sat in a large chair, holding her on his lap, and she huddled against him, her legs doubled under her. She crouched on her knees, her arms about his neck, clutching him fiercely.

She could not speak. She burrowed against him. The doctor now appeared.

"My lord, she must expel what she can!" the doctor urged.

Kathryn, ignoring the sharp pains in her stomach, ran for a bowl. James forced Maggie's head up, forced her clenched jaws open and bent her double. She began to retch.

The doctor stood over them. This was the only thing to do; there was nothing more except to pray. Maggie's mouth was wiped with a towel dipped in rose water.

"Let me lay you down so you are more comfortable," James said. His voice was thick with the emotion he was trying to control.

"No," Maggie whispered. She wanted to cling to James as long as she could, for she felt the truth even though no one else would admit it. Her life was ebbing. Her regret was for James.

In the next room they had already covered Eufemia's and Sybilla's bodies. The maids wept, James could hear their sobs, and he felt as if his heart was being rent by the talons of a fierce beast.

Kathryn and Anne had barely sipped the wine, but already both could feel the gripping pain knife through them. Fear touched them both.

Maggie's eyes had closed, her face looked sweet and peaceful.

Kathryn and Anne vomited up their breakfast. Both told the doctor how much wine they had drunk. He did not seem to worry for them.

"The sisters died almost instantly," the doctor answered Kathryn's question.

356

"Is . . . is there any hope for Maggie?" Anne gasped as another sharp pain made her grasp her stomach.

"None," the doctor said quietly. He lifted the curtain so they could look into the next room.

James was laying Maggie on the bed and pulling the white sheet over her body. Anne noticed his dark hands against the white material. He did not cover her face, but tucked the sheet gently about her. Then he crossed her hands over them. He knelt by the bed, and laying one hand over hers, he kissed her cheek and laid his head next to hers on the pillow. The watchers could see the broad shoulders shaking and hear the ragged weeping. It seemed torn from him in wave after wave of bitter pain.

For the rest of the day James remained at Maggie's side, refusing food or drink. Mourning like a man demented, he roared his refusal when they came to get Maggie and prepare her for burial. Everyone seemed filled with the same fear. James, grieving so deeply, was not going to let them bury the woman he loved.

Everyone was distraught and sought a way to get James to relinquish Maggie. Finally it was Anne who took matters into her hands.

Anne had been ill for two days as she fought off the poison. It was early evening and she had listened to the stories of James's grief. She rose from her bed, weak and trembling, and walked down the dark hall to the room in which James kept his vigil.

A few candles had been lit, but no one dared approach the bed by which James knelt.

Tears formed in Anne's eyes as she could almost feel the pain that emanated from him. At first he didn't seem to notice her, but as she drew close he turned to look at her. His eyes were red rimmed and two days' growth of beard made him look as if he did walk the narrow edge of sanity.

"My lord," Anne said gently.

"Go! Leave me alone."

"I cannot, sire. I have come to prepare Maggie."

"No!"

"Sire, Maggie would weep to see you thus. Is your love for her so small that you would refuse her the honor of a burial so that her soul can seek freedom?"

This stung, and again James turned a feral glance on her. He rose slowly, his hand gently slipping from Maggie's. He looked as if he were going to strike Anne. His teeth were clenched and his eyes filled with fury.

"What know you of my love for her?" he snarled. "What was good in my life has been snatched from me by the hand of a fiend."

"Yes, sire, that is so, but consider Maggie. Would you have her be there unattended? She needs to be honored for the good and loving person she was. Like this, none can show both their respect and love for her, or for you. Maggie is gone. But, sire, you hold her memory in your heart and in your hands. Honor her. Give her what those fiendish creatures would deprive her of. Release her, my lord." Anne's voice was gentle and understanding.

His huge body seemed to quiver and tears rolled down his cheeks. Anne felt she had never seen such pain before.

"I cannot," he choked, "I cannot. How shall I face another day without her? Without her smile, her warmth, her love. I cannot."

"Consider, sire, that few have had the love you and Maggie shared. Even if you shared it for so little a

358

while. Hold to the memories, and let us give Maggie rest, for she has battled a world so the two of you could share the time you had. Now it is up to you to show the world what Maggie really was and how you two truly love." The last words were a half sob and James realized for the first time that Anne felt pain with him, that in his dark world, someone seemed to understand. He held out a hand to her as he again sagged to the floor. Anne held his hand tightly as she knelt beside him.

"It is my guilt that has taken her away," he muttered. "It is because of me she had died."

Anne began to protest, but soon she was shocked to silence by the bitter flow of guilt that washed from James's mind. After a while he seemed not to know she was there. He poured his grief and guilt out and Anne listened in silence. She felt his pain and ached to be able to ease it somehow.

After a while he was silent and even though he continued to clutch her hand, he drifted into an exhausted sleep.

Before the first light of dawn reached them James stirred awake. He looked into Anne's eyes and felt the easing of his burden.

"You have sat here all night?"

"You needed me, sire," Anne said simply.

James sighed, then rose and sat on the edge of the bed, looking down at Maggie's face.

"I loved her so much," he said bitterly.

"Aye, my lord. I know."

He turned to look at her and believed that she truly did. "And what is there left for me?"

"To be a king," Anne replied. " 'Tis what Maggie would have wanted."

He inhaled deeply and gave a ragged sigh. "Aye . . . I suppose you are right. You have her gentle heart, Lady Anne. I am grateful."

"I only wish you peace, my lord. May I call for help so that we can prepare Maggie?"

James was silent for a long moment; then he bent slowly to kiss Maggie's cold lips. He rose. "Aye. It pleases me that you choose to do so. You will always have my respect and my gratitude."

"Thank you, my lord."

James turned and walked from the room and Anne remained silent in the wake of the grief he left behind. He would be a kind and good king, but he might never love again.

Five days later James Stuart rose from a chair and walked to a window. The day was dying and miles away at Dumblane Abbey, the priests would be chanting a mass.

Under the stone floor of the abbey was interred the body of Maggie Drummond. Hers was the middle grave. Her sisters rested on each side of her. The graves were marked with blue flagstones. Each dawn and each dusk masses were sung for her. James could hear again the thin singing he had heard five days ago at Maggie's grave. The only thing that eased the situation for anyone was the order that James had given. There would be no celebrations . . . no births celebrated, no feast days . . . and no weddings for at least three months.

Anne hated the fact that she had had a reprieve through Maggie's death but she was grateful to James for the time. She only wished there was some way to get word to Andrew. Surely he felt she was yet to be married in a matter of days. She wondered where he was and what he was doing. Only thoughts of Andrew and her love for him kept her going.

360

Jeffrey Sparrow tented his fingers and rested his chin on them, staring over them at a very changed Andrew.

Andrew was beside himself with anger at his own king. With proof of the traitor's willingness to betray their king in his hands, he and his advisers lingered over the details of the agreement that was to be presented to James.

The days were growing short and so was Andrew's temper. Within two days Anne would be wed and unless he was there to stop it . . . He raged even more at the thought.

"Andrew, sit down. This pacing and fuming does no good."

"Damnit, man, can none of you understand? There is no more time! For Anne the time is running out."

"And you think she will believe you have abandoned her?"

"No, Anne knows better than that. Don't you see, Jeffrey, she has surrendered all hope. If there was just a way to control James . . . or McAdam. To put a stop to the wedding. At least—"

He was interrupted by a knock on the door that surprised both men.

"Come in," Jeffrey called.

The man who entered bowed to both Jeffrey and Andrew.

"There is a courier who had just ridden in from Scotland, Sir Jeffrey. He says that it is urgent he speak with you at once."

Andrew and Jeffrey exchanged puzzled looks.

"Send him in at once," Jeffrey said.

The courier was a young man and he looked as if

he were in a state of total exhaustion. He bowed stiffly to both men.

"You have news," Jeffrey urged.

"Yes, sir. There is serious word from Scotland."

"What news?"

"James is in mourning. He will receive no one for the next three months. It seems as if affairs of state have come to a stop temporarily."

"In mourning," Andrew said sharply. A tingle of premonitional fear coursed up his back. "In mourning for whom? Who has died that it brings such action?"

"Lady Maggie Drummond, sir."

"Maggie," Andrew breathed. "How?"

"She was poisoned, sir. It seems she and four other ladies were having breakfast and the wine was poisoned."

"Four other ladies," Andrew repeated. His heart felt as if it were swelling, pounding against his ribs. "Who were they?"

"Lady Maggie's sisters, Lady Eufemia and Lady Sybilla."

"And . . . ," Andrew prompted urgently.

"Lady Kathryn and Lady Anne."

"Dear God," Andrew muttered as he sagged into a chair. His face had gone white and his hands were clenched into fists. "They are dead?" he asked in a low whisper.

"I don't know, sir."

Andrew was on his feet at once. He grabbed the courier by his doublet and nearly jerked him from his feet. "What the hell do you mean, you don't know!"

"Andrew! Let go of him," Jeffrey cried.

Andrew released the frightened courier, who quickly backed away, putting some distance between himself and this dark, infuriated man.

"Explain," Jeffrey urged.

"When I left, Lady Eufemia, Lady Sybilla, and Lady Maggie were dead. But Lady Kathryn and Lady Anne were very ill. I do not know if they have died since . . . but it is most likely that they did. The poison was a very deadly one, sir."

Andrew suddenly felt as if all the strength had been drained from his body. He had fought a marriage, but even the king could not do battle with death.

The courier was sent away quickly by Jeffrey, who turned then to face Andrew. He had never seen him in a state such as this.

Andrew had buried his face in his hands, feeling as if his whole world had crashed about him.

"Andrew?"

"I must go," he said as he stood. "I must ride back now. I must know."

"I don't understand. If Lady Maggie is dead, of what use can you be there? If you do not have the king's treaty in your hands, and you are caught, you will be executed."

"I regret Maggie's death, she was a fine person. But I must know if Anne is . . ."

"But—"

"Don't, Jeffrey. Don't tell me not to go. If it were the last breath in my body I would have to surrender it before I could not go. I must know if she is dead."

"Can you tell me . . ."

"That she is everything," Andrew said bitterly. "That if she is dead my life is over as well. That I love her. She is more important to me than any king or country, anyone."

The strength of his words, the way he stood, and the resolution in his voice told Jeffrey everything.

"What can I do for you?" Jeffrey's voice was laden with sympathy.

Andrew was grateful for his understanding. He shook his head, then considered the question again.

"I shall ride to Hermitage. From there I can find out . . . all I need to know. Send someone there with the papers. I will do my best to carry your plans through, but I must go now."

"God speed you, Andrew. I will pray that your lady has survived."

"I too will pray. But if she . . . if she is not, do not expect my quick return. I have an idea who might have been the assassin and I will make sure he does not survive either."

"We are trying to make peace. If you cause an incident . . ."

Andrew turned a very cold and angry face to Jeffrey. "If Anne is dead I do not care who is guilty, he will die, your politics be damned."

"I know how you must feel but—"

"No, Jeffrey, no. You do not know how I must feel. No man is more loyal to his king than I. You must admit that I have asked for nothing and have done all in my power to accommodate your plans. But to give up her life so casually, not even to go back to see if she is dead . . . Don't you think you . . . and my king . . . are asking a little bit too much?"

"You love her so much that you would sacrifice your life?"

"Yes. I would trade my life for her in a moment if it were possible." He strode to the door. "I shall be at Hermitage. Send the papers and I will face James Stuart or Patrick Hepburn or even that accursed Donovan McAdam and put your plans in motion. But do not expect me to return until the person responsible for this has met the fate he deserves."

Andrew left, and Jeffrey looked at the closed door for a long while. The diplomat, the political maneuverer extraordinaire, the man who could move kingdoms, prayed deeply for the girl who held the heart of his friend.

Andrew rode like the wind. He rode until his horse was lathered and he was so tired he could barely move, yet he could not stop.

Nightmare visions hovered before his eyes, drawing him on and on. When he reached Hermitage it was the dead of night. He left his horse at the stable and crossed the courtyard.

He expected to find many of the traitorous group inside but was surprised to find no one but the servants.

Where were Fleming and Lord Douglas?

He questioned the servants and found that the conspirators had left the morning after he had. He was more than certain at whose hand the tragedy at Edinburgh had occurred.

He had to have answers . . . more answers, but he had to form some kind of plan to be able to get them. If he rode to the castle he would not have the time to utter a word before Donovan would have him back in a cell, and he was sure the cell would be a less pleasant one . . . and the stay a great deal shorter.

He questioned the servants as thoroughly as he could without making them too suspicious and all the answers he got only did more to make his fears grow deeper.

Yes, there had been a tragedy, they said. Yes, James had lost his Maggie . . . but no one knew the fate of Lady Kathryn or Lady Anne.

He was frustrated, frightened, and filled with a kind of grief. He had to refuse to think back too far, or he would come face to face with his darkest and most painful thoughts: that he was so filled with his own importance, so secure in his ability, that he had left Anne to a horrible fate.

He ordered wine, for he knew he would have to wait for the return of Fleming and Lord Douglas in order to get some word. But the wait was hardly bearable.

As he sat and drank he allowed the warm, poignant memories of Anne to flood his mind. From the first moment he had seen her he had known a beauty that had been beyond his dreams. He relived the perfect and magical night she had come to him, trusting him, loving him beyond anything he had ever known.

He laughed bitterly at his useless vows. I will get free, I will come back for you. Why the hell hadn't he just taken her with him? Once in England he could have put her safely in his home and returned to finish his work.

It was then he heard the noise of new arrivals. There seemed to be some confusion and a great deal of commotion before Douglas and Fleming walked into the room.

"Ah . . . Sir Andrew," Fleming said. "You . . . ah . . . have arranged everything in England?"

"Aye, 'tis all done. The king is quite pleased and intends to act on the information as rapidly as possible. In fact I await a courier with word soon. Then . . . we will move."

He'd chosen his words well and had not said anything that was not true. Now he desperately needed his own information.

366

"It seems there have been some unexpected events at the castle since I've been gone," he began.

"Unexpected?" Fleming smiled. "Yes, I suppose death is unexpected."

"You speak so casually." Andrew tried to smile but at his side his fist was clenched in a supreme effort to keep from leaping at Fleming's throat. "One death is one thing . . . but five? Really Lord Fleming."

"Five?"

" 'Tis what I heard," Andrew replied hopefully.

Douglas and Fleming exchanged a glance and Andrew could have easily murdered the both of them where they stood.

"My dear, Andrew. You must come with us. There is something we have to show you."

"What?"

"Just come. You will most likely find it very interesting."

Andrew rose and walked beside them. He was puzzled, and anxious for them to clear up what they said. As they walked out into the courtyard Andrew froze in his tracks and stared in awe at the sight before him.

Fleming chuckled. "It seems, my dear English friend, that we have some guests."

Chapter 23

If Andrew was beside himself with panic at the fact that Anne had been poisoned, Donovan was even more so when word was brought to him about Kathryn.

At first he too misinterpreted the news and for one heartrending moment he thought it was Kathryn who had died. The stark terror that filled him as he raced to her was balanced only by the rage that filled him. The urge to kill blossomed in his mind like a gray thunderous cloud.

When he reached the room in which the women had sat down to breakfast, Maggie and James were already together and Kathryn and Anne were being hovered over by wailing and helpless maids.

But Donovan pushed them aside and ran to Kathryn, who was leaning weakly against the door frame. Her face was white and beads of perspiration coated her face. Her arms were wrapped about herself and she was clenching her jaw against the shards of pain that tore at her.

Anne was being helped to a chair. She was trembling in fear, but neither she nor Kathryn had drunk enough to kill them as quickly as it had the others. But would they still die . . . slowly?

"Kathryn," Donovan breathed her name in a kind of agony as he went to her. She looked up at him and for the first time in her life real fear was reflected in her eyes. He saw pain there too and it was as if something tore at his vitals as well. He would not let her die! He could not!

He swept her up in his arms and carried her to their bed, where he laid her gently against the pillows. His mind spun. How could he save her from possible death, or even from the pain he saw etched on her face?

He shouted orders, sending for brine or anything that would make her vomit. He had no way of knowing she had retched until she was weak. When it came he forced the liquid between her lips, then held her as she immediately retched. He cradled her bent form until he was sure no more would come. It frightened him that so little was expelled. Had the rest had its time to work? Would it be fatal? Something deep within him cried out in anguish at this thought.

Her body shook, so he rapidly stripped away the soiled clothes. He wrapped her in a blanket and sat on the edge of the bed, holding her close, rocking her against his hard frame as if he could force vitality from him to her.

He made everyone leave. He would fight for Kathryn's life, but if she died . . . he wanted to hold her.

She moaned softly and in the silence of the room it echoed like a thunderclap.

"Kathryn . . . Kathryn love, can you hear me?"

"Yes," she whispered, too frightened to hear his soft word of endearment.

"Did you drink the entire goblet of wine?"

"No."

"How much did you drink?" She inhaled as another sharp pain made her grasp him spasmodically.

369

He tightened his hold on her. "Kathryn, you must tell me. How much did you drink?"

"Just . . . just a sip or two," she whispered.

He felt a surge of hopeful relief. He could win her life. Even if he could never win her love she would be alive. He could not bear the thought of her death.

He stood with her in his arms, turned and laid her gently on the bed.

"Donovan." It was a cry of fear so totally alien to her that Donovan was torn with it. Kathryn had never tasted fear, and she needed hope . . . she needed him.

"Listen to me, Kathryn," he said urgently as he sat beside her and held her hand in a firm, steadying grip. "We are going to fight this, you and I, and we're going to win. You won't die. I won't let you. You must do as I say."

Her eyes were half-closed as she tried to focus on him and what he was saying. "I'll . . . I'll try."

Kathryn was in a haze combined of fear and misery. But Donovan's broad-shouldered form hovered near, and she reached for him as for a lifeline.

He bathed her completely, washing away the poisonous perspiration. Again he wrapped her in a blanket. She wanted desperately to curl up against his warmth and sleep, but he wouldn't let her.

Despite her moans and efforts to deny him, he got her to her feet and made her walk. With his arm supporting her, he forced her to move back and forth across the room.

He could feel her resistance, but he was far stronger, so she had little choice but to obey. Any other time her forced obedience might have amused him, but now he was too filled with worry to be thinking of anything else.

They worked for several hours until Donovan could feel the strength returning to her legs and until her resistance became more lucid . . . and she became more verbal. Only then did he put her back into bed.

He covered her with several blankets, hoping to sweat out what poison was left in her body. She fell into a deep and restless sleep, and he kept a close vigil the balance of the day and into the night.

Maids came to light the candles, but after they had done so Donovan ordered them away, and one look at his face was enough to put an end to any of their arguments.

As night fell Kathryn slept on, but he was relieved to see that her skin was cool and her breathing was regular. By morning the danger would be past.

He undressed and slid under the covers beside her. He put his arms about her, gently cradling her against him. Now he was caught by the thought that he had come so close to losing her. He had to face his own truth. Whether she loved him or not, or whether she loved Andrew, were both unimportant; she belonged to him and he would not let her go. He resigned himself to the fact that the balance of their lives might be a continual battle, but the emptiness she would leave behind was beyond his capacity to face. At least, he thought in grim amusement, life with Kathryn would never be dull or tame. He thought of the children they might have and it excited him. They would be spectacular if they had only half of Kathryn's wit or courage.

But these thoughts led to the echo of Kathryn's words. That she would bear him no children, that he would have no legal heirs to all he had achieved. Was she doing something to prevent conception? He would have to find out. Although he would refuse to give her the satisfaction of telling her so, he could not picture life without her . . . or children that were not hers.

He could not deny the fact that he wanted her even more now than he did the first time they met. He wondered if the time would ever come when he did not want her.

But then his thoughts returned to Andrew. Andrew, the handsome English spy. He cursed the day he had ever seen him and promised himself that the next time they crossed paths he would see him dead. Maybe if his blood soaked into the ground and he were finally cut away from Kathryn, she could face the truth . . . or maybe, his black thoughts taunted . . . he would be a martyr and Kathryn would never be able to forget him.

"Curse you, you damn betrayer. Will you always be a ghost to stand between us? Will you always remain locked in a place that I cannot enter? Damn you."

Kathryn had dreamed wild, disoriented dreams. Everything was a jumble. Music and dancing swirled into a mist-filled morning, and she was dashing through the mist, mounted on her trusty black stallion. Someone rode beside her and she didn't know who it was. Yet she heard his deep laugh and the whisper of her name.

But then she was no longer riding. The horses were tied nearby and she was waiting. But she didn't know what she was waiting for.

The mist swirled about him and he stood immobile. Then he reached one hand for her and spoke her name softly. "Kathryn."

She wanted to go to him. Somehow she sensed all

the questions could be answered, all problems would be solved. But the ground before her had opened and a deep chasm grew between them.

She could feel tears on her cheeks and an ache grow within her.

As suddenly as he had appeared he was gone, and the mist formed into other things. Like the bright colors of a kaleidoscope, scenes appeared and disappeared. But no matter where she wondered and who drifted through her dreams, the ache continued to grow. She wanted something . . . someone . . . but she didn't know who or what. All she really knew was that she was lost and only the dark-shrouded, mysterious form knew the way to the sunlight.

Kathryn blinked, then opened her eyes. The morning sun streamed through the windows. At first she was disoriented, and for a minute she not only didn't know where she was, she couldn't remember what had happened.

She turned her head and looked toward the windows and saw Donovan standing there gazing out, unaware that she was awake.

He looked as if he had not slept in some time. He was fully dressed, yet he looked as if he had done so without thought.

Pieces of what had happened began to come together in her mind, yet from the time he had come to her when she was in such pain, she remembered very little.

Donovan stood looking out at the brilliant day with eyes that saw little of the beauty before him. He knew Kathryn had won the battle for her life, just as he knew he had to win the battle to keep her.

"Donovan."

He spun about at the sound of her voice and for a minute the mask of indifference fell and Kathryn could catch a glimpse of warmth . . . of need . . . of something else. Then it was gone and the mask was back in place.

She felt the hard lump in her breast. If only he could let go of his arrogant pride and say one word of love. But she knew he couldn't, and she could not surrender all while he surrendered nothing.

Donovan walked to the bed and sat down on the edge.

"Kathryn, how do you feel?"

"So . . . so weak . . . and thirsty."

He rose and went to a nearby table, where he poured some water into a goblet and carried it back to her. She smiled as she took it in both hands.

" 'Tis better than wine. I don't know if I will be able to ever drink wine again." She drank a bit. "Donovan . . . Maggie is truly dead?"

"Aye . . . It's terrible, James has been inconsolable. You and Anne were both lucky. Maggie's sisters were not."

"James?"

"Is finding his grief almost too much to bear."

"It could so easily have been him."

"It was meant for him."

"What will he do?"

"What can he do? There is no way to know who the villain was. If he could find out who was responsible he would kill them with his bare hands."

"I don't blame him," Kathryn said vehemently.

"Nor I," he answered quietly. The thought again came to him that if Kathryn had died he would have torn the world apart to find the one responsible. "Nor I," he repeated as he rose. "I'll send for some food. Do you think you can eat? It would be good if you could."

"I'll try."

He walked to the door.

"Donovan?" He turned to face her again. "I remember so little . . . you . . ."

"I did what had to be done."

"Did you? I seem to recall a doctor was present."

"There was a lot of confusion. The doctor could not take care of everyone and Maggie was his prime interest at the time. Two were already dead, the doctor was with Maggie, and your sister was getting care. You needed help."

"Will you not even allow me to thank you?"

"I don't want you to thank me, Kathryn. You are my wife."

"Yes . . . I'm your wife." Her voice was soft with a hurt he refused to recognize.

"Kathryn."

"What?"

"I won't forget that, and I won't let anyone else forget it either. Not you . . . not anybody. Remember that."

He left the room and Kathryn closed her eyes. Hot tears slipped from beneath her closed lids to run down her cheeks. She didn't even wipe them away.

It was two days before Donovan would let Kathryn out of bed. But even when she did get up she was shaky and weak. After a few steps Donovan lifted her in his arms and carried her to the window where she could enjoy the breeze.

She could feel her heart race as he held her, the strength of him seeping into her like a slow-moving warmth. Neither could find words and neither seemed to have the power to bridge the emptiness that stood between them.

It was another day before Kathryn really took notice of the fact that Donovan was hovering protectively over her. So protectively that she was becoming unnerved, with every touch. Every moment together she wanted him more, but her fierce pride would allow her no room to retreat.

But the growing desire was not hers alone. It smoldered within Donovan like a simmering volcano.

By the next day Kathryn's nerves were being stretched to a breaking point. She had to put some room between herself and Donovan before she said things she knew she would regret.

When the door opened that evening she felt as if she were about to scream. But to her relief it was Anne who stepped inside and closed the door.

Anne was a little pale, but she was feeling fine, and she was pleased to see Kathryn was completely recovered as well.

"Kathryn, it's so good to see you looking so well."

"I'm fine, and I can see you are able as well. You have no idea how glad I am to see you." Anne sat down near Kathryn before the huge fireplace. "It was such a terrible thing. Anne . . . we have left our home unattended for too long. I'm sure the servants have cared for it, but . . . I would really like to go home for a day or two."

"What of Donovan?"

Kathryn's voice was almost angry. "I must get out of here, even if it is only for a little while. I must!"

"Oh, Kathryn, of course we'll go if you want to. I had planned on returning home tomorrow anyway. We can leave in the morning. The ride and the fresh air will do you good."

"Yes," Kathryn said. She sucked in her breath in a

deep sigh as if she were filled with relief at escaping something.

"Are you really all right, Kathryn?"

"Yes, really, I'm fine. Like you say, I need to ride and get some air. Anne . . . ?"

"What?"

"I . . . I wish you wouldn't mention it to anyone that we're going. You and I haven't had a chance to talk for ages. I would really like it to be just us."

"Of course, if that's what you want. But . . . what of Donovan?"

"Especially him. He . . . he needs to . . . to have time too."

"Kathryn . . ."

"Don't . . . Don't ask me questions now. I don't have any answers. I just need . . . some peace."

"All right. We'll ride tomorrow."

"Thank you," Kathryn said softly. She reached out to lay her hand over Anne's. "Anne . . . what of you . . . and Andrew?"

"Andrew," Anne repeated with a faraway look in her eyes. "Andrew is gone . . . and he shall not return. There can be nothing for us. I must learn to resign myself to the life fate has chosen for me, as you have done."

Kathryn did not want to say that she was certainly less than resigned to the life she was caught in.

A young maid came in to bring a tray of food for Kathryn. She set it on a table near her and walked to the door.

Anne and Kathryn resumed their conversation, but discussed Andrew from a more abstract and gossipy point of view. They were both well aware that castle walls had ears, and young maids had bigger ones, with loose tongues as well.

The maid took as much time as she possibly could

377

to exit the room, anxious to hear some tidbit of gossip she could pass along. But what she heard was what she already knew about: the mysterious escape of the handsome English spy, Andrew Craighton . . . and the whispers about Donovan. Other whispers linked the McLeods to scandal, but no one could pin them down.

Outside the room she drew the door slowly closed and walked down the hall humming softly to herself. She was caught up in her thoughts and nearly ran into Donovan before she realized he was there.

"Lord McAdam."

Donovan totally ignored the flirtatious gleam in her eye and questioned her. "You've taken Lady McAdam her dinner?"

"Yes, sir."

"She was up?"

"Up and dressed, sir. She has a visitor."

"A visitor? Who?"

"Her sister, Lady Anne."

"Ah, I see . . . I imagine Lady Anne was sharing the latest gossip with her." He smiled to cover the fact of his avid curiosity as he drew a coin from his purse. "Was the gossip . . . interesting?"

" 'Twas naught, sir," she said thinking he wanted to know if his wife spoke of him. After all they were so newly married. "She spoke of the English spy that has escaped. They were talking about him when I left."

Donovan stood immobile and watched her take the coin and walk away. Even when he was gone Andrew still lingered with Kathryn. He began to walk slowly toward her room, determined to rid her mind of Andrew Craighton once and for all.

He remembered when he had asked Anne if Kathryn had sent her to find out about Andrew's imprisonment and to find out what was going to happen to him. Obviously Anne had lied to him when she said no . . . and just so obviously Anne was Kathryn's confidant and knew that Kathryn and Andrew were . . . He refused to acknowledge this.

He walked abruptly into the room and Anne and Kathryn almost leapt apart in surprise that to Donovan looked like guilt. Then Anne rose to face him. She smiled, feeling herself the only one in the room who realized these two loved each other.

"Lord McAdam," she said.

"Lady Anne," he replied, but his eyes were on Kathryn. "I'm sorry to interrupt your reunion, but I would like to speak to my wife . . . alone."

"Of course." Anne felt a strange kind of pity for the strong, proud, and forceful man who was caught in something he couldn't understand. Love was too soft an emotion for the warrior to do battle with.

She pressed Kathryn's hand, then left the room, closing the door quietly behind her.

"You look much better, Kathryn. There is color on your cheeks," he smiled, "or is that temper?"

"Why should I be angry at you, my lord. I owe you my life."

"Your sister looks well also. Is this the first time she has visited you?"

"Yes . . . why do you ask?"

"Oh," he shrugged, "no reason. I suppose you have a great deal in common to talk about."

"What concern is our conversation to you? You have much more important things to concern yourself with, I'm sure." She looked to the window and stood with her back to him. "Donovan?" she questioned without turning to look at him.

"What?" He sat down in the chair she had just vacated and leaned against the back, gazing at her.

The moon was low on the horizon and it cast only enough light to highlight the glow of her hair, but it framed her in the huge window, like a portrait. He sat very still, realizing that a fierce desire was gnawing at him, a desire to make love to her until Andrew Craighton ceased to exist. He wanted her with a heat that he found hard to contain and he wanted not to want her.

"I want a favor from you," she said.

He laughed a short, mirthless laugh. "That comes as a surprise. I never expected you to ever ask me for anything again."

"I don't find it funny."

"What do you want, Kathryn?"

She turned to face him, her face unreadable. "I want to return home with my sister."

Donovan expected something he would not like . . . but the last thing he expected was this. "Are you trying to tell me that you plan on leaving?"

"It's not exactly like that."

"Then how is it?"

"I just want to go for a few days. Oh damn! I hate begging you for what I should have the freedom to decide myself."

"You needn't beg for anything. What, it seems, you really need to remember . . . is that you are my wife and I do not intend to let you go . . . for . . . or to . . . anyone."

"To . . ." Her eyes widened and her cheeks flushed with the beginnings of real anger. "Are you suggesting that I . . . that I have a . . . a . . ."

"A lover? I'm not *suggesting* anything. I am only warning you."

"You should heed your own warnings. How is your beautiful mistress anyway? Is she pregnant yet? When will your first bastard be born? I must send an appropriate gift."

He almost leapt from the chair, and in seconds he crossed the room and was beside her. It was so fast that Kathryn had time only to suck in her breath. He grasped her shoulders and drew her to him until she was only a breath away.

"I told you once that if you kept pushing me one day you might get treated the way you have been asking to be treated."

She saw the blaze in his eyes and felt the force emanating from him and for the first time she regretted her words. Even she could no longer understand why she needed to taunt him, to hurt him. A part of her wept in frustration.

"Let me go," she half whispered. But their eyes were locked. She watched as the fury was forced under control and a new and much more dangerous emotion replaced it. Yet she continued. "You have what you wanted from me. All that the McLeods had is now yours. What more do you demand!" Kathryn had no way of knowing she was saying precisely the wrong thing and definitely at the wrong time. Donovan's battle with his own self had his nerves raw and his battle with her was now at a point that he could not accept.

"What do I want from you!" he rasped. "To stop denying the truth. To face reality."

Your reality, she wanted to scream, your truth. Say one word of love, say one word that will tell me this is more to you than a tumble in bed with any other woman. Tell me you want a wife not a whore to warm your nights! Tell me I am not bought and sold like so much baggage! She wanted to demand what she knew he would not give.

"Keep your realities for yourself to face. You bought me! Don't expect more than what you have paid for."

She fought tears with the same effort that he was fighting his senses.

For a long moment their eyes held while a battle raged. Then he spoke with a deadly gentleness. "If that is your will . . . I will expect what I paid for."

His arms were about her now, and she found it hard to breathe as his mouth lowered to cover hers.

His arm was clamped about her waist, and as her head fell back under the fury of his kiss, she was aware of the hard, muscular promise of his body against hers. Why did it always have to be this way? It was humiliating and degrading to be forced thus into the full realization of her own weakness and the almost sordid sensuality that his touch could arouse in her.

She was nearly past reason when the kiss ended, and still breathless as if she'd run a long distance. Her cheeks wore a feverish blush and her eyes, which a moment ago had appeared as a soft, cloudy green, seemed to darken like the surface of the sea when a storm approached.

She backed away from him as a shaft of sheer anger cut into the bleak cloak of lethargy that had enveloped her.

He had felt the frantic beating of her heart, like a captured forest creature, against his chest. He remembered small, incoherent moans through parted lips. Kathryn, the kind of woman who could lead a man to destruction. How she could curse him, scream and fight him, only to yield with complete abandon the next. How she continued to elude him even when he managed to force the surrender of her body.

But again the thought of Andrew intruded, and he lost the battle of control. He would not let her go!

He reached for her again so quickly that she hardly had time to gasp his name. He seized her head between his hands and kissed her again, deeply and fiercely, drawing from the depths of her the very essence of her being.

She reached for words, words that could deny what he said, words that would let him know of the pain and misery she felt when she thought of he and Jennie together. But she was choked to silence by his intense gray gaze that had the ability to look into her soul. For no matter how much she felt that he was lying about Jennie, she loved him, and she could not deny it.

She tried in vain to hold back the flood of emotions that swept her up and carried her away. She tried to resist the firm insistent mouth that ravaged hers with calm deliberation. The battle was over, all her defenses were shattered, all her resistance melted by his passionate assault. His arms loosened their hold, but when her arms crept about his neck, she did not know. His hands slid down the curve of her waist and rested on her slim hips, drawing her tight against him.

She was held pinned against the length of his body, and he kissed her savagely, demandingly until she could feel the fevered pounding of her blood and her legs grow so weak she had to cling to him for support.

He seemed to sense the moment her body surrendered, but the battle continued as his hands caressed her, and he kissed her over and over. . . . She struggled to rally her heart's defenses, but after a while a soft sound told of her failure. She felt all protest slipping away . . . to be replaced by a wild and explosive warmth that seemed to uncoil within her.

383

Donovan could only think of the miracle that seemed to occur when he held her. He knew her body yielded . . . but would Kathryn ever yield completely? Would Kathryn, the sweet essence of her, this maddeningly unpredictable woman, ever truly yield?

When she was in his arms like this, her mouth opening under his, her body arching to press closer to him, she drove every other rational thought from his mind.

It was easy to lose sight of their battle and its causes when she filled his senses to capacity.

He could do nothing more than to take her and lift them both to the magical plain of forgetfulness where they did not have differences, where only the brilliance of their blending was truth.

His hot mouth found her rapid pulse at the base of her throat and groaned, almost a sound of agony as he tasted her flesh.

His hands moved on her body, releasing her clothes and seeking soft warmth. His fingers teased and aroused her senses until she trembled in his arms, desiring release from this fiery furnace. She whimpered against his mouth, craving more and more of this delicious and tumultuous desire.

Now he began to move slower, taking his time, playing with her, teasing her with hands and mouth until she was twisting and turning beneath him. Her world filled now with nothing but him and the violent pulsing need.

His lips skimmed down her body, nipping her flesh; then he was caressing with his tongue until she wanted to scream at the ecstatic torment.

Gently he caressed her thighs, separating her legs. His lips stroked her flesh, gentle and seeking, until he found the pulsing center of her sensual being.

Then he was a hot probing sword that sliced her soul and sent her senses screaming for release. He was fierce and possessive, and hands that wanted to push away drew him closer. When she felt she could stand no more, when she stood on the edge of oblivion the torment ceased . . . but only for a moment.

He was deep within her, his hard maleness driving into her again and again . . . endlessly, demandingly driving her higher and higher.

She could hear her own voice from a great distance, sobbing and begging. He whispered incoherent words of love and desire into her ear as they both dove beyond the boundaries of reason.

It was nearly violent, the explosive release that tumbled them from the brink of supreme ecstatic fulfillment to the world of reality.

Her reality was a cold agony as feelings of shame and revulsion engulfed her. She wept in uncontrolled misery. She had been exactly what he had wanted her to be. With the touch of his hand and the power of his kiss, he had reduced her will to ashes about her. She wept, knowing he thought of her as a convenient object, a passing pleasure he could have when he chose.

The moment had gone from the most remarkable pleasure to one of doubt and insecurity.

He knew she wept, and he had no words that would change anything. She rolled away from him, and it was a long time before she slept. But he couldn't sleep. As the sleepless night grew longer and longer a revelation within him grew as well. At first he refused to see it. But if he closed his eyes the battle raged. He lost. And the reality was so brutally fierce that he could barely breathe. He loved her . . . more than he had ever loved Jennie or any

385

other. He loved her and tomorrow he would have to know the deepest truths . . . Did she truly love Andrew . . . and could he give her up for her happiness, or would he cling to her for his own. Tomorrow . . . tomorrow he would know for certain. It was nearly dawn before he slept.

Chapter 24

Dawn had barely streaked the morning sky when Kathryn slipped silently from the bed. Dressing carefully, she went to Anne at once. Anne was awake, and this surprised Kathryn. She had no way of knowing Anne found sleep a difficult thing since Andrew's escape. She spent hours praying alternately for Andrew's safety, for Kathryn's happiness . . . and for her own ability to face what must be faced, life and marriage without Andrew.

If Anne was surprised at Kathryn's early arrival she remained silent. She knew the unsettled state of Kathryn's mind and heart.

"Kathryn, I'm afraid I'm not quite ready."

"I'll wait here. Please hurry, Anne."

"I will," Anne agreed. She dressed as quickly as she could. But she watched Kathryn, who paced the room like a caged tigress. It was always Kathryn's way to expend the pent-up passions she felt in movement.

Kathryn wanted to be gone before Donovan wakened. She meant to go to her old home for only a short while, then to go on, putting as much distance between herself and Donovan as she could and keeping the distance for as long as possible, even if that meant extended visits to her many relatives scattered across Scotland.

Kathryn's nerves were stretched taut by the time

Anne was ready to leave. Servants and stable hands looked at them in silent surprise both because they were riding out so early and because they were riding out unescorted.

They rode without speaking for some time. Anne was aware that Kathryn's emotions were in a turmoil, but she, as a younger sister, could hardly advise if Kathryn asked for nothing. Kathryn had always been the leader, the one able to control any situation, and now Anne was sure she was finding her position a very difficult one.

Anne was also sure that Kathryn was in love with her husband. Her stubbornness was an obstacle few had ever been able to conquer. Of course Anne didn't know for certain how Donovan felt, but she sensed that he too was caught in the dilemma of an inability to put into words an emotion that must be driving him frantic.

"Kathryn?"

"What?"

"Are you . . . well, are you planning on staying at home with me for a while?"

"Not for very long."

"Good." Anne breathed a premature sigh of relief. The relief was short lived.

"I intend to go on to Napier."

"To Napier?" Anne was surprised. "Whatever for? . . . I mean . . ."

"To visit our cousins," Kathryn said obstinately.

"Cousins. You have never cared that much about them before."

"I don't intend to stay there that long either."

"I don't understand."

"There is little to understand. I intend to travel for a while."

"Without packing your clothes or bringing servants? Without any one to ride with you, and without . . ."

"Without my husband," Kathryn finished. "Yes, I

388

intend to do just that. I have brought money and some of my jewels with me. That should be sufficient to keep some distance between us. If it's necessary I shall find passage to join Eric. One way or the other I shall be rid of him."

"Kathryn . . . are you really sure this is what you want? I have never seen you run away from anything in your life."

"Anne . . . in this situation it is the best thing to do."

"Are you sure?"

"Yes, I'm sure."

"I don't think Donovan will remain silent on this matter."

"He has what he wants. What wealth we had is his. Our land, our home, our name and prestige. That is good enough for him."

"I don't believe that."

"You are so . . . trusting. But take my word for it, it is so."

"Kathryn . . . why don't you tell him you are leaving?"

"And give him an opportunity to imprison me more securely than I already am."

"Imprisoned? If you were imprisoned would you be able to ride with me like this, unescorted? I think you see a prison that is not there."

"It is there," Kathryn said softly.

"Maybe it is in your heart. A prison of your own making."

Kathryn looked at Anne in surprise. Anne was proving to be a much different person lately.

"What do you know of my situation?" she lashed out, somehow suddenly afraid Anne had the key to many locks.

"Being forced to marry a man not of my choosing," Anne said, a touch of anger in her voice. "Loving someone else you cannot ever share a life with. Being afraid for him and not knowing where he is or what he's doing. Yes, I know much of your situation. But mine is worse, because I cannot ever love the man I am promised to. But you . . . you love Donovan McAdam."

There was a potent silence when Anne finished talking. She thought she would feel some regret for lashing out at Kathryn in such anger, but she did not. The anger remained.

There were tears in Kathryn's eyes, but she clenched her teeth and lifted her chin.

"And that is the worst thing of all, dear sister," she said quietly.

"How can you think that?"

"Because it is so. Donovan has told me himself. He thinks of love as a foolish entangling emotion. He wants little to do with it. He married me for . . . for breeding purposes. We had hardly been married for a month when he took a mistress. His old love, Jennie Gray. He loved her once and wants her now and there is nothing I can do about it." Anne could hear Kathryn's injured pride in her voice.

"Is there something you *want* to do about it?"

"I will not beg him!"

"Your pride can often be a monumental folly, Kathryn." Anne was exasperated. "How sure are you he has taken a mistress? I have heard nothing of it at court and gossip is rampant. I think you are seeing shadows that are not there."

"Do you really?" Kathryn laughed bitterly. Then she continued to tell Anne of the rides Donovan and Jennie had taken and how disheveled she had been when they returned.

"Did he explain it to you?"

"A feeble explanation about finding her unhorsed on the road. But she looked . . . as if she were more than satisfied." She continued by telling Anne what she had done.

"Oh, Kathryn, how . . . how aggravating. Maybe he was telling you the truth. Maybe, knowing Lady Gray, someone has been just a little more clever than you."

"He . . . he has gone to see her many times since that day. One night he did not return to our room at all." There was a thickness in Kathryn's voice that brought a half-smile to Anne's face.

"You are jealous," she said quietly. "You are jealous and too stubborn to fight for what you want."

"I don't want him!"

"You don't? Where is the honesty that has always been between us?"

It was then that Anne saw one tear escape to trace down Kathryn's cheek. "What good does it do, Anne? Donovan has made it more than clear. He does not love me, he will not love me, and he thinks of love as some sort of trap. I cannot live like that. How can you live day in and day out with a man to whom you would give everything . . . and who wants nothing. I cannot."

"Tell him."

"No!"

"Kathryn, don't let your pride spoil your life. Tell him!"

"It isn't pride, it's knowing the truth. I would be doing more for him if I were out of his way. He has all he wants, and he can have his mistress as well. He will be happy."

"And you will be miserable. It's funny. I thought you had much more courage than this. I'm disappointed."

"That's unfair."

"From the time we were children I have never seen you give up on anything you ever really wanted. I've always admired you for that, considered you an example I've always tried to follow. I can't see you letting this break you, Kathryn, and I can't see you giving up what you want as badly as I know you want this."

"I'll admit it now. I'll say it now, to you, but I will never say it again. Yes, I love him, but I must learn to live without his love and the only way I can bear it is to put some distance between us. Anne, please help me, please understand."

This was a new and much more vulnerable Kathryn and Anne's sympathetic heart could not refuse.

"Of course I understand," Anne said quietly. But within she was pondering the idea of facing Donovan herself and seeing what the truth really was.

They were a short distance from their home but both were still content with each other's company for a while, so they decided to stop and enjoy the beauty about them and talk some more. They rode their horses to a clump of trees and dismounted, tied their horses, and sat in a secluded grassy meadow. Neither was aware that they had been followed almost from the moment they had ridden from the castle, nor were they aware that several men were approaching them silently.

They were laughing together over some childhood memory when an amused voice interrupted.

"How convenient to catch two birds together."

Both Kathryn and Anne turned to face the speaker.

"Lord Fleming — Lord Douglas — you ride early also." Kathryn tried to be nonchalant, but something in the eyes of the two men and in the attitude in which they surveyed her sent a tingle of apprehension through her.

"Anne, 'tis best we go now."

"I think not, Lady Kathryn," Fleming smiled, "at least not toward your proposed destination."

Kathryn realized both men stood between she and Anne and their horses . . . and both men were well armed. The two men who accompanied them already held the reins of their horses. There was no chance to retrieve them even if they could get past Lord Fleming and Lord Douglas.

"Let us pass, Lord Fleming," she said coldly. It brought a chuckle to Fleming's lips. Then he strode toward her and Douglas walked just as purposefully toward Anne.

The first thing that touched Donovan's consciousness was the fact that Kathryn was not beside him in the bed. The second thing was that more of the day was spent than he had planned on. It was late morning; how late he didn't realize until he rose.

He suspicioned she had left their bed with a purpose not to return to it. But he had other plans and this time force, not even the king's power, had anything to do with it. He meant to break his own vows, to tell her how he felt about her and ask her to stay.

He could explain to her a lot of reasons for the terrible start they had had in their marriage, but that would come later. For now he had to tell her he loved her. It was an urgency in him that would not be denied. He felt it overpower him. At the same moment he felt a strange kind of tension, as if something told him to hurry, that Kathryn was slipping away from him.

He was dressed and walking to the stables less than half an hour later. He had not taken the time to eat breakfast. He could eat breakfast with Kathryn at her home when they had talked and all their problems were safely dealt with.

"Lady Kathryn and Lady Anne rode out alone this morning?" he questioned a stable boy as he saddled his horse.

"Aye, they rode uncommon early as well. The sun was hardly up."

"Then she must be home by now," he said, half to himself as he mounted and rode out.

It was a considerable ride to the McLeod home and

it gave Donovan plenty of time to think, and to put the words in his mind in some kind of order that Kathryn might accept.

He thought of the short time they had spent together and the traumatic effect she had had on his life. He tried to consider how it might be if she left his life forever. It was an impossible thought, one he could not accept.

At that moment he realized he would do whatever needed to be done to bring Kathryn back.

He rode at a steady pace, his horse eating the distance rapidly with his long strides. When he arrived he was mildly surprised that he had to pound on the door to get attention. Surely the household was in attendance to their mistresses. It made him uncomfortable and he didn't know why.

When the door was opened he strode inside, removing his gauntlets as he did. "Tell Lady Kathryn that I wish to speak to her," he ordered a puzzled servant. When the servant did not move at once Donovan leveled an inquisitive look at him.

"Lady Kathryn, sir?"

"Are you dense this morning? Aye, Lady Kathryn. Be quick about it. Tell her it's important."

"Lady Kathryn is not here, sir. She has not been here since she was wed."

Now Donovan was more than certain that Kathryn had given him orders to tell anyone who came that she was not there. But Donovan was in no mood to be playing any cat-and-mouse games. The time for them was over.

"Whatever orders you were given must be disobeyed. I come in the king's name." He was certain James's name would bring quicker results. But the servant remained just as puzzled as before.

"But sir," — the servant was getting nervous under Donovan's intense gaze — "Lady Kathryn has never returned from the castle. She is not here!"

A tremor of apprehension tingled through Donovan, but he fought it. Of course she was here. She had just given orders that he was to be told different. He could not blame the servant. Kathryn was not a mistress to be disobeyed.

Determination moved him and he strode toward the stairs with an anxious, hand-wringing servant following in his wake.

But a thorough search revealed nothing but more curious and worried servants. It was true: neither Kathryn nor Anne was there.

He pondered this for a while, then came to the conclusion that they must have stopped somewhere along the way and he had ridden past them. He left a household of uncertain and anxious servants.

He rode back toward the castle very slowly, watching each area where they could be, searching each copse of trees. But, as he neared the castle, anxiety was turning into a shadowy fear. Something had happened to them along the way.

The castle was suddenly bustling as he gave orders for search parties. But hours fled and the searchers returned unsuccessful.

By now a multitude of insidious thoughts had swirled through Donovan's mind. They were not injured or someone would have found them . . . or had they been injured and someone had? He found the pictures in his mind unbelievably painful. Kathryn hurt, needing help, and he unable to do anything.

Then, the worst picture of all exploded in his mind: Andrew Craighton! Had she run to him! At first the thought paralyzed his whole being. Then anger swelled within him. Why had he not killed the cursed English spy when he had the chance? How easy it would have been to eliminate him, wipe him from Kathryn's life forever.

Self-flagellation followed the anger. If he had been different with Kathryn, if he had told her last night how he felt, maybe she would not be gone today. Or would she have chosen to go anyway? Every bitter word, every moment that he had forced her to his will, tore at him until his spirit was bloody and his heart squeezed into a hard knot of misery.

By early evening Donovan was actually contemplating going after Kathryn if he had to follow her into the court of England. He was a mass of confused emotions that kept everyone at a distance. Servants tiptoed about and friends who had come to help sat in the great room and drank, waiting for a word from Donovan that they should ride out and search. One word from him would raise a hundred swords to his aid. Half of them were convinced something had happened to Kathryn and the other half convinced she was displaying her formidable temper. None of them gave one thought to the fact that Kathryn would betray either her husband or her country. They may have been either annoyed or amused at her escapade, but they believed in her.

Donovan alone faced his fear. Kathryn had gone to Andrew. It tormented him as nothing else had the power to do.

Night shadows grew longer and Donovan sat before the huge fireplace, brooding and struggling both with his own conscience and with the plans he was making. Kathryn was his wife and if he had to ride into Buckingham Palace he would. He realized he faced a life that seemed to have had the light taken from it.

Two of his closest friends, Ian Knox and Brian Argyll, sat some distance away. They watched Donovan carefully for, knowing him as well as they did, they realized he was not a man to sit and allow something he wanted to be snatched from his grasp.

Still time ticked by and Donovan did not rouse from his black thoughts. He ignored the bringing of his evening meal. Food was unimportant now. Torches were lit and the hearth blazed with light.

Donovan was mentally traveling every route they could have taken, touching on anyone that might have the arrogance — or the stupidity — to do something to Kathryn . . . his wife.

Despite all, the friends around Donovan had liked Kathryn. She was easier with them than with Donovan. She had smiled, seen to their comfort and welfare, and had a kind word and gentle hand when necessary. They had seen a side to Kathryn that Donovan was not given. Now they wanted her back almost as badly as Donovan did. Besides this their respect and admiration for Donovan made it impossible for them to accept the situation. They were prepared to ride out at a word from him.

And at last he seemed ready to give it. He stood, jaw clenched and white-hot fury dancing in his eyes. He had made a decision.

Both men rose as well in anticipation, but before Donovan could speak a servant entered and walked swiftly to him.

"M'lord," the servant spoke so his voice would not carry to the men on the other side of the room. Donovan read more in the servant's eyes than was there. His heart began to pound. Was she found injured somewhere . . . dead? The thought was so brutal that everything in him denied it. But the worst thought had to be faced. He took the message the servant offered. Was it written by Kathryn? Was it a message that would tell him she was leaving his life forever?

The servant left his silent master and Donovan stood a long time looking at the message. Then, slowly, he unfolded it and read.

The ones you seek are safe as long as you follow orders. Ride to Hermitage. Ride alone or they will die before you can reach them. Come unarmed.

So Anne had been taken with her sister. Was this an accident because she had just happened to be with her, or was Anne part of a scheme, too?

At first Donovan was flooded with relief. Kathryn had not left him of her own accord. She had been taken. Fear was soon to follow. Taken by whom? He knew he had a number of mortal enemies. He also knew that if Kathryn's life hung in the balance he could do nothing but obey the message. It was a trap set for him and he knew it. But if he could trade his life for Kathryn's he meant to do it. He also had no doubt that his friends would offer their swords and strong arms without question. He folded the note and slid it within his doublet.

He started from the room, but as he knew they would, the two men started to follow. He turned to face them.

"I go alone," he stated.

They exchanged glances as if they were agreeing on a single thought.

"The message was about Lady Kathryn?" Ian Knox asked.

"Aye."

" 'Tis a trick to get you alone," Brian Argyll stated.

"Most likely. But her life is not worth guessing about! The threat is to kill her if I do not come."

"Then you must go, but not alone," Ian argued.

"Alone is how it must be. I have to find out just what these bastards have in mind, and who they are."

"Ye know what they have in mind: your life. The king would forbid it."

"The king need not be told."

"Damnit, man, we cannot let you walk into a trap like that!"

Donovan smiled grimly and placed his hand on Ian's shoulders. "And if you were in my boots, Ian, if it meant your Margaret's life. Would you be standing here arguing about it? I must go. I have some enemies I know, but surely they know if I die that James would leave no stone unturned until he found them. There is something more here than my life or Kathryn. Someone wants to reach James somehow. By attack or by betrayal. Maybe they want me alive more than dead."

"You think they might want to deal with James through you?"

"It's a good thought. I don't think they know our Jamie as well as they believe they do. I'll put some hope in that. But whatever reasons are behind it I have to go, and I have to go alone. Whatever answers there are I mean to find them . . . and I mean to bring Kathryn back . . . where she belongs." He had never felt the truth of those words so strongly as he did now. Within he flayed himself for not seeing the truth of it a long time ago. For the first time he recognized the cause of Kathryn's tears. He had taken her so casually, as if there was no feeling, no emotion behind it. He had held himself away from her. Taken, but never given. He mentally groaned under the weight of his guilt.

Just a few words might have been enough. Instead he had driven Kathryn away from him and if anything happened to her he knew how impossible it would be to ever forgive himself.

"Aye, my lord," Ian said quietly, "where she belongs."

Donovan looked closely at Ian. So everyone knew what was happening.

"You remained silent and loyal my friend, even in the face of my stupidity."

"Aye," Ian grinned. "Stupidity not to see that Lady Gray could not be fit to polish your Kathryn's boots."

"Lady Gray has naught to do with any of this."

"No? Let me tell you, laddie boy, that to bring your mistress into the same household as your wife was the height of folly. My Margaret would have had my head on a platter. Your Kathryn showed uncommon control."

"There was never—." He paused. Guilt would not allow him to go any further. Of course he had used Jennie. Used her like a weapon against Kathryn. No explanations, no promises, no denials. He inhaled a ragged breath. He had driven her toward Andrew as surely as if he had planned it. Could he blame her for wanting to be with someone else when he gave her so little for their marriage to build on. "I must go . . . and I must go alone. I have been responsible for enough pain. At least if I can bargain for her life it will be enough."

" 'Twould be a fairer thing if you'd let us go with you."

"No, Ian. If they see others with me they will kill her, and I'll never get a chance to tell her . . . No, I must go alone."

"You're playing into their hands. Whoever it is they've no consideration or they wouldn't have taken advantage of a woman. They would have met you face to face like men of honor. They are less than men, and they deserve to die."

"I'll not argue with you. What you say is so. But I must take the chance that I can get safely away. It's a slim chance but one I have to take."

Ian sighed. There had never been any changing of Donovan McAdam's mind when he set it upon something and there would be no changing of it now. He simply nodded, hoping Donovan's mind was so intent on his plans that he overlooked the fact that Ian had not agreed not to follow him.

Donovan walked away and Ian and Brian stood together.

"Ian, surely you do not plan to let him walk into some trap alone?"

"I would no sooner let him walk into one than I would let James. 'Tis just that we must not be hasty.

The lad has quite a temper, and he also has a sword I would not care to tangle with."

"So we will follow?"

"Aye, you and I. And as soon as we know where they are and who they are you'll return and bring word to James. I'm sure he'll find a way to serve out some justice."

Brian nodded. The two men walked toward the stables, remaining in the shadows until they saw Donovan leave. They saddled their own horses quickly; then, keeping away from the main road that Donovan followed, and following Donovan by watching through the trees, they remained a distance behind. Just enough distance that Donovan was unaware of their presence.

Donovan rode at a steady pace, grimly aware that this might be the last ride of his life. Yet he would not change his mind or his goal. He had to see Kathryn again. He had to hold her once more and at least try to tell her that he loved her, maybe to get some forgiveness for the bitterness in their relationship.

Ian's words were like thunderbolts. Of course he had sensed Kathryn's feelings about Jennie. But he had felt then that a taste of the jealousy he had felt about Andrew was what was necessary. But he was the one who had been brutally stung by it.

He was not too sure Andrew was not a part of the traitorous business he was walking into. At least he hoped so. He wanted at least one chance to cross swords with him again.

The nagging thought that Andrew had shown a sense of honor at their first confrontation escaped him now in the face of his black jealousy and his fear of losing Kathryn.

What puzzled him was the purpose behind taking Kathryn. Of course there were many who wanted him dead, but there were ways to kill him without using Kathryn or Anne. No, there was another purpose. Kathryn and Anne were bait. Someone wanted another kind of contact except murder. The only person he could think of was Andrew Craighton. Who but Andrew Craighton would want more? He would want Donovan on his knees. He would want to look into Donovan's eyes and see the knowledge that he had power over him.

At that moment he really would have gone down on his knees and begged Andrew if he thought it would do any good. But it wouldn't do any good. . . . It wouldn't because he stood between Kathryn and Andrew.

Another question appeared. If it were just Andrew then the threat to kill Kathryn and Anne was a useless one. Andrew would never kill Kathryn. So there must be others who were powerful enough to hold Andrew Craighton in check. If so they would have to be very powerful indeed.

He tried to work this puzzle out in his mind. Kathryn was not one to betray her country or her king. Would loving a man like Andrew make her do that? Or was it balanced the other way? Did she love Andrew that much?

Regret made him jerk the reins in a sudden convulsion and the horse danced sideways on the road. Regret . . . he who had been so self-assured, so in charge of his life and the lives of those in his power, was now flooded with regret for the mistake of forcing Kathryn to his will.

One picture after another flashed before his eyes, and he groaned mentally with the weight of the misery they caused. Kathryn, with the sun in her hair, riding her stallion. Kathryn, laughing at some nonsense someone had said. Kathryn, warm and responsive in his bed.

He remembered the note: ride to Hermitage, ride

alone. Hermitage. When he rode up to it he would be an open target. If someone wanted him dead he could never stop him. He had to hope that someone had more than just his murder in mind.

Ian and Brian rode in the depths of the woods that lined the road. They rode very carefully. Friends though they were, they had no intent of rousing Donovan's anger. Still they wanted to do what they could to either help him or protect him. They were as sure as Donovan that he was riding into a trap, but they knew him well . . . too well.

Someone had taken something from Donovan. Someone had struck him a blow that had shattered his control. What he was using now was sheer courage. He was placing his life before his enemies with the very slim idea that he could snatch away Kathryn and Anne and come out of it alive himself. It was the slimmest chance in existence, and worse, they knew Donovan knew it as well.

"Ian?"

"Aye?"

"Who do you think is behind all this?"

"I've no way of knowing. I only know Donovan suspects that English spy that got away."

"What was his thought, man? He had only to ride over the border to be free. Why this?"

"I think . . . mayhap there's more between these two than English or Scot," Ian said thoughtfully. "Aye, a whole lot more."

"There's death for someone in Donovan's eyes. I'm only hoping he isn't the one to die."

"Damn. If we only knew his destination."

"It would solve a lot of problems. One of us could follow him the rest of the way and the other ride back for help."

"I can't even make a guess at this point. The road

goes to so many places."

"But some miles ahead," Ian said, suddenly excited, "the road splits. If he takes the left road, it can only lead one place."

"Hermitage."

"Do you think it's possible?"

"More than possible. But it won't be too long until we find out for certain."

They rode as carefully as possible, still keeping Donovan in view through the trees. If Donovan had not been so caught up in his own thoughts and worries it would not have taken him long to realize he was being followed. But Kathryn held all his thoughts now. Ian sensed more than knew what Donovan was going through. He abhorred the agony his friend must be feeling, but for the moment he was grateful it held all of Donovan's attention.

It seemed to the two men who followed that it was hours before Donovan approached the place where the road would split. Both men watched Donovan expectantly and both breathed a sigh of relief when, without hesitation, Donovan took the road to Hermitage. Ian turned to Brian.

"Go back and gather some men. Not too many and keep to Donovan's personal guards. We need men we can trust."

"I shouldn't tell the king?"

"He would raise an army and both Kathryn and Anne might be dead before we get to them. No, this is a place where using our heads will be more valuable than using an army."

"All right." Brian was about to turn away when Ian reached out to grip his arm.

"Brian, be very careful. There is more going on than we know, and I'd hate a careless word or action to warn anyone. Too much is at stake."

"Aye, Ian, I'll be careful."

"Good! Now ride as if the devils of hell themselves

are behind you."

Brian nodded and was gone without another word. Ian felt more secure now. There was no need to ride so close to Donovan. He knew more than one less-traveled path that led to Hermitage. If he quickened his pace he might just arrive there before Donovan did.

He also knew a great many of the household at Hermitage and could wangle his way within the castle walls. There he could find some answers for himself, and he would be in a much better position to help Donovan.

Donovan whipped his thoughts into control. He was completely uncertain of the situation he would find. He had to have answers and there was only one way to get them, whatever the answers might be. If Kathryn truly loved Andrew, if she was his supporter in this . . . the thought was brutal and he could only hope to counterbalance it with the same hope: that Kathryn was innocent and he could bargain his life for hers. At least then he might have that one moment to hold her . . . to tell her all he should have told her a long time ago.

The morning sun was a red rim on the horizon and dawn cast deep shadows as he drew his horse to a halt and looked at the dark, formidable castle of Hermitage that stood before him.

Chapter 25

Andrew had never been so shaken, nor had to struggle so hard for control, as when he came face to face with an angry and disheveled Anne and Kathryn.

He wanted to rush to Anne, to crush her in his arms and kiss her over and over. He could have wept with the relief of knowing she was alive.

But he had to keep his emotions in check. His face remained impassive, but a fury was raging in him. Fleming and Douglas had manhandled Anne, it was obvious by the women's outraged looks and their condition. Even the tears that glistened in Anne's eyes were evidence. Andrew made some vows to himself that would have shaken Douglas and Fleming if they had known.

"What the bloody hell do you think you're doing?" he demanded. "This was a foolish thing. You'll have Donovan McAdam on your shoulders. He's no man to take anything from, much less his wife."

"Donovan McAdam is the reason we've taken them," Fleming smiled. "They played so conveniently into our hands by riding out alone."

"I don't understand." Andrew was now well aware of the shocked looks in both Anne's and Kathryn's eyes. It had just occurred to them that he was not in hiding here, that he was a part of Fleming's and Douglas's plans, and those plans could only be treason.

At first Anne was shaken, but her love for Andrew and her faith in him made her unconsciously deny it all. Andrew had not lied to her. She would not believe it. But she could not say anything to Kathryn, who was looking at Andrew in narrow-eyed scorn.

"And so you have found your own level, m'lord." Her voice was chilled. "Dogs run with dogs. It seems I was mistaken. I never should have helped you escape. Donovan should have executed you."

There was little Andrew could do to defend himself from the sharp blade of Kathryn's scorn. He felt the wound of it go deep. Could Anne be thinking the same thing?

"What are you going to do with them?" Andrew demanded.

"We will discuss our plan with you. But not in front of them," Fleming replied. He called for guards. "Take them up to the tower. I want them separated."

This alone frightened Andrew. Neither Douglas nor Fleming were above rape, and separated, both women were more vulnerable. They could not even depend on each other. He knew Anne must be frightened and he felt a surge of helpless anger. No matter what it cost he would let no harm come to her. Even if it meant sacrificing all he had worked for.

Kathryn and Anne were dragged away and the last view he had would be stored in his memory forever. Anne . . . her eyes holding his. What was she saying? That she still trusted him? That she didn't? Maybe that she felt betrayed and now hated him. His confusion only added fuel to the anger that was building in him.

Now Andrew turned to Douglas and Fleming: "I think you'd best explain what your plans are. Our agreement did not include kidnapping women, especially the wife of Donovan McAdam. That is a dangerous thing to do and could well ruin all our plans."

"McAdam has always been a thorn in our side,"

Douglas complained.

"Now was not the time to pluck that thorn. You might just find yourself bleeding to death because of it." Andrew scowled.

"You are too hasty, Andrew," Fleming laughed. "We are going to pluck the claws of this threat instead."

"How do you propose to do that? Surely there is a hunt on for the women by now."

"Not for a few hours. They were on their way to their home, so they won't likely be missed for some hours. By then our plans will be moving."

"What plans?"

"We intend to rid ourselves of the small problem of Donovan McAdam."

"You harm one hair of his head and James will see you torn limb from limb."

"Not if James is confused about McAdam's motives."

"Do you intend to confuse me more or tell me what you have in mind?" Andrew was reaching ultimate disgust at his own tolerance of Douglas and Fleming.

"Consider this," Douglas chuckled. "Donovan McAdam is found to be a traitor."

"Unbelievable. James would never swallow that, not for a minute."

"Even," Fleming said softly, "if his name was signed to a copy of your . . . ah . . . agreement."

"And he'll just walk in and sign it for you. Not likely either . . . unless . . ."

"Unless his wife's life means something to him."

Andrew was silent, his thoughts churning furiously. "Go on," he said, reaching for time to gather his thoughts.

"If Donovan McAdam wants to keep his wife alive, he will sign the copy we made of your document."

"And after that," Andrew offered, "he need only deny it."

"He won't be around to deny it."

"You mean to kill him."

408

"Of course. That's the only way James will accept the evidence."

Andrew paced the floor for a minute, then turned to look at the two betrayers. "First he will never sign your paper. He won't put his name to a thing like that. And second . . . he and his wife have not had a very . . . stable relationship. Their marriage was an arranged one. Besides, he might have an army gathered already."

"Again you are wrong," Douglas said. "He has been sent a message. It will guarantee his arrival here . . . alone."

"You see," Fleming added, "I have been at court long after you left. Things between Donovan and his wife are not what they seem. There are those who say he loves her."

"He would be the first to deny it."

"Even so," Fleming said coolly, "he will come."

Andrew sighed. He needed time to think and somehow he needed to get to Anne. He had to make her understand that he was not as guilty as he appeared to be. He was reasonably sure there was not much use in trying to talk to Kathryn. She certainly wouldn't believe him.

He had to find a way to get Kathryn and Anne free . . . and to get to Donovan at the same time. He laughed bitterly to himself. He needed to be two men.

"Maybe you're right. How do you propose to carry this out?"

"We will let him smolder for a bit, let him worry. Then a message will be delivered. I expect by dawn he will be outside our gates."

"And the two women?"

"They will be held . . . alone. It will frighten them. I suggest by dawn they will both be ready to do whatever we say," Fleming said.

Andrew could have smiled, but he restrained it. It was obvious to him that neither Douglas nor Fleming

409

knew or understood Anne or Kathryn very well.

"They are creatures of comfort, these two," Fleming continued. "All day and all night without word, without food or water, locked in and unsure of their fate, will bring them into submission."

"So what do you plan on doing with them?"

"They are lovely creatures . . . both of them." Fleming's voice was heavy with suggestion and Andrew struggled to control his anger. "Both will need husbands. With Eufemia dead . . ." Fleming shrugged, then he laughed. "Don't worry your head about them. By the time McAdam is cold and buried, both women will be wed . . . to Douglas and me. They stand high in James's court. What better place for us? All our plans will work out very well, very well."

Andrew's face wore a smile, but at his side his fist was clenched. He had been angry his share of times in the past but never had it threatened to overpower all his senses as it did now. The pictures that flashed in his mind of Douglas and Anne or Fleming and Anne almost made him strangle with the heavy fury that filled him. Men who betrayed king and country would not hesitate to betray a woman.

Anne and Kathryn had no time to speak to each other, to even offer each other some kind of consolation or courage. They were dragged apart and locked securely in two separate rooms.

At first both women were stunned. Being kidnapped was a shock in itself, but to come face to face with Andrew and realize he was somehow involved in some scheme was really shattering.

Of course Kathryn's first response was anger and self-recrimination. She knew Anne had been stricken at seeing Andrew there and she was in a mood to kill him for betraying Anne. She also felt helpless, and that was unusual for Kathryn. She wanted to be with

Anne, to try and bolster her courage and help her face the fact of Andrew's position and the reality of it. She knew Anne must be in tears by now.

But Anne wasn't in tears. In fact she was strangely calm. That one moment of doubt had vanished as quickly as it had come. She loved Andrew, and she would not deny that until she faced him and he told her he was truly involved in more of a plot than he had first said.

She walked to a window and stood looking out, refusing to surrender to thoughts that could only torment her. She allowed only the memories of that sweet fleeting moment she and Andrew had shared to fill her mind and her heart.

Time moved slowly for both women. Enforced solitude made the stress of waiting worse with each passing moment. No food or drink were brought, so both women were hungry and thirsty by the time the day came to an end.

Andrew had refrained from rushing to Anne because he knew how suspicious that might look. But his every thought was with her. He knew food and drink had been deliberately withheld from them and he made some plans to get some. He simply had to wait for the right moment. But it was near midnight before it came.

Douglas, Fleming, and Andrew had sat down to a late supper where wine flowed freely. Andrew made sure he drank little, and he also made sure that both Douglas's and Fleming's goblets were kept full. By the time the eleventh hour came both men had celebrated their good fortune to the point that they were nearly incapacitated. Andrew smiled grimly. He felt he knew Anne, Kathryn, and Donovan much better in a short while than these two men who had known them so much longer. They would need all their wits to defeat a man like Donovan McAdam . . . and tomorrow their wits would be dulled by the results of all this drink . . . not to mention tonight when they should have been planning.

He meant to put an end to whatever plans they had as quickly as possible, but for now contact with Anne was his most important plan.

When he realized both Fleming and Douglas were beyond caring what he did he stood up, unsteadily, as if the wine had gotten to him as well.

"My head swims and I feel in need of my bed before I find myself sprawled on one of these hard tables. My back would be complaining in the morning."

Douglas, who was fondling a young maid who had made the mistake of getting too close as she served wine, was laughing. "Find yourself a softer bed, my friend."

Andrew smiled through gritted teeth, then staggered clumsily across the room and out the door. Only then did he move swiftly toward the room where he knew Anne was held.

He took steps two at a time. The key was with the guard who watched the two rooms. They were opposite each other, so the guard could easily see both doors from his place. He sat on a heavy stool, his back braced against the wall. He was totally relaxed, in fact half-asleep, when Andrew approached.

Now Andrew pretended drunkenness again and the guard remained relaxed and somewhat amused as Andrew bumped the walls in his unsteady move toward him.

"A bit too much to drink, sir," he chided.

"Aye . . . a bit," Andrew chuckled. "But it's just warmed up my interest. Unlock the door. I would visit the pretty Anne McLeod." At the jailer's doubtful look, Andrew laughed again. " 'Tis all right, Lord Douglas has agreed. She will belong to one of us eventually, and he is not greedy. A taste or two won't hurt the merchandise. He'll still bed her and most likely wed her when the time is ripe. For tonight he has . . . other plans, so the little visit won't bother him much — though I expect it will bother the lady a bit." He winked and leered at the guard. "Ye won't disturb us should you hear any unseemly noises. I'll . . . I'll have the lady under control and I wouldn't want to be distracted."

The man licked his lips and returned Andrew's look with a lascivious look of his own that made Andrew want to kill him where he stood. Then to Andrew's relief he removed the key from his pocket and unlocked the door. Andrew stepped inside and the door closed behind him. He stood immobile, just inside the door, until he heard the lock click.

Anne, who had been pacing the floor, froze in her track. Her eyes met Andrew's across the room that was heavy with silence.

Kathryn tried to think logically, forcing her fear and all other emotions aside. They had refused to speak of their plans in front of her, but she was not so foolish that she could not imagine what they intended. Only they didn't make sense to her.

If they meant to capture her to use as a hold over Donovan, she felt they were in store for a rather large surprise. Neither Donovan nor James was about to pick up a sword over her. Her wealth was already in their hands and she was bitterly sure she was no longer of enough value or importance that Donovan or James would allow her to be used as a pawn.

What she truly feared was the fate she and Anne would face once their captors realized that taking them had been a worthless effort.

Up until now she had tried to keep her feelings for Donovan at bay. But here alone, unsure of any future, she allowed him to walk through the shadows of her

413

mind.

She had loved him. She could deny that to all but her innermost self. She had never been defeated by anything or anyone in her life until now. But, she admitted miserably, Donovan had succeeded where no one else had.

She had wanted him in passion and in promise. The passion was all that he could give and all that he chose to take. There was no promise, no future, nothing but blackness, and the wound of this was deep.

What would they do when Donovan refused to bargain with them? What would they do when James laughed at their efforts to get some hold on him? And what would they continue to do if they were not stopped?

That they had betrayed their country to England was obvious just by Andrew's presence here. How far did that betrayal extend? Did it extend to James? Her heart began to pound; did it extend . . . to death?

Much as she knew her position, she could not face the idea of Donovan's death. She could not bear it. Kathryn did not love easily, and when she loved it was not easily destroyed. She had been alone many times, but never had she felt loneliness before. The taste of it was bitter.

She refused to cry, but the tears blinded her eyes and she slowly sat down in a chair to consider what kind of a battle she would have to face . . . and how to face it. Whatever it was she knew that Donovan was something she had to lock away in that secret center of her. For it was only there that he could live. He was a dream that she would have to surrender and the surrendering was the hardest thing she had ever done.

Andrew stood motionless, paralyzed with the fear that Anne truly believed he had betrayed her, al-

414

lowed — no — aided in bringing her here. He found it hard to draw each breath and had to lick dry lips before he could speak her name.

"Anne," he whispered hoarsely, and he began to search for the words that could convince her.

But Anne had read his heart long ago and had put her faith in it. Now she read his eyes, and knew what lay behind them. She moved slowly across the room and into Andrew's arms.

With a ragged sob he crushed her to him, rocking her in his arms and reveling in the relief that flooded him.

"Ah, Anne . . . love. I thought I'd never hold you again."

He tipped up her chin so he could kiss her. Again and again his lips found hers. He kissed her forehead, cheeks, eyes, and returned to her mouth as if he was drawing his life from her.

Anne too was overwhelmed with the joy of being in his arms. She wept tears of pure pleasure and surrendered to his touch, feeling the strength and warmth of him flow about her like a protective shield.

When finally the burst of relief was over he cupped her face in his hands. "You know, do you not, that I would never betray you like this? You know that what I told you before was the truth?"

"Aye, Andrew. I know. I know you to your soul. And I know that I love you now as I loved you before. That will never end."

"Then you still trust me, Anne?"

"Aye."

"I'll find a way to get you away from this, I swear. Believe that, no matter what, none of them will harm you. I just need some time to find a way. I don't want you afraid, even if I must leave you alone a while longer. Remember that I am near."

"Oh, Andrew, can you not stay with me a while?"

He flushed, but held her eyes. "I . . . I must stay a

short while. So . . . so the guard will believe the story I gave when I came. I hate to shame you like this before anyone, but it was necessary."

"You told him that you . . . ?"

"Aye," he finished, "that I would bed you for sport."

"To lie with you will never shame me, Andrew. No matter where. What he believes comes from the darkness of his own mind. We know the truth."

Again he kissed her, this time gently, taking pleasure in her surrender and the sweet giving taste of her. "Anne girl, I love you like the breath in my own body. I will not let any harm come to you. You've trusted me this far. Will you trust me a little longer to play their game? A message was sent tonight, a message that will bring Donovan McAdam into a trap. I have to stop this as well."

"What are you going to do?"

"I don't know yet."

"Andrew . . . they could kill you if they knew."

"Aye, but they don't know. By the time they do I hope to have this puzzle solved."

"You are one and they are many!" Alarm was in her voice. "How can you save three of us alone?"

"If I can reach Donovan . . . get a sword to him, it will be two."

"But he believes you . . . Andrew! He would turn on you too!"

"No, I think not. Once I tell him I intend to help him set you free he will be more accepting. Whatever it is that stands between us will be settled by us later. For now it is one step at a time. You and Kathryn are first."

"All right, I will do whatever you say."

His heart warmed at her confidence. "There is so little time right now. I cannot go to Kathryn. We will have to hope she will stand firm and not be too frightened. If I go to her, questions will be asked that I don't care to answer right now. Besides, these few

416

minutes with you are too precious. I am too selfish not to want to hold them a while longer."

His arms tightened about her and her parted lips welcomed the heat of his kiss with a responding promise that set his senses spinning into another time . . . another place. . . . Soon, she would be his again.

It was over an hour before he rapped sharply on the door to be let out. He had told Anne to get into the bed so that the scene that might meet the guard's eyes would be more believable.

He was right. The guard looked past him and smiled. He believed the rumpled bed and the silent woman who lay there had been victim to Andrew's lust.

Andrew stepped out quickly and drew the door shut. "Lock it and guard her well," he threatened. "I would have more of this one and I wouldn't want her touched until I am finished with her. Mark you . . . no one goes in there but me."

"Aye, sir." The guard was obviously disappointed. But he expected to be rewarded later . . . and he would be, Andrew promised himself, but not as he imagined.

Andrew had intended to return to the main room to see what Douglas and Fleming were doing. His mind was on Anne. He really wished he could have gone to Kathryn, but it would have been a drastic mistake.

The night was going to prove to be very long. There was no way he could sleep, so he decided to examine the castle. It was his military background. He needed to know any possible escape routes, how fortified the place really was, and what chance he might have to get Kathryn and Anne out. But from what he could see the chances were pretty slim.

He drifted about to find the actual strength of arms enclosed in these walls. There was a formidable supply of men. He ran across a few engaged in tossing dice and spoke a few words to them. Only as he started to walk away did he notice another small group standing a little distance away. Feeling his eyes on them, they turned their attention to him. He was puzzled. There was something he should recognize . . . or somebody, but . . .

Then suddenly recognition broke through. He was shocked, but refused to let it register on his face. He held the man's eyes across the narrow, semidark court for several seconds, then turned and walked away. But his heart was pounding.

The sun would rise soon and he knew as sure as he knew its arrival that Donovan McAdam was not going to be far behind. What gave him real pleasure was to know that he had one other friend inside these walls. He had not been mistaken. The man leaning against the wall was a very close friend of Donovan McAdam . . . Ian Knox.

Andrew sat in his room trying to contain his nervous tension as time slowly moved on. Anne was so close, yet so far away. All he could think of was her, yet he knew he should be centering his thoughts on other things, such as what was going to happen when Donovan arrived. He would need every ounce of luck and every drop of ability he had to keep this situation from developing into a disaster. If he failed . . . his mind could hardly contemplate the result.

It was some time before he noticed the room was growing a little lighter. He rose and walked to the window. In the distance he could see the rider approaching. Fate had dealt the hand and now was the time to play out the game. Donovan had come for his woman, and to end the lives of the ones who had threatened her and, through her, him. Andrew knew he was in for more than one surprise.

Kathryn had not closed her eyes for a minute of sleep. She couldn't. Anxiety over Anne's welfare battled with her thoughts of Donovan and what he might be doing. She remembered so many things about him now and was surprised at the poignancy of the memories.

She thought of the night they were married and how he had come to her not as a master but as a lover. She remembered the way his laughter could rumble from deep inside. It surprised her that she remembered so many little things about him. No matter how she had threatened to hate him forever she could not fight the whispers of beautiful, sensitive moments that swirled about her.

As sweet as they were, the reality of his true motives and true feelings was always there. She loved him and she would deny it no more, just as she would no longer deny the fact that he did not love her and there was no future for them together. She could not bear living with him, lying with him, and knowing it meant nothing to him.

The long night gave her a chance to make decisions. Of course, the possibility that she would ever leave this place alive was remote; still she planned for the possibility.

If she found freedom she would leave. It was the only thing she could do. She would find her brother and share his exile with him. She would go on the best way she could, but it had to be without Donovan. She knew that if she remained with him she would surrender to his will because of her love for him, but with each moment of surrender she would die a little, for love tossed on barren ground could never flourish. In time it would be too painful a situation to bear. It would drive her to insanity.

She sighed deeply as she watched a black sky slowly begin to turn gray with the first sign of dawn. She rose and walked to the window. As she looked down, the shadows seemed to flow and separate. She gasped and the whisper of his name was almost a sound of pain.

"Donovan."

Was it true? Was he really there or was it a wishful dream, something she wanted so badly that she conjured it up from her own mind?

But no, the first rays of the sun touched him, glistened in his tawny hair and brought his broad shoulders into startling relief. It was Donovan.

Joy was replaced by terror. He was riding to his death calmly, as if it were any other day and nothing was amiss.

The window was locked and there was no way for her to open it. She wanted to warn him, to send him away, to keep him safe. If it cost her life she didn't care. It would be better to be alone and know he was alive. But she couldn't. Even though she cried out his name he couldn't hear her. The tears that fell were unseen.

Donovan paused for a few moments, then kicked his horse into motion and rode to the gates. It did not surprise him when they were opened at once. They had been watching for his arrival. Most assuredly they were amused at what looked like foolhardiness on his part.

Maybe it was, he thought, but he could not deny the hunger to see Kathryn again. There was another hopeful hunger too. If Andrew Craighton was here, one way or another he could come face to face with him, and one way or another Andrew would pay some part of his debt to Donovan before he died.

He rode through the gates slowly, with a cool, self-controlled arrogance that set Fleming's teeth on edge. This attitude was one of the things he had always admired about Donovan. No matter what the situation he always seemed to find some way to control it.

Donovan reined in his horse in the seemingly deserted courtyard. He dismounted and walked a short distance from his horse.

Although he was being eaten by anxiety he slowly removed his gauntlets as if they were his only serious consideration at the moment.

"Welcome to Hermitage, m'lord."

Donovan turned around. If he were surprised to see Fleming and Douglas standing there he didn't show it.

"Your invitation left me little room to refuse . . . m'lord." He deliberately paused at the title and his voice held a sneering challenge.

"You sound upset," Fleming grinned. "Are you afraid by any chance?"

Fleming was pushing him and Donovan knew it. But he still felt the anger beginning to broil inside of him. He would have loved nothing better than to draw his sword and kill Fleming then.

"Where is my wife?" he grated.

"Ah, yes, your wife and your sister-in-law. They are safe . . . and out of your reach for the moment."

"If you've harmed her I'll . . ." Donovan started toward them.

"Don't come any closer, m'lord. We want to talk to you and would hate to have your wife pay for your hasty temper."

Donovan paused. "Where is she? I want to see her now."

"In time," Fleming said, then motioned to a door. "Come inside."

Donovan knew that death was not far away but to irritate Fleming he smiled and walked toward the door. When he pushed it open and walked inside he was immediately surrounded by Fleming's men. His arms were roughly pulled behind him and bound. Donovan turned to look at Fleming and Douglas, who had followed him inside.

"Men of honor," he sneered. "Why not face me sword in hand like a man?"

"Unnecessary," Fleming answered smoothly. "Why

should I use a sword when I can kill you so many other ways?"

"There is only one way to die."

"Is there?" Fleming's voice was filled with a subtle amusement. "What if I should let you watch your lovely wife die slowly before we kill you. Maybe you will understand more clearly."

Donovan's eyes narrowed. He stood silent for long enough to make Douglas, who was already tense, even more nervous. Then Donovan spoke softly.

"You want something from me before you kill me, don't you, Fleming? What is it? What do you want? Mayhap . . . we can bargain."

"Bargain," Douglas laughed.

"Be quiet," Fleming said tonelessly. "We need one little thing from you. Your signature on a paper we have prepared."

"And you think I will sign it . . . just like that." Donovan was the one who laughed now and the laughter was like a blade.

"You find that amusing?" Fleming said casually.

"Remarkably."

"Don't be too amused, that could be costly."

"Stop dallying with your petty threats, my Lord Fleming. Get to the point. Your reticence bores me."

Fleming flushed with anger and the desire to kill Donovan was visible in his eyes. He might have lost control of his temper but another voice came from nearby. Donovan turned to face it.

"Maybe I can ease your boredom, Lord McAdam," Andrew said. He watched Donovan reach for control.

"Englishman," Donovan said in a chilled whisper. "So we meet again. I should have known you were somewhere in this."

"I serve my king as you do yours," Andrew said mildly. "There is something we wish from you as you have said, Lord McAdam. I think it would be very wise if you paid very close attention to what I want. It